FLASHING BLADES!

Tazendra, after having made a great show, charged Kurich's longsword, which was flashing in such an intimidating manner that she was forced to back out again. She charged once more, but was again forced to retreat, this time trailing blood from a deep cut on her left shoulder.

"First blood to me!" cried Kurich.

"But last to me," said Tazendra, striking with such force that the Dragonlord's weapon was brought far out of line. . . .

Also by Steven Brust

To Reign in Hell
Brokedown Palace
The Sun, the Moon & the Stars
Cowboy Feng's Space Bar and Grille

The VLAD TALTOS sequence:

Jhereg
Yendi
Teckla
Taltos
Phoenix

THE PHOENIX GUARDS

STEVEN BRUST,
P.J.F.

A TOM DOHERTY ASSOCIATES BOOK
NEW YORK

THE PHOENIX GUARDS

A Tor Book
Published by Tom Doherty Associates, Inc.
175 Fifth Avenue
New York, N.Y. 10010

Tor® is a registered trademark of Tom Doherty Associates, Inc.

Cover art by Sam Rakeland

ISBN: 0-812-50689-8
Library of Congress Catalog Card Number: 90: 29900

First edition: August 1991
First mass market printing: June 1992

Printed in the United States of America

0 9 8 7 6 5 4 3 2 1

For Maria, CB

Acknowledgments

My thanks to Dawn Kieninger for some translations, and to Betsy Pucci who helped with medical information. To David Dyer-Bennet for keeping the machine running, and to Dan Goodman who let me steal a line or two. Thanks also to Valerie Smith who keeps me eating and allows me not to think about the more depressing aspects of being a writer. My sincerest appreciation to copy editor V. Fleming and proofreader Don Kellor for excellent work. Apologies and thanks are due Rich Adamski and David S. Cargo who tried to help me with palace architecture.

As always, I am deeply indebted to the Scribblies: Emma Bull, Pamela Dean, Kara Dalkey, and Will Shetterly; to my editor, Terri Windling; and to Fred A. Levy Haskell. I cannot describe just how helpful and patient these people have been, nor how much fun it is to work with them.

Thanks, all of you.

Steven Brust, P. J. F.

The Phoenix Guards

Touching Upon Certain Events Which Occurred
in the Year of the Phoenix,
In the Phase of the Phoenix,
In the Reign of the Phoenix,
Of the Cycle of the Athyra

Submitted To the Imperial Library
By the Sliptower Estates
House of the Hawk
On This Eighth Day of the
Month of the Jhegaala
In the Year of the Lyorn
In the Phase of the Dragon
In the Cycle of the Phoenix
In the Great Cycle of the Dragon,
Or, the Three Hundred and Ninth year
Of the Glorious Reign of
The Empress Zerika the Fourth

By Sir Paarfi of Roundwood
House of the Hawk
(His arms, seal, lineage block)

Presented, as Always, With Humble Respects
To Lady Parachai of Redstaff
In Hopes that it will Meet with her Approval

Cast of Characters

The Court
His Majesty Tortaalik I—*The Emperor*
Her Majesty, Noima—*The Imperial Consort, Tortaalik's wife*
Her Excellency Lytra e'Tenith—*The Warlord*
G'aereth—*Captain of the Red Boot Battalion*
Lanmarea—*Captain of the White Sash Battalion*
Gyorg Lavode—*Captain of the Lavodes*
Duke Wellborn—*The Imperial Discreet*
Count Shaltre—*An advisor to His Majesty*
Her Ladyship Seodra—*An advisor to His Majesty*
Lord Garland—*The Favorite*

House of the Phoenix
Illista—*Khaavren's lover*
Allistar—*Brother of Illista*

House of the Dragon
Marquis of Pepperfield—*Deceased*
Uttrik e'Lanya—*Son of Pepperfield*
Kathana e'Marish'Chala, Baroness of Kaluma— *An artist*
Jenicor e'Terics—*Fifth in line as Dragon Heir*
Diesep e'Lanya—*A friend of Jenicor*
Adron e'Kieron,
Duke of Eastmanswatch—*Dragon Heir to the Throne*

Guardsmen in G'aereth's Company
Aerich
Fanuial
Frai
Khaavren
Pel
Tazendra
Tuci

Guardsmen in Lanmarea's Company
Dekkaan e'Tenith
Kurich
Sergeant Lebouru
Rekov
Thack
Uilliv

House of the Iorich
Guinn—*A jailer*

House of the Jhereg
Corris—*A gaming room operator*
Fayaavik—*Friend of Seodra*
Tukko—*Runs the Hammerhead Inn*

House of the Teckla
Srahi—*A servant woman*
Yini—*Maid of Jenicor e'Terics*
Mica—*A peasant*

Easterners
Crionofenarr—*Leader of an Eastern army*
Ricardo—*Librarian at the Zerika Library*

Preface

*In Which Discussion is made of the Sources
Which Led to the Document that Follows*

I T HAS NOW been a mere two score of years since we
had the honor to have our work, *Toward Beginning
a Survey of Some Events Contributing To the Fall of the
Empire*, rejected by Lord Tri'ari and Master Vrei of the
Institute. We may say that we are in complete sympathy
with their desire to have our work expanded by an additional eight or nine volumes prior to its appearance in
the Imperial Library in order to ensure that certain details
are sufficiently clear and that our annotation is complete.

But should he who holds the present sketchpad of
words in his hands wonder how it came to occupy such
a place, we should explain that it was one of our note-
books while we were preparing for the longer work mentioned above. Yet Master Vrei, who happened to see the
notebook one day while we discussed the volumes in
question, and read it on the spot, announced that, by
itself, it would, if not provide an accurate look at certain
aspects of court life before the Interregnum, at least be a
possible source of, in his words, "enlightened entertain-

ment." It was with this in mind that, for the past twenty-one years, we have had the honor of refining, or, if we are permitted, "honing" the notebook, and preparing it for the publication we humbly hope it merits.

We pray, therefore, that we may strain our readers' patience long enough to give a brief explanation of how this particular notebook, or, if you will, sketchbook, came to exist.

It may be hoped that the reader has had the pleasure of perusing Master Kesselroi's *Survivors of the Fall*. If not, we wish to express the earnest wish that he[1] will make for himself a note to do so. In any case, it was our pleasure and honor to read this manuscript some decades prior to its publication, when it author was kind enough to send us, via our common patron, Parachai, Countess of Sliptower, a handwritten copy, which we eagerly devoured, being familiar with the author's earlier works in history and poetics.

One thing that caught our eye occurred in the sixty-third or sixty-fourth chapter, where mention was made of a certain Tiassa who "declined to discuss the events" leading up to the tragedy. While the notion of a reticent Tiassa is startling enough, it also brought to mind at once a passage in the ninety-third stanza of Mistress Fornei's poem, "Return to Me, My City," where we find the lines, "Yet you survived, for far away/ Walking out upon the silent road/ Where quiet Tiassa for you waits/ With Yendi and gallant Lavode."

This intrigued us so much that, when Master Kesselroi refused, quite properly, to directly identify the Tiassa in question, we could hardly fail to find and study the entire poem. And, while noting no other references to a Tiassa, we did find reference, in the eighty-eighth stanza, to one

---

[1] Translator's Note: The Dragaeran language uses the symbol "gya" to represent someone of unknown sex. Since English lacks this convenience, I decided to use the word "he" for all such occurrences.

Aerich, which name stuck in our mind as having to do with certain events transpiring nearly five hundred years before the Disaster and the Interregnum.

Unable to stop here, we searched for references to Aerich where we could, and discovered that he was, in fact, a Lyorn, and associated with a Yendi, with a Dzurlord who, some time later, became a Lavode, and with a Tiassa. A little more work told us the name of the Tiassa, and yet more work, some of which is of a nature we are not prepared to discuss, procured for us copies of certain letters to and from him, mostly written early in his career, which provide much of the basis for the work you now hold in your hands.

We must beg our readers' indulgence, of course, if we have used other sources as well. Many of the events herein described are matters of public record, and we can hardly claim to be the only historian who has chosen to discuss them. Furthermore, the Yendi who was mentioned in the poem has left many records and missives behind, some of which, no doubt, are accurate, at least in part. In addition, we have more accounts that we can make use of for such matters as the geography of the Imperial Palace and Dragaera City; and many of the events were witnessed by such chroniclers as the Marquis of Windhome, and, in some cases, by Sethra Lavode herself. We also took the trouble to conduct interviews with the Duke of Y_____ and the Baroness of D_____, whose memories were graciously placed at our disposal. Yet, for the most part, it was the occasional journal entry by the Lyorn, Aerich, and letters (home and abroad) by the Tiassa himself that have given us this look at Imperial life before the Interregnum.

As a last note, we would like to say that we have every intention, for our own enlightenment if for no other reason, of continuing our researches into the lives of these personages. We have, even now, reason to believe that some of them may have had an influence on the events at Court beyond the account contained herein, perhaps even exerting their influences as far as the Interregnum itself.

With this in mind, we hope our reader will take some degree of pleasure in our relation, or, if you will, *collation* of these events, and, perhaps, even to such a degree that we may feel justified in continuing our researches.

—Paarfi
309 (2/1/2/3)

BOOK

ONE

Chapter the First

*In Which We Introduce Several Persons
With Whom, In the Hopes of the Author,
The Reader Will Wish to Become Better Acquainted*

I T HAPPENED THAT on the sixth day of spring, in the first year of the reign of His Imperial Majesty Tortaalik I of the House of the Phoenix, a young gentleman entered a small hostelry, in the village of Newmarket, some sixty leagues from Dragaera City. The inn was called The Three Forts, and its sign depicted three tall fortresses with doors flung wide open. The name was taken from those fortresses built during the War of the Barons, in which the district had been much involved, that could be seen from the west end of town.

The village (and, consequently, the inn) was located in the wide valley between the Yendi and the Shallow Rivers, a region renowned for its wheat and maize fields and for the unique odor of its kethna farms. If we go on to say that Newmarket was in that portion of this valley which was located within the County of Sorannah, and that within the Duchy of Luatha, we hope we shall have identified the place well enough to satisfy all but the most exacting of our readers.

As for the village itself, it should be said that there was little to distinguish it from other villages in the area. That is, it had its inn, it had its leather-worker, it had its mill and bins. It had no sorcerer, but did have an augur and a healer. It had no steelbender, but did have a smith and wheelwright. It had no packing-house, but did have a smokehouse. It had no mayor, but did have its Speaker, with a low Speaker's House that was the only building of stone in the town. It had one street, that for half the year was mud and for the rest was the good, black soil of the district. It was near enough to the Imperial Highway that a coach came by the inn every morning and evening, but far enough away that it was a good refuge for the few bandits and highwaymen who dared to brave the wizards of the Athyra Guard, just lately retired with the turning of the Cycle from the Athyra to the Phoenix and with the ascension of the Emperor Tortaalik.

This day was the thirteenth of Tortaalik's reign, and this reign the eighteenth of the House of the Phoenix. The inaugural festivities still had four days to run their course. So it was that the young gentleman found New-market in a state of quiet and serene celebration.

This gentleman, to whom we now have the honor of returning, was, we should say, dusty. In those days, before the Interregnum, a gentleman who had been traveling on foot was easily seen to be poor. And yet he was surely of gentle birth. He had long, curly black hair, parted at his noble's point; soft brown eyes; and a rather long, pleasant face, distinguished by the creases in the forehead that show high intellect and by the strong chin that indicates determination and will. To these features, add high cheekbones, a proud nose, and a fair complexion, and it will be seen at once that he was not only a gentleman, but clearly of the House of the Tiassa—which was proved by the color of his garments, where they could be discerned beneath the dust he wore as his outer, and, no doubt, inner, layer of clothing.

His tunic was of white cotton, with puffed sleeves, and

was drawn tight around the waist. He had a light woolen overtunic of pale blue with wide lapels. The tunic ended in a short flared skirt without fringe or tassel. Beneath, he wore hose of the same shade of blue, and lyornskin boots, undyed, with low heels and rounded toes. A chain of flat links around his waist held a light sword of good length. The chain also held a thong which ran from scabbard to belt, preventing the sword from scraping the ground when he walked, as well as a sheathed dagger next to the sword, and a purse on the opposite hip. The purse, upon close inspection, looked rather anemic.

He was of medium height, but well built and athletic-looking. He wore neither jewelry nor hat—this last because it had been lost in a gust of wind two days before. To round off our description, with which we hope our readers have not lost patience, we will say that he had a clear, friendly eye, an open countenance, and a frank, pleasant smile. With these things and a sword of good length, much can be done, as we will, by and by, endeavor to show.

The Tiassa, whose name was Khaavren, entered the inn, and stood for a moment to let his eyes adjust to the darkness. On one side was a table where sat the host, waiting for travelers. On the other was a single large room, lit by kerosene lamps and containing four long tables. At first glance, every chair seemed to be occupied, but a closer look revealed a few empty places in the farthest corner. Khaavren made his way there, smiling his apologies to a Jhegaala and a Chreotha, into whom he could not help bumping. Since the inaugural festivities continued, and since the Tiassa's countenance was one of friendliness, neither one was inclined to take offense, so he soon found himself seated on a plain, hard-backed wooden chair.

At length, he identified a servant who seemed to be keeping the patrons supplied with cheer. This servant, however, was on the other side of the room, so Khaavren relaxed, making up his mind to wait patiently. To pass the time, he looked around, his gaze slipping by the numerous Teckla to dwell on persons of more interest. To his right a wizard of the House of the Athyra sat drinking alone, staring into his cup, and, we must assume, thinking deep and subtle thoughts. Next to this wizard was a Vallista with her head on the table, snoring loudly. To Khaavren's left was an attractive young lady of the House of the Dzur, who was engaged in a game of three-copper-mud with a Lyorn and two Hawks. As Khaavren's eye was about to pass over them, the Dzurlord suddenly stood, a hand on the greatsword she carried over her shoulder. Several pairs of eyes turned to her as she frowned at one of the Hawklords. The Hawk at whom she stared seemed suddenly pale.

"My lady," he said in a raspy voice. "What troubles you?"

The Dzur, as Dzur will when in the presence of someone showing fear, allowed a smile to play about her lips. "It is very simple, my lord," said she, in a strong voice. "I have an amulet, given me by my uncle, Lord Tuaral." She paused here, evidently to see if the name produced an effect. When it didn't, she continued. "This amulet emits a small sound, which only I can hear, whenever sorcery occurs near it."

"I fail to see," said the Hawk, "how I am concerned with an amulet given you by your uncle."

"Ah, but you soon will."

"How so?"

"Well, this way: four times now, you have made very difficult throws. Twice, you managed three Thrones over my split high; once, you achieved three Orbs over my three Thrones; and now, just lately, you threw three Orbs followed by a split high after my three Orbs."

"That it true," said the Hawk. "But how does this concern your amulet?"

Khaavren, who saw things faster than the Hawklord pretended to, drew in his breath and leaned forward.

"It concerns the amulet," replied the Dzur, "in that at each of the throws I have just had the honor to describe,

I have heard that sound. Had it been only once, I should have thought nothing of it. Even hearing it twice, no action would have been called for. But four times—come now, my lord. Four times is excessive, I think."

The Hawklord seemed to understand at last. His brows came together. "I almost think you accuse me," he said.

"Well, yes," said she.

He glanced around, then said to the other Hawklord, "Will you stand for me, my lord?"

"Gladly," said the other. Then the latter turned to the Dzur and said, "Have you a second?"

"I have no need," she said, "If this gentleman"—here she indicated the Lyorn next to her—"will be so kind as to judge for us."

The second Hawklord turned to the Lyorn. "My lord?"

Now, all this time there had been more and more interest in the proceedings from those nearby, until nearly everyone in the room was watching the interplay. But the Lyorn, who had been one of the players, had shown no sign of interest save for a slight, sad smile which flitted across his face, rather like the small, red daythief across an afternoon sky. When spoken to, however, he shrugged. Then he said to the Dzurlord, in a quiet, melodious voice, "Do you accuse?"

"I do," she answered, with a toss of her head that sent her dark hair from one side of her neck to the other.

He turned to the second Hawklord while pointing to the first. "Do you deny?" he asked.

They looked at each other, and the principal nodded. "He does," said the second.

"Well, then," said the Lyorn, and drained his glass in one motion, his throat bobbing smoothly. He set the glass down gently and stood up. "Perhaps the street," he suggested. He looked around, his eye coming to rest on Khaavren. "Would you care to draw the circle?"

Now, we would not be faithful to our role of historian if we did not say that Khaavren was young, and, moreover, had come from a noble family, albeit one that had fallen on hard times. He had been as well-educated as his poverty would permit, but the Fallen Nobility, as they were beginning to be called in that day, usually had little experience with the ways of Court, or even the ways of the more prosperous of the aristocracy; yet they invariably craved such knowledge and experience. A young gentleman, such as Khaavren, could hardly be made such a request without being delighted. He nodded.

Remembering what was involved as best he could, he walked out into the street, which was, fortunately, rather wide. He noted the size of the Dzurlord's blade, estimated the distance between the hostel on the one side and the livery stables on the other, and decided that it would do. He took more pains with his task because, in addition to other factors, he had been living far out in the country, and, in his ninety-five years, he had never been this close to a duel. To be sure, he had once, as a child, peeking over the stone wall that surrounded his home, had occasion to see his father beat a neighbor with the flat of his sword over some insult, but that was hardly the same as a duel, with all of the formalities that, like war, make legal and proper injury or death inflicted on one's fellow man.

As he was making his observations, the Dzurlord emerged, speaking to the Hawklord's second, apparently deciding on the terms of the engagement. The Lyorn came after them. Khaavren looked at the latter briefly, noticing the short, straight brown hair brushed back off a high forehead, the thin face, the small chin, small mouth, and hooked nose. These, along with the dark complexion, identify the Lyorn even without his costume. This Lyorn, who was very tall for one of his House, seemed to be a warrior, as he was wearing soft leather boots, a plain red blouse, and a brown skirt that came to his ankles. He had no visible weapon, but wore a pair of copper or bronze vambraces.

The Tiassa turned back to his task then, and drew his sword. He found a spot to make the corner, and lowered his blade to begin drawing the line. He was interrupted, then, by a low, soft voice near him: "No, not your sword."

He looked up and saw the Lyorn standing near his elbow.

"No?" he inquired.

"Use your knife," said the Lyorn.

"Why?" asked Khaavren.

The Lyorn smiled sadly. "Name?"

"Khaavren of Castlerock."

"Aerich," said the other, accompanying the word with a gesture to indicate himself.

"But," said Khaavren, "about the sword—"

Aerich gestured at the weapon's point. "This is your honor," he said. "It must never touch the ground. Use your knife."

Khaavren looked at Aerich for a moment, trying to decide if the Lyorn were jesting. But then, he thought, Aerich was the judge. He sheathed his sword, took out his dagger, and drew a line across the width of the street, then one along the side, twice seventeen paces in length, then crossed the street again, and back to where he had begun to complete the rectangle. He straightened his back with some relief and looked up at Aerich, who nodded solemnly.

Aerich turned and gestured to the combatants, indicating where they ought to stand. The Dzurlord removed her doublet and folded it carefully, setting it on the street outside of the circle. She drew her sword from behind her back. The weapon seemed close to her own height, yet she had no apparent trouble wielding it. The Hawk had a short broadsword, and a dagger in the other hand. Aerich looked at the Hawklord's second.

"Terms," he said.

The other Hawk frowned. "We have agreed—"

"State them aloud, please," said Aerich.

The Hawk nodded. "Plain steel weapons, sword and dagger, to first blood, no healer present, but a healer may be summoned at once upon conclusion."

Aerich looked an inquiry at the Dzurlord, who seemed disgusted, but nodded. The Lyorn stood between them, so they were each separated from him by five paces, and from each other by ten. He raised his hand.

"As your chosen Imperial intermediary, in accordance with the laws of the Empire, I ask if you will not be reconciled." His tone of voice indicated a certain lack of interest in the answer.

"No."

"No."

"Very well," he said, and lowered his hand in a motion that was at once graceful and sudden.

Both Hawk and Dzur seemed to be startled but the Dzur recovered first. With a yell, she sprang at her enemy, her blade visible only as a blur. The Hawklord barely had time to assume a defensive posture, and at once there was the ringing sound of steel on steel, which sent a thrill through Khaavren's heart.

The Hawk stepped back, and swung his blade wildly—and from so far away that Khaavren could see it was a useless gesture. The Dzur smiled contemptuously and stepped in, and, to Khaavren's inexperienced but expert eye, she moved with a grace and fluidity that would have made her a worthy opponent of his own sword-master.

With her next step, she beat aside the Hawklord's sword and, with the same motion, gave him a good cut across his right shoulder and down to his chest. The sound that came from his throat was more squeak than moan as he fell over backward, the point of her sword still lodged in his chest, breaking two ribs and nearly cutting open his lungs.

The Hawklord's weapons fell from his hands as he lay on the ground, staring upward in horror as the Dzur pulled her sword free and raised it for the killing stroke.

"Lady!" called Aerich, in a tone that was far sharper than Khaavren would have suspected possible from the quiet gentleman. It was used to good effect, too, as the

Dzurlord stopped, looked at him, then sighed and nodded.

"Ah, yes," she said, with a hint of contempt in her voice. "First blood."

Then, turning her back on the fallen Hawklord, she walked back into the inn, stopping only to clean her blade and retrieve her doublet. The Hawk's second approached his principal and dropped to his knee, looking at the wound.

"A healer!" he cried.

The village healer, such as he was, was sent for, and Khaavren returned to the inn, following Aerich back to the same corner he had occupied earlier. They sat down next to the Dzur, who had already resumed her place with an air which indicated that the battle in which she had just been victorious was not even worth the trouble to discuss. Aerich picked up the three copper pieces they had been playing with, threw them into the air, looked at the result, and carelessly set out two silver orbs.

"With only two players?" asked the Dzur, who was gathering the Hawklord's winnings over to her side of the table. Khaavren studied her for the first time. Her hair and eyes were quite black, the hair hanging straight down to well below her shoulders without evidence of a curl. Her cheekbones were high, and she had the upward tilting eyes of the House of the Dzur. She was fully as tall as he, with a dark complexion. Her nose was long and straight, her chin strong. She wore a black doublet of finely woven linen, which came to just below her waist. The collar was high, but she had no ruff. The sleeves were nearly as puffed as Khaavren's own, with a bit of white lace at the cuff. The buttons on the doublet seemed to be of gold, and had inlay work that looked to be Serioli in style. Her belt of black leather was wide with brass buttons. He couldn't see her legs, but his memory told him that her hose were of silk, and finely knit. She wore gleaming black boots with cuffs just below the knee.

Around her neck was a pendant on a silver chain, with the face of a dzur pictured on it.

Aerich shrugged and looked an inquiry at Khaavren. The latter felt himself blushing. "Lord Aerich," he said, "I do not play."

Aerich studied him, then wordlessly drew several coins from in front of him and set them in front of Khaavren.

"My lord," said Khaavren, as he tried to decide if he ought to be offended that his lack of funds had been discovered. "I could not—"

Aerich cut him off with a smile and a shake of his head. Then he pointed to the three copper coins. "Split high," he said. He pointed to the coins he had placed in the middle of the table. "Two," he added.

Khaavren swallowed, and pushed two silver orbs into the center of the table. The Dzur had already done so. Aerich passed him the coins, and Khaavren gathered them clumsily into his hand. He licked his lips, and tossed the coins half a meter into the air. They hit with the high, tinkling sound of light copper, two of them showing orbs and one showing the throne, the same as Aerich's.

The Dzurlord said, "Split high. You match."

"Hmmmm," said Khaavren, struggling to remember the little he knew of the game. "I'll hold."

The Dzurlord threw next, splitting low, leaving her out. Aerich threw and split low. He shrugged, and passed a hand over the table indicating that he would hold.

Khaavren threw and achieved three thrones. He looked at Aerich, who nodded. Khaavren collected the silver. The Dzur gave him a smile, then called in a loud voice, "Bring us wine, by the Orb! I'll not be penniless and dry at once, eh?" Then she turned to Khaavren. "What is your name, my friend?"

He told her. She said, "I am Tazendra." Aerich gave her, for only an instant, a singular glance, but said nothing. Khaavren noticed this look and wondered.

The tinkling of coins continued, and the pile of silver that Aerich had given Khaavren began to diminish. Khaavren, it should be noted, was hardly concerned, since the money had not been his to begin with. He had, in his purse, some ten silver orbs, which he had no intention of using in this manner. Thus he could only gain. And, he realized, should fortune smile on him, he'd be able to purchase a horse. This, if it wouldn't make his journey shorter, would at least make it more comfortable.

As they played, Khaavren addressed the Dzur, who was by far the more communicative of the two. "Lady Tazendra," he said, "how do you come to be here?"

"Eh?" she said. "But I live nearby. My—" she paused, then continued. "My home is only a few leagues away."

Khaavren chewed his lip. It seemed to him that she had been about to say something else. "Ah, I see," he said to himself, remembering the strange look that had passed over Aerich's features. "You are doubtless the daughter of the lord of these lands, and our Lyorn friend knows it, but you wish to keep it a secret. Very well, we will see if we can discover the reason behind your reticence."

Now Khaavren, we should understand, had one of those searching, inquiring minds which, in a more serious or studious person, leads to work in some of the more strange and esoteric branches of magic, and perhaps the discovery of spells that had never been thought of before. But, Tiassa that he was, he had not the disposition for it. Still, he was intrigued, and he resolved to discover what he could about the lady who called herself Tazendra. None of this passed over his countenance, however, as he turned to Aerich and said, "And you, my lord? What brings you here?"

His sharp eyes noted that Tazendra seemed curious too, from which he deduced that, if Aerich knew about Tazendra, Tazendra didn't know about Aerich. But the Lyorn only shook his head and said, "Me? Why, I am here—because I am here. It is your throw, my good Marquis."

"Yes and—but hold, I believe you have addressed me as 'Marquis'."

"Why, yes, I did," said Aerich.

"How did you know?"

Aerich shrugged, a gesture he seemed to be fond of. "You call yourself Khaavren," he said.

"Well, and if I do?"

"Khaavren is the largest district within the County of Shallowbanks."

"And if it is?"

"The Count of Shallowbanks always gives his eldest son one of his districts and the title of Marquis."

"But," exclaimed Khaavren, "County Shallowbanks was sold back to the Empire nearly a thousand years ago!"

"Yet," said Aerich, "it has not been given to fiefdom to another. You perceive, therefore, that you are entitled to the name."

Before Khaavren could argue further, Tazendra said, "And whither are you traveling?"

"Eh? To Dragaera, of course. With a Phoenix on the throne, there will be places in the Guard, and I think I could use such a place."

Aerich frowned. Tazendra said, "In the Guard? But why?"

"It surprises me to hear a Dzur ask," said Khaavren. "But still, I can hardly live off lands we no longer own, and I must do something. I think my sword is long enough, and I am tolerably well acquainted with its use."

"But the pay, I'm told—"

"It's bad, I know. However, that is a beginning only. By the Orb! I don't intend to be a mere man-at-arms all my life."

"You will be competing with Dragons, however."

"So much the better," said Khaavren. "They will have many Dragons, but few Tiassa. Therefore, you perceive, I will stand out. Someone will notice me, and I will take the opportunity to distinguish myself, and my career will be made."

Tazendra's eyes grew wide. "Why, now," she said. "That is hardly a plan with which I can find fault."

Aerich nodded, "A career in arms is certainly worthy for one of gentle birth," he said.

"There was a young Guardsman here, just yesterday," said Tazendra. "Was there not, good Aerich?"

"Not a Tiassa," exclaimed Khaavren in alarm.

"I hardly know," said Tazendra.

"He was a Yendi," said Aerich.

"A Yendi!" said Tazendra.

"Indeed," said Aerich.

"Bah! How could you tell?"

"By the Phoenix, I think I could tell that he wasn't a Teckla; noble birth cannot be hidden. And he was not a Jhereg, or I should have smelled it. Every other House may be identified by face and clothing, save the Yendi."

"That is well," said Khaavren. "I have no fear of my place being taken by a Yendi."

"Yet," said Tazendra, "why should a Yendi wish to join the Imperial Guard?"

"Ah, perhaps I will see him and ask," said Khaavren, who, talking about his plans, became filled with the desire to reach the end of his journey.

"Yes," said Tazendra. "We will find him and ask him."

"We!" exclaimed Khaavren. "Excuse me, but I nearly think you said 'we'."

"Why, I did at that," said Tazendra.

"*You* join the Guard?"

"And by the Orb, why not? Your plan sounds to me to be a good one."

"Well, I think it is."

"Therefore, I shall subscribe to it. Come! I have money, if our friend the Lyorn doesn't win it all from me, and I can pay for a coach for both of us."

"Ah!" said Aerich. "You say 'both'."

"Well, and if I do?"

"Both means two, I think."

"So it seems to me, good Aerich."

"Well, I think we are three."

"You mean to join us, then?" cried Khaavren happily,

for, in playing, he had begun to admire the Lyorn's coolness more and more.

"You have understood me exactly," said Aerich.

"Come then," said Tazendra. "Let us drink to this plan!"

"Rather," said Aerich, "let us drink to our friendship."

To this they agreed, and it was no sooner said than acted upon. But Khaavren said to himself, "Come, Aerich my friend, there is some mystery here. I will certainly find you out in time."

And yet, as they drank the dark, sweet wine of the district, Aerich seemed so pleasant, though he still spoke little, that, by the third bottle, any mistrust Khaavren may have had of him vanished, and never returned as long as they knew each other.

Chapter the Second

---◆═══◆═══◆═══◆───

*In Which Our Friends Take a Journey
Which is Not as Uneventful as One Might Suppose*

A T THE TIME of which we have the honor to write, there were, in general, six varieties of coach in use throughout the Empire. The one- or two-horse coaches in the large cities, that allowed intercourse among the streets and alleys thereof, were often only bare frames of soft wood, with highly decorated but poorly built square boxes nailed to the top. At the other extreme were the privately owned and built coaches, such as the famous twenty-two-horse carriage of Lothinor, Duke of Needle-At-The-Top, made of blackwood braced with iron, with a box of oak, maple, and silver, with six separate compartments, each with its own door, and six sets of wheels, each with its own brake, that required three expertly trained coachmen to keep on the roads, and was capable of such speed that it nearly made the jump across the Lonely Ridge in the Kanefthali Mountains.

The coach in which our friends found themselves early in the morning of the next day fell squarely between these extremes. It was built upon fine maple braces, each of which had a strip of good iron for additional support, and above these were set long pieces of leather on which the cab rested, to provide ease for the passengers from the tribulations of the journey. The cab itself was large enough for eight persons—that is, four on either side—to journey in great comfort, with room for all of them to stretch out their legs, a great boon on long journeys. Above each passenger was a small cabinet supplied with several wines of various potency and sweetness, along with good bread, fruit, and dried meat. Luggage was cleverly placed on top of the cab, behind the driver, surrounded by an oak railing that prevented it from sliding or toppling onto the driver or the road.

The driver, a surly Teckla who wore the black that has been the garb of coachmen for as long as coachmen have existed, casually threw Khaavren's valise up to the top, followed by the small pack that Aerich bore. Tazendra, it seemed, had no luggage at all. Khaavren and Tazendra removed their swords and set them inside near to hand. A light but steady rain, typical for that part of the country in that season, fell against the wooden cab. The driver assisted the passengers up the iron stairway and into the cab, then closed the door and pulled the stairway back up to fasten against the single door until it was needed again. He then climbed up to his box, and allowed the passengers to make their own introductions as they would.

The coach rolled smoothly out of the yard behind the inn, with Khaavren sitting next to one window, Aerich next to the other, and Tazendra between them. Across from them were the only other occupants of the coach, a man and a woman. Both wore the white and green of the House of the Issola, had the light brown hair and eyes that most Issola have, and the gentleman even had an issola engraved on a ring he wore on the least finger of his left hand.

To Khaavren's eye, the gentleman was pleasing enough; that is, his movements were slow and practiced, he smiled with both sides of his mouth at once, his fingers were long and graceful, and his attitude was easy and relaxed.

It must be added, lest we be reproached for leaving out details important to our reader's understanding of subsequent events, that the lady seemed to have all the attributes of beauty, grace and charm that make a young man's heart beat faster and cause his eyes to widen, lest they miss the least nuance of expression or gesture. It need hardly be added that Khaavren was just of the type to appreciate all of these qualities; that is to say, he was young and a man, and had, moreover, a vivid imagination which allowed his thoughts to penetrate, if not the mind of the lady opposite him, at least the folds and angles of her gown.

"Good morning," said Khaavren. "It seems we are to travel together. I am Khaavren, and these are my friends, Aerich and Tazendra."

"A pleasant morning to you, also," said the lady. "I am Nylissit, and this is my husband, Hrivaan." Hrivaan nodded pleasantly to them, then leaned his head against the well-padded seat back and closed his eyes. Khaavren's heart sank when he heard the word "husband," yet he kept his disappointment from his features. "My husband," continued the lady by way of explanation, "is very weary from the revels of the last night, which were spent in Pondview, just a few leagues from here."

Khaavren nodded. "We also spent the evening well. Are you traveling, as we are, all the way to Dragaera City?"

"Indeed we are," she said. "We have accepted positions in His Majesty's Diplomatic Service."

"Ah," said Khaavren. "How fortunate."

"Indeed," said Nylissit. "It is fortunate. My cousin was acquainted with His Majesty some years ago."

"That is splendid," said Khaavren. "We, also, intend to serve His Imperial Majesty, by becoming part of the force of city guards, or the Rovers, or perhaps the army itself."

"Indeed?" she said. "And yet, none of you are of the House of the Dragon."

"So much the better," said Khaavren, and he explained his reasoning, aided now and then by a comment from Tazendra, and this quickly passed on to a discussion of the affairs of the day and predictions about the Reign of the new Emperor. Thus they passed the first stage of the journey in amiable companionship among the three of them, while Aerich watched the countryside, and Hrivaan dozed.

They stopped at an inn along the highway for the afternoon meal of corn-bread and the local kethna sausages, which were bland but satisfying. During the meal, the couple left for a walk around the inn to observe the countryside, giving Khaavren the chance to ask Aerich what he thought of their two companions.

"What do I think?" said Aerich. "It is odd that you ask. What do *you* think?"

"Well, I think they are very odd for Issola."

"Ah, and what makes you think so?"

"As for him, what Issola would sleep rather than converse pleasantly with strangers?"

"Well taken," said Aerich. "And her?"

"As for her, well, did you not observe some moments ago, that a single strand of gold hair peeked out from beneath the brown?"

"No, I did not observe this, good Khaavren. You have keen eyes."

"Speaking of eyes," said Tazendra.

"Well," said Khaavren. "Speaking of eyes?"

"Did you happen to notice the eyes of the gentleman, when he first opened them as we stopped here?"

"No," said Khaavren. "What of them?"

"Well, when he first opened his eyes, I should have thought they were of a golden color, such as one sees in those of the House of the Phoenix, or in certain paintings rendered by artists who wish to show purity of character without concern for accuracy."

"Yet," said Khaavren, "I had thought I perceived that his eyes were brown."

"Indeed yes," said Tazendra. "That is why I was startled. And, to be sure, when I looked a second time, they did seem brown. And yet, at that same moment, I heard the sound emitted by my amulet when in the presence of sorcery."

"Well," said Khaavren to Aerich, "what do you make of it?"

"What do I make of it?" said the Lyorn. "Only this: any sorcerer can change the color of his eyes, and anyone can wear whatever clothing he chooses, and anyone can wear a wig, and anyone can wear a ring. But only a Phoenix can carry that air of majesty which I observe in both of them."

The discussion was interrupted at this point by the return of the couple in question. Shortly thereafter the Teckla coachman emerged from the kitchen wiping his face on the sleeve of his dirty black tunic, and they set off again. The meal seemed to have thoroughly refreshed the one who called himself Hrivaan. They continued the conversation as if there had been no interruption, aided this time by Hrivaan contributing his own ideas on the upcoming Phoenix Reign. "We who serve the Emperor," he said, "must be strong from the very beginning, to hold back the darkness as long as possible."

"Come now," said Khaavren. "You speak of some darkness?"

"I do indeed," said the other.

"Tell me what it is, then."

"Why, simply this: is His Imperial Majesty not of the House of the Phoenix?"

"He most certainly is."

"And does not the Phoenix represent both rebirth and decay?"

"Well, yes, it does."

"And is it not the case that every Phoenix Emperor except Zerika the First, who founded the Empire, grew decadent, and began practicing evil arts, and neglecting

pire, until at least he was removed by the turn of
Cycle and the arrival of the Dragon?"

"Well, that seems to be true."

"And is this not the eighteenth time the House of the
Phoenix has taken the Orb? That is, the first time after a
complete Cycle?"

"It is indeed."

"Well, then, it seems clear that we can expect this Emperor to act as all the others have, if not even more so,
and that the Empire will be neglected, and nearly fall into
ruin."

"You think so? Perhaps, as we start a new cycle, we
will have a Phoenix Emperor much like the first, of whom
no ill can be spoken."

"Well, you may be right, but I think it likely that the
end of this Phoenix reign will, in fact, be worse than any
other in our long history."

"And, if it is?"

"Then it is our task, we who serve His Majesty, to hold
back the darkness as long as we can."

Before Khaavren could speak, Aerich stirred himself
from the window and said, "Sir, you are nearly correct."

"Ah, you say, nearly."

"Yes."

"But then, have I erred in some way?"

"A small but significant way, my lord."

"Well, tell me what it is."

"You said that we serve the Emperor."

"And if I did?"

"We do not."

"We do not?"

"No."

"But, then—"

"Rather, we serve the Empire. The distinction is small,
but, you perceive, important."

Hrivaan frowned, as if this method of thinking were
new to him, but Nylissit laughed. "Well spoken, good
Lyorn. You reason like an Athyra, yet speak like a Dragon,

straight to the target, all the more appropriate as we now begin the reign precisely between those two Houses."

Aerich bowed his head to acknowledge the compliment. "Spoken," he said, "like an Issola." If Khaavren noticed the hint of irony in this speech, it was only because he was looking for it, and had come to know the Lyorn's moods rather well for the short time they had known each other.

A certain amount of time elapsed then in which no one spoke. During this interval, Khaavren happened to notice Tazendra who, after the change in seating which followed the meal, was sitting next to the window, as well as next to Khaavren, who can thus be seen to have been in the middle, well situated to observe the Dzur, who was, in turn, well situated to observe the fields and meadows of Sorannah slowly pass by. After this interval, Khaavren remarked, "My good Tazendra, I believe I heard you sigh."

"Well, and if I did?"

"It is, if I am not mistaken, the third time you have done so in these last few minutes."

"Perhaps it is."

"Tell me, then, for I am curious, why you are sighing."

"It is only that this is the first time I have left my home, good Khaavren, and I believe that I shall miss the spine-trees, and the song of the follow-me, and the candlebud, which grows nowhere else."

During this speech, with which Khaavren was in full sympathy, as similar thoughts had crossed his mind several times since he'd left home, he happened to notice that Nylissit gave a small start, as if pricked by a needle carelessly left by a handmaid, and, at the same time, Hrivaan had suddenly placed his hand against his chest, as if to assure himself that it remained adjoining to his shoulders, or, thought the Tiassa, as if to assure himself that something concealed within his cloak was still in place. Khaavren pretended not to have noticed, however, and contented himself with murmuring sympathetically to Tazendra.

He considered the words which had caused the simultaneous reaction in his fellow-travelers, and decided that it was upon the mention of the word "candlebud" that the reaction had occurred. Now Khaavren was also from this general region, which was the only area where candlebud could then be found; he therefore turned at once to the two of them and said, "Have you, perchance, ever seen the candlebud? It is a small flower, yet remarkable in its own way."

"Why, no," said Nylissit coolly. "I have never seen one."

"It grows only on the eastern slope of a hill or valley," said Khaavren, watching them carefully. "And always near running water, though never too near. The stalk is pale green, and rises to the height of a man's knee. In the fall each plant produces small, purple berries, tart and full of juice. Yet what is remarkable, my friends, is the color. For at the top of each plant, in the early spring, is a small bud that is bright yellow in the morning, and changes, as the day grows older, to orange, and at last to a shining red. But that is not all, for when darkness is full, the bud gives off a light of its own, so that there are whole valleys that shimmer in the night, and are so well lighted one can find the small paths left by the antelope and the tsalmoth. It is a shame that we have no more time here, for they are just now in bloom."

"A most remarkable flower it must be," said Hrivaan. "But come, it can not be the only unusual feature of this region. What else grows or lives here that is worthy of mention?"

This led them off to a discussion of the history and character of Sorannah, which occupied the rest of that day's journey, and continued well into the next day. During the subsequent hours, while they spoke together of many things, as good travelers ought, they never came back to the subject of the candlebud, nor did Hrivaan or Nylissit ever speak of their own history.

Chapter the Third

In Which, Upon Arriving in Dragaera City,
We are Introduced To a Notable Personage
In the Imperial Guard

THE ACTUAL ARRIVAL of Khaavren, Aerich, and Tazendra in Dragaera City, which occurred early in the morning, was uneventful. They gave courteous farewells to their traveling companions, who, notwithstanding that they seemed to be in a great hurry to be about their business, returned the compliments nearly as well as the Issola they pretended to be.

The coach stopped on a narrow street, and was surrounded by urchins of the House of the Teckla who begged driver and passengers for coins. On this occasion they were disappointed, as the driver chased them away before any of the travelers could bring forth whatever alms they might have wished. When the urchins and the supposed Issola were gone, Tazendra and Khaavren took a careful look around. On one side of the street were small structures of wood and stone, most of which appeared to be homes for two or three families, save for one that displayed the Nut and Raisin emblem of the grocer. On the other side the buildings were taller and darker, and made of brick, and one of these claimed to be an inn.

"The Imperial Palace," said Aerich, "is this way."

"Good," said Khaavren. "Let us adjourn thither, for I tell you plainly that arriving thus, a full week sooner, due to your courtesy, than I had thought to, has only increased my desire to enter the Guard as quickly as possible."

Without another word, then, they set off, taking up most of the middle of the street, Khaavren with his arms linked with Aerich to his right and Tazendra to his left. They were nearly marching as they stepped through the long, winding street. On either side of them, inns, shops, and houses appeared, though Khaavren noticed at once a lack of any facilities for horses, which, as he subsequently learned, were forbidden to be stabled near the Imperial Palace, because of the odors they produced and the pests they attracted.

Most of the structures in this area had been built while the Idyllic School of the House of the Vallista was in fashion, as one could see from the semicircular archways, the wide, enclosed courtyards, and the impossibility of determining what was a carefully hidden support as opposed to a decoration. Furthermore, as they came closer to the areas of the city dominated by the Imperial Palace, they began to notice that there were no wooden buildings to be seen, but rather, everything was of carefully wrought stone. Khaavren looked around in wonder until, while passing a large, white building which proclaimed itself The Campaigner, he felt his arm grasped by Aerich, which he took as a signal to halt, and which signal he simultaneously passed on to Tazendra.

"Yes?" he said to Aerich.

The Lyorn made a gesture, then asked Tazendra, "Is that he?"

She leaned forward. "Kieron's Boots, I think it is."

"Who?" asked Khaavren. "The small fellow holding a gold cloak, and speaking to the Chreotha?"

"The very one," said Tazendra.

"Well?" asked Aerich.

"Let us hail him," said Tazendra.

"Yes, indeed," said Khaavren.

"Very well," said Aerich.

They quickly approached him. But, as they came near, he happened to turn away, so he didn't see them. When they were close by, they could hear him speaking in a firm but pleasant voice. "My dear lady," he was saying to the Chreotha, "regulation cut is all very well, to be sure, but I have no doubt that you perceive that a half-cloak, coming only to the tops of my thighs, would but ill suit my physique. Now, I beg of you, make it only a little longer, and I promise you that no harm will come of it. On the contrary, my Captain will be delighted that his Guard is looking well, for it is certainly a poor reflection on him for one of his regiment to stand out unpleasantly. You see my logic, do you not?"

"My lord," she said, "you argue most convincingly. But I assure you that I have been told, and in the strictest terms, to—" She stopped then, not from seeing the approach of the three friends, but because of the sound of coins clinking on the table in front of her where she sat before the building she shared with several other merchants, artisans, and mendicants who served the Imperial Palace in varying capacities.

The worthy Chreotha stopped, as we have said, and cleared her throat. "Well, after all," she said, "if you can promise me—" This time she did, in fact, stop because she had caught sight of the three friends approaching her. Seeing her glance over his shoulder, the other turned around, and Khaavren saw a young man who, while small, appeared to be perfectly proportioned. His face, in addition, was regular and handsome, with wide-set blue eyes and a well-formed nose. He was dressed in a marvelous tailored silk doublet of white, with lacing around his small, delicate hands. He wore hose and pantaloons of black, and tall, shiny white boots with pointed toes. His doublet was embroidered with black and red abstract designs. He bore a sword of medium length and weight, with the bell guard that has been called the "dueler's grip," and a ruby set into the hilt.

He bowed to Khaavren, Aerich, and Tazendra, showing no sign of embarrassment. His bow, moreover, was graceful, left foot forward and right hand nearly touching the ground while his eyes remained on the faces of the companions. While he did not, as we have said, show any embarrassment, the Chreotha more than made up for this lack by flushing and stuttering enough for several court functionaries.

"A good day to you," said the Guardsman. "I believe I have seen two of you before, in the village of Newmarket, have I not?"

They nodded. "I am Aerich, and this is the lady Tazendra, and the Marquis of Khaavren." They bowed in turn, and he acknowledged.

"I am Pel," he said. Khaavren had, by this time, learned to watch Aerich whenever an introduction was made. He was rewarded in his vigilance by seeing the tiniest furrow cross the Lyorn's brown. Pel continued, "What brings you to the city?"

"Why, the same thing that brings you," said Tazendra carelessly.

"You must excuse me if I fail to understand your meaning," said Pel. Khaavren was certain there was a tension apparent in Pel's face and voice as he said this.

"Why," said the Dzurlord, "to join the Guard."

"Ah!" said Pel, his expression clearing. Khaavren glanced at Aerich. They caught each other's eyes for a moment, and Khaavren knew that Pel's reaction had not been missed by the sharp-eyed Lyorn. "That falls out well enough," said Pel. "For I am fortunate enough to be on tolerably good terms with G'aereth, who is a captain, and is just now looking for recruits to fill his posts. I should be happy to introduce you. Now, two of you," he indicated Aerich and Tazendra, "I know to be excellent companions, from having seen you at play but two days ago. And as for you," he nodded to Khaavren, "I must say that your face pleases me. So if it is agreeable to join the regiment in which I have the honor to serve, it is as good as settled."

They quickly agreed to this, whereupon Pel smiled and turned back to the Chreotha, who had recovered and was patiently awaiting the end of the conversation. "Come, now," said the Guardsman. "I will return for this cloak two hours after noon. I think you can have it ready by then, can you not? I'm certain I can have still more business for you, if you do."

For a moment, the Chreotha flushed with embarrassment, but the thought of preparing uniforms for three more Guards apparently decided her and she agreed.

"Come then," said Pel, "and I'll lead you to the captain." So saying, he began walking down the street. The three companions followed. Tazendra caught up to him, and they began talking as they walked. Khaavren dropped back and made a sign for Aerich to do the same. When the latter did, Khaavren spoke to him in a low voice.

"I could not help but notice, my friend, that you started when our friend gave us his name."

"Well," said Aerich. "And if I did?"

"I should be happy to know why."

Aerich shrugged. "I am a Lyorn, and we are taught all that we need to know of the lines of the Houses. Now, I know very well that there is no 'Pel' belonging to the House of the Yendi. Therefore, he did not give us his true name."

"Ah," said Khaavren. "But what then? He is a Yendi."

Aerich had no answer to this, so they continued in silence toward the Imperial Palace.

The Imperial Palace was begun shortly before the reign of Emperor Jamiss I, and the earliest version was completed toward the end of his reign, which encompassed, in its nine hundred years, the entirety of the reign of the House of the Vallista in the First Cycle. The story has come down to us that the Tsalmoth Emperor who proceeded him, Faarith I, took possession of the Palace before it was habitable, and that he was killed by falling masonry as he directed the installation of the throne. That the Imperial Orb, which was even then beginning to show its marvelous attributes, didn't save him, was taken as a sign by Jamiss, the engineer who was directing the building. He thereupon claimed the throne and the Orb for his own. While this tale smacks of the apocryphal, we cannot deny that it has a certain charm.

At any rate, the aforementioned Vallista reign saw, in addition to the construction of the Imperial Palace, the creation for the first time of forts and fortresses (the distinction, certain comments by the Lord of Snails notwithstanding, having nothing whatsoever to do with the presence of breastworks, nor the size of buttresses) along what was then the Eastern border. The construction of the Great Houses around the Imperial Palace did not begin until the Second Cycle, with the reign of Kieron the Younger, of the House of the Dragon. He ordered the building of the Great House of the Phoenix, opposite the Palace, as a tribute to Empress Zerika II, or possibly as a bribe to persuade her to relinquish the throne—history is unclear on this. The other Houses were built over the course of the Lyorn, Tiassa, and Hawk reigns during this Cycle, and doors were added to the Imperial Palace which looked out on each. Streets were laid on each side of these Houses, so that if one left the Palace by, for instance, the Athyra Door, one would pass the House of Athyra on one's left.

It is not our intention to weary our readers with a description of each Great House in the Imperial Circle, but we beg leave to make a hasty sketch of the Palace itself.

The Palace was built before the Vallista architects had split into the Idyllic and Realist camps (and therefore, of course, long before the Reunification and subsequent splits), but the seeds of both major styles could be seen quite clearly, as Mistress Lethria has shown so well in her recent treatise. By the time of Emperor Tortaalik—that is, by the time of which we have the honor to write—the Palace had long since reached its final form, and the original building was a mere nucleus within, holding the throne room, the personal chambers of the Emperor and his family, kitchens, and a few small audience chambers. The larger Palace rose nine stories into the air, contained full courtyards at each door, a separate four-story wing (with associated minister) for each House, dozens of balconies (pillared and plain), hundreds of stairways (circular, curved, twisted, and straight), thousands of windows (round, oblong, triangular, rectangular, octagonal, and square), nine libraries (public and private), four indoor gardens and arboreta, twelve major indoor baths, sixty-five towers, twenty-seven minor domes and three major ones, and was, in the famous words the Empress Undauntra I, "the most bleeding indefensible structure it has ever been my duty to occupy."

In those days, no one familiar with the Imperial Palace spoke of going there. One went to the Dragon Wing, if it was a matter of war, or the Iorich Wing, if it was a matter of law, or the Central Palace, if it was an Imperial matter, and so on.

It was to the Dragon Wing that our friends found themselves traveling. Khaavren knew some of this, from having been told of it, but he had no comprehension of it until, walking around the immense complex of buildings, looking for the Street of the Dragon, he realized he was seeing one massive structure.

"It's amazing!" he cried to his companions.

Pel smiled complacently, but Tazendra touched his arm and said in a low voice, "Come! Not so loud. Everyone will think that you come from the duchies."

A puzzled look crossed Khaavren's countenance. "But I do come from the duchies."

This time, the look of puzzlement crossed Tazendra's features, while Aerich smiled.

In due course they came to the Street of the Dragon.

They walked along it until they came to the gate into the Dragon Courtyard. Eight guards were stationed on the walls of this gate, dressed in the black with silver trim of their House. Each carried a pike and had a sword at his side.

As the companions came near, one of the Guards said, "Who approaches the Gate of the Dragon, and by what right?"

"The Cavalier Pel, Guardsman of the company of G'aereth, with potential recruits, to see the Captain."

"Enter," suggested the guard.

They passed beneath the arched gateway, which had not been closed. Khaavren found himself, to his own annoyance, nervous. For the first time, he began to wonder if he could make his mark in an organization filled with such men and women as these. But he resolutely put these thoughts aside.

They were challenged once more before being admitted into the wing itself. They were in a hall wide enough for a party twice their size to walk abreast. The walls were of marble, and unadorned save for occasion oil paintings of great battles, none of which, we are forced to admit, Khaavren recognized.

The apartments of the captains of the Imperial Guard were located in the west sub-wing of the Dragon Wing of the Palace, which was reached through a wide hallway that jutted off from the main entrance at a sharp angle, passing beneath a plain arch and sweeping in a gentle curve away from the central area of the Palace. In it, each of the captains had apartments arranged in this way: a large foyer or waiting room, a private audience room for the captain, and audience rooms for up to six lieutenants. Behind the captain's audience room was a stairway, leading up to the captain's living quarters. Each captain also had a small stairway which communicated to the audience quarters of the Brigadier-General of the Imperial Guard, to whose person and household the entire third floor of this sub-wing was devoted. The fourth and top floor was a vast meeting hall, where the Brigadier could address as many as three thousand Guards at once.

There were quarters in the Palace for six captains, although there were, at present, only two. Each captain could command as many as six lieutenants, although Pel's captain, My Lord Count of Gant-Aerethia (or G'aereth, as he was then known) had only troops enough for one, and had therefore chosen to have none. We should note in passing that this decision of Captain G'aereth's had the effect, not entirely accidental, of leaving his troops with the belief that anyone who could show himself worthy would be promoted to fill the spot.

Khaavren and his companions entered the foyer of this captain, which was nearly empty except for them, and Pel addressed a few words in a quiet voice to one of the Guardsmen. This man, a tall Dragonlord with two short-swords, nodded and stepped over to the Captain's door. More words were spoken quietly, then the Dragon nodded to Pel, who motioned his companions forward. Khaavren's heart was pounding as they stepped toward the door, but he attempted to look as cool as Aerich, or, failing that, as haughty as Tazendra.

However, before they reached the door, there was the sound of commotion behind them, and a cry of "Make way! Make way for Lord Shaltre. Make way!"

Khaavren, whose keen eyes missed nothing, saw Aerich's back tense as this name was pronounced, but the Lyorn coolly moved to the side when Pel, who was leading them, did so. Khaavren and Tazendra followed this lead, and as they did, two things happened. The first was that an old, powerfully built Dzurlord appeared from the door in front of Pel, walking quickly into the middle of the room. This was plainly the Captain. His eyes were fixed on the opposite door, so Khaavren looked there also. A man and a woman, both Dragonlords and both in Guardsmen's cloaks, entered and stepped to the sides. Then another came through the door, dressed in the golden-brown and red of the House of the Lyorn, but wearing long, loose breeches instead of a skirt, and no vambraces. Khaavren glanced quickly at Aerich, but the latter's face showed no expression.

The Lyorn noble and the Captain looked at each other, then nodded and the captain signaled that the other should enter his audience chamber. This chamber, we should note, was supplied with a hard oak door, on leather hinges, set into a wall of stone, so nothing said within could be heard from the antechamber, unless one pressed one's ear directly to the door.

Pel shrugged, as if to say, "Well, it may be a while then," and walked casually over to the woman who had accompanied the Lyorn. As he did this, Khaavren leaned over and whispered to Aerich, "Who is he?"

In a tone without inflection, Aerich said, "The Count of Shaltre, Marquis of Deepsprings, Baron of—"

"Pardon me, good Aerich," said Khaavren. "But you perceive that these names tell me nothing."

"Well, he is a chief advisor to His Imperial Majesty."

"Ah!"

Then Khaavren noticed that Pel was in deep conversation with the woman who had escorted the Lyorn. She smiled and shook her head, and, from the back, Khaavren fancied he could see Pel smiling at her. After a moment, Pel shrugged and seated himself next to the door, and leaned back as if resting—with his head remarkable close to the door itself. Aerich and Khaavren exchanged a glance full of meaning.

"Well?" said Tazendra to Khaavren.

"Well?" said Khaavren. "I should think we could wait. What is your opinion, Aerich?"

In answer, Aerich seated himself and said, "This appears to be a waiting room."

Khaavren nodded and also sat down, on a backless stone bench that caused him to wonder briefly who had done the labor of bringing it there, how many it had taken, and if they were well-paid for their trouble. Tazendra looked unhappy but also sat down. A moment later, Pel stretched lazily and leaned forward, and at just that moment the door opened and Count Shaltre emerged. His eyes flashed fire, but he said nothing. He collected the two Guards who had escorted him and departed.

Tazendra said, "Well, should we—"

"Hush," said Aerich. Pel turned back to them and sat down next to Tazendra.

"Well?" said Khaavren. "What did you learn?"

"Learn?" said Pel, frowning. "Do you pretend I learned anything?"

"I nearly think so," said Khaavren. "Or, at any rate, I should think you were trying to."

"Not the least in the world, I assure you," said Pel.

Before Khaavren could answer, the Dragonlord who had been in the room said, "The Captain will see you now." The four stood as one. Pel led the way into the audience chamber, with Tazendra close at his heels, followed by Aerich and Khaavren.

They found themselves standing before a long desk, covered with papers. Behind the desk was the Captain, and behind him a window that looked out into a courtyard, where several Guardsmen could be seen engaged in sword practice. A cool breeze came through the window, disturbing the papers, which were only held in place by stones set on them.

G'aereth gave them a greeting with his hand. Pel said, "My Captain, I have the honor to present to you the Cavalier Aerich, the Cavalier Tazendra, and the Marquis of Khaavren."

"Welcome, my friends, welcome. So, you all wish to join his Imperial Majesty's Guards?"

They signified that this was, indeed, the case.

"Well, well," he said. He addressed Aerich. "It would appear that you have no blade."

Aerich bowed as a sign of agreement.

"Can you use one?" asked the Captain.

Aerich shrugged, as if to say, "Who cannot?"

"Are you then, a sorcerer?"

This time when Aerich shrugged it meant, "Only a poor one." Aerich, as we can see, was very expressive with his gestures.

The Captain looked at him closely for a moment, his keen eyes taking in the skirt that is the mark of a trained warrior of the House of the Lyorn. Then the Captain grunted, as if to say, "I have no worries about your fighting abilities, my friend." The Captain's grunts, as we can see, were nearly as expressive as the Lyorn's shrugs.

G'aereth turned his attention to Tazendra. He said, "I see that you have a blade."

"Well, so I do."

"Can you play with it?"

"Yes," she said.

"Ah! And are you a sorcerer?"

"If my lord would be good enough to try me—"

The Captain grunted, which meant, this time, "There is no need for the moment."

He continued, "Can you ride?"

"I was born on horseback," she said.

"Hmmm. And you, my good Khaavren?"

"My lord?" said Khaavren, who felt a sudden tightening in this throat. "Yes, I ride."

"Are you a sorcerer?"

"No part of me, I must admit."

"And your swordplay?"

"I only ask that you try me, my lord."

"That's well," he said. "That is what we'll do." He reached into a cupboard that was next to his chair and found three purses. He passed one to each. "Guardsmen Pel will show you where you may purchase uniform cloaks. Come back when you are attired, and we will give you a trial duty, during which each of you will experience a patrol as a Guardsman, and a report will be made of how well you perform your duties."

"Thank you, Lord," said Khaavren, taking the purse. Aerich bowed his head, which amounted to the same thing.

Tazendra, however, bowed without accepting the purse. "I am well provided for," she said. "I have no need—"

"Ah! So much the worse!" said G'aereth.

"So much the worse?"

"Yes. It is my wish that I, and I alone, you perceive, outfit and equip my Guardsmen. I wish them to be dependent upon me, as I am upon them."

"Oh. Well then—"

"Yes?"

"I shall give up my funds from this moment."

"That would be well. And I have just remembered something else." He found, from within the same cupboard, a handful of gold Imperials, which he gave to Aerich. "These are to allow you to purchase a sword."

Aerich shrugged again, this time to indicate, "I will obey, naturally."

At this, they understood the interview to be at an end, and filed out of the room, after bowing to the Captain.

"Come now," said Tazendra to Pel, "let us adjourn to the tailor with whom we saw you speaking earlier. The sooner we are outfitted, the sooner we may be tested. And the sooner tested, the sooner we shall be able to cover ourselves with glory."

Aerich shrugged again.

Chapter the Fourth

In Which Aerich Acquires a Sword
And our Friends are Assigned their Duties

ON THE WAY to meet with the Chreotha tailor, Pel had occasion three times to point out to Aerich that they were passing a weapon-smith, but each time the latter merely shook his head. The third time, Pel said, "I should mention, I think, that the Captain expects you to be armed."

"I will be," said Aerich laconically. Even as he spoke something seemed to catch his eye, for he stopped, and indicated a door leading down into the basement of a hostelry. They were on a tiny, unnamed street between the Street of the Dragons and the Street of the Seven Trees, perhaps half a league from the Dragon Wing. The hostel was a squat, two-story building, of whitewashed brick, and had a large sign depicting a fat partridge. The door to the basement had a small sign, depicting a simple longsword.

"Here?" said Pel.

"Do you know this smith?" asked Aerich.

"K'sozhaleniju, I do not," said Pel, falling for a moment into the Serioli speech then fashionable at court.

Aerich, without another word, made his way down the stairs. The others followed, and found themselves in a small, stuffy basement, which would have been damp, smelly, close, and dark, were it not, in fact, well-lit, which prevented it from being dark. An old Vallista, with scraggly grey hair and bright eyes, sat at a table honing a hiltless blade by use of a small whetstone. As the four friends entered, he looked up and pursed his lips, as if trying to decide why someone could be coming to see him. Then he shook his head and said, "May I have the honor to be of some service to you, my lords?"

Aerich nodded. "I would like a sword," he said. "It is to be three and three quarter pounds, forty-seven centimeters of blade. The width is to be a uniform three and one half centimeters. The steel must be Kanefthali, tempered in the Dui'clior way and crystal-forged. The balance must be within one centimeter of the guard, which must be plain. Double-edged, oak-covered hilt."

The Vallista listened to this quietly, then bowed, "Length of the hilt, lord?"

"Anything within reason."

The smith nodded. "I have one that is made of a fine alloy, woven, as is said, in the technique of—" He paused, seeing that Aerich was uninterested in these details. He continued, "It fits all of the particulars you mention save hilt and balance."

"Balance is necessary," said Aerich.

"Of a certainty it is, lord," said the Vallista. "But with a few words, I think, I can satisfy you."

"Pray do so, then."

"I shall."

"How?"

"Well, this way: I shall removed the hilt and replace it with one of oak, and I will hollow this out and fill it with lead shot until the balance is correct. You perceive, then, that we will have solved both problems at once."

"Admirable," said Aerich.

"To be sure, I will also sharpen, clean, and polish it. Would you like leather grips on the hilt?"

"Exactly."

"And will you have a stiffened scabbard? Or perhaps a soft leather sheath?"

"Just so," said Aerich.

"A belt then as well, with a small chain for a side draw?"

"Precisely."

"Very good."

The Vallista disappeared into a back room, whence the sound of sawing could be heard for a few minutes, then other sounds which Khaavren recognized as smoothing and polishing. The companions occupied themselves by describing the coach-ride to Pel, and discussing their strange companions, who were dressed as Issola, yet seemed to be Phoenix. When Khaavren explained his observations about the candlebud, Pel's brow came together, and then Khaavren observed a faint smile and upon his lips, hover for a moment, and fly off. Yet when he asked about it, Pel denied having any thoughts on the matter; Tazendra, we should add, was amazed that this deception had taken place before her, and demanded several times of Khaavren and Aerich if they were certain of the truth of their observations, to which they replied without hesitation that they were.

In a surprisingly short time, the smith appeared with sword and sheath, along with belt and chain. Without deigning to inspect any of them, Aerich placed on the table the Imperials he had been given by the Captain for the sword. The Vallista seemed satisfied, and bowed deeply. Aerich led them out of the basement.

"Come then," he said. "Let us see about our uniform cloaks."

This was done in due course, after which they repaired to The Campaigner, which inn they had noted earlier, and had a meal while waiting for their cloaks to be finished. Their host brought them several bottles of wine from the Ailor region, and a dish involving darr meat rolled around chunks of delicately seasoned beef and covered with a sauce in which butter, cream, and tarragon figured prominently. For a while, the only sounds from the four friends were those scrapings, of wooden spoons in wooden bowls, so beloved of the hungry, the epicurean, and the cook. At last Khaavren gave forth a sigh and announced that he was finished with the meal.

"That is well," said Aerich, "for I think it is time we take our uniform cloaks and return to the Captain who will, no doubt, assign us trial duties."

"Well spoken!" said Tazendra. "For my part, I am quite ready to begin."

"As am I," said Khaavren.

Using the money given them for the purpose, they paid their account, and picked up their cloaks from the Chreotha across the street. Each cloak was made of linen and silk brocade, of a fine golden hue, and was fastened at the neck by a cunning clasp made of copper and inlaid with a stylized phoenix. On the left breast was a small pair of boots, embroidered in red thread. Khaavren, Aerich, and Tazendra had half-cloaks, while Pel's was knee-length.

After settling with the clothier, they returned to the Imperial Palace and informed G'aereth that they were prepared to take up their duties.

We will pause, then, long enough to say two words about Captain Gant-Aerethia. He had arrived in Dragaera City, the poor younger son of a poor Dzur baron from a marshy south-western lake region, late in the Seventeenth Teckla Republic. He joined the army of the Jhegaala, and was involved in the fall of the Republic and the establishment of Empress Viodonna the Sixth, of the House of the Jhegaala. He then enlisted in the armies of the Empire under the command of Lady Yaro e'Lanya, and came to her notice during the Island Wars, especially at the Battle of Near P'iensotta, where he received a battlefield promotion to officer. He ended the Wars on Lady Yaro's staff, and it was actually in his arms that she died in the famous Charge of the Brown River.

At the end of the Wars, and the subsequent beginning of the Reign of Cherova III of the House of the Athyra, the entire battalion that had been Lady Yaro's was eliminated, but by then Lord Gant-Aerethia had earned many friends at court, not the least of whom was Sethra Lavode herself, who served as Warlord during the last half of the Island Wars. For these reasons, then, Empress Cherova was unable to dismiss him. She finally found a spot for him commanding her personal guards, thinking thus to keep him from doing anything noteworthy. When she next noticed him, these guards had become an elite fighting corps—none other, in fact, than the famous Featherhats, although this name wasn't given them until hundreds of years later.

After that, he was involved in the Lavode scandal, although in what capacity is not clear. He emerged in good form, however, appearing, somehow, not to have made an enemy on either—or, rather, any—side. When the fires died, as the saying is, he had earned such powerful friends among the courtiers and allies of the Empress that her own personal dislike for him was unable to harm him.

Among his friends for many years was the young Prince Tortaalik, to whom he had, in fact, given some lessons in swordplay before the Prince became Phoenix Heir. Their friendship grew no weaker as the years wore on, and Tortaalik never stopped admiring G'aereth's blunt manner, harsh tongue, and fiery temper. G'aereth became Captain of the Gold Cloaks the very day Tortaalik took the Orb.

This Captain, then, this G'aereth, was just coming into his prime, just arriving at the station for which he had worked all his life, and he accepted this as he accepted everything life threw at him: with a bold eye, good humor, a clear sense of what mattered, and unbending principles. Thus his first words when the friends arrived were to say to Pel, with something of a glint in his eye, "Your cloak appears somewhat different from those of your comrades."

Pel bowed. "I am honored that my Captain should deign to notice."

G'aereth chuckled, but said no more about it. Khaavren said, "My lord, we are prepared to assume our duties."

"That is well," said the Captain. "Are you aware of what these duties consist?"

"No, my lord," said Khaavren frankly.

"But we hope to learn," said Aerich with a slight bow.

"Then I will tell you," said G'aereth. "There remains two more days of festivities in the city. Those who enjoy these festivities may, in their enthusiasm, become a menace to the other more restrained citizens. It falls upon us, then, to make certain there are no, or at least few, needless injuries. We must also strive to our utmost to see that the dueling code is upheld."

They nodded.

"Very well," said the Captain, "you are to enforce the laws of the Empire."

"And what laws are these, Captain?" asked Aerich.

"Heh," said G'aereth. "Use your judgement. If it looks illegal, then it probably is."

"Very well."

"Furthermore, if necessary, you may act as judges and Imperial Witnesses, but only if no other duty presses you."

The four friends nodded once more.

"And remember, from this moment forward, your lives belong to the Emperor first, to the Warlord second, to me third, and to yourselves last. Is this plainly understood?"

They all agreed that it was.

"That is well. Now, have your found lodgings?"

All except Pel shook their heads.

"Well," said the Captain, "the evening's revelries will not begin for yet a few hours. Make use of this time to secure lodgings. Then you will meet outside of the Dragon Gate. Here you will find those I have chosen to be partners for each of you. Be warned," he added sternly, "that your partners will report to me on how well you have carried out your duties. You perceive that admission to the Imperial Guard is not a favor to be earned lightly—especially when it is to my brigade that you wish to attach yourselves."

They all bowed. The Captain's words suited Khaavren well, for he would have found little value in a prize too easily won. Something occurred to him, then, and he said, "All of us? Isn't Pel admitted?"

"He is, yes," said the Captain. "His test was completed two days ago. But he has not yet made a patrol, and I wish for him to be guided by someone with experience."

"I understand," said Khaavren.

Pel, in his turn, said, "How long will this patrol last, my Captain?"

"You will begin as I have indicated, three hours hence. Continue until dawn, then you may retire. Tomorrow, present yourselves to me again. You, Khaavren, at this hour. Tazendra at the next hour, and Aerich one hour later and Pel last."

There being no more questions, then, the foursome took their leaves and went out to secure lodgings. This was quickly done, but, as we have already taken up much of the reader's valuable time with descriptions, we do not intend to try his patience with yet another at this moment—rest assured, however, that we will return to the matter of lodgings soon enough, as it plays a part in the history we have the honor to relate.

Chapter the Fifth

In Which Method is Applied to Mayhem, and Khaavren, To his Advantage, Recalls Certain Filial Advice

I N THE MEANTIME we will leap ahead, with our readers' kind indulgence, to the early evening, when a cool breeze from the east blew across our friends before the high wrought-iron and stonework Dragon Gate of the Imperial Palace. They had just settled down to wait when four Dragonlords appeared from within. They approached the four friends and, without arrangement or study, each stood before one and bowed.

The young man who bowed to Khaavren wore knee-length black boots, heavy black hose, a black, cheaply woven and loosely fitting cotton doublet with copper buttons and silver-colored strips along the side and at the cuffs. He carried a heavy broadsword at his side. Khaavren at once determined that he was the sort of fellow whose arrogant blue eyes and quarrelsome countenance would have already earned him scores of duels.

"Good day, my lord," said our young hero. "I am Khaavren."

"I am Frai e'Terics," said the other. "If you would be so kind as to follow me, we can begin at once."

"I should be honored," said Khaavren.

"Yes," said the other.

Khaavren looked at him quickly, but saw no trace of a smile. He shrugged to himself, however, and allowed the Dragonlord to lead him toward the Street of the Nine Pleasures. This was a narrow, east-west running street that had been named for the inns, brothels, gaming halls, and other entertainments that could be found there. No one knew what all of the nine pleasures were, and much entertainment was derived among the lower classes (and, we are forced to admit, sometimes the upper classes) by speculating upon what these pleasures were, or imagining that a tenth had been found. One that was often spoken of, in jest, was the pleasure provided by the narrowness of the street, which hardly permitted the passing of a single hand-cart.

The pleasure provided by this feature was that of standing in a doorway when two nobles, particularly two Dzurlords, met; especially if each had a greatsword worn in such a way that it would project out to the side. When this occurred, as it did several times a day, one of the nobles would be obliged to turn to allow the other to pass, thus being subject to the loud hoots and jeers from hidden onlookers; or else both must stand fast, in which case it was unlikely that both would resume the journey under their own power. It is certainly true that there were other streets in Dragaera City as narrow, but none as narrow and as well-trodden by the nobility.

To this street, then, came Khaavren and Frai. On this evening, ribbons had been hung from building to building—ribbons of all colors, but gold predominating; buildings of all types, but square wooden frames of two or three stories and round balconies being the most common. During the walk, they had not said a word to each other, Khaavren contenting himself with watching the festivities. These, it should be said, ran the gamut from public, with hundreds of revelers singing songs together, attempting to reclaim in volume whatever might be lost in pitch, to private, with a single Teckla holding a bottle of wine and laughing uproariously at a joke only he understood. Sometimes, the revels were organized, as the parade they passed which included bits of wood and wax thrown from buildings, and fireworks shot back and forth between the balconies of opposing inns in a sort of mock battle, at other times to the completely disorganized, as the bathing party in the public fountain near Maretta's House.

After some few minutes of walking along the street and watching the festivities, Frai indicated that they should enter an inn beneath a sign which showed an issola contorting itself around a thin tree. The Inn was crowded, as all such places were on this evening of celebration. The patrons were of mixed Houses, but Khaavren noticed a high proportion of Dzur and Jhereg. He mentioned this to Frai, but the latter gave him a look which said, as plainly as Aerich could have said it with a shrug or the Captain with a grunt, that the observation was useless.

The host, who stood behind a long counter nearly as high as his chest, noticed the two men in gold cloaks at once, and nodded to them. Walking down to the end of the counter and reaching under it, he appeared to pull on something. Khaavren was at a loss to know the result of this at first, but Frai continued to the far wall, through a door in it, and came at last to a hallway, where he stopped opposite a part of the wall that appeared no different from the rest of the passage. Frai glanced at Khaavren as if to say, "watch closely," then clapped his hands five times in a particular sequence. Almost at once, a door was revealed in the wall, and the two Guardsmen passed through.

Khaavren found himself in a large room set in the back of the inn. There were six or seven round tables, and seated at each were five or six persons, mostly Jhereg and Dzur, and they appeared to be playing with the Sivali-

Yangorra Stones, which were at that time becoming one of the more popular means of parting with or gaining excess funds.

For an instant, Khaavren wondered why the gamblers had taken the trouble to conceal themselves, as apparently they had done, but the idea suddenly came to him that a game thus concealed would be safe from Imperial taxes, and this would allow the inn to keep a larger portion of the profits. He was on the point of asking Frai how he had uncovered this place, and if they were to arrest all of the participants as well as the owners, when he noticed that no one in the room seemed surprised or concerned by their presence. In fact, at that very moment, a short, pale Jhereg approached them, with an ingratiating smile on his lips.

"Good evening, my lords," he said.

Frai said, "You will be so kind, my good Corris, as to keep your pleasantries to their home within your mouth, and merely hand over to me that for which I have come."

"With pleasure, my lord," said the Jhereg, giving Frai a moderately heavy purse. "Is it your pleasure to stay for a few hours and increase this amount, or to offer us the chance to regain some portion of it?"

Frai only growled and signified to Khaavren that the interview was at an end. As they passed back into the main part of the inn, and presently, back onto the street, Khaavren said, "Tell me, my friend Frai, does what I have just had the honor to witness represent a common occurrence?"

They crossed the street and were immediately inside another inn, almost identical to the first, save that the counter was lower, darker, and on the other side of the doorway. The floor had once been tiled, which indicated that the inn used to be of the expensive sort, but the tiles were now broken and chipped, and the plain hardwood of the walls seemed in need of some repair. Light was provided by lamps hung along the walls, as well as a large one in the center of the single large room. This hostelry was, like the first, filled nearly to overflowing, although

Khaavren noticed only a few Chreotha and Vallista among the throng of Teckla.

"I do not believe, my lord Tiassa," said Frai, "that I have done you the honor of calling you my friend. And as to your question, I think you will soon learn the answer."

"A moment, sir," said Khaavren, who suddenly felt his blood rushing to a spot behind his eyes. "Could it be that I have the misfortune to have done you some injury of which I am unaware? If so, I hope you will do me the honor of telling me of it. Yet, if I may say so, it seems unlikely that I could have yet had the chance to have given you an injury, since all we have had to do with each other is to collect a few gold Imperials, which you have not even deigned to share with me, as, I think, a good comrade would."

"You have done me no injury, sir," said Frai, who, stopping just inside the doorway of the inn at the beginning of Khaavren's speech, had become more than a little warm by the end of it. "You have done me no injury, yet I confess that I think little enough of you."

"Indeed," said Khaavren haughtily. "If you would be good enough to tell me the reason, perhaps we can come to an accord of some kind."

"Reason?" said the other, in fully as haughty a manner as Khaavren's before him. "I need no reason. You are a Tiassa; that is sufficient."

"You pretend, then, that there is some blemish upon my House?"

"Not the least in the world. Only—"

"Well?"

"You are not a Dragon. Hence, you see, you have no place in the Imperial Guard."

"And yet, it seems to me that membership in the Guard is open to all who earn it."

"Oh, as to that; that is a matter of law. I speak of what is proper."

"Sir," said Khaavren, only keeping control of his temper with great difficulty, "I am anxious to improve your opinion of me."

"That is unlikely," said Frai.

"I know a way," said Khaavren.

"I should be happy to learn of it."

"It is the only way a man of honor has to repair an insult to his House, or rid himself of an annoying companion."

"I annoy you then?" said Frai with some surprise.

"What do you expect?" said Khaavren. "I am, as you have done me the honor to notice, of the House of the Tiassa, and furthermore I am from the Sorannah, where no one utters careless speech, for we are all as warm as the winters are cool, and consequently we let little pass."

"You wish, then, to play at sport?"

"Exactly. And of a particular nature."

"Well, I find myself suitably equipped."

"Where shall we play, then, my lord? Perhaps a stroll out into the evening is in order?"

"For what reason, my lord? Here is fine, I think."

"And yet, need we not find seconds, and a judge, and a witness, to stay within the agreements of the law?"

"How then?" said Frai. "Who is likely to arrest us?"

"That is true," said Khaavren. "For my part, I am unlikely to arrest myself, and you will soon be in no condition to arrest anyone."

"That is unlikely," said the Dragonlord. "And as for seconds, well, as you are only lately come from the duchies you have had insufficient time to make friends; it would therefore be unbecoming of me to have the advantage of a second when you have none."

"You speak with courtesy as well as wisdom, my lord."

"And, as to whether I will, as you suggested, be in no condition to make an arrest should I wish to do so, well, it is likely that you are mistaken."

"Come, then, let us find out," said Khaavren, stepping into an aisle between rows of tables, and backing to the far end of the room, where he removed his cloak, and drew his sword.

The Dragonlord moved to a spot in the same aisle, near the door, and removed his own cloak. It should be added that the guests, so numerous the moment before that movement was all but impossible, had, by the particular magic of crowds, made a large clear space for the contest without any of them actually leaving the room.

"Have a care," said Frai. "I should hate to take advantage of you by breaking your stick."

"Oh, that is of no consequence," said Khaavren, taking his dagger into his left hand. "If you will be so kind as to draw, you will make me the happiest of men, I assure you."

"I am only too delighted to please you, sir," said Frai, and took his heavy broadsword into both of his hands, weaving it through the air quite expertly. Khaavren noticed that, with the Dragonlord's doublet as apparently ill-fitting as it was, there was no need for it to be removed to allow him full freedom of motion. Khaavren's tunic, of course, made no interference with his own motion.

Meanwhile, the patrons of the inn, delighted by the rare spectacle of a contest between a pair of Guardsmen, drew well back and cleared away several tables. The host, while worried about damage to his inn, was also aware of how good it would be for his business for weeks to come to have such an event occur there.

Khaavren, watching Frai's blade-work, would have been frightened at the skill the Dragonlord was showing, except that his anger, by this time, had passed beyond the reach of fear. He stamped his foot, then, and said, "Sir, I am awaiting you impatiently."

"Oh, there is no need of that," cried Frai, and immediately charged, sweeping his broadsword down at an angle to strike Khaavren's neck on the left side, which would have ended the discussion at once.

Khaavren, however, not wishing to feel the bite of such a large blade in the region of his neck, and knowing that his thin blade could hardly parry a strong cut from the larger broadsword, took half a step backward. Now, although he was quite warm, Khaavren's sense had not deserted him, and he knew that he must consider carefully his approach to the contest. First, he noted with pleasure that the other's blade was no longer than his. Second, he observed that both of his opponent's hands were involved in maneuvering the heavier sword, while he, Khaavren, had his left hand free to use his dagger. Third, the broadsword was considerably heavier, but then, it ought to be slower, notwithstanding the fact that the Dragon was using both of his hands.

As Frai struck again, this time for the other side of Khaavren's neck, the Tiassa continued observation. "From the blades," he said to himself, "let us pass to the wielders. Now, I am in extremely good health, and ought not to tire easily, yet I would be surprised indeed if he were not. So. Yet he is larger than I am, and, moreover, his arms are longer than mine, so I ought to contrive to position myself closer to him than he is to me, to make up for it. This, alas, is unlikely. However, I ought to be that much quicker. We can call that even as well. So much for the questions of reach and endurance.

"Now," Khaavren continued to himself, "he is quite as good as I am in his handling of the blade, so I can expect no advantage there. But, we must not forget, he is a Dragonlord, and will hardly think of me as a worthy opponent, especially since I have now retreated from him twice. Well then, if I defend myself only, I will increase his self-confidence, and then he will betray himself. Yet, thinking again, this plan will result in a long engagement, and my father (who should know, I think) says that long engagements are decided by a mistake, rather than by skill, and each of us is as likely to make a mistake as the other.

"So, then! Instead, if I were to cut him a few times, he will grow angry, and as I play with some skill, I will encourage him to make errors due to anger, and this will humiliate him, and lead him to make more mistakes, and then I will commit the final humiliation of passing my sword through his body. Come, this is the plan, I think."

Having settled on this idea, Khaavren put it into action at once. As Frai cut for his stomach, the Tiassa stepped back again, but only so far as to make sure the sword missed by the smallest possible margin. As the Dragonlord pulled his blade back for another cut, his left elbow was, for a moment, unprotected, and Khaavren reached out, without changing his footing, and scratched it.

Frai bared his teeth as he felt the scratch, and swung straight down for Khaavren's head. This maneuver forced the Tiassa to step backward, because merely tipping his head back would have allowed the blade to continue downward along his breastbone. He stepped back, then, but immediately recovered his place, and, almost delicately, put a cut across Frai's right wrist.

At this point the Dragonlord stopped, and looked at Khaavren with a grimace of rage. He still had enough of self-possession, however, not to charge into the quick hands and supple wrists of the Tiassa. Therefore, he changed his tactics, and began making quick thrusts with the point of his broadsword for Khaavren's head, chest, and abdomen.

This was no better, however. For without the weight of the blade and the force of the long swing behind it, Khaavren was able to use his sword to parry the thrusts—with some effort, it is true. On the fourth of these thrusts, aimed at Khaavren's neck, the Tiassa managed to push Frai's blade to the right, while maintaining his own sword in a position on top of his opponent's. This, for an instant, left the Dragonlord's body open. Khaavren stepped in and thrust with his dagger at Frai's throat, a blow which the latter avoided by leaning backward and bringing his sword up. Then Khaavren dropped the point of his sword and stepped forward again while thrusting.

The Tiassa's blade penetrated a good inch into the middle of the other's chest. Frai scrambled back, while Khaavren continued forward with a thrusting motion. His steps were of a strange cadence: right—leftright—leftright—leftright, and so on, and each time his left foot was forward he struck with his poniard, and each time his right foot was forward he struck with his sword.

Frai continued to retreat for a moment, then, gnashing his teeth, he seemed to lose his temper at this upstart Tiassa who was forcing him to retreat. He moved in, while whirling his blade in a continuous circle, so that any weapon coming within it would be struck by the full weight of his blade, and, almost certainly, dropped or broken.

Khaavren stopped his advance and Frai's eyes lit up. But the last Count of Shallowbanks, Khaavren's father, had told him of this maneuver, saying: "I only mention this because it is an error even a skilled swordsman may make, not for you do it yourself. It is easily defeated. . . ." And, remembering this lesson, Khaavren matched the motion of the broadsword and, following the inward motion of a screw, ended, after three orbits, by passing the greater part of his blade through the body of the Dragonlord, who cried out, fell against the serving-counter, and collapsed in a heap next to it.

Khaavren rushed over to this counter, set his weapon on it, and knelt down by the injured man. Frai looked up at him and blinked, not seeming to recognize him at first. Then he saw him and said, hoarsely, "Give me your hand, good Khaavren." Khaavren gave his hand to the Dragonlord, who pressed it. "It was well fought," he said. "I am proud to have fallen by your hand, and it would please me indeed if you would, hereafter, think of me as your friend."

"Is there anything I can do for you, good comrade?" said Khaavren.

"Ah! By the Lords of Judgement, I think you have pierced by lung."

"A healer!" cried Khaavren. "Find a healer!"

A healer was sent for. Frai, who was well acquainted with wounds, was correct: Khaavren's blade had been traveling up, and had passed just to the right of the clavicle, between the second and third ribs, puncturing a lung, missing the pulmonary artery, it is true, but making small cuts in the aorta and esophagus, and had exited near the backbone, below the neck. We can see, therefore, that while his lung was, indeed, damaged, he was bleeding internally as well.

It may be supposed that a soldier as experienced as Frai would have recognized the signs of such wounds, but he said nothing to Khaavren, merely smiled and pressed his hand until, just as the healer walked into the inn, the Dragonlord coughed bloodily and expired. The healer, a man of fair, delicate skin dressed in the white and red robes of the House of the Athyra, merely shrugged upon seeing the body.

Khaavren stood up. "Very well, then," he said crisply. He pointed to four of the persons who stood watching with great interest all that occurred. "Bring him with me."

He sheathed his sword after cleaning it on a towel provided by the innkeeper. Then he donned his cloak and with a fair imitation of the flourish he had noticed in Tazendra as she had first donned hers. The four he had spoken to hadn't moved. He drew himself up. "On the Imperial Service!" he cried, putting a hand to the hilt of his sword, whereupon they shuffled forward and picked up the body. Khaavren found the purse that Frai had received from the Jhereg, and drew a single gold coin from it, which he presented to the healer. "For your trouble," he explained, and, with a last glance at the Athyra, he led the way out of the inn.

Chapter the Sixth

*In Which the Results of the First Patrol
are Discussed At some Length with the Captain,
Who is Less than Pleased*

THEY WALKED BACK to the Dragon Gate, and into the sub-wing of the Imperial Guards, where Khaavren paid each of the four two orbs from the same purse. They left the body in Captain G'aereth's antechamber, and told the attendant that he wished to see the Captain. This worthy looked at the body and went to give the message. He returned at once, and signed that Khaavren should enter at once.

"Well, my good Tiassa," said the Captain, motioning Khaavren to a chair. "It seems that something has happened. I am anxious to hear the details."

"My lord," said Khaavren, "I will tell you of the entire affair."

"That is precisely what I wish to hear," said the Captain.

"That is well. Here it is, then." And he explained exactly what had occurred, with the precision of detail only a Tiassa is capable of. As he spoke, G'aereth's eyes became hard. When he had finished, the Captain opened his mouth to speak, but they were interrupted by the attendant, who said that the Cavalier Pel wished to be admitted.

The Captain shrugged, and signed to Khaavren that he should be patient. "Very well," G'aereth said to the attendant. "Send him in."

Pel bowed to the pair of them.

"Well?" said the Captain.

"There has been a small misadventure, my lord," said Pel.

"A misadventure?"

"Precisely."

"Of what kind?"

"On the part of my partner."

"Your partner?"

"Yes."

"She is hurt?"

"Ah! You say, hurt."

"That is to say, injured."

"It seems likely."

"But not badly?" asked G'aereth hopefully.

"On the contrary, my lord."

"On the contrary?"

"Yes. It is very bad."

"But, she still lives, does she not?"

"Oh, as to that. . . ."

"Well?"

"I regret to inform your lordship—"

"Lords of Judgement! She is dead, then?"

"It is my sorrowful duty to say it, my Captain."

"But how did it happen?"

"Oh, it was a strange thing."

"Well?"

"Well, as we walked along the perimeters of Castlegate, where the revelries of the season were just beginning, my partner and I were discoursing on some subject—"

"On what subject?"

"That is to say . . . on the subject of . . ."

"Of dalliance, Cavalier?"

"Oh, certainly not, my Captain!"

As he said this, Khaavren noticed a flush on the pale features of the Yendi, and wondered if the Captain had seen it, too. Pel continued, "It was on the subject of sorcery, my lord."

"Of sorcery?"

"Yes, She pretended that no one who was not an accomplished sorcerer could have a place in the Imperial Guard."

"Well, and?"

"I had the honor to inform her that the reign of the Athyra had ended fifteen days ago."

"Ah."

"I feel she took my words amiss, for she raised her hands, as if she would cast a spell upon me."

"Ah! And you?"

"Well, your lordship must understand that I could hardly permit a spell of an unknown sort to take effect on my person. It could have harmful effects. I had no choice but to draw my sword."

"Oh, but you stopped with drawing it, I hope."

"Most certainly, my Captain. I recovered myself, and I pleaded with her, as eloquently as I could, not to set out on this hasty course, from which no good could possibly occur."

"And she? Was she convinced?"

"Entirely."

"Well?"

"Well, upon seeing the wisdom of my words, she rushed to embrace me, and, in doing so, spitted herself upon my sword."

"My good Pel!"

"It is as I have the honor to inform you, my Captain."

"And yet—"

"We were observed by many, my Captain. There should be no difficulty in confirming what I have said."

"You may assure yourself that I will investigate her death as thoroughly as I investigate the death of Frai."

"Frai?"

"Khaavren's partner, whom you doubtless observed in the ante-chamber."

Pel gave Khaavren a glance full of meaning. "Has your partner also had an accident then?"

"Not at all," said Khaavren. "We had occasion to fight."

"Yes," said G'aereth. "In fact, I was about to say—"

"Hold a moment," said Pel. "I believe your attendant is calling."

In fact, at that moment, the door-warden approached to announce the arrival of Aerich.

"Send him in, then," said the Captain.

Aerich entered, and bowed gracefully to the room at large and to each man present.

"Well," said G'aereth. "What have you to report?"

"My Lord Captain, it is with sorry that I must report the death of my partner."

"Her death?"

Aerich bowed.

"But how did she die?"

"I killed her," said Aerich coolly.

"What?" cried the Captain. "This is infamous!"

Aerich shrugged. Pel and Khaavren exchanged glances.

"How did it happen, then," said G'aereth. "Did you quarrel?"

"Oh, as to that," said Aerich. "It took place on the Street of the Cold Fires, at the Circle of the Fountain of the Darr. It was not, you perceive, in a private place, so no doubt you can discover any details that interest you."

"But I, sir," said the Captain. "I wish to hear of it from you."

"Very well," said the Lyorn, losing none of his coolness. "We did quarrel."

"Ah! And what did you quarrel about?"

"Diamond mines."

"Diamond mines?"

Aerich bowed his assent.

Beads of sweat broke out on the Captain's brow. "How did you quarrel about diamond mines?"

"Your lordship is aware, perhaps, that there have been diamonds discovered in County Sandyhome?"

"I am indeed aware of it, sir, but I am anxious to learn how you became a party to this knowledge."

"I was told of it."

"By whom, then, were you told?"

"By my partner."

"Ah! Well, she told you that diamonds have been discovered. Then what?"

"Your lordship is, no doubt, aware that County Sandyhome, once in the possession of the Empire, is now in the possession of the Easterners."

"Yes, yes, in fact, it was a Dzur who led the expedition which discovered the diamonds."

"Furthermore, my lord, you may be aware that there are so many Easterners there that it would be a major campaign for the Imperial army to remove them?"

"I know that indeed, sir."

"My partner, then, said that the Emperor wished to do exactly that—to mount such a campaign to take this area which has no military value—"

"Oh, as to that. . . ."

"Yes?"

"It has immense economic value."

Aerich shrugged to signify that he had no opinion of his own on this subject.

"Go on, then," said the Captain.

"My partner felt that this would be a useless waste of the Imperial armies, when our real project ought to be— you understand, Captain, that these are her words—ought to be the defense of the Pepperfields, which are necessary to the security of the Empire."

"She is entitled to think whatever she wishes," said G'aereth.

"That was my opinion, my Lord Captain. I am delighted to find that it coincides with yours."

"Well, go on, then."

"It was then, Captain, that my partner made certain statements slandering the character of the Emperor."

"Ah!"

"We were, as I have had the honor to inform you, in the Circle of the Fountain of the Darr, that is, in a public place, and a place, moreover, filled with Teckla of all sorts. I therefore hastened to inform her, in a quiet voice, that it was the duty of all gentlemen to support and defend the Emperor, and that for those who had the honor to carry a sword in his name, this was twice as true."

"And she said what to this?" asked the Captain, on whose brow beads of sweat could still be seen.

"She said that her opinion was that of the lady Lytra, the Warlord of the Empire, and that it was not my place to dispute her."

"And then you said . . . ?"

"I replied that the lady Lytra had not said anything of the kind in my presence, and I doubted that she had said so in a public place, nor would she approve of saying so."

"And your partner?" asked the Captain, whose breath was now coming in gasps.

"She asked if I pretended to teach her manners."

"And you?"

"I assured her frankly and sincerely that I was only acting as any gentleman ought to act."

"By the Orb, sir! She drew her blade, then?"

"Excuse me, Captain, but her blade had been out since I questioned her first statement."

"Ah! Had you drawn, as well?"

"Not at all," said Aerich.

"Well, did you then draw it?"

"My partner became adamant on the subject; I felt it rude to refuse."

"Then she attacked you?"

"Oh, she attacked me, yes."

"Well?"

"She was very fast, my lord. I was forced to pierce her heart. I called for a healer at once, but, you perceive, it was already too late. I paid a pair of Teckla to keep watch upon her body so it may be brought to Deathgate Falls, should her House deem her worthy of it."

"But then, among the three of you—"

"Excuse me, Captain," said Pel, mildly. "The four of us."

"What is that?"

"I believe I hear the attendant announcing the lady Tazendra."

G'aereth shook his head. "Send her in, then. I hope she, at least, has a different tale for us."

Aerich shrugged. Tazendra entered, then, her eyes flashing with the cold anger of a Dzurlord. "My Captain," she said.

"Yes?"

"It give me great pain, but I must make a complaint."

"What? A complaint?"

"Yes. Against the individual with whom I was partnered."

"The Cavalier Fanuial?"

"Yes, that is his name."

"Well? And your complaint?"

Tazendra drew herself up and flung her long hair over her shoulders, and thrust forward her fine jaw as she said, "He is no gentleman, my lord."

"How is this?" asked the Captain, astonished.

"My lord, I will tell you the entire history."

"I ask nothing better."

"Well, it fell out in this manner. We began our patrol in the hills of the Brambletown district. We arrived, and had hardly set foot upon the Street of Ringing Bells when I saw a young gentleman walking toward us, who seemed to be looking at me quite fixedly."

"In what way?" asked the Captain.

"Oh, as to that, I am too modest to say."

The Captain's eyes traveled from Tazendra's thick black

hair to her finely shaped legs, stopping at all points of interest in between. "Yes, I understand, madam. Go on."

"I stopped to speak with this young gentleman, who appeared to be a count—" she glanced quickly at the others, cleared her throat and amended, "or perhaps a duke. Yes, undoubtedly a duke, of the House of the Hawk."

"Well?"

"Well, my partner made remarks about this young noble of—of a particularly rude and personal nature."

"I see. And what was your response to this?"

"Well, I was tempted to fight, Captain."

"But you didn't, I hope?"

"I could not, Captain. You understand, do you not? I am a Dzurlord, he only a Dragon. It would have been dishonorable to attack him."

"I quite agree," murmured the Captain. "What did you do, then?"

"Do? Why, naturally I suggested that he find four or five friends, and that, if they would do me the honor to all attack me at once, I would engage to defend this young Hawklord of whom he had spoken so disrespectfully."

The Captain buried his face in his hands. Out of respect for him, no one spoke. After a moment, the Captain lifted up his head and said, in a tone noticeably lacking in hope, "He attacked you then?"

"Attacked me? I almost think he did. He drew his sword, which was of tolerably good length, my lord, and rushed me as if it were the Battle of Twelve Pines."

"And you?"

"Well, not having time to draw my own sword, you understand—"

"Yes, yes, I understand that."

"Well, I was forced to use a flash-stone."

"And?"

"I think the charge tore his throat out."

"Oh," groaned the Captain."

"And part of his chest."

"Oh."

"And penetrated his lungs."

"Will you have done?"

Tazendra looked mildly startled. "That is all, my lord."

"I should hope so, for the love of the Emperor."

Tazendra bowed.

The Captain stood up, and looked at the four of them. "If this is a conspiracy, on the part of Lanmarea or anyone else, I promise you that all of your heads will adorn my wall."

At the word "conspiracy," Aerich's brows contracted. Khaavren managed with some difficulty not to look at the wall to see if there were heads adorning it already. But the Captain said, "I fear, however, that after interrogating what witnesses I can, I will discover that you have all told the truth. And then, my friends, then what am I to do?"

They didn't answer. He looked from one to the other. "If that is the case," he said at last, "it seems plain that, whatever you do, you are so valuable that I must either have you with me or have you dead."

He chewed his thumb. "It is also plain," he said, "that I cannot have you on duty with my other Guardsmen— we can't afford it. In the future you must patrol and team only with each other."

Pel bowed low at this and looked in the Captain's eyes. He said in his mild voice, "Captain my lord G'aereth . . ."

"Well?"

"We ask nothing better."

Chapter the Seventh

*In Which We Discover How Lodging Was Arranged
and Something is Learned
of the Structure of the Imperial Guards*

AND NOW AT last we return to a discussion of the lodging which our friends found for themselves. It was located on the Street of the Glass Cutters, barely a mile from the Dragon Gate, off the Street of the Dragon itself. Just across the road was the hotel of a private army which hired out to the Empire for certain kinds of duties, and from which the coming and going of Dragonlords, often in a state of heavy intoxication, could be seen at all hours. Further down the Street of the Glass Cutters was a small private hospital about which, when it was pointed out to Aerich, he had said, "That's lucky." Behind the house, facing onto the Street of the Dragon, was a small but prosperous temple dedicated to the Goddess Verra, and which was nearly as much of a gathering place as the inn, identified by the sign of a mallet, which was directly across the street from it.

This, then, was the neighborhood in which our friends found lodging. The house itself had first been built by a wealthy Jhegaala merchant for his retirement, which occurred during the last Teckla Republic, and it had been either occupied or rented out by his heirs since his death some three hundred years later. It was of the Early Volanthe style, displaying the fondness for towers, rounded walls, and painted stonework so typical of that period of Imperial architecture.

It was open and airy in front, with a circular porch, while in back it was enclosed entirely by large twostem bushes and was shaded by three giant oak trees, spaced in an equilateral triangle, and one sugar maple, set in the middle, all of which had been planted hundreds of years before, at the beginning of the Athyra reign. The result was that our friends could sit in front of the house and watch the antics of the soldiers across the street, or, looking a different way, watch the comings and goings toward the Dragon Wing of the Palace; or they could sit in the peaceful garden in back, drinking and engaging in the pleasant conversation that is the means by which friendship, created by the haphazard twistings of life, nourished by shared experience, becomes deep and lasting.

They had decided, in order to save expenses, to rent a single house. Pel took for himself the isolated chamber in the back, which let out by its own door into the garden. He explained that he found the breeze from the back window cleared his mind for the philosophical studies he pursued from time to time. Khaavren and Aerich exchanged looks but said nothing.

Khaavren chose for himself a room on the second story that had its own balcony, allowing him to stand or sit and gaze at those passing in the street, and create fanciful stories of their histories to amuse himself.

Aerich took the long, narrow room next to Khaavren's, and arranged it neatly and precisely, with a few tasteful ornamental vases, some landscape psiprints of the northwestern Great Woodlands, a shelf for his books, and some very comfortable chairs, which made it the room in which, as often as not, the four friends would meet to talk, even though there was a perfectly good living room below.

Tazendra's room was next to Aerich's, and took up a small portion of the back wall, as well as a circular tower that protruded above the rest of the building and had been at first intended to be servants' quarters, for which reason it had its own stairway directly to the kitchen. Tazendra made this upper room her own, furnishing it with soft pillows upon which guests could sit; and filling the room with candles, a collection of daggers she sent for from her home and set about the room, and all sort of liquor bottles hidden in unlikely places, so she could reach out a hand and emerge with one at the proper moment in a conversation.

The one other sleeping chamber was taken by a Teckla woman called Srahi, to whom they had offered room and board in exchange for keeping some semblance of order to the house and cooking one meal per day, if the Guardsmen could manage to procure the food. It should be noted in passing that this history begins only forty years after the Revolt of the Livery, so personal lackeys were, just at that time, out of fashion. Srahi was small and mouse-like, with wide eyes and a lip that curled in a way quite out of keeping with her status or House, yet very much in keeping with her voice, which was at once sharp, loud, and nasal.

Each day, Khaavren rose between the eleventh and twelfth hours after the midnight bell. On some occasions Pel would be up and wandering around, or reading in back; at other times Pel would be gone. Tazendra would invariably be up, and outdoors, or in back, or in the sitting room, or drawing pictures or modeling in clay. Aerich arose at around the same time as Khaavren, and would usually spend some time alone in his room, sitting in a chair and breathing deeply, as if gathering the strength he would need for the day.

And so it was on this basis that the household was erected, with four personalities at such variance: Pel planned out his life in careful stages of which he didn't speak, and, if one might suspect that he had more affairs of the heart than any ten normal men, at least no one could prove any of them. Tazendra never planned, but always attacked life as if the world existed purely for the pleasure it afforded her to tramp through it, laughing and gambling and loving; doing all of these far less, be it understood, than she claimed, but nevertheless enjoying the claims as much as another would have enjoyed the deeds. Aerich was of a dark disposition that seemed to thrive on the pleasures of his friends, as if pleasure for its own sake was impossible for him; yet he could take a certain measure vicariously, as it were, so that when his friends were happy, he was happy, and when his friends were sad, he was sad. Khaavren, we know, only rarely planned anything; his preference was neither to sculpt life, nor to attack it, but rather, to take everything, a blow or a kiss, just as it came, and to contrive as best he was able to take as much joy or opportunity, or as little pain or damage, as he could.

Aerich and Khaavren took to walking together around the neighborhood, or stopping in small klava holes. Upon returning, Aerich would sit and work at crochet, while Khaavren and Tazendra would often retire to the back garden to take a few passes with their blades—Khaavren forcing Tazendra to work to her utmost, while Tazendra would show Khaavren certain tricks of defense she had learned from the exclusive Dzur sword-master with whom she had studied. Srahi would rise last of all, usually not until the afternoon, and she would lounge about the living room in a tattered yellow robe until it came time to prepare the afternoon meal, following which the Guardsmen would be off to the Palace until their duties ended. On their return, Srahi would sometimes be gone, and sometimes be sleeping, but the house would, to a degree at least, be clean, leaving them no cause for complaint.

As to their duties at the Palace, we must pause here to

explain something of the structure of the Imperial hierarchy at that time.

At the top was, of course, the Emperor himself, though he played little enough part in day-to-day military affairs unless the almost constant skirmishing that occurred on the seas, in the outlying Duchies, and along the Eastern border had managed to elevate itself to the point where he was willing to consider it a war, which required him to involve himself in it enough to prevent its being effectively carried out, and thus to extend its length and cost enough to justify his involvement. The Warlord, then, was, in reality, in charge of the military might of the Empire, except for the Lavodes, who were at that time still in existence, and were led by their Captain, one Gyorg, Sethra having resigned upon being banned from the court many years before. The Warlord, a Dragon who was called Lytra e'Tenith, had, in theory, two subordinates, one being the captain-general of the Imperial Army, the other being the brigadier-general of the Imperial Guard. It should be noted that, at this time, both of these posts were vacant, so all of the subordinates of each branch reported directly to the lady Lytra.

Of these subordinates, one was G'aereth, who commanded the Red Boot Company of the Imperial Guard (thought it should be noted that no red boots had been worn for more than four hundred years). After the coronation festivities in the city were over, the battalion was, variously, assigned patrols through the city streets, or escort duties for certain nobles, or guard duty at the Iorich Wing, or to serve as Honor Guards for the Court, depending on the day of the week. Those who didn't have duty would lounge around the sub-wing, drinking, gossiping, gambling, or taunting the Guards of the other Captain, Lanmarea.

G'aereth's battalion numbered some sixty or seventy Guardsmen in all, while Lanmarea's company, the White Sash Battalion, numbered nearly two hundred. This gave to G'aereth's company the impression, which the Captain encouraged, that they were, in some way, an elite force, a feeling which the other Guardsmen quite understandably resented. In addition, we should note that the two captains were in competition for the post of Brigadier, which had been vacant for nearly a thousand years at this time. And finally, we must point out that it was Lanmarea's company, that is to say, the White Sash Battalion, that had been granted the honor of guarding the person of the Emperor, a most sought-after position.

This state of affairs had come about because Lanmarea, a close friend of Noima, the Imperial Consort, had begged this boon of the Emperor. Tortaalik, himself, as we have had the honor to mention, a close friend of G'aereth, was constantly seeking the opportunity to give this duty to the Red Boot Company, but had, since his coronation (some weeks past, at this time), been unable to find a pretext. As a result, there was considerable rivalry between the companies; rivalry which had led to drawn swords several times, and twice had led to spilt blood. It need only be added that Lanmarea's Battalion had been victorious on both occasions to allow our readers to see that there was, at this time, considerable anxiety among those Guardsmen who served under G'aereth.

As for our friends, one may suppose that, after the incidents of their first patrol became generally known, they were but ill-received by their fellows, yet nothing could be further from the truth. By the strange psychology peculiar to men of the sword, the foursome were looked upon with, at first, a certain respect, and, eventually, with friendship.

Khaavren's case was easy enough, for he was an instantly likable young man, and after proving himself by killing Frai (who was not, to be sure, especially liked by the company), his naturally pleasing personality won him as many friends as he could wish. Tazendra was respected as all Dzurlords are respected by soldiers, and, moreover, her beauty made her the subject of much attention and interest. The women of the Imperial Guard, fully a third of the total, at once attached themselves to Pel, who took the greatest possible care of his physical appearance, and whose gentle speech and conduct won him hours of delightful conversation. As for Aerich, he was accorded the honor with which everyone looks upon a Lyorn, and soon his fellow Guardsmen began to come to him with questions of conduct, rank, etiquette, history, and advice on dealing with an errant wife or husband, mistress or lover.

Khaavren slowly learned that the greater part of a Guardsman's income came from the collections he made from those who wished to keep their activities secret. He learned that accepting gold to help conceal a crime was, if not unheard of, at least frowned upon, but, at the same time, he came to understand that the Guardsmen did not consider efforts to avoid the Imperial Tax Collectors to be a crime, a philosophy to which, after some reflection, he began to subscribe.

Nevertheless, Khaavren was unable to bring himself to accept these gifts, so instead he preferred, at least while on duty, to avoid the establishments which allowed such behind-the-walls enterprise. Pel, on the other hand, haunted such places in particular, but never accepted payment in money. It seemed to Khaavren that Pel had some sort of understanding with these people, and the Tiassa resolved to keep a close eye on the Yendi, to try to determine the nature of this understanding.

Aerich staunchly refused to have anything to do with those who bribed the Phoenix Guards, though he seemed to have no quarrel with the Guardsmen around him who felt differently. Tazendra, alone of the foursome, was delighted with the practice, and regularly accepted these gifts of money, which she happily returned by losing most of it playing shereba, which game, played with cards, was well in fashion just then.

Often the other three would sit near the table while Tazendra played, drinking wine and discussing affairs of the Empire, or the nature of their duties, or speculations on when they would have a chance to gain notice in the eyes of their superiors.

It is worth our while to mention that the inn closest to their home, whose sign, as we have mentioned, showed a hammer in the act of striking a nail, held a back room where shereba was often played under the watchful eye of a ruddy-faced Jhereg named Tukko, who had somehow acquired a partnership in the Hammerhead Inn, as it was called. Whenever the Dragons from the mercenary army were in funds, the entire inn was crowded with singing, drunken warriors, and the back room, which was a favorite haunt of Tazendra, became even more crowded than the common room.

It had been observed more than once that when a room is crowded with drunken Dragonlords, and a Dzur is gambling, it is a good time for any peace-loving individual to discover that his business has called him away. One day, some three weeks after our friends' arrival in the city, this observation was shown to be particularly astute, as we will take it upon ourselves to demonstrate.

Chapter the Eighth

In Which It is Shown That
There are No Police in Dragaera City

ON THIS PARTICULAR evening Tazendra was enjoying a run of luck at shereba, a game in which the caprices of chance measure themselves against the nerve of the player, so that a momentary failure of confidence can bring down the entire financial edifice that has been built up by hours of painstaking calculation, yet a sudden change in the draw of the cards can, if played boldly and steadfastly, cause a fortune to move from one side of the table to the other—such as happened to Paluva, Count of Cloverhill, in the well-known epic.

And yet, as we have said, Tazendra was this time enjoying the luck of the cards, and, moreover, was playing at her best, because if there is anything that will inspire a Dzur more than being outnumbered, it is being outnumbered by Dragonlords. And her opponents were, in fact, all of the House of Dragon, there being three women and one man from the Army of the Thorny Rose, and she had been steadily drawing coins from each of them into a pile in front of her.

We should note that this game was, in the strictest sense, illegal—that is, it was not reported to the Imperial Tax Collectors, but the reader ought to be aware in addition that such laws are given only the merest nod during an Athyra reign, and hardly more during the reign of the Phoenix that follows. It is when the cold and rigid Vallista brings an Emperor to the throne that such laws are enforced in all their vigor, which enforcement puts gold into the treasury of the Jhereg, who eventually make use of it to buy their way into positions of power until they can pick their own Emperor, from which we can learn that it is the Jhereg, along with those corrupt officials who lack only the colors to be Jhereg themselves, who gain from the enforcement of laws designed to limit an individual's pleasure.

The significance of this fact for our purposes—for we assure the reader that it is the relation of historical fact, not the exposition of political reality, that we have set as our task—is that, the Phoenix Guards having been paid, there was little danger of a raid or an investigation by the Empire; hence the doors were all open and there was constant intercourse between the common rooms and those rooms set aside for games of chance in this inn. In fact, at the very moment at which we are looking, Khaavren, Aerich, and Pel are standing behind Tazendra, watching her play, and discussing a matter of some moment to them, that being the question of Srahi, the Teckla, whom Pel pretended was far too recalcitrant to be a servant.

"It is a problem," said Khaavren to Pel, while looking over Tazendra's shoulder at a lay of cards, featuring three House cards and the Ace of Fire, that promised no good to her opponents, one of whom was betting heavily on what looked like a flood but probably wasn't. "For it is obvious that she ought to be beaten, and yet, it is a sad thing, but in this modern age in which we find ourselves, a gentleman may not lift his hand to a woman, whereas before only a lady was excepted. And yet it is entirely proper for a lady to correct a servant of either sex. Am I not correct, my dear Aerich?"

"Exactly," said the Lyorn, "although I hasten to add that this rule hardly applies when the lady in question is armed, as on the battlefield or the field of honor. But this is clearly not the case."

"But then," said Pel, "if we cannot thrash her, surely we can convince Tazendra to do so."

"I?" said Tazendra, turning around and frowning. "Strike a defenseless servant-woman?"

"It is as I thought," said Khaavren. "A problem."

"Perhaps," said Pel as Tazendra turned back to her game, "we ought to hire a man who is not a gentleman, and can therefore be instructed to thrash Srahi when it is called for."

"I think," said Khaavren, "that the state of the treasury will scarcely permit that."

"Well," said Tazendra, as the lady across from her cursed at the card she had drawn and threw the remainder onto the table, "that problem may be on the way to solving itself."

"Perhaps," said Pel. "But you must admit, my dear friend, that you are likely to lose tomorrow what you have won today."

"Well, and does that matter?" said one of the ladies who had been steadily losing to Tazendra. "You police are no doubt able to make as much as you require in your agreements with Jhereg such as our fine Tukko here, which agreements allow us the opportunity for this agreeable play, in which, you perceive, you cannot lose, as you do not gamble with your own money, but, rather, with ours."

Tazendra slowly turned her head, which had been directed to Pel, until she was facing the lady who had spoken. Meanwhile, Khaavren, Aerich, and Pel took a step forward at the same moment to position themselves behind Tazendra, who said in a voice that was at once soft and menacing, "Would you do me the honor to say once more what you have just said? Perhaps my hearing was at fault."

The Dragonlord tilted her head and said, "Have I in some way insulted you? Do you pretend that you are offended at my suggestion that you are paid by Jhereg who wish to hide from the Imperial Tax Collectors?"

"Not in the least," said Tazendra.

"Well?"

"But I nearly thought that you used the word 'police'."

"And if I did?"

"I have the honor to inform you," said Aerich coldly, "that there have been no police in Dragaera City since the Revolt of the Livery, some forty years ago."

"Well," said another Dragonlord, "but it seems we are looking at some now."

"It is not a word," said Pel, tossing his cloak over his shoulder so that the elegant hilt of his blade was visible, "that pleases my ears."

"Well," said the lady who had spoken first, "I confess that your ears are of only a little concern to me."

"But," said Pel, bowing politely, "your tongue is of great concern to me."

"For my part," said Khaavren, "I am concerned with her feet."

"How," said Aerich, who stood between Pel and Khaavren. "Her feet?"

"Indeed. For if she will use them to move from these cramped quarters, well, I will do her the honor of showing her what my arm can do."

"You?" said Pel, indicating that, while he agreed with object and predicate in Khaavren's speech, he differed from the Tiassa as to subject.

"My friends," said Aerich softly, "our lives are His Majesty's, remember." He then bowed to the lady and said, "You are doubtless unaware that by calling us police, you are not merely insulting us, but also the Warlord, Lytra e'Tenith, to whom we owe allegiance, and also His Majesty, who has done us the honor to take us into his service as soldiers."

"Not at all," said another of the lady's companions. "The Warlord may hire all the police she wishes without dishonor."

"And," said another, "His Majesty may call them soldiers if he wishes to; that is the privilege of royalty."

"Aerich," said Pel, turning to the Lyorn, "you do not believe that we can allow this conversation to continue, do you?"

"But then," said the lady who had just lost to Tazendra. "Who could stop it?"

"I, for one," said Khaavren, with a bow.

"You?" said the lady scornfully, at which her companions laughed. "That would be amusing; to see an officer of the police fight a warrior."

Aerich drew in his breath sharply, but put a gentle hand on Pel's shoulder. "Easy, my friends," he said. "Remember our duties—"

"Bah," said Pel, shrugging off Aerich's hand. "Our duties do not require us to allow ourselves to be insulted by every little Dragonling who believes she knows which end of the sword is sharp."

"How?" said the lady, standing up, at which her friends stood also, leaving only Tazendra still seated. "Dragonling? No gentleman is required to take such words from—"

"Stop," said Khaavren. "For if you utter that hated word once more, which it sounds very much as if you are about to do, I believe that I will separate your head from your body without the formalities that are so beloved by the lawmakers. You perceive, then, that I am doing you a favor by interrupting you."

"Oh," said another Dragon, "formalities mean little enough to me or my friends; our swords don't require them."

"Although," added another, "we understand that this attitude is different among the police."

Now, there is no question that, with this last utterance of that word which is so justly hated by all good persons of all times and places, a duel would have followed immediately, if there had not come an interruption at that moment. The interruption came when Tazendra, who had been trying to maintain her calm so that she would have the privilege of dueling with a Dragonlord, rose with a great cry, drew her sword from her back, and, with a shout, gave such a blow to the lady who had spoken that it would have certainly split her skull had she not leapt backward, upsetting her chair and bumping into a patron who had come to watch the hostilities. Because she was not there to interrupt the determined progress of the sword, however, it continued into the heavy oak table at which they had been playing and very nearly split the table instead of the skull at which it had been aimed. Coins and glasses splattered, tinkled, and rolled onto the floor.

The four Dragonlords recovered quickly, drew, and placed themselves on their guards. Khaavren and Pel drew as well, and even Aerich was sufficiently exasperated to take his sword into his hand.

"I'm stuck," said Tazendra, who was unable to extract her weapon from the table-top.

"So much the better," said her antagonist, and aimed a terrific blow at her body, which would certainly have killed her had Pel not interfered by giving the Dragonlord a good cut on her shoulder, which caused her to gasp and drop her weapon.

"Thorns, to us!" cried the Dragonlords.

"Guardsmen, to us!" cried the Guardsmen.

Of these two calls, the former was the more effective. There were nearly a score of soldiers of the Army of the Thorny Rose who were in the hostel, whereas, to our friends' chagrin, there were no other Guardsmen there at all. As a result, within seconds Khaavren, Aerich, and Pel found themselves backed up against the far wall of the room, while their antagonists pressed forward, hampered only by their numbers, the size of the room and the table itself, for reasons which we will hasten to explain.

Tazendra had also decided to retreat, but was unwilling to leave her sword behind, and so she dragged it, table and all, to a position in front of her friends. Now this table, we should say, was supported by stout wooden legs, which curved outward from a common support in the center of the underside. Because of this design, the table overbalanced, with the result that it became an effective shield, reaching to the height of Tazendra's breasts.

Therefore, for a few moments there was something of a stand-off, with the Dragonlords only able to attack around the sides of the vertically positioned table and the Guardsmen unable to attack at all. Then a Dragonlord cried out, "Press them, press them; let us finish this before more of these police come to rescue them," which was not only a dire threat, but a fresh insult which aggravated the Guardsmen beyond endurance.

Tazendra, who had been frustrated in any case by her inability to free her sword from the table, gave a cry like an enraged dzur and began pushing the table forward into the throng of Dragonlords. Khaavren immediately put his shoulder into it as well, while Pel and Aerich stood by its sides, cutting at any who dared to press too close. In this way, Pel gave one of them a scalp cut which bled profusely and left the victim lying senseless on the floor, while Aerich nearly struck another's hand off, this in addition to a number of small wounds they inflicted.

After the first moment of the charge of the table, the Dragonlords began to fall back, and three of them lost their footing, whereupon Khaavren and Tazendra happily trampled them on their way past.

The counter-attack (or, if the reader prefer, table-attack) went well until the Guardsmen had succeeded in pushing their enemies to the far wall of the room, whereupon two things happened: first, the press of bodies and the force of the charge itself served to squeeze soldiers around the side of the table and put them in a better position to attack the Guardsmen from the flanks, and second, Tazendra's sword, as if offended at being used as the grip of a moving barricade, slipped free from the table, which promptly fell backwards, its feet sticking up into the air. Suddenly, then, the momentum shifted, and the four friends were at once surrounded.

They wasted no time in considering strategy, however. Tazendra, delighted to have her blade free, charged at the largest group she could find with such vigor that they fell back before her, momentarily confused. Khaavren found himself facing one of the original four antagonists, and, in the time it takes to draw a breath, cut her twice on the arm, once in the face, and then struck her fully in the body, at which time she fell like a coal-sack. At this same time, Aerich wounded a man with a cut in the neck, and Pel felled another by burying his poniard in her chest, for which he paid by a long scratch down the side of his face and a light cut in his left shoulder.

Now the innkeeper, not knowing what else to do, had dispatched a servant to bring the Guard, who were fortunately close at hand, so that the cry, "The Watch! The Watch!" was taken up by the patrons who were nearest the door and the cry was quickly spread throughout the hostel. Our friends, hearing this cry, took the opportunity to make a retreat into the common room, and afterward fell in with the pair of Guardsmen who had been summoned, and who were of their own company. No words were necessary to show the newcomers the situation, so they at once drew and stood next to their friends. The numbers, while still not equal, were at least a little more balanced, so that the Dragonlords, of whom perhaps a dozen remained, standing, hesitated before attacking.

"I think," said Khaavren, "that it is not time to withdraw."

"Bah," said Tazendra. "The game is only beginning to grow warm."

Aerich said, "I, for one, agree with Khaavren."

Pel said, "Whereas, my dear Lyorn, I find that on this occasion I am entirely in accord with Tazendra."

The two Guardsmen also agreed with Tazendra, saying that they had had no chance to fight. Aerich said, "That is true, but you are on duty, and ought to attempt to quell disruptions rather than contributing to them."

"Ah, that is true," they said regretfully.

"But," said Pel, "I do not believe these fine soldiers have any intention of allowing us to leave in a peaceful way."

"I nearly think you are right," said Tazendra happily, as their foes seemed about to make a charge.

Aerich said, "You can delay them, Tazendra."

"I?"

"Well, are you not a sorcerer?"

"Ah, that is true. Very well."

She raised her hands and muttered under her breath, whereupon the room was almost instantly filled with smoke, which appeared to have no source other than the air itself; and, moreover, there were flashes of light, all the more frightening because it was impossible to determine whence they came or what effect, if any, they were having.

"Now," said Tazendra, appearing to be pleased with herself, "we can charge them on a more equal basis."

"Now," said Khaavren, "we can retreat—for I believe we have successfully stated our views to them, and they still outnumber us two to one."

Pel, Tazendra and the two Guardsmen who had been summoned argued briefly, but, largely because Aerich agreed with Khaavren, prudence won on this occasion, and, upon gaining the street, they hastened to join up with another pair of Guardsmen who, when informed of the situation, went off to rouse several more. The soldiers, content with having driven the enemy from their encampment, made no pursuit. In a short time, there were some twenty-eight or thirty Guardsmen gathered together at a klava hole several doors down from the Hammerhead, where they made plans to assail the arrogant warriors when they made their appearance.

However, and it is probably fortunate that it was so, they took to consuming great quantities of wine while they waited, so that Khaavren eventually realized that the only battle that would be fought that evening would be against the ground, which promised to strike the imbibers as they attempted to return home when the revelries finally broke up. Khaavren mentioned this to Aerich, who agreed with his assessment, and passed it on to Pel and Tazendra.

And so the four friends quietly slipped away and returned to their home, where they spent several anxious days waiting to see if there would be repercussions either from the Army of the Thorny Rose or from Captain G'a-ereth, but at length it appeared that they had escaped the consequences of the disturbance.

"Well," said Khaavren, "I have learned, at any rate, that one ought to be careful with whom one gambles."

Pel, whose face and shoulder had been almost entirely healed, remarked, "I have learned that Dragonlords are not pleased when their diction is brought under scrutiny."

"And I," said Tazendra, "have learned that tables have more uses than I should have dreamed."

"All in all," said Aerich, picking up his crochet hook, "a most educational experience."

Chapter the Ninth

In Which Certain Persons Attempt
to Hold a Private Discussion, And the Results Thereof

THE DAYS BECAME weeks, as they will when allowed to heap themselves upon one another unattended, and these weeks, likewise, turned themselves into months of seventeen days with no regard for the hours and minutes they used up in doing so. Khaavren, when duty did not take him into what was called "the City," which meant any part of Dragaera that was out of sight of the Palace, industriously explored, first the Dragon Wing, then portions of the rest of the Palace. The uniform of the Phoenix Guards was as good as a password or Imperial seal for a great deal of the Palace, and Khaavren had resolved to use this freedom to learn what he could of the geography of the institution to which so much of his life was now committed.

It was on such an occasion, then, that he happened to be in an area where a short but wide corridor, sloping down and gently curving to the right, connected the second floor of the Dragon Wing to the third floor of the Imperial section. He passed below an arch and noticed a small, unmarked passage jutting off at an angle. Since it is axiomatic that such corridors lead to more interesting places than large, well-trampled ones, he resolved at once to see where it led, and this decision was no sooner reached then acted upon.

After twenty paces, the passage abruptly turned, then equally abruptly ended in a plain wooden door, before which was planted a Guardsman Khaavren had not seen before, but whose insignia indicated he was part of Lanmarea's company. Khaavren noted at once that he was carrying, not only a sword, but a pike, which weapon indicated that he was performing a function associated with the security of the Empire.

"Name and business," said the Guardsman brusquely.

"My name? It is Khaavren, good sir. But my business, in truth, I think is my own."

"And yet, since you are here at my station, and clearly desire to pass, it is necessary that I discover it, and that quickly."

"Well, you are mistaken."

"Mistaken? How?"

"I have no desire to pass. Rather, I shall turn around and walk the other way."

The Guardsman, a short, heavily built Dragonlord with red hair and a pale complexion, frowned at this and said, "You have, nevertheless, appeared where you ought not to appear unless you have some pressing business with those inside. I begin to think you have none, whereupon I am still required to know your purpose in being here."

"Come, then, give me your name."

"I am called Dekkaan e'Tenith."

"Well, good Dekkaan, I have made a wrong turn, that is all there is to it, so by your leave, I will now make a correct turn, and that will be the end of it, don't you think?"

"Not the least in the world, my good Khaavren. In fact, what I must do now is summon a comrade, who will escort you to our Captain, Lanmarea, whom you must satisfy as to your innocence or guilt."

Khaavren frowned in his turn. "And yet, I think I've told you that I am here by accident. As I am a gentleman, I see no reason for the matter to go any further. Do you?"

"Well, I almost think I do, for I begin to think you fear an interrogation, which makes me wonder what you have to conceal."

At the word "fear," Khaavren began to grow warm, and he placed his hand upon the hilt of his rapier. "Conceal?" he said. "You may observe by my countenance that I am not one who often conceals his ideas. I do myself the honor to suggest that you, yourself, rarely conceal your ideas. In your case, doubtless, it is because ideas so rarely come to you that you have never needed to give thought to concealment; but in my case it is because, being a gentleman, as I have had the honor to inform your lordship, my affairs are always handled in a frank and honest manner. Nevertheless, you ought to be able to tell the difference between someone who is, like yourself, a servant of His Imperial Majesty, and a spy."

"Spy?" said the other ironically. "I never used the word—you have brought it up yourself. I nearly think there is reason why this word was uppermost among those ideas which you have done me the honor to discuss."

"My lord, you are rude."

"Well?"

"Well, I think—" began Khaavren, when the door Dekkaan was guarding swung open and a tall, haughty-looking young Dzur of perhaps five hundred years of age stepped through, saying, "What is this disturbance?"

Dekkaan turned and bowed low to the new arrival, saying, "My lord, this man, called Khaavren, a soldier, apparently, of G'aereth's company, came upon this door, and refuses to state his business or to be questioned on his reason for being here."

While he spoke, Khaavren took the opportunity to study the man. He was, as we have said, of a haughty mien, with short, dark brown hair beneath his beret, and piercing, slanted eyes beneath very thick brows. He wore black, and the only decoration was the seal of the Lavodes fixed upon the beret. He carried a broadsword strapped to his back, and in his hand was a wizard's staff. Khaavren's eyes quickly traveled from this figure to the room behind him, which seemed small and only sparsely appointed, but what caught his attention was the appearance of a very old woman, who quickly turned from Khaavren as if to hide her features. And in fact, at that very moment, the newcomer shifted his position as if to shield the interior of the room from Khaavren's eyes.

"My Lord," said Khaavren, bowing, "as I have had the honor to explain to this Guardsman, I was merely walking through the Dragon Wing and took a wrong turn. Bloody Throne, my lord, I have not been here long, and you must know how easy it is to become lost here."

The Dzurlord frowned, then nodded. "Very well, then. You may go. But I will remember your name."

"I can ask no more, my lord."

"Well. And why don't you leave, then?"

"My lord, I will do so at once, but my business here is not complete."

"How, not complete? Have you not claimed to be here by accident?"

"Indeed, yes, my lord, and I even repeat it. Yet there remains for me the task of assigning myself a meeting with my dear friend Dekkaan, which I do myself the honor to hope he wishes for as much as I."

Dekkaan, in his turn, bowed, saying, "My friend, my duty ends at the ninth hour, and I shall be most happy to be your servant at that time."

"That falls out admirably. You have, I hope, some friends?"

"I can find two or three, I think. One is only a few feet away from me now, guarding the other door to this room, and the other two will be awaiting us when I am off duty."

"Three is just the right number for me," said Khaavren.

"There remains, then, only the task of deciding where we shall meet."

"Well, do you know the courtyard behind the South Door of the Dragon Wing?"

"I am acquainted with it."

"Well, behind that courtyard is a practice range for archers, which I think will not be in use at that time."

"I will be awaiting you at the tenth hour, then, my lord."

"I shall endeavor to be punctual."

"Until then, good Dekkaan."

"Until then, dear Khaavren."

Whereupon Khaavren turned and walked away. When he was out of earshot, Dekkaan bowed to the Dzurlord and said, "I hope I have not unduly disturbed you, lord."

"Not at all, only—"

"Yes, my lord?"

"I think that Tiassa has seen things which he ought not to have seen."

"And so?"

"If you would be so kind as to kill him, well, you would be doing me a great service."

"I shall endeavor to please you, my lord."

"That would be excellent, my good Dekkaan."

Khaavren, who heard nothing of this conversation, proceeded at once to find his friends. Aerich and Pel were at home, and Khaavren was about to explain to them the service he required for the evening's entertainment when Tazendra arrived in Aerich's room, where they were conversing.

Khaavren said, "My dear Tazendra, you seem rather warm."

"Well, I am."

"Ah. Tell us the cause then, for we are very anxious to know."

"The cause is that I have been treated rudely today."

"You? How did this come about?"

"In this manner. I was carrying on a conversation with

a certain gentleman today, in the Round Room adjoining the West Tower of the Dragon Wing."

"I know the place," said Pel. "It is very private, is it not?"

"Well, often it is so, but today our conversation was interrupted not once, not twice, but four times."

"But then," said Khaavren, "one cannot always have the privacy one desires."

"And yet," said Tazendra, with a toss of her head, "this gentleman, who was, I might add, a Count of the House of the Issola, was determined that our discussion not be interrupted."

"I can understand this desire," said Pel.

"But what steps did you take?" said Khaavren.

"Well, my friend, the Count of T_____, suggested a place he knew in the Imperial Wing, which is very private and rarely used."

"And," said Pel, "did you, in fact, find it empty?"

"Not the least in the world. We arrived to discover a Guard stationed there."

"Well, and what then?" said Khaavren. "Did you leave?"

"Indeed, we were going to, but this Guardsman, whose name is Kurich, insisted making observations which were entirely unnecessary."

"I begin to see," murmured Aerich.

"You attacked him?" said Pel.

"He was armed, you understand, with a pike, whereas I had a sword of good length, so—"

"A pike, you say?" said Khaavren.

"Exactly."

"So he was guarding someone on Imperial business."

"Cracks and Shards, good Khaavren. We were in the Imperial Wing; what would you?"

"Exactly," said Khaavren. "So then—?"

"Why, then we were interrupted by an old woman of the House of the Athyra, who bade us leave off our play at once."

"Ah, so you arranged matters for later?" said Khaavren.

"Precisely."

"And at what time?"

"At the eleventh hour past noon."

"And where?"

"We have agreed to meet in the foyer of the Dragon Wing, and will determine a meeting place at that time."

"Well, and had he some friends?" asked Pel.

"His number was three, which could not be better."

"And was," said Khaavren, "one of his friends on duty very near him, even at the other side of that very room?"

Tazendra stared. "You must be prescient," she said.

"This falls out rather well," said Khaavren. "Come, we are close to the appointed hour, and I will explain matters as we walk."

So it was that, by the time they reached the archery range, they were all acquainted with the matter. They arrived somewhat early, but had only to wait a few minutes before their opponents arrived.

"Well, my lord," said Khaavren, "I believe we know the issues that stand between us."

"I think so," said Dekkaan. "And, likewise, some of our friends are already acquainted. For the rest, I present for you the Count of Uilliv, and the Lord Rekov."

"You do us honor," said Tazendra. "This is the Cavalier Pel, and Aerich."

"Very well. And for the judge and the Imperial witnesses?"

"Why," said Khaavren. "I have brought none. And you?"

The one called Kurich, who faced Tazendra, shrugged. "What would you? I have no desire to wait. Let us deal with matters as they stand. Come now, to arms."

Tazendra received this compliment in her usual manner; that is, she took her blade into her hand and commenced flashing it about, while making a great show of pretending to study Kurich's body, as if deciding where to make her marks. Kurich himself, apparently undisturbed by this display, drew his longsword, saluted, and put himself on guard.

Khaavren said, "Well, then, let us be about it," and drew himself, moved off to the side, and made a hasty salute to Dekkaan. Pel drew also, and indicated that he would fight with the Dragonlord called Uilliv, who had a reputation as a hot blade, thus making Pel eager to try him out. Aerich studied the gentleman called Rekov and said coolly, "Well then, shall we fight, or merely watch?"

Rekov shrugged and said, "For myself, it has been some time since I've had a blade in my hand save for practice, and I shouldn't be sorry to puncture you a few times."

"Very well, then," said Aerich, and, after drawing and saluting, put himself onto the guard position of the Lyorn masters; that is, with his sword and poniard crossing his body, his vambraces meeting before his neck.

The first to clash were Pel and Uilliv, which fight was also the shortest, as Pel put on such a fierce expression and charged so strongly, that, after only a few passes, Uilliv stumbled backward and lost his sword. Pel knocked aside the other's knife and placed the point of his own weapon against his opponent's neck, whereupon Uilliv promptly admitted to being beaten.

Aerich, having assumed a defensive posture, awaited Rekov's attack. The latter, apparently wishing to end the combat quickly, made a strong attack which, however, was brushed aside by Aerich's vambraces, which he used in lightning-fast but graceful sweeping motions, each one of which created an opening for either his sword or his dagger. The Lyorn warriors, however, are trained to kill or disable at a single stroke, and disdain openings that will not end the combat.

Rekov, at first puzzled by Aerich's failure to attack, and disturbed by the cool expression on his countenance, began to attack with less caution, until Aerich saw the chance he was waiting for, when Rekov's sword was caught between Aerich's vambraces and yet Rekov's dagger was far out of line, holding his balance. At this time, Aerich made his first move forward, a single step that caused Rekov to twist to his left, presenting Aerich with his back. Since this was what he'd been waiting for, Aerich lost no time in striking downward with his poniard past Rekov's collarbone, while simultaneously cutting into his side with his sword. The Dragonlord gave a low moan and crumbled to the ground.

Tazendra, after having made a great show, charged Kurich's longsword, which was flashing in such an intimidating manner that she was forced to back out again. She charged once more, but was again forced to retreat, this time trailing blood from a deep cut on her left shoulder.

"First blood to me!" cried Kurich.

"But last to me," said Tazendra, striking with such force that the Dragonlord's weapon was brought far out of line, whereupon she charged yet again and, in backing up, Kurich tripped over Rekov's body, at which time Tazendra nailed him to the ground with her greatsword, which had a specially sharpened point for just such maneuvers.

Khaavren and his opponent had similar styles; that is, they both covered a great deal of ground, chasing each other all about the area, stepping around or over obstacles, and engaging each other with quick strokes, using mostly the tips of their blades, and searching for openings on the wrist or the leg. Dekkaan, in fact, had already scored two light scratches on Khaavren's knife hand. Khaavren, however, seemed not to notice, but still smiled fully into the smile of his opponent.

After some length of time, Dekkaan said, "I believe you are bleeding, my friend."

"Well," said Khaavren, "it doesn't disturb me."

"That's well. I'd hate to lose you easily."

"The Gods," said Khaavren. "I hope to give a good game."

"Then you should have a care for your knife hand, which you hold too low."

"Good," said Khaavren. "You give me a lesson. That's kind. But then, you perceive, with my knife low it is ready to flick at a good angle any time you cut for my side, and the proof is that you have not done so in some time."

"Well, but then your head is exposed, and I would think you need it."

"Certainly, when you try to take it, ah, there it is!" As he said this, Khaavren ducked below a sweeping cut for his head and stepped to his left, causing Dekkaan's right side to be exposed. Rather than attacking, however, he took half a step backward, for the Dragon, realizing how exposed he was, made a panicked sweep with his sword which ended far out of line to the right. At this point Khaavren moved in and cut Dekkaan's knife arm, while burying his poniard in his body.

The Dragonlord groaned and fell to his knees, dropping both of his weapons. "Cracks in the Orb," he said. "I think you've killed me."

Khaavren knelt beside him and said, "I don't think so, my friend, for I felt my knife was stopped by your ribs."

"Well, then, I give you the contest, but if you love me at all help me to a physicker."

"I can do that, I think, the more so since my friends are able to help me." Then he looked up and said, "Come, let us get these brave men to a healer."

"Well," said Tazendra, "I'm afraid I've killed mine, but I'll help with the others." Whereupon Khaavren and Tazendra assisted Dekkaan, while Pel and Aerich carried Rekov, with assistance of Uilliv. Afterwards, clapping each other on the back, they wen to celebrate at an inn favored by G'aereth's Company, and allowed those of the troop who were there to buy them as much as they could drink.

Chapter the Tenth

In Which we Learn a Bit of Personal History about Tazendra

THAT CELEBRATION CONTINUED well into the night, until everyone had either been taken home by friends or had passed out at table. The only ones still awake, in fact, were Khaavren, who never drank excessively due to an experience early in his childhood, and Tazendra, who seemed able to drink the Dragaera River, were it wine, and still retain most of her faculties. The innkeeper himself, overcome with fatigue from supplying the necessities for a festival of which he'd no advance warning, was sitting on a chair in the corner, snoring as loudly as any of his patrons.

Khaavren set his glass carefully on the table, for though it was only his fifth in as many hours, still he felt that his head was beginning to swim. "Well," he said carefully, "it was a well-done piece of work today."

"You think so?" said Tazendra.

"I am sure of it."

"Well, then I'm satisfied. The Orb! Did you mark our friend Pel?"

"What of him?"

"The look on his face while he fought. Who would have thought such a thing of a Yendi? We had not yet engaged, so I was able to observe his battle, and hang me for a thief if I'd not have surrendered myself if I saw his countenance charging me, as if all the were-beasts of the Paths had been let loose. And then, when his man had surrendered, he was as polite as an Issola. 'Good sir, you have given me your sword, be assured I will keep it among my valued heirlooms.' Were those not his words, good Khaavren?"

"To the very expression, Tazendra. And did you not as well admire our friend Aerich? He stood like a mountain of iron, impervious and unmoved, and then, when he saw his chance, Kieron's Boots! Such speed!"

"That is true. He reminded me of—" Tazendra abruptly broke off her speech and turned red.

"Well, of who?"

"Ah, it is of no importance."

"Come now, good Tazendra. Let there be no secrets among us."

"No, no, it matters not. Come, let me get you more wine. But what is this, there is no bottle and the inn-keeper asleep? Well, we will help ourselves, then, and here's some good sausages to go with it, for you know I dislike drinking without eating at the same time. It is said to be bad for the health. Hence, we will satisfy our gastronomical needs and our palates at the same time."

"Tazendra, you reason like an Athyra. Yet don't expect me to match you glass for glass; you are aware that I drink but a little."

"My god, I think so! Here I am with the remains of four good bottles of Ailor, and you have only finished a bottle of Khaav'n, which, if I am not mistaken, our good friend Tuci helped you with."

"But what then, we can not all be Dzurlords."

"Ah, that is true, and, if truth be known, I think it would be a dull world if all were." Tazendra, who had drained her glass and filled another by this time, went on to say, "My mother, the Countess, used to say, 'Remember, we are only one part of this great body of Empire. And if we hold on to the valor, then others must needs take care of the rest.'"

"A wise woman, your mother," said Khaavren. "And, no doubt, a valorous one."

"Of a certainty she was. Who would have thought she—" and Tazendra broke off here, frowning.

"You were saying?" said Khaavren.

"I? I was saying nothing."

"Oh, indeed, you were speaking of the valor of your mother."

"Bah! It means nothing."

"Oh, but come, Tazendra, she must have been bold enough for two Dzurlords; where else could you have gotten such courage? For we all know that character passes from mother to daughter, just as from father to son. Cracks in the Orb, haven't the Dragon wizards proved it?"

Tazendra said, in a whisper Khaavren could barely hear, "And yet she ran."

"Bah. From what?"

"From a battle she was losing."

"What? Is it true?"

"It is what I was told. One day while I was still a child, barely thirty years of age, in fact, there was a great rumbling which woke me up. My mother and father and my nurse came into my chamber, and I remember my mother was wearing her cutting sword, not the thrusting sword, and my father wore a leather harness from which hung his greatsword and a dagger. I said, 'But why are you armed?' They only shook their heads, and hugged me and entrusted me to the care of the nurse."

"Well, and what then?"

"Then I was taken out of our castle, and I never saw them again. I was later told that they had been attacked by an army of Dragonlords hired by someone who coveted our holdings, and that they had been cut down by sorcery as they'd tried to flee the battle."

"But what of their own army?"

"Army? They had no army."

"But then, it was the two of them against a battalion of Dragonlords?"

"Exactly."

"And you think they should have fought?"

"Well, they should not have run."

"I will never understand the Dzur," said Khaavren. "But then, who was this enemy?"

"That," said Tazendra, "I never found out, though I long to know."

"But, if he took your holdings, couldn't you find out who now owns them?"

"Well, I was, in fact, just setting out to discover this when I happened to meet you and Aerich in that charming little town. But now that I have joined the Guards, my time is not my own."

"Cha! We are allowed leaves from time to time. You could use one for your search, could you not?"

"I nearly think so. Will you help me in this search?"

"I should be delighted to."

"Well, we will consider the matter to-morrow, then."

"We will do so."

It happened, however, that Tazendra, who had had a great deal to drink, didn't recall this conversation for some time, and since Khaavren had also been drinking, the thought likewise didn't cross his mind.

Nevertheless, it is the case that from this day forward the four friends were firmly and irrevocably accepted into the brotherhood of the Red Boot Company of the Imperial Guard, and passed many a gay evening dicing, playing cards, and drinking with their new comrades.

On one such occasion, at an inn which was called The Rose Bush, Khaavren chanced to be sitting near a window with Aerich on his right and Pel on his left as they watched Tazendra, who was engaged in losing a good sum of money, playing with two gentlemen of the House of the Iorich. Pel had engaged Khaavren in an animated discussion comparing two of the more common breeds of horse, about which Pel seemed to know enough to startle Khaavren, while Khaavren was expert enough to surprise Pel. Aerich, as was usual, merely listened.

"You cannot deny," said Khaavren, "that the Megaslep is rather slow, and, in fact, has little endurance."

"I do not deny this," said Pel. "Yet it is of high intellect, and can be trained easily."

"Oh, as to training, yes. But the Browncap can also be trained, save for the stallions, which are often unmanageable. The Browncap is, moreover, faster for shorter distances, can ran longer, and carry more weight. Should I be called upon to enter into battle on horseback, its courage would serve as well as its other virtues."

"Well, then," said Pel, "I admit to you that were I to enter a campaign, as seems likely enough, I could wish for nothing more than a Browncap mare or gelding, and yet—"

"Well," said Khaavren. "What then?"

"I only wish to say this: there are other uses for horses than to ride to campaigns upon them."

"Indeed, yes," said Khaavren. "You refer to draught animals, or to carriage beasts?"

"I was thinking more of the pretty little Megaslep."

Khaavren shook his head, "And of what use is such an animal, then?"

"Well, you understand, the Megaslep is a fine animal to be seen on, both for its features and its gait. And under certain circumstances, one might wish for nothing more than a fine-looking animal, impractical though it may be."

"Under what circumstances are these?" asked Khaavren, as Tazendra won a small sum back and began her turn at dealing out the cards.

"Well, for example," said Pel, "if you will look out on the street there, you will see a young man of the House of the Phoenix, leading a Longear mare. The gentleman is engaged in an animated conversation with a lady of the same House. It seems that, should he actually wish to impress her, he might have a little Megaslep to dance for her, and bow its—but stay, good Khaavren, what is the cause of that remarkable expression which has just crossed over your features?"

For, in fact, Khaavren was staring quite fixedly at the Phoenix lady his friend had just pointed out, and he realized that she was none other than the lady with whom he had traveled, she in the guise of an Issola, on his journey to Dragaera City. "A moment, good Pel," he said, "but I believe I recognize someone I have seen before. Allow me a moment to discover if I am deceived."

Chapter the Eleventh

*In Which the Plot, Behaving in Much the Manner
Of a Soup to which Corn Starch Has been Added,
Begins, at Last, to Thicken*

WITHOUT AWAITING AN answer, Khaavren ran from the inn. Once outside, however, he paused long enough to ask himself what he would say to her, to whom his thoughts had returned on more than one occasion since they had parted company. Therefore, it was with hesitation that he approached, stopping only when he was close enough to hear the words being spoke, with the intention of stepping in at the exact point in the conversation when he should deem it most propitious. This did not, however, prevent him from taking the opportunity to listen to the discourse, in which, at this moment, the lady was speaking.

"But then, dear brother, you say she scarcely noticed you?"

"Hardly, my sister. That is to say, she caught my eye once or twice, but, beyond the barest flicker of her brows, which could (I must say it) have been only an imagining on my part, she hardly acknowledged me or my gift."

"A woman of frost!"

"Well, I haven't given up."

"Well then, brother, what next?"

"We must either surrender the battle, or find a new means of attack."

"Surrender, my brother, is impossible. You know what is at stake: for you, for me, for our friends, for the Empire. I repeat: surrender is impossible."

"Then a new direction must be found."

"Well, have you one in mind?"

"I, sister? But it is always you who have the ideas."

"And, in truth, you have seen how far my last one took us. Come, you must find one of your own."

"And, if I do?"

"Then I will endeavor to support you with all the means at my disposal."

"Well then, here is my idea: we must find a way to give her that which she most wants."

"That is not badly taken, brother. But what is it that she wants more than anything else? Had she only her husband's love of jewels, the answer would be simple."

"No, it is not the jewels she wants. It is something else."

"But do you know what it is?"

"Well, my sister, I think I do."

"What? You know?"

"Yes. And not only that, but so do you."

"You mean—?"

"Exactly."

"Ah! But how?"

"I don't know. I will consider. Do you, on your part, consider also."

"Well, I will. We will speak together to-morrow, at the place you know, and discover if our thoughts have brought us anything."

"Excellent, then. Until to-morrow."

"Until to-morrow."

Upon saying this, the cavalier turned, mounted his horse, and rode off down streets which had not been designed for a horse to travel on, forcing him to pick his way carefully among pedestrians, hand-carts, and door-steps. Khaavren was able to observe, as he went by, that this brother was the gentleman who had been her pre-tended husband on the coach-ride. We must add, then, that, upon discovering this, the first idea that crossed Khaavren's active mind was that if he was her brother, perhaps she had no lover; for it is clear that it is easier to fill a position for which a vacancy has been posted than to replace someone who has been carrying out his duties in a satisfactory manner.

As passers-by scurried into doorways to avoid the horseman, the lady turned away from him and was thus face to face with Khaavren, whom, to judge from the ex-pression which crossed her features, she recognized at once. "Sir, Guardsman," she said, "Did we not meet some weeks ago?"

Khaavren bowed low. "Your memory is as perfect as—" he caught himself, and blushed. "That is," he amended, "you are correct."

The Phoenix, either unobservant or tactful, gave no appearance of noticing Khaavren's discomfort. "Your name is Khaav'n, like the wine, is it not?" she asked.

"In fact, my lady, you remember nearly exactly, for though I style myself Khaavren, still the wine that calls my name to your thoughts is produced from grapes that grow in the very district from which I take my name. That is, the names are identical, but their pronunciation differs slightly. And now that my identity has been established, I am most anxious to learn yours, for I can hardly call you by the name you gave while pretending to be an Issola, and yet I must know your name so I can happily offer to perform for you any service you might require."

A slight flush came to her cheeks when he called to mind the deception she had practiced, yet she did not deny it. She merely said, "My name is Illista. And did you mean what you just said?"

It took Khaavren a moment to realize to what she could

be referring, and when he did, his heart gave such a leap that he was barely able to nod in answer.

"Come," she said, "walk with me to my carriage, for I have things to say to you."

Without a glance, then, at the companions he was deserting, Khaavren fell into step next to Illista. "Do you know," he said, "that you have a lovely name? It recalls to me the waterfalls from the Trior River, a tributary of the Shallow River which flows near my home."

"Oh," she said. "Do you think so?"

"I do think so. Illista. It flows from my tongue."

"You will make me blush," she said.

"Oh, never," he said. "But, you perceive that we have arrived at your carriage. What did you wish to say?"

"Pray get inside, and I will tell all."

"You see, I am entering just as you wish, for I trust you completely."

"Oh, you are too good."

"Not the least in the world. But do not keep me waiting. What is it you have to say to me?"

"Only this:—oh, I cannot."

"You cannot? That is what you wish to say to me?"

"No, I cannot say what I wish to say to you."

"How, cannot?"

"Oh, but I must."

"Must what?"

"Tell you."

"Tell me what?"

"I cannot say."

"My lady Illista, it nearly seems as if you are in some distress."

"Well, and if I am?"

"Then I only ask to be told the nature and cause of this distress, that I might remove it."

"Oh, if only you could."

"I can. I will. I swear to it. If it is a man, I will destroy him. If it is a thing, I will obtain it. If it is a cause, I will champion it. If it is a god—"

"Well?"

"Well, if it is a god, I will take him from his seat and escort you there, though all the phantoms of the Paths should guard the way."

"So you say. But what will you do?"

"Ah, you wound me."

"I?"

"Try me, that is all I ask."

"You swear you can be trusted?"

"I will hold your secrets dearer than the whispers of my heart."

"Well then, I will tell you. But not now."

"Well, name for me the time and place."

"Do you know an inn where, some few weeks ago, you killed a man called Frai?"

"Indeed, I could hardly forget it. But how do you know of it?"

"Oh, as to that," she said, "I know a great deal of what happens in the city. But since we are agreed as to the place, be there to-morrow when night falls, and I will whisper in your ear."

"I will be there without fail."

"I count on you, then."

"Not in vain."

"That is well. Go now."

"I go, as I arrive, at your bidding." With these words, he leapt from the carriage and dashed back to the inn where his friends awaited him. Tazendra immediately began to question him, but he indicated with a sign that he would discuss the matter later.

"Very well, then," said Pel. "We were discussing, I believe, horses."

"But rather than that," remarked Aerich, "we ought to discuss the aftermath of the little affair at the archery range."

As we pronounced the words, "archery range," the two Guardsmen with whom Tazendra was playing smiled, as, in fact, did Tazendra. Pel and Khaavren, however, frowned, as they had sufficient perspicacity to catch something in Aerich's voice when he pronounced the word, "aftermath."

"What of it, then?" said Pel.

"The Captain did me the honor to speak to me of it today."

Khaavren shifted uncomfortably and said, "Does he know, then, that we were involved?" He had just recalled that the fight had taken place without the sanctions required by Imperial Law.

"How could he not?" said Pel. "Do you pretend he is deaf and blind?"

"But then, why are we not arrested?" said Khaavren.

"That is," said Aerich, "G'aereth knows; the Captain is, as yet, ignorant."

Khaavren nodded. "Then this discussion was without the Orb, as the saying is?"

"Exactly."

"Well then, what did he have to say?"

"That someone wounded the Cavalier Dekkaan."

"And you said?" asked Pel.

"I said it was a most unfortunate thing."

"Well, and did he agree?" said Khaavren.

"He did more than agree, he concurred."

"Well?"

"He said that the Cavalier Dekkaan is a hot-blooded gentleman, who will not take a blow easily."

"This doesn't surprise me," said Khaavren, who had tested him thoroughly.

"Moreover, there is the matter of Kurich."

"Stay," said Tazendra, turning around suddenly. "I think I know that name."

"You should; you killed him," said Aerich.

"Ah," said Tazendra, "that is it, then," and she returned to her game.

"Well?" said Khaavren, "what of Kurich?"

"He was the younger brother of Her Excellency Lytra e'Tenith, the Warlord."

The three of them looked at one another soberly. Tazendra continued to lose money after the fashion of someone accustomed to doing so.

"But then," said Khaavren, "it was a fair fight, and it is only necessary to ask Uilliv and Rekov in order to prove it."

"I told the Captain as much."

"You told him?"

"In terms of speculation."

"Ah. And he said?"

"That this was what had kept the perpetrators—that was his very word—alive to this date, but, that if they were wise, they would guard themselves closely."

"Well, we will do so, then," said Pel.

"But there was more."

"How, more?" asked Khaavren.

"We have also annoyed someone else."

"That being?"

"Gyorg Lavode."

"Captain of the Lavodes?" asked Pel.

"Exactly."

"But, how have we done so?" said Khaavren.

"The Captain had no idea in the world."

"Tell me, Pel," said Khaavren, "you who seem to know the courtiers as well as my hand knows the grip of my sword, would you know Gyorg Lavode to look at him?"

"Of a certainty."

"Well, is he a Dzurlord of perhaps half a millennium, rather taller than Aerich with fiery dark eyes, a hooked nose, and thin lips?"

"You have described him exactly."

"Well then, I have some idea that we might have annoyed him."

"He can be a bitter enemy," said Pel. "He is, after all, both wizard and warrior, as are all the Lavodes, and this is not a matter to be taken lightly."

"So much the worse," said Khaavren.

"What then should we do?" said Pel.

"I have no plan," said Aerich.

"Allow me to consider the matter," said Khaavren. "Perhaps I will find a solution. But I think this discussion would be best concluded at home, where there are fewer ears about."

"That suits me," said Pel. "We have only to await our friend the Dzurlord."

Tazendra shrugged. "I have lost all my money, so there is no reason for me to remain," she said, turning around and proving that, if she was uninterested in the conversation, she was at least not deaf to it.

They returned, then, to their home, which was nearby, and sat in worried comfort in Aerich's room, where Srahi served them wine. "Thank you," said Khaavren, still politely when she had finished. "That will be all."

Srahi sniffed. "More of your private discussions?" she said. "Well, it is all very well to leave me out of them, but you must not expect me to fight off brigands for you, or to patch you up when you return here as full of holes as the Ballinni Tower."

"We should not ask you to do so," said Khaavren politely. "And yet, one would think you should be happy to know nothing of a business which can hardly interest you, and which, at the same time, could be fraught with danger to anyone who knows about it."

"Ah, then I am right," she cried. "Mark me, young man, you will find—"

But she got no further, for Aerich cut her off with a gesture. While she appeared to be insolent to Tazendra, and haughty to Khaavren, and suspicious of Pel, yet her attitude toward the Lyorn was formed mostly of fear, with some measure of worship. When he signed that the discussion was over, she gathered herself together and left the room without another word. Aerich then picked up his crochet hook and began to work with it, making Khaavren knew not what, while nodding to Khaavren that he should speak.

"Well," said Khaavren, "I do not know that the dangers

of which I spoke to our good Srahi are real, yet I am not certain that they are not. I am, in fact, worried about this news we have received."

"As am I," said Pel. "But you must not forget to explain to us what you were doing when you ran off. If, in fact, it is something you can discuss without compromising your honor as a gentleman."

"Oh, there is no fear of that. I will explain at once."

"Do so, then," said Pel.

"You see," said Tazendra, "that we are giving you our full attention."

"Do you recall our traveling companions on our journey here?"

"I think so," said Tazendra. "They were two Issola bound for the court, who you have said were in fact Phoenix. I've often wondered if we would see them again."

Aerich nodded.

"Well," said Khaavren, "I have just spoken with the lady, who appears to be in some difficulty, and I am to meet with her in hopes of giving her aid."

At these words, Aerich allowed himself a smile, while Tazendra and Pel merely nodded. Silence fell, while Khaavren considered many things that had happened since his arrival in the village of Newmarket, and realized that there was still a great deal that he didn't understand about the affairs of court, and why it could be that a Phoenix would pretend to be an Issola, and why, furthermore, he might have annoyed such an illustrious person as Gyorg Lavode.

He considered these matters carefully, and determined at last that it would be unwise to speak more of the Phoenix lady until he could discover something about what might be in progress around the court. He further considered how the conversation could be brought around to this subject. The others watched him closely as the echoes of his thoughts flitted across his features, until at last he said, "My friend Pel, for so I hope I may call you—"

Pel signified that he could, "—I have yet to thank you for your introduction to the Captain."

"It was nothing," said Pel.

"I beg your pardon, but it was a great deal."

"I am entirely of Khaavren's opinion," said Aerich.

"And I, too, friend Pel," said Tazendra.

"If you wish," said the Yendi, permitting himself a graceful, depreciating bow. "I assure you that I am only to happy to render any service of which I am capable."

"Ah!" said Khaavren. "In that case, if you would be so kind as to be of further help to me, I assure you that I would consider myself your friend for life."

"Konechno," said Pel. "I would be my pleasure. What is it you wish?"

"Just this," said Khaavren. "I am from a duchy far from the capital."

"Of that I am aware."

"We hear very little of what is transpiring here in the capital of the Empire."

"Well?"

"I should be happy to learn something of what has occurred of late, especially during the weeks before our arrival here, so that I shall appear less the fool when others chance to speak of such things."

"Nothing is easier, my dear Khaavren."

"You will do so, then?" cried Khaavren.

"Why, certainly," said Pel. "And at once, if you would like."

"You see that I am anxiously awaiting your every word."

"Well, then, the items of news are these: Empress Cher-ova the Third vacated the throne and Tortaalik the First ascended it some eleven weeks ago."

Aerich sat back in his chair and drained his wine cup. Tazendra leaned forward anxiously. Khaavren, also lean-ing forward, said, "With this piece of intelligence I was already acquainted. It is, in fact, why I am here."

"Indeed?" said Pel.

"Certainly," said Tazendra. "You know that an Athyra

Emperor has little use for Guards who are only swords-
men, but a Phoenix—"

"Of course," said Khaavren. "But about the Empress—"

"Oh, as to the Empress," said Tazendra, addressing Pel.
"We knew about that."

"Yes, but do you know the reason for Empress Cherova's abdication?"

"Ah! The reason?" said Tazendra, looking at Khaavren.
"You ask if we know the reason?"

"I had assumed," said Khaavren, "that it was due to the
turning of the Cycle."

"Yes," said Tazendra. "After all, when the Cycle turns—"

"Well, yes," said Pel. "But you know that a turn of the
Cycle is always indicated by some tangible event, and
that it is this which leads to the next House assuming the
throne and the Orb."

"Of course," said Khaavren, who had known no such
thing. "There was a tangible event, then?"

"Very tangible," said Pel, studying his long, graceful
hands.

"And it was an event?" put in Tazendra, determined
not to be left out.

"I can think of no other way to describe it than as an
event."

"Well, then, what was this event?"

"The Baroness of Kaluma has struck off the head of the
Marquis of Pepperfield."

"Ah!" said Khaavren. "And this has caused the Empress
to see that the Cycle had turned?"

"Well, why should it not?"

"Yes," said Tazendra, who was beginning to look
flushed. "Why should it not?"

"But I don't see—" said Khaavren.

At this point, Aerich interjected, "The Baroness of Kaluma is perhaps better known as Kathana e'Marish'Chala,
of the House of the Dragon."

"Oh, in that case I see plainly," said Khaavren, who

was as confused as ever. "But, what was the cause of the quarrel?"

"The Baroness," said Pel, "that is to say, Kathana, is, as you know, an artist. She had just completed an oil commissioned by Lord Rollondar e'Drien. The oil depicted, as I recall, a wounded dragon. She brought it to the Palace, to hang in the Dragon Wing."

"Well, and then?" said Khaavren.

"Well, it happened that the Lord Pepperfield was at the Palace to visit the Warlord. He chanced to see it, and made comment on it."

"Ah!" said Khaavren. "He didn't like it?"

"He felt it was too melancholy to be a dragon, and not fierce enough. The Baroness, I am told, wished to demonstrate that she knew as much about ferocity as did he, and removed his head with her broadsword in the course of demonstrating this."

"And it was well done, too," affirmed Tazendra. "I'd have done the same, only—"

"Yes?"

"I don't paint."

"But," said Khaavren, "how did this cause the abdication of the Empress?"

"In this way: Pepperfield is a far eastern fief, held by the House of the Dragon in its own name. It had been given to the Marquis who is, I believe, of the e'Tenith line—"

"E'Lanya," said Aerich quietly.

"E'Lanya, then," said Pel. "In any case, with his death, argument broke out within the House of the Dragon over who should be the new duke. The Dragon Heir, being of the same line as Lord Pepperfield, wished to continue the duchy within his line, but another line, I believe the e'Kieron branch, objected."

"Well," said Khaavren, "I still do not understand."

"This will make it as clear as the Threefalls River: the fief of Pepperfield lies in a small valley, between two impassible mountains, on the eastern border of the Empire. As such, it is a very important area strategically."

"Go on, good Pel, I am exceedingly interested."

"Furthermore, this area has been subject to more invasions throughout the history of the Empire than any other. Why it is, we do not know, but it is for this reason, you understand, that the land was entrusted to the House of the Dragon to be defended. The Empress, upon taking all of these facts into account, decided that it was a dangerous situation, and conjoined with the Carriage House Uprising, which was then proceeding in all its vigor, required an Emperor with, perhaps, less knowledge of sorcery, but more skill as a diplomatist, to settle the problem before the accursed Easterners take it into their minds to invade."

Khaavren looked quickly at Aerich, who was absorbed in his crochet work. "Ah! Now I understand," said Khaavren.

"That, then, is the state of things today."

"But what of the lady Kathana?"

"Oh, the new Emperor immediately ordered her arrest."

"Arrest!"

"Certainly. She had mortally wounded a man without following the dueling code. And, as his spine was severed, and as, moreover, she had put several paint brushes into his eyes after beheading him—"

"What?"

"It is as I have had the honor to explain. As she had done these things, his life could not be saved, and he was brought to Deathgate Falls, to enter whatever afterlife awaits him. There was no choice, then, but to order her arrest."

"She has been arrested, then?"

"Ah! As to that, I don't say she was."

"What? She is in hiding?"

"She is on tolerably good terms with Captain Lanmarea, and as it was to Lanmarea that the order for the arrest was given, why, it is hardly surprising that no arrest has taken place."

"Now I understand," said Khaavren. "And yet, why has the order not been given to G'aereth, if Lanmarea has failed?"

"My good Khaavren," said Pel, "the Emperor could hardly deliver such an insult. To ask G'aereth to accomplish this task, after having first given it to Lanmarea, would destroy the delicate balance of policies that he is, even now, working to accomplish."

"And yet," said Khaavren, "could he not assign the task to the Lavodes?"

"It is clear that you are only lately come to court," said Pel. "Even the Emperor cannot assign a task to the Lavodes. They take after their first captain, the Enchantress of Dzur Mountain, and accept what tasks they wish, and ignore those that don't please them."

"But then, has he asked them?"

"Well, I don't say that he hasn't."

"And?"

"The Lady Kathana, it seems, is a friend of The Enchantress, and though The Enchantress is banished from court and from her command, still she has great influence with the Lavodes."

"But suppose," said Khaavren, "that certain Guardsmen under G'aereth's command should find this fugitive and bring her to justice? What then?"

"Do you mean," said Pel, "without acting under orders from their Captain, that is to say, from Lord G'aereth?"

"You have understood me exactly," said Khaavren.

"Well, in that case," said Pel, frowning. "In that case I nearly think they will have done Lanmarea and her White Sash Battalion a severe disservice, while pleasing G'aereth to the same degree. As well," he added, with a quick glance at Aerich, "as annoying certain others."

"And," put in Tazendra, "they will have gotten themselves prudently out of the city for a while."

"Which says nothing," remarked Aerich, looking up

from the crochet work in which he was currently engaged, "of the service we will have done for the Empire."

"Ah," said Khaavren, "you have said *we*, I think."

"Well," said Aerich. "I did."

"Do you, then, propose an expedition?"

"That is hardly necessary," said Aerich with a smile. "It seems that you have already done so."

"Blood of the Horse," said Khaavren, "I think I did. Do you accept?"

"I am entirely in favor," said Aerich.

"As am I," put in Tazendra. "It is, after all, just the sort of adventure for which I came here."

"And you, good Pel?" asked Khaavren.

"Oh, I? Well, if the rest of you are determined on such a course, I will hardly speak against it."

"Then it is settled," said Khaavren.

"Nearly," said Aerich.

"What remains to be decided?"

"Two things," said Aerich. "The first is, how are we going to convince the Captain to give us the leaves of absence we require, without telling him our plans?"

"I had not thought of that," said Khaavren.

"I have a way," said Pel.

"Excellent," said Khaavren. "We'll leave it to you. And the second, good Aerich?"

"The second issue," said the Lyorn, "is this: just exactly how are we to find Kathana e'Marish'Chala in order to effect her arrest?"

"Oh, as to that," said Khaavren.

"Well?"

"You may leave it entirely in my hands."

Chapter the Twelfth

━━◆═══◆━━━━━━━━━◆═══◆━━

In Which Khaavren Attempts To Learn
The Whereabouts of Kathana e'Marish'Chala

W E TRUST THAT our readers will forgive us if
we have not lingered over every aspect of
the day to day lives of those personages
whose history we have chosen to explore. It is our con-
tention that, facts being as numerous as grains of sand in
the desert of Suntra, mere recitation of detail will both
weary and confuse, whereas careful selection will entertain and enlighten. Thus, we have not deemed it necessary to educate our readers on exactly how it was that
Srahi came to find a launderer, nor on the means Pel used
to select perfumed note-paper on which to write to his
mistress, nor on the treatment for the leather Aerich used
on his boots to prevent them from leaking when it rained,
nor on how Tazendra would contort in preparation for
her morning exercises.

Yet we are forced to admit that, from time to time, we
will discover that a detail of no more moment than these
will take on a far greater importance than we had ever
thought to assign it. When this happens, we find our-

selves hesitant to amend what we have already written, but will instead go forward, forward, ever forward, as Undauntra would say, and let the stragglers fill the gaps.

It therefore becomes our duty to confess that we have erred in failing to mention that Khaavren had spent some portion of nearly every day in one of the Imperial libraries in the Palace. It had occurred to him that Pel had his secrets, Aerich his contemplations, and Tazendra was happy to gamble and carouse while she waited for the opportunity to gain glory with her sword, but if he, Khaavren, were ever to achieve greatness, he must at once remedy the ignorance which afflicted him. His impoverished family had barely been able to afford to send him to a classroom tutor, from whom we had learned to read and to calculate sums along with the children of Vallista and Chreotha, which hardly provided him the knowledge he craved; he therefore arranged his time so he could spend some portion of every day with books in each of the five great categories; magical and natural science, history, philosophy, books-written-to-be-performed, and books-written-to-be-read.

What is significant was that, as he approached these studies, darting from one to the other as a bee in a flowerbed, he would, naturally, meet librarians. He had, in point of fact, met several. In the Caffissa Library, taking up the first three stories of the southern quarter of the Athyra wing, all of the librarians were Athyra, and they were only as polite to Khaavren as was necessary to avoid the challenge which any astute observer could discover always waiting on the wings, as it were, of the Tiassa's countenance. In the halls of Silver Library, outside the Palace proper but quite close to the Lyorn Wing, all of the librarians, themselves Lyorn historians, were helpful, but often too helpful, and Khaavren frequently became lost in their recommendations and counter-recommendations, and corrections and notations.

But in the Zerika Library, in the basement beneath the Imperial Wing, there was an Easterner, one Ricardo, a rotund fellow with, as is common with those of his short-lived race, more hair growing on his face than on the top of his head. His walk had a trace of the waddle one finds in the smaller species of wildlife that dwell long the Yellow River, and the tip of his tongue appeared to have made a permanent home between the teeth on the right side of his mouth. Yet in him, Khaavren found a veritable fountain of information, which, at the least pressure, that is to say, at the slightest provocation, would gush forth until the Tiassa thought he might drown in it. For while the Phoenix rate philosophy very high among the branches of knowledge, still it was as yet the aftermath of the reign of the Athyra, a House with as little use for impractical knowledge as the House of the Dragon would have for anything which didn't cut or thrust. All of this had the result of leaving poor Ricardo destitute for patrons in a poorly maintained library, and one which was visited but seldom; hence his high regard for Khaavren when the latter first appeared.

It need hardly be added that the young Tiassa benefited greatly by the association; where by nature he was inclined to flit from book to book and from thought to thought with no order or method, the Easterner displayed some of the characteristics of a tsalmoth—attacking any problem from a dozen angles simultaneously, but never letting go until it was solved. The result is that Khaavren, though he never developed more than a passing interest in philosophy, that is, in the science of science, still he received two benefits; the first being the acquisition of some skill in how to approach a problem, the second being the friendship of this learned Easterner.

It was to Ricardo then that Khaavren went, and brought with him news of the crime of Kathana e'Marish'Chala. Ricardo listened to the entire history as he listened to everything, with his whole attention, asking no questions, his eyes fixed on Khaavren's mouth as if he were reading the words as they emerged.

When Khaavren had finished, the Easterner suggested

that Khaavren return in several hours while he, Ricardo, requested of one of the records libraries certain documents which he claimed would be most revealing. To this Khaavren agreed, and, after a light luncheon of fruit and cheese in one of the small inns connected to the Phoenix Wing, he returned to find Ricardo bent over a large stack of folios, with slips of paper, red, brown, green, yellow, or blue, emerging from them like the tongues of snakes. Upon closer inspection, the folios were filled with columns of numbers, names, dates, and locations. Raising his eyes from these, Ricardo looked at him blankly, as if forgetting who Khaavren was and why he was there. Then he gave his head a small shake and said, "Ah, you are back."

"That is true, good Ricardo," said the Tiassa. "And it seems you have something there."

"These documents I requested from the Imperial Records Service, which oversees all matters pertaining to taxation."

"Ah. Taxation."

"Exactly."

"But, if you will pardon me Ricardo, what has taxation to do with the whereabouts of Kathana e'Marish'Chala?"

"Oh, it has everything to do with it."

"How is that?"

"Well, I will explain."

"Do so, please."

"What you must remember, young sir," said the Easterner, forgetting that Khaavren was, in point of fact, rather older in years than he was, "is that Dragonlords never hide. Therefore, if your quarry seems to you to be in hiding, to her she must be doing another thing entirely."

"And what might that be, good Ricardo?" inquired Khaavren, patiently allowing the librarian to arrive at the point in his own way.

"Any of a number of things are possible. And yet, she is an artist. So, what would be the most natural thing for an artist to do, if she wished to remain out of sight for a long period of time?"

"Well, she might go paint a picture," suggested Khaavren.

"Exactly my thought," said Ricardo.

"But, you perceive, she could paint it anywhere."

"She could, but she wouldn't. That is, she is actually in only one place."

"With this, I agree. But how are we to determine where? That is, after all, the very question with which I came to you."

"And it is the question which I now propose to answer."

"What, now?"

"Indeed, yes."

"How, then?"

"By making a determination."

"Ah! A determination."

"Yes. By determining for whom she is working. I have here the reports on all expenditures within the last month for every one of the ten thousand wealthiest nobles in the Empire. These reports are broken down into categories, and each details the expenditures made by that individual. One category on which these people must report is the amount spent on cultural matters."

"That is true, Ricardo; for the Empire is always interested in encouraging culture among the nobility; hence the lack of taxes on any such expenditure."

"Precisely."

"And you have looked through ten thousand of them?"

"Oh, hardly that. The Emperor would be saddened to learn how few have actually spent anything at all on improving their knowledge of the arts; but for us, why, we are pleased, for there were a scant thousand, and most of those could be dismissed at a glance."

"I see. So, you have discovered who has spent money on artistic pursuits."

"Yes. And more."

"What, more?"

"Of a certainty. The Empire requires more than the bare amount; on the contrary, anyone wishing to avoid these taxes must include the amount spent, the type of work, and the name of the artist."

"Ah, the name of the artist!"

"Exactly."

Khaavren considered for a moment, and said, "But surely she would not be listed by her own name in such a thing."

"It is necessary that she be so listed."

"Well, then?"

"Do you know by what means an artist earns his livelihood?"

"Well, by being paid for his art."

"But then, who pays him? One can hardly expect an artist to put his work out for sale in the market, as if it were a clutch of eggs."

"No, the artist must have a patron who agrees to purchase the work, or else must make an agreement beforehand."

"And will this agreement state the amount to be paid for the work?"

"Assuredly, though one expects to pay more than the agreed-upon price."

"And do you suppose that an artist who is also a Dragonlord, such as Kathana e'Marish'Chala, would, even in hiding, accept a fee below her usual standard?"

"Why, I should not expect so."

"Well, there you have it. We need only look for who has commissioned a painting within the range that the Baroness of Kaluma, that is, Kathana e'Marish'Chala, generally commands."

"And it is just such a list that you have, my good Ricardo?"

"Indeed, Sir Khaavren, and I have already perused it."

"And you have a result? That is to say, you have discovered her whereabouts?"

"Oh, as to that, I could hardly be certain of such a thing. And yet I have discovered that Baroness Kaluma has received, for her last several works, payment between one thousand three hundred and two thousand one hundred Imperials."

"Blood! So much?"

"It is so."

"And you have found someone who has commissioned a work for that amount?"

"Many, in point of fact."

"Then we must determine which it is."

"Your pardon, but I have already done so."

"Done so!"

"Indeed."

"But how?"

"Why, when I looked at the names of the artists listed, there were some few I recognized."

"Ah, the those could be eliminated at once."

"Exactly."

"And then?"

"Well, then I looked at the others."

"And what did you find?"

"One, I found, was called, Fricorith."

"Very well, one is called Fricorith."

"Exactly."

"But I fail to see—"

"Ah. You do not yet comprehend."

"You are correct; I do not comprehend."

"Fricorith, in the old North-western tongue, which is still preserved by the House of the Dragon, as well as the House of the Lyorn, means, 'Nearly-the-end-of-Winter.'"

"How is it you know this, good Ricardo?"

"Why, it is in this language that most of the library documents are written, since most Lyorn still speak it, as I have had the honor to mention."

"I see. But then, how did this information help you make your determination?"

"By the simplest means. The Baroness of Kaluma is of

the e'Marish'Chala line; that is, she was named after Marish'Chala, who was Warlord of the Empire during the fourth Dragon Reign. At that time, she, that is, Marish'-Chala, was called Marishori Cvorunn Chalionara, which name I took the precaution of looking up against the chance that it would be useful to know."

"And that was well thought."

"I am gratified that you think so."

"But, then, tell me what it means."

"I will do so. Marishori is a Northwestern name that signifies 'keeper of trust.'"

"And yet, good Ricardo, I do not see how this is of help to us."

"It is not. But then, I did not stop there."

"You did not?"

"No. I acquired translations of the other names as well."

"And what did you find?"

"Cvorunn, I found to be very close to the Serioli Kvirinun, which means, 'time of melting snows,' that is, spring. And Chalionara is similar to another Serioli word, that being Shuloon!re, which means, 'to arrive prematurely.' The combination, you perceive, would be 'spring arriving early,' and at what time of year would spring arrive early?"

"Why, late winter, of course."

"Exactly. Now, you perceive, it is significant that I have found an artist whose name, Fricorith, means, 'nearly-the-end-of-winter.'"

"Ricardo, you are a marvel!"

The old Easterner bowed, and his face actually became slightly pink. "I think," he said at last, "that we may safely assume that the Baroness of Kaluma is dwelling in the far Eastern keep of Redface, home of Adron e'Kieron, of the House of the Dragon."

Chapter the Thirteenth

In Which, to our Regret, We are Forced to Leave our Heroes for a Brief Time

Now, AS KHAAVREN runs up the narrow circular stairway to the level of the Street, and sets off at a run through the maze of the Imperial Wing, around the South Cornerstones to the Long Corridor, there to burst out in the Phoenix Courtyard and begin the dash toward the rendezvous set for only an hour hence, his hand clutching his sword to keep it from between his feet, his head fairly exploding with ideas and intentions—now, we say—we will turn our gaze to a place far back in the Palace, and much higher than Khaavren has ever ventured.

Here, in the labyrinth where the Imperial Family makes its home, in one of the numerous tower chambers that provide such an excellent view of much of the Palace and a fair portion of the city, two persons were sitting on the thin, yellow marble tiling of the tower floor. One, dressed in the full regalia of the House of the Dragon, complete with "bombast," that is, with the patches and medallions and insignia of her campaigns and the honors she has won in them, was none other than Lytra e'Tenith, the Warlord of the Empire. The other was a dark figure, in the hooded robe of an Athyra, it is true, but without mark or insignia upon her garments. The hood hid her face, but her hands were old and wrinkled, yet her voice was strong without any hint of age.

The Athyra said, "The news, Excellency, is of the most recent variety."

"But, dear Seodra, I am not asking how recent the news is, I speak of the news itself."

"And you wish to know, Excellency?"

"I wish to know how this could have happened."

"I assure Your Excellency that, if I were able to explain this, I would do so, and that directly. Perhaps one of the gods had a hand in it."

"Should that prove true, Seodra, we must enlist another, or, at any rate, a demon."

Seodra chuckled, which sound might have sent a cold shiver of fear down the back of anyone who chanced to be listening; indeed, Lytra herself could scarcely keep a singular expression from crossing her countenance. "Have you a god in your pocket, Excellency?"

"Hardly," said the Warlord.

"Nor, you perceive, have I."

"Well?"

"Well, then we must find another means of protecting our investment."

"Investment, Seodra? By the Orb, you sound like a merchant."

"After a fashion, Excellency, I am a merchant, although the merchandise in which I have the honor to deal can be neither tasted nor smelt, and the coin in which I am paid does not shine like gold."

Lytra shifted uncomfortably, as if she had no wish to penetrate Seodra's metaphor. "Perhaps," she said, "it was not a god; perhaps there is some sorcery that pierces the veils you have cast about our friend."

"That is possible, Excellency; in any case I am not offended at the suggestion. But be it sorcery, the act of a god, or merely the caprice of fortune, we must act in such a way as to repair the damage."

"I ask for nothing better. Have you a suggestion as to how we may go about doing this?"

"It may be, Excellency, that a simple warning will do. He is neither Dzur nor Dragon."

"And then?"

"Well, he may have some sense."

Lytra stared at the old woman, her brows coming together. "Seodra, are you attempting to offend me?" There was now an edge to the Warlord's voice.

"Not in the least," said the other. She chuckled. "After all, where would be the profit in that?"

"Profit," said Lytra scornfully. "You *do* speak like a merchant, dear Seodra."

"That's as may be, Lytra, but may I do myself the honor to suggest that we concentrate on the issue which has come before us?"

"Someday, Seodra, you might succeed in making me angry. And do you know what would happen then?"

"Why, then the Emperor would either lose a skilled Warlord, or he would lose ..." Her voice trailed off, as if she was unwilling to describe what else the Emperor might lose.

"And yet," said the Warlord, "this possibility does not in any way appear to concern you, Seodra."

"Thank you very much, Excellency. Shall I arrange for this warning, which I have just mentioned, to take place?"

"By all means."

"That is well, Excellency."

"And if the warning doesn't work, Seodra? What then?"

"Then? Why, we follow through on the warning, that is all. You have a tolerably long reach, have you not? And my own is hardly shorter. We have each our arms, our eyes, and our tools. You are the Warlord, and this, it would seem, is war."

"Indeed it is, Seodra, but an amusing war."

"Amusing? In what way?"

"Why, amusing in that we are going to a great deal of trouble to protect this little Kaluma, and yet it is we who are going to destroy her."

"But it must be we ourselves, and none other, Excellency, for as you know, if anyone else destroys her, we lose our best bargaining piece in the real game, and it may not be so easy to find another."

"That is true, my ally. Which bring us to the question of Viscount Uttrik."

"Yes, the poor son of the late but scarcely lamented Marquis of Pepperfield, he whose head Kaluma so conveniently removed for us."

"Exactly. He is undoubtedly looking for Kaluma even now, and if he finds her—"

"If he finds her, he will challenge her, and she will kill him. He is a pompous fool."

"He was. He has seen battle recently; perhaps he has changed."

"Impossible. He was a pompous fool, he remains a pompous fool."

"But, for a Dragon, not an exceptionally brave one. He may call the authorities in, rather than challenge her himself."

"Impossible, Excellency! No Dragonlord could do such a thing, as you should know better than I."

"And yet, I must ask: can we take this chance? Such an error could be the undoing of all our plans."

"How, then you have something to propose? If it is assurance you want, there are those in the House of the Jhereg who would be anxious not to be in my debt any longer."

Lytra struck her chair with her fist. "No!" she cried. "No assassination! Do you understand me, Seodra? There are depths to which I will not plunge. I will break you, and let all of my plans fall into pieces before I will countenance the use of assassins."

"Very well, Excellency. Then what?"

"There are other ways. A duel, for example."

"With whom? You? Would you expose yourself that way? And on what grounds is this duel to be fought?"

"A pretext can be found easily enough. And as for whom—well, I will consider that."

"Ah!"

"Excuse me, Seodra, but you said, 'ah.'"

"And so I did, Excellency."

"You have, then, an idea?"

"Indeed I have."

"Well, tell it me."

"I shall do so."

"Begin, then."

"Well, this is it: my arts have revealed that a certain individual has just discovered the whereabouts of she whom we wish to keep hidden."

"So you have just informed me, Seodra. What then? We have said that we shall warn him away."

"And so we shall. But we will also arrange to put the headstrong Uttrik in his path. And, should Uttrik somehow kill the young Tiassa—"

"The discoverer is a Tiassa?"

"Exactly. A member of the Red Boot Battalion of the Imperial Guard, in fact."

"I see. Go on, then, Seodra. You interest me exceedingly."

"Well, should Uttrik kill him, then we will have eliminated one problem, and should the Tiassa win, we will have eliminated another. We will then meet again to discuss the remaining problem."

"An excellent idea, Seodra." She laughed. "Perhaps, if the gods smile on our plans, they will do each other in, and this will solve things neatly."

"Exactly, Excellency. That was my own thought precisely. It is easy to see that, though you are of the e'Kieron line of the House of the Dragon, you nevertheless have some of the e'Lanya blood flowing through your veins, for your grasp of tactics is without fail."

"A truce on flattery, Seodra. Tell me instead how we are to arrange for this duel to occur?"

"In the simplest possible manner: we will let Uttrik know that the Tiassa is looking for Kaluma."

"How will that help us?"

"Because we will also allow him to think that he is seeking her in order to aid her, rather than the reverse. He will be most anxious to stop him, and they will fight, and one of them will kill the other."

"Very well. An excellent plan. But stop, is this Tiassa called Khaavren?"

"Why, that is the very name, Excellency. Is there some problem?"

The Warlord laughed. "Problem? Not the least in the world. All the better, in fact. See to it."

"I will do so, Excellency."

"Then let us pass on to other matters. What of His Imperial Majesty?"

"What of him?"

"As of our last conversation, he was making warlike noises."

"Well? The right war, or the wrong war?"

"The wrong war."

"He must be brought around then, Excellency."

"And how can we accomplish this, Seodra?"

"Well, am I not his eyes? And are you not his hands?"

"But them has he not ears as well? And even other hands?"

"If you would be so kind as to speak plainly, Excellency."

"I was merely continuing your simile, Seodra. But very well. Have you forgotten the Lavodes? The Guards? The Palace gossips and courtiers who have his ear?"

"The Lavodes are on our side, Excellency. Do you forget who their Captain is? Their *true* Captain? We need not worry about them. And the gossips are merely so much wind; they will only fill His Majesty's ear if there is nothing of more substance to take their place."

"Well?" said Lytra. "And the Guard?"

"They take orders from you, Excellency. Have you somehow contrived to forget this?"

"Not the least in the world. But tell me, Seodra, for I wish to know, what order am I to give them? Do you pretend that I can call Lanmarea and G'aereth into my chambers and say, 'You will take no action against this and such person, or this and such occurrence'? In two minutes, Seodra, I would no longer be Warlord, and you would find all of your creeping vines had buried themselves in their own roots."

"Lanmarea we can ignore for reasons you know as well as I do, your ladyship."

"Well, yes. And G'aereth?"

"G'aereth, I confess, is a problem. He must be given other things to think about."

"Have you something in mind, Seodra?"

"Hmmm. Well, you could send him out to look for something such as, say, candlebud."

Lytra stared at the hooded figure for a moment, then a slow smile spread across her face, which grew gradually broader until it erupted into laughter, which filled the small tower chamber above the Imperial residences.

Chapter the Fourteenth

*In Which it is Shown that Eleemosynary Behavior
is Sometimes Rewarded In This Lifetime*

As this conversation was taking place, another conversation, equally private if less sinister, was occurring within G'aereth's apartments in the Dragon Wing.

"Come in, Cavalier," said G'aereth to open the discussion. "Pray, be comfortable. I have been given to understand that you wished to have two words with me."

"This is true, Captain," said the visitor, who was none other than Pel. "I wish to share with you a thought that has just recently crossed my mind."

"Well, and what thought is it? For you know that I expect my Guardsmen to use their heads, and I think yours is a tolerably long one."

"Thank you, Captain."

"But, as I have asked, tell me this thought."

"Well, I will. It is this: I worry about dispatches."

"How, worry?"

"It seems to me, Captain, that, when six men witness

an event, there will be six different reports on what has happened."

"That observation is just, I think."

"Now many Athyra, and some others, most notably the philosopher Hydragaar, believe that this proves that six different events have occurred, and all have the same truth."

"Well, and you?"

"I, Captain, believe, along with Daridd of Diar-by-the-Bennaat that these Athyra are overreacting."

"I perceive that you are well-read in the classics."

Pel bowed. "I have had the honor to receive some small education. But, Captain, if I may be permitted to ask you a question, I am curious as to your position on this matter."

"Mine? Well, I believe I must side with you and Daridd on this issue."

"I am gratified that you do."

"But explain to me, Cavalier, how these epistemological issues relate to dispatches?"

"In this way, Captain: I have spoken with four men, all of whom have just returned from garrison duty in the east."

"In the east?"

"That is to say, in the area around . . ."

"Around?"

"Around Pepperfield, Captain."

"Ah. Just so."

"Would you be interested to know what I have learned?"

"Why, yes, if it would please you to tell me."

"Well, I have learned that there are a thousand thousand Easterners preparing to invade the Empire."

"Ah!"

"And I have learned that there are no Easterners within a hundred leagues."

"Go on."

"I have learned that the garrison is strong, and that it is weak."

"Well?"

"That it is well-commanded, and that there are no leaders who are prepared for any sort of engagement."

"I understand what you are saying, Cavalier. But, speak plainly, it seems to me that you are moving in some particular direction. Tell me what you want?"

"What I want?" said Pel, with an expression of innocent surprise on his features. "How, you pretend I want something?"

"Well, don't you?"

"My Captain, the very philosopher whom we were just discussing spoke of the importance of charity, and good works, and serving others."

"Well?"

"I want only to serve His Imperial Majesty, Captain; that is all."

As we could not possibly add anything of importance to this declaration, we will now return to Khaavren, whom we left traveling at as great a speed as he could manage toward his rendezvous with Illista. He arrived out of breath, yet early enough that he could refresh himself with a glass of dark red wine while he waited. He also, as was his wont, inspected those around him. Now that the festivities were well over, the inn had reverted to its usual clientele, mostly of the House of the Teckla, with an occasional Chreotha or Jhereg. The tavern itself was large and had a rug covering a portion of the floor, presumably, thought Khaavren, to hide the bloodstains left by his encounter with Frai. The innkeeper appeared to recognize Khaavren at once, to judge from the expression of unease that crossed his countenance, but the host made no remark.

Darkness was just falling, and those whose work ended with the light were beginning to trickle in. It seemed to Khaavren that this was an odd place for a lady of the House of the Phoenix to request a meeting, but perhaps, if she wished for privacy, just such a place would be best. It was only then that he was struck with the realization that the day's activities had temporarily driven from his mind—that is, the thought that soon he would be meeting her, Illista, whose voice had already imprinted itself on his mind, whose bright, narrow eyes and delicately molded features swam before his imagination, and if, in his imagination, she looked at him with an endearing expression that she had, in fact, never bestowed upon him in real life, who can fault him for this? It is our prerogative to imagine in one we love all of those gentle feelings that hope can supply, and to continue to do so until harsh reality intervenes with it war-chariots and spears, with its broken assignations and revealed deceptions, crying, "Here I am! You must face me whether you will or nill!" Is there one among you who has never built such imaginary worlds for yourself, even though, like Khaavren as we observe him with his wine and his dreams, his mocking smile and the slow shake of his head, you may chide yourself for your illusions?

For we know that now and then, here and there, it may happen that the dreams become real, and that our love is returned, and the one we love may bestow that very look that we have imagined. And, rare though it may be, it is still that knowledge that allows us to continue to hope, and to bare our breasts to the spears of reality, crying, "Do your worst! I will risk all in order to cling to the barest, thinnest thread of a chance at ultimate bliss!"

It was in such a mood, then, and with such bittersweet thoughts, just as Khaavren was beginning to wonder if Illista would never appear, and if his hopes were to be dashed even as he was beginning to savor them, that his reveries were happily interrupted by a waiter who came to his table and said, "My lord, if you will do me the honor to accompany me to the back room, a lady wishes to speak with you."

To his credit, Khaavren gave hardly any reaction to this message save a curt nod, though his heart pounded like the hooves of a maddened horse. He rose, finished the last sip of his wine and said, "Very well." The servant led him to the rear of the inn, through a curtained doorway, through a narrow, well-lit room, to another room, curtained on both sides and lit only by a single candle high on the wall. A small, hooded figure sat at the far end of the long table that, save for a few chairs, was the only furnishing the room offered.

Khaavren frowned. "Illista?" he said hesitantly.

She brought her finger to her lips to indicate silence, then pulled the hood back so he could see her face. "Don't speak my name so loudly here," she said.

He rushed to her and knelt at her side. "I will not, but I fear my heart may be heard, for it cries your name aloud with each beat."

"Oh, come," she said, blushing. She suddenly seemed younger than she had before. "Sit next to me," she said. "We must speak."

"I am eagerly awaiting your every word, for the sound of your voice is sweeter to me than the ringing of the bells of Scansni."

"Please."

"I cannot refuse you. I will speak no more of your charm, your grace, your beauty, the shiver that passes through me when I hear your voice, the throb in my breast when your eye meets mine; I will say nothing of these things, but instead I will sit and listen patiently to what you have to tell me. You see? I speak no more, but merely listen."

And, true his word, he sat quietly, watching her every expression, waiting for her words to fall, like water from the Everlasting Fountain of Prince Westmount, into his waiting ears.

"I have a friend," she began.

"A friend?" said Khaavren.

"Yes."

"How? Do you mean a lover?"

"Oh, that you should ask! Haven't you just promised to listen?"

"Your pardon," said Khaavren, blushing. "The thought forced its way from my heart to my mouth, never stopping in my brain. You perceive, I always speak my heart; it is a defect, I know."

"It is," she said, "a charming defect, it is true, but still a dangerous one."

"Ah, you think so?"

"I am certain of it."

"Well, then I will bridle and rein these wild feelings, and listen, only."

"Well, then I continue."

"I await your words. You have a friend who is not a lover."

"Yes. She is in trouble."

"Well?"

"The Empire has taken an interest in her."

"An unkind interest?"

"As unkind as possible: they wish to arrest her."

"Ah! But haven't you friends at court who could protect her?"

"Indeed, I thought so; I have the ear of the Consort herself."

"I would nearly think that sufficient."

"But it is not."

"How, not?"

"Because her enemies have the ear of the Emperor."

"That is a problem, yes. Of what crime is your friend accused?"

"She is accused of nothing short of murder, my friend."

"Good heavens!"

"Ah, you exclaim. Are you horrified?"

"Horrified? No, I am delighted."

"How, delighted?"

"I am delighted that, just now, you called me your friend."

"Oh, as to that," said Illista, blushing. "But what of the crime?"

Khaavren lifted his shoulders and brought them down again, like Aerich. "All murders are not the same. Some are cowardly, such as the killing of Lady Yurrota, that had the court in turmoil for days. Others are merely duels without the formalities such as that recently committed by Lord Porishtev in his killing of Gerand of Kor. Still others, such as the matter of the Baroness Kaluma, are—"

"What name did you say?" cried Illista.

"Baroness Kaluma, who is better known as Kathana—"

"Yes, yes, I know. But how did you come to mention her?"

"Why, surely everyone is acquainted with the matter?" said Khaavren, who had not heard of it two days before.

"And what is your own belief on her crime?"

Khaavren frowned. "Well, it was hardly a duel, and yet it seemed to me perfectly justified."

"Then you believe she should go free?"

"Oh, I don't say that."

"You don't?"

"Well, it was a killing, after all."

"Then I am undone!"

"How?"

"You were my last hope."

"I was? But I no longer am? You speak in riddles."

"And can you not solve the riddle?"

"The Gods! How can I—? But wait, could it be that your friend's name is Kathana e'Marish'Chala?"

"Ah! You have guessed it."

"But then, this changes everything."

"What has it changed? You perceive that I am most eager to hear your answer."

"A moment ago, I was considering mounting an expedition to capture her."

"What, you?"

"Indeed yes. But I no longer hold with this plan."

"And have you another?"

"I have. Instead of capturing her, I will save her."

"But, why?"

"Because she is your friend, and you—" Here Khaavren broke off, stammering.

"Yes, I?"

"Oh, I cannot say."

Now it was Illista's turn to blush, but she said, "How can you save her? I don't know where she is."

"Ah, but I do."

"You do? How can that be?"

"In the simplest possible way: I have discovered it."

"But then, where is she?"

"She is at Redface, the home of Adron e'Kieron."

"What? Are you certain?"

"As certain as if I'd seen her there."

"And you will save her?"

"I answer for it."

"But what of those who plan to arrest her?"

"I will foil them."

"And if they attack you?"

"I will defeat them."

"There are many of them, and they are powerful."

"I am not without friends."

"Can you count on them?"

"Assuredly. But tell me, who are these people who are many and powerful and will attack me?"

"Oh, I cannot tell you that!"

"You cannot?"

"I cannot."

"But why?"

"It's not my secret."

"Whose secret is it?"

"But I cannot tell you that and still keep faith."

"Ah. Yes, I see that. Well, then, I will simply perform."

"Then you are resolved to help me?"

"Resolved! Yes, that's the very word."

"You are kindness itself!"

"Is it not a gentleman's duty to be charitable to those in need? And I nearly think you are in need."

"Oh, you are so good to me."

"No, it is you who are good to me, for you have allowed me the privilege of helping you. And furthermore—"

"Yes? Furthermore?"

"You are about to allow me to kiss your hand."

"Oh." Illista looked away and blushed.

"Well?"

She said nothing but extended her hand to Khaavren, who reverently placed his lips upon. "Ah!" he cried, "And now, I must leave at once to go about this errand, lest I grow so overcome with emotion that I am unable to move from this spot."

"Yes," she said. "Go. And I—"

"Well, and you?"

"I will await your word."

"You will not need to wait long," he said, and sprang through the door, only to stop just past the threshold and return.

"Your pardon," he said.

"Well?" she said.

"If I am to get word to you, how shall I find you?"

"Oh. In the easiest possible way. You shall ask after the Marchioness of the Twicetied Hills, in the House of Phoenix."

"I will not fail to do so," he said, bowed low to her, and sprinted through the door, through the inn, and out into the evening air.

Chapter the Fifteenth

*In Which Khaavren Receives a Warning
And Aerich tells a story*

KHAAVREN'S FEET SEEMED to him, insofar as he concerned himself with their activities, to have developed their own brain, complete with memory and will, as they transported him through the narrow, curving streets, and up the gentle slopes toward his home. Khaavren himself, as we have already had the honor to imply, was mostly unaware of their activity, as he had things of more moment with which to concern himself; to wit, the brush of soft fingers against his, the touch of his lips against a hand, and the contact, fleeting, but no less powerful for that, of his eyes with those associated with the fingers and hand to which we have just referred.

It remains true, however, that an inconveniently placed railing or sharp corner will not remove itself from the path of a drunkard, even if that drunkard is unaware of the obstacles on the path he has set for himself; in other words, no matter to what degree we are oblivious to the world, it makes its own choices as to how oblivious it will be to us. Khaavren discovered this fundamental truth of human existence when, as he carried himself rapidly through the streets of the Palace District of Dragaera City, or, more specifically, as he went breezing by a certain narrow gap between a tinsmith's shop and a belt-maker's, his flight was suddenly arrested by a pair of rough but very strong hands which landed upon his collar and abruptly yanked him into the narrow gap we have already had the honor to mention. Furthermore, before he could recover himself, he found that there was a heavy and rather sharp blade of some sort pressing against the back of his neck in a manner indicating that his spine could be severed with the greatest of ease.

Khaavren gasped—the combination of his reckless run and its sudden stop having left him temporarily out of breath—and saw a figure before him in a dark grey hood. The figure was slightly shorter than he was, and moreover had its head bowed a little so that Khaavren could not discover its face beneath the hood. Whoever was behind him seemed to be large and was unquestionably strong.

The figure Khaavren could see, the one in the hood, spoke in a whisper that Khaavren could barely hear over his own gasping. It said, "Sir Khaavren, you perceive that, although we have you at our mercy, we do not kill you. We have not been sent to kill you, but rather to speak with you. Yet rest assured that if the results of our conversation prove unsatisfactory, as evidenced by your future action, we will be forced to take your life at that time. Do you understand?"

The pause after the question was Khaavren's first chance to regain his equilibrium, and it took a moment for the events of the last few seconds to assemble themselves in his mind. By the time they had done so, and he was beginning to consider what sort of reply he ought to make, the individual in front of him had begun speaking again. "You have chosen to look for a certain person—you know who I mean, do you not?"

"That is," began Khaavren. "I assure you—"

"Do not trifle with me, young man. You know of whom I an speaking."

"Well, and if I do?"

"You must stop. There are deep matters here, and you are likely to drown in them. I am, you perceive, doing you a service when I tell you that you must stay away from these intrigues; you ought to thank me. It is for the best if you listen. Is it clear to you what I am talking about?"

"It is clear," said Khaavren. "It is also clear that you are no gentlemen."

"Well, that is true," said the other, "but I think you will be as dead if killed by me as if you were killed by a gentleman."

Khaavren saw the extreme justice of this observation. It came to his mind to tell them that he did not place such value on his life that he would allow strangers to dictate his actions, but it seemed likely that if he expressed this thought they would kill him, which would allow him no chance to pursue any course of actions at all and would, moreover, give him no chance to punish these men who had laid such rough hands upon him, so he merely said, "I admit the truth of what you say."

"That is good," whispered the figure in front of him, and made a sign to whoever stood behind Khaavren, of whom the Tiassa had had not a glimpse. For a moment the knife at his neck loosened, and Khaavren was considering how to twist away from the grip when something dealt him such a blow on the back of the head that he at once fell senseless to the street.

He awoke, some time later, to several sensations, including that strange disorientation which comes upon waking up in a place other than one's bed, and the discomfort of sleeping in an unusual position, and the chill of the evening breeze, now that dusk was beginning to draw its curtain over the city. Yet what he noticed most of all was the throbbing pain in his head, and it was in attempting to determine its cause that the events of his last few conscious moments began to come back to him.

His first thought, even as this occurred, was to wonder if he'd been robbed while lying there helpless, but, perhaps because this part of the city was better patrolled than many, perhaps for fear that he might awaken suddenly and use the longsword that lay on his hip, perhaps because he was somewhat hidden, or perhaps because of a combination of reasons, his possessions and his meager purse were safe.

As his memory began to clear, and he remembered the events which had led him to that place and time, he looked around to see if his attackers were still there. "Well," he said to himself, "I perceive they are gone. They are cowards, but at least they are not murderous ones. But stay, how could they have come to learn that I am in pursuit of Kaluma? Could someone be spying on me? Or is there some dark sorcery at work here? Surely, this will take more consideration than I can give here and now; I must return home, traveling with more care than I did when last I was headed that way. Will my legs bear my weight? Why should they not? It was my head, not my legs that suffered the attack. Well, let us see. Ah! They obey my commands. Excellent! Homeward, then, legs, but not so fast that my eyes and ears cannot exercise all the caution that circumstances warrant."

He arrived home without further incident, although whether we may attribute this to his caution we cannot know. Upon arriving, he found that Pel and Aerich were anxiously awaiting him. Tazendra, who was snoring softly in the corner, woke as he shut the door, blinked blearily and tossed her head. "Ah. I was correct," she said. "Here is our missing friend, none the worse for having missed our company this evening. Am I not correct, good Khaavren?"

"Well," said Khaavren, as he sat in his favorite chair and took a deep breath, "I seem to be healthy in all my parts, excepting only the headache, yet if, as I perceive, some of you were worried about me, then I can say that it was not without reason."

At this cool announcement, Aerich's brows came together, Pel leaned forward, and Tazendra stared. "Well?" said the Yendi after a moment.

"Since I left this morning," said Khaavren, "I have learned where the Baroness Kaluma is hiding, been asked to help her, warned to stay away from her, and attacked in an alley. That, I must beg you to understand, includes only part of the day's activities; the rest being of a nature that I do not care to share with you at this time." At this last statement, Tazendra smiled knowingly, while Aerich looked sad.

Pel said, "A busy day, indeed. I hardly know where to begin asking questions."

"You might ask what our intentions are toward the Baroness Kaluma," said Khaavren.

"Well then," said Pel with a smile, "I ask."

"And I answer thus: I no longer know."

"How? You don't know?" cried Tazendra.

"It has become confused," said Khaavren.

"I am not good with confusion," explained Tazendra.

It was at this point that Srahi entered the room, dressed in her faded and tattered housecoat but looking quite wide awake. "So," she said to the room at large. "He has returned. But little damaged, I trust, master? You were, no doubt, at an inn? Or having some secret tryst with a lover? Or being chased all around the city by brigands? Well, you're home now, not caring about the hour, and no doubt will want tea with sweet wine. Very well, very well, I'm on my way to the kitchen. But mark my words: you will not be young forever, and someday you will come to regret having wasted your youth—"

"Srahi," said Khaavren, "if you will be so kind as to bring me a damp cloth to put on my head, well, I will appreciate you the more for it. And, if you will do so silently, well, I will consider myself deeply in your debt."

She left the room still muttering to herself. "The gods,"

said Aerich under his breath. "I nearly think she guessed the entire tale."

"Perhaps," said Tazendra, "we should ask her how to proceed."

"Then again," reflected Pel, "perhaps not."

Srahi returned with the cloth, which Khaavren placed about his head, and to her credit, she said nothing more.

"Tell us, good Khaavren," said Aerich when the servant had left, "why you are concerning yourself about our intentions toward the Baroness."

"Well, in the first place, I have been asked to protect her."

"By whom?" said Pel.

"A certain lady of the House of the Phoenix whom some of us have met."

"Ah," said Aerich.

"My dear Khaavren," said Tazendra, frowning. "Are you well? Your face has become quite red."

"Hush," said Pel.

"That is—" began Tazendra.

"I agree this is a view from another side," said Aerich.

"And there is more," said Khaavren.

"Well?" said Aerich.

"Well, as I was returning home, I was attacked."

"Blood of the Phoenix!" said Tazendra. "By whom?"

"That I cannot say. It was a treacherous attack, from an alley, and there were two of them. They held a knife at my neck and warned me not to become involved in the matter of Baroness Kaluma."

"Indeed," said Aerich.

"But, which side were they on?" said Pel.

Khaavren shook his head, then winced from the effect this had on the injured area. "They said nothing which would tell me. Furthermore, the one I could see was cowled the entire time, so I couldn't see his face."

"That's too bad," said Tazendra. "For it seems clear that we ought to oppose them, and that is difficult to do if we don't know who they are or what they want."

"No doubt they were merely ruffians hired for the purpose," said Pel. "Orca, no doubt, or perhaps even Jhereg."

"I am not entirely certain that we should oppose them," said Aerich slowly.

"How?" said Tazendra, amazed, and Pel frowned at the same time, and even Khaavren felt some surprise that the Lyorn seemed to be willing to let them be frightened off.

"It is all very well to say, 'Come, let us not be afraid of anyone low enough to employ Orca or Jhereg to do their fighting for them.' But consider: they could have killed Khaavren had they chosen. Can we stay on our guard all the time? Do we have the littlest idea of the forces which are arranging themselves against us?"

The others started to speak, but at that moment Srahi returned with a pot of strong tea which had been fortified with wine. After serving them, she started to sit down with them, then, looking at their faces, gave a snort and left the room instead. At this point, before anyone could speak, Aerich gestured for silence.

"Let me tell you a story," he said.

"Ah," said Tazendra. "I should like to hear a story."

"Well then, here it is. Once there was a young man of the House of the Lyorn. He was raised in a proud family, and brought up in all the ways he ought to have been. That is, he was taught history, poetics, philosophy, sorcery, swordsmanship, penmanship, and the thousand other things necessary for one who is to rule over the lands and vassals he will someday inherit—for he was the eldest child, in fact, the only child of this family."

He paused to sip his tea. Khaavren thought he detected an odd tremor in the Lyorn's hand. He said, "Pray continue, good Aerich. You perceive we are all listening most adamantly."

"Well, it so happened that at just about the time this gentleman reached the age of eighty—that is, well before, by the custom of his House, he was considered to have reached maturity—his father became involved in court politics. To be precise, he was called in by His Majesty,

Cherova, for advice on settling matters with the King of Elde Island, whose name, I regret to say, escapes me."

"I think it is not important," said Khaavren. "Please continue."

"Yes. Well, a certain individual, also of the House of the Lyorn, had, until that time, been advising His Late Majesty on the subject, but m—, that is to say, the young man's father proved more able to conduct negotiations."

"Well," said Khaavren, "it would seem that this would be all to the good."

"So it would seem, good Khaavren. Yet there times when it is dangerous to succeed where another fails."

"Ah. There was jealousy?"

"You have it exactly," said Aerich. "And not only jealousy, but the power to act on it. The discredited advisor was not above using subterfuge and hiring known thieves. It began to appear as if the successful advisor were unscrupulous. The evidence mounted until, driven to distraction, the gentleman began to fight back in ways he would never have thought himself capable of using. Of course, this was discovered, and, in less time than one would have thought possible, the successful advisor became the discredited one, and, furthermore, all of his lands were taken and he died a broken, penniless man, leaving his son trained to rule a fief that was no longer in the family."

Khaavren studied his friend for some moments, then said, "And the unscrupulous advisor, could his name, perhaps, have been Shaltre?"

Aerich stared at him coldly. "I have no idea to what you could be referring. I was telling a story, to illustrate a point."

"And the point, good Aerich?"

"The point is that it is sometimes dangerous to meddle with those who have fewer scruples than you do; you may lose more than your life. You may lose a stake you didn't know you had set onto the board."

"And yet, good Aerich, was the Lyorn wrong to have done what he could for the Empire?"

"Ah, as to that, I do not say. I merely bring up a matter for you to consider before you dive headlong into danger of an unknown sort, from an unknown quarter. We have no worry for our lives, after all; they have belonged to the Empire from the moment we took our oaths. But what are we prepared to risk, my friends? Surely this deserves some consideration."

As he spoke, Khaavren felt a sudden chill, as if, in the winter, a window had been left open and cold air, unmistakable in feeling yet indefinite in source, had touched the back of his neck and sent its tendrils down his spine. He sent a glance at Pel, who was frowning and staring at the floor.

Tazendra, however, said, "But consider that, if we do nothing, we are giving in to fear of the worst sort—the fear of unknown dangers. We may scorn a man who runs from a battle he cannot win; how much more should we scorn a man who runs from a place where he thinks there might be a battle that perhaps he cannot win?"

Khaavren stirred. "I think our friend the Dzur has the right on this, good Aerich."

The Lyorn sighed. "Yes," he said. "I'm afraid I agree. And you, good Pel?"

The Yendi made a dismissing gesture with a wave of his hand. "We are young, we are brave, and we are four together. If we let fear direct us now, what will we do when we have lived a millennium or two, and know the full measure of terror? We will be afraid to throw a stick in a river, lest we be splashed by water that has somehow been poisoned. I agree with Tazendra."

Aerich sighed. "Yes, my wise friend, I don't dispute you. Well then, if we must, let us be about it. How shall we begin?"

"Ashes!" said Tazendra. "We must first decide if, when we find this artist, or killer, we are to arrest her or prevent her arrest."

"Not at all," said Pel.

"Well?" said Tazendra.

"It seems we must find her first. Then we can decide what to do with her. You say, Khaavren, that you know where she is?"

"It is likely," said Khaavren.

"Then we must go there."

"And yet, it is not easy to get a leave of absence from our duties."

"Is it not?" said Pel, with a smile. "Did I not say that I would attend to it?"

"Indeed you did," said Khaavren. "Have you, then, done so?"

"After a fashion."

"After what fashion?"

"Why, I have procured for us a mission which will require us to be gone for an unspecified length of time."

"A mission? Of what nature?"

"Are you aware of the trouble brewing around the estate of Pepperfield?"

"Indeed I am," said Khaavren.

"As am I," put in Tazendra, who seemed anxious not to be left out of the conversation.

"Are you aware of the nature of the trouble?"

"Yes," said Khaavren.

"Oh, the nature of it," said Tazendra.

"Well?"

"That is to say, not entirely."

"Well, it is a dispute over which line of the House of the Dragon is given the area to rule. It is further complicated because, as you know, diamonds have been discovered nearby, in a place called Sandyhome, and the Emperor is considering raising an army to secure Sandyhome which, although it is hardly fifty leagues away, is of sufficient distance to leave the Pepperfields only poorly defended."

"Ah," said Tazendra. "Now I understand. But how does this concern us?"

"Doesn't it seem to you that it might be worth the Emperor's while to send someone to look the area over, and find out just what the situation is?"

"That seems reasonable," said Khaavren, smiling. "And you suggested to the Captain that we would be well-suited to such a task?"

"My dear Khaavren, you have it exactly."

"And yet," said Tazendra, "doesn't the Emperor have soldiers near the area from whom he can get reports, merely by asking them through the Orb?"

"Ah, but how reliable are they? There are always conflicting reports, my dear lady, depending on whom one asks. But a member of his own regiment, well, that would be an entirely different matter. Or so our Captain thinks."

"So," said Khaavren, "we are to go east."

"Yes, taking as much time as necessary. If our route happens to bring us in an entirely different direction for a while, well, we are not expected to report for quite some time at any rate."

"It is well then," said Khaavren, "that our route takes us almost to that very place."

"Cracks in the Orb," said Tazendra. "It does?"

"Indeed," said Khaavren. "We are bound for Redface, less than fifty leagues from Pepperfield."

"Fifty leagues of the city, or fifty leagues by the Easterner's reckoning?" said Aerich.

Khaavren shrugged. "A day's brisk march by the footpaths, so I'm told, or else two days' quick ride by the horse-trails."

"That falls out rather well," said the Yendi.

"Indeed it does," said Khaavren. "Have we horses?"

"My dear Khaavren, we will have the choice of the stables, as well as Cards for Passage for the posts, and letters of credit to see us on our way."

"My dear Pel, you are a marvel. Then we can set off in the morning?"

"I can see no reason not to," said Pel, bowing his acknowledgment of the compliment.

Aerich, who had not spoken until this time, said, "Then I shall prepare myself by sleeping. I suggest the rest of you do the same."

Tazendra and Khaavren agreed at once, though Pel claimed he had an appointment with a tailor who had agreed to make dresses to Pel's designs, and that he must meet with this person before his departure. He left, then, while the others, before preparing for sleep, held a brief discussion over plans, the content of which, be assured, we will return to in due course, after which Tazendra and Aerich went off to their chambers and at once to sleep.

Khaavren did not have such an easy time of it. He remained awake for some time, his thoughts flitting about like a hobird; hovering for a moment on the dark words Aerich had spoken, flapping about the plentiful unknowns contained in the mission they were preparing for, touching lightly on plans and preparations for the morrow's departure, and at last resting calmly on his memory of Illista's sweet lips, and the way her brows rose so charmingly when she smiled into his eyes. In this way, he passed finally into a dreamless sleep.

Chapter the Sixteenth

In Which we Learn What it Means
to be Half an Emperor

WHILE KHAAVREN SLEEPS the sleep of the young and brave, we must, like the hawk, whose eyes can see through the overcast to spot a norska who can not see him, even should the norska think to look up, send our gaze winging through the city, up Kieron's Hill, past the Jungle of Ferns where Tuorli sat for week after week composing a cycle of love-poems to her errant lover the Marquis of Gwethurich, down Backside Hill, around the Nine Bridges Canal where Lord Brythor, Dzur Heir to the fifteenth throne, lost his future and his life in the six-hour-long duel with his cousin the Duke of Kl'burra, until we arrive at an unprepossessing hostelry built of arched wood on the Avenue of Urtiya the Sage. Here, making good use of our capacity of imaginary observer, we will, without mounting by staircase or wall, without passing through door or window, nevertheless arrive in a second-story corner room, where a young girl, scarcely two hundred years in age, is making her toilet with the help of a maidservant who is even younger than she.

"Well, Yini," said the girl, "have I nothing whatsoever that will set off this gown?"

"Madam," said the maidservant, "since you do me the honor to ask my opinion—"

"Of course I do, silly girl."

"Then I think the small sapphire brooch, given you by Count N——, will complement the red of the gown nicely, as well as setting off your eyes."

"You may be right, Yini, but what about House insignia? I can hardly have the Duke of G——call upon me when when I am wearing nothing to show my Dragon heritage, can I? Yet the pendant would scarcely look right when placed against the silver of the ruffles."

"Is then madam not going to wear the black sleeves with the silver lace?"

"Cracks and Shards, Yini, I think I am."

"Then perhaps madam could wear the ring instead of the pendant, since silver always looks well against black, and they are, after all, the very colors of your House."

The girl considered for a moment, then said, "Very well, Yini. Fetch it, then help me with my hair. Shall I put anything in it, do you think?"

"Little if anything, madam; I believe that on this occasion the elegance of a simple knot, with perhaps one comb, would be best. Perhaps a comb with a few small sapphires, to set off the brooch."

"Excellent, Yini; I think your plan will be a good one."

"Thank you, your ladyship."

The lady, who was none other than Jenicor e'Terics, completed her toilet by smoothing one side of her hair with water, gave her lovely face a last approving look in the glass, and left the room to await her visitor in the receiving room that had been included in the apartments she had rented.

Now, considering that this was a part of Dragaera City that had once served as a market for the Teckla from the south-west, and, that since the completion of the Hawk's Landing Road it had become less and less frequented so that by the time of which we have the honor to write it was a part of the city that a nobleman would visit only if he felt an uncontrollable need to find the poor so he could give them alms, one might well wonder what Jenicor e'Terics, Marchioness of Sharp Bend Cave and Environs, future Duchess of Highland Reef, and, even then, only five steps removed from the Dragon Heir, would be doing in such a place. For the answer to this question, the reader need only wait patiently while she puts on a silvery mask to hide her features.

We should note that in those days the masks actually concealed the identity of the wearer, whereas today they are only symbols through the use of which certain nobles pretend to be excused for conduct which would be unforgivable without this "disguise." In those days, in which one could use such a word as "honor" without feeling one's face becoming red, a noble who allowed himself to be recognized while engaged in scandalous activity risked his reputation, his fortune, even his right to Deathgate.

So it was that Yini set the mask over her lady's features, carefully arranging the cord so as not to dishevel her hair, and succeeding in hiding those features which would have identified her, unless one knew her so well that her small, pouting lips and dimpled chin would have been sufficient. Yet none of those were required to see that she was a lady; the merest glance at the trim ankles that appeared beneath her broad-shouldered, tight-waisted gown or the long fingers whose outlines were clearly discernible beneath her neatly seamed silk gloves gave unimpeachable evidence of noble birth, even if one were inobservant enough to miss the full, thick texture of her hair, which achieved, through no artifice except nature, that fine shade of brown that almost appears red beneath the natural orangish light of day.

At the exact moment that Yini was completing her task

of fastening the mask there came the sound of a soft, fine, almost feminine clapping outside the door.

"It is he!" whispered Jenicor. "The Duke of G——!"

"Shall I open it, then?" asked Yini, also whispering.

"No! Retire to the common room, but return here in two hours."

"Yes, madam. Shall I use the other doorway?"

"Of course, silly girl. Be off, now." At which time the clapping was repeated, perhaps a trifle impatiently, to judge by the increase in volume. Jenicor hurried to answer it. "Who is there?" she called.

The answer came in a voice low but clear. "It is I, madam, who come, once more, to worship at the feet of my goddess."

At these words she flung open the door, which revealed a man covered in a large brown woolen cloak, with a hat pulled down well over his face. "Ah, Cavalier," she cried, "it is you at last," proving that he was both expected and recognized.

"It is," he said. "Are we alone?"

"Indeed we are. I have sent my maid down to the common room."

"But then, you wear a mask?"

"Well, and you wear a cloak and a hat."

"That is true, but I have been walking through districts where it would be useless to be recognized."

"And I?"

"You, madam, seem to be alone in your room; hence, there is no one to recognize you. And the proof is, see, I remove my hat."

"But suppose I were to wish to visit the common room, Cavalier. Surely you cannot expect me to remain in my chambers, alone, with you?" Here a singular smile, at once innocent and flirtatious, sped over her lips.

"Ah, madam, you wound me."

"I?"

"Assuredly. How can you doubt your safety with me?"

"Well, if you recall our last meeting, at the keep of the Baron of R——, you will recall—"

"Bah! I was drunk."

"You? Drunk?"

"On the splendor of your eyes, madam. They are intoxicating."

"Cavalier, you must not speak so!"

"But I must, for you have not allowed me the honor of kissing your hand."

"Well, then, here it is."

"Ah, I touch my lips to perfection. You see, I do so again. There. And again. And—"

"Stop, now. You must desist."

"Well, then, let us sit down together and speak like brother and sister, if you will have it so."

"I will."

"Shall I pour you wine?"

"Only a little. And have a care, lest you become drunk again!"

"Ah, madam, if you knew how your jests are as poniards to me—"

"Stop, then, and let us speak, Cavalier, as you have said."

"Very well. Since we must, let us speak of the court."

"Of the court? Why of the court?"

"Why? Because I wish to be half an Emperor."

"How? What can you mean, half an Emperor?"

"I shall explain, if you like."

"Please do, because I am most curious."

"Well, allow me to begin by asking you a question."

"Your explanations often begin that way."

"Are they any less clear for that?"

"Not at all. Ask your question, then."

"Well, this is it: what does the Emperor have that I am lacking?"

"That is not difficult: In the first place, the Orb."

"Well, that is true, and after the Orb?"

"Power."

"What is power?"

"Power is to give an order and have it obeyed."

"What order, then?"

"Any order."

"But, by way of example, madam, I ask you to instruct me."

"Well, suppose someone were to say, 'You, of the Guard, go and conquer that duchy.' Now, if he were an Emperor, the Guard would jump to obey, and the duchy would fall. That is power."

"You reason like Clybru, the chief of Mathematicians."

"Well then, are you answered?"

"Almost. Tell me this, why should he wish to conquer the duchy?"

"Why? Perhaps he has said to the duke, 'I require five hundred tons of wood be sent to my ship-builders in the south,' and the duke has failed to do so, but instead has begun building up an army of his own, like the Count of Endmarch did less than two hundred years ago."

"Well, but how would the Emperor know these things?"

"How would he know? He would be informed."

"By whom?"

"By those whose duty it is to inform him."

"Why would they do so?"

"Because he is the Emperor, and the Emperor must be well informed, or how can he make his decisions?"

"So, the Emperor is the one who, first, has the Orb, and, second, is sufficiently aware of what is going on around him to know how to deploy his forces."

"That is it exactly."

"You perceive, then, that I wish to know what is going on at court, so I may be half an Emperor."

Jenicor was so impressed by this logic that she at once said, "Well, I understand. What, then, do you wish to know?"

"Tell me of the cabals."

"You pretend there are cabals?"

"Cabals, intrigues, call them what you will."

"You seem certain there must be such."

"It is a court; there must be cabals and intrigues."

"Of what fashion?"

"Of all fashions. Alliances of mutual love; alliances of mutual hatred; most of all, alliances of mutual benefits. Come, you must be aware of some."

"But, good Cavalier, where would I look for them?"

"*K'luno*, dear one," said the Cavalier, "everywhere. But, if I were to start, I would always begin with the Imperial Consort."

"Well, she is very beautiful."

"And she is powerful, by reason of having the ear of the Emperor, as well as two good ones of her own, making three ears in all, which, by the logic I have shown you, makes her half an Emperor herself."

"I nearly think you are right."

"So, who flocks to her banner?"

"Well, it is said that there are those who wish to take her as a lover."

"Ah. And does she maintain her virtue?"

"Some say she does, but only because she cannot make up her mind among the suitors."

"And the Emperor, is he jealous?"

"Only of his friends, it is said."

"Naturally; one is always jealous of one's friends."

"How would you know that, Cavalier? You have none yourself."

"You are wrong, my lovely Dragon, and the proof is that I have three."

"What? Three friends? Surely not those you live with, and who only know you by your assumed name?"

"None other."

"What is the name they call you? It is the name of a valley to the west, is it not? Kor?"

"Pel."

"That is it. But then, you say they are your friends?"

"They are; so much so, that I would risk my life for them."

"But would you risk your ambitions?"

"What? You pretend I have ambitions?"

"Assuredly. You are ambitious of being half an Emperor."

"Ah, you have caught me, lovely one. I do have that ambition. But tell me, what names are attached to the hopeful lovers of the Consort; for surely the court gossips cannot fail to include names."

"Well, there is a Dzurlord, the Marquis of L_____. And a Tiassa, Lord N_____. An addition, there is talk of the Dragonlord, Adron e'Kieron, and a certain Lyorn called the Count of Shaltre. And even a Phoenix, a certain Duke of Threewalls."

"Stay, then. Threewalls?"

"Why, yes, that name has come up. I believe he is called Allistar."

"You interest me greatly; for I believe I know him. Has he a sister, who is Illista, Marchioness of the Twicetied Hills?"

"The very one. It is said, in fact, that this sister schemes on her brother's behalf, in hopes of raising the fortune of their branch of the family."

"Does she? Does she go so far as to help him bring to the Consort rare flowers of which she is fond, such as candlebud?"

"Cavalier, you have been toying with me, for you already know the court gossip. Therefore, I will tell you no more."

"If you will not, then it only remains for us to pass from discussion on to other matters."

"Cavalier, you begin to alarm me!"

"Why? Are my kisses so unwelcome to you? Are you unhappy that I do this? And this? And—"

"Wait, I hear something!"

"I hear nothing save the sound of your gentle breath in my ear."

"No, it is my maid, Yini, returning from the common room. Come, we must separate for now."

"Separate? Fresh wounds in my heart!"

"What? You think nothing of my reputation?"

"With your maid? Hardly."

"Do you think maids do not speak to other maids? And these maids do not speak to their mistresses? I assure you, I have enough duels on my hands to last me until the Dragon reign, I have no need to seek more because I have changed from a purveyor of gossip to a subject of gossip."

"Well, then I will leave."

"And that, I hope, quickly."

"Very well. My cloak and my hat?"

"Here they are."

"How do they look?"

"They suit you admirably."

"Well, and your hand to kiss?"

"Here it is."

"Farewell then, my tormentor, until the next time."

"Until the next time, wicked man."

And with these words, they parted, the door closing behind Pel even as Yini came into the room from the other door, and found her mistress staring wistfully at the spot the Cavalier had so recently occupied.

"Someday he may be more than half an Emperor," she said her herself with a small smile. "Even now, he is more than half a lover."

Chapter the Seventeenth

*In Which Discussion is Made
of Mathematics and Philosophy
As our Friends Prepare for Departure*

WE WILL NOW return to the house on the Street of the Glass Cutters and inform our readers of the conversation that occurred during Pel's absence, which was, we should add, both noticed and wondered at, since the worthies therein had not the abilities we have granted ourselves to flit carelessly about the city and look, unnoticed, into whatever odd corners our caprice takes us. Khaavren, Aerich, and Tazendra, then, sat in Aerich's chambers and laid down what plans they could. Khaavren positioned himself on the couch, where he lay with a damp cloth, supplied by the sullen but silent Srahi, wrapped about his head.

"We shall set out, I think, in the morning," said Khaavren.

"Very well," said Aerich.

"To-night, then, we must prepare for our departure."

"Prepare?" said Tazendra. "In what way?"

"Why, in all ways that seem good. That is, we must gather whatever we determine we shall need."

"Well, then—" began Tazendra.

"If you please," said Khaavren. "Not so loudly. My head still gives me pain."

"Ah, yes," she went on in a softer voice. "I will remember."

"That is good of you. What were you saying?"

"I was saying," said Tazendra, "that I shall need my sword."

"That is right," said Khaavren.

"Shall I also need a flash-stone?"

"A flash-stone will be welcome, I think," said Khaavren. "Several, if you can get them."

"Get them? My dear Khaavren, I make them!"

"What, you?"

"Indeed yes; you know that I am a sorcerer."

"That is true; I had forgotten. Well, and how long does it take you to make one?"

"Well, to charge a single stone with enough force to knock a man from his horse, and, if well aimed, to leave him stretched on the ground, will require, first, three hours to prepare the stone, next, two hours to beg the stone to receive the charge, and, last, a single hour to acquaint the stone with the means of releasing the charge."

"Well, that is six hours, then."

"Why yes, I think it is. How curious."

"And why is it curious that it is six hours?"

"Well, I have often noticed that it takes me six hours to charge a stone."

"And? What then?"

"Well, it is curious that you have arrived at this number after hearing only the several parts of it."

"You know, Tazendra, that I am an arithmetist."

"Ah, I hadn't known that. All is solved then."

"But tell me this. If we should require a stone with

enough of a charge to knock two men from the saddle, or even five, then how long will it take to prepare?"

"Well, for a stone with twice the charge, it will take four hours to prepare, four hours to set, but still only a single hour to arrange the release."

"That is, then, nine hours."

"Why, yes, I believe you are correct. Blood of the Horse, you *are* an arithmetist."

"I can figure sums like an accountant, but, I confess to you, little else. Fortunately, that is all that is generally required."

"Yes, you are right. I have heard it said that all other branches of arithmetic are properly the province of philosophy, and ought not to be considered by a gentleman at all."

"There is some justice in that remark."

"I think so."

"But, good Tazendra, let us return to the subject of flash-stones."

"Oh, now that is a subject that I know better than I know philosophy or arithmetic."

"Well, here is my question then: is it not the case that one can prepare a single stone to hold two, three, or even four charges?"

"It can be done."

"And the preparations?"

"Well, for small charges, an additional hour for each charge is required to prepare the stone, and, above that, each charge placed in the stone will require an additional four hours."

"And the release?"

"To inform the stone that it must release the charges one at a time is a singular challenge, my good Khaavren."

"Well?"

"Two charges, then, require three hours of work. Three charges require five hours, and four charges would require eight hours."

"So, then, a stone with three charges would require, in all, more than half a day to prepare."

"That is true."

"Well, then, we haven't the time. We shall have to do without the flash-stones."

"Not at all, for I have already prepared a stone with two small charges, and two others, each with a light charge. If I prepare one more small one, then we shall each be equipped with a flash-stone for our journey before to-morrow."

"Excellent, Tazendra. Let us then be about it."

"I shall begin at once."

"But wait a moment; we must decide what else we will need for our journey."

Aerich, who, for want of anything to say, had maintained his habitual silence until this point in the conversation, said, "Money."

"Cha!" said Khaavren. "That is true. We shall need money. Have you any?"

"Little enough," said Aerich, digging through his pockets and placing a single Imperial along with a few scant orbs on the table.

"At that," said Khaavren, "you are richer than I am." He dug in his pocket and placed a share of pennies next to Aerich's money, in which company two single orbs shone with greater pride than perhaps they truly merited. "And you, my good Tazendra?"

"Oh, I have plenty."

"Ah, plenty?" said Khaavren. "You have then, enough?"

"Certainly. Here it is," and she majestically laid down a newly stamped Imperial, showing the face of his Majesty Tortaalik, and with it three or four silver orbs.

"Well, is that all?" said Khaavren.

"Hardly. There is also this." And she put a scrap of paper on the table, which Khaavren hastily took into his hand and studied.

"The Gods!" he said. "It is a draft on the Dragon treasury in the amount of three hundred orbs!"

"Three hundred orbs?" said Aerich. "Well, that is a tolerably round sum. Whence comes this draft, Tazendra?"

"Why, I assure you I have no idea, save that it was brought around by the post this very evening."

"To whom did it come?"

"In faith I don't know; it was rolled up and sealed, with a ribbon about it and no name. Since it was I who took it from the hand of the post officer, and since it bore no address, I thought to open it, and I did."

"And you did right," said Khaavren.

Aerich picked up the paper, looked at it, and shrugged, "Well, it is signed and stamped, and even chopped; therefore it as good as coinage for our purposes."

"I suspect," said Khaavren, "that our captain does not wish for our journey to fail due to lack of funds."

"What," said Tazendra, "he considers it important?"

"I think so," said Khaavren. "And this proves it, does it not?"

"I nearly think it does," said Tazendra. "Pel has done well in speaking to the Captain."

"Yes, but that makes me think: where is Pel?"

"At his tailor's," said Tazendra, with a smile which indicated that, in some matters at any rate, she was no dupe.

"He will be here," said Aerich, "when he is no longer busy elsewhere."

"Which is to say," said Khaavren, "that he is not here because he is not here."

"Well, do you deny the justice of this remark?"

"No," said Khaavren. "I think it entirely correct. And yet, it does not relieve me of worries."

"Bah. Were it you, or even Tazendra, I might worry. But there is no occasion to worry about Pel when he is out; he has many calls."

"Many mistresses, that is," said Tazendra. Aerich shrugged.

"Yes," said Khaavren, "you are right. We need only wait,

and I am sure he will be here. And while we wait, let us continue to reckon up what we will need."

Tazendra said, "We are going east, are we not?"

"Yes," said Khaavren. "You're memory is like the Orb itself."

"In that case," continued Tazendra, "we must also go north or south, unless you intend to travel through either the desert of Suntra, or the jungles."

"Well," said Khaavren, "I have always believed that the desert would be a fine place as soon as it could be contrived for someone to bury sufficient bottles of wine amid the sand, and likewise, the jungles, as soon as they could be rid of those animals which are rude enough to wish to eat men, rather than peaceably allowing the reverse, which is as nature intended."

"And yet," said Tazendra, "since there is no wine in the desert, and since there are wild beasts in the jungles, you no doubt wish to travel either north or south, in addition to east."

"You are correct, good Tazendra; I have chosen to travel south around the desert through the *pushta*."

"Well, then, there is no need for warm clothing."

"But then there are the mountains."

"Ah, yes, well then, I shall bring my cloak which is lined with the fur of the fox and the norska."

"And you will be wise to do so, Tazendra."

"What else do we need?"

"A map, I think," said Khaavren.

"I have one," said Aerich.

"Is it a good one?"

"It is by the Baron of Portsfree, and bears the seal of my House."

"That is well," said Khaavren.

"And then, what else?" said Tazendra.

"Our swords, our daggers."

"That is natural."

"Horses," said Tazendra.

"The Emperor will supply them."

"How?"

"You forget that we are in the Guards?"

"That is true, but if one should become lame?"

"Bah! We will then buy another."

"With what?"

"We will find the money. Haven't we already found three hundred orbs that we didn't expect to find?"

"He is right," said Aerich. "It is wrong to doubt a providence which has already provided so much."

"Very well," said Tazendra, who didn't appear to be entirely convinced. "What else?"

"Rope," said Khaavren.

"For what?" said Tazendra.

"Well, I don't know, but shouldn't travelers in the mountains always bring rope?"

"I, for one, do not anticipate climbing on the mountains, but merely walking in them."

"Very well," said Khaavren. "Should we bring pavilions in which to rest at night?"

"How?" said Tazendra. "Are there not inns?"

"For the most part I think there are."

"Well, then?"

"But should we be caught in the mountains between inns?"

"Then we shall make a fire."

"Then we must bring an axe."

"Very well," said Tazendra. "I agree with the need for an axe."

"Extra girths, reins, and tools for repairing saddle and bridle."

"How, do you know how to use them?"

"I do," said Aerich.

"Then I agree with the tools," said Tazendra.

"Wineskins," said Khaavren.

"Certainly, wineskins," said Tazendra.

"Means of making fire," said Khaavren.

"I am a sorcerer," said Tazendra.

"That is true. Bandages?"

"Indeed," said Tazendra.

"Cooking gear?"

"I," said Tazendra, "intend to eat at hostelries along the way."

"And, if we are between hostelries?"

"Then we shall bring bread and cheese."

"Very well," said Khaavren. "Then we also have no need for napkins and tablecloths."

"That is true."

"Oiled cloaks in case of rain."

"That is well thought. What else?"

"That is all, I think."

"In that case," said Aerich, "it is time we got some rest, for we must awaken, in any case, when Pel returns, so that we may acquaint him with all that we have decided."

At which time they did, as we mentioned above, retire for a few hours. Khaavren was the first to wake when Pel returned, and hastened to collect the others, who, notwithstanding that they were still tired, made haste to the parlor.

"My dear Pel," said Tazendra, "is that you?"

"It is," said the Cavalier.

"But," said Tazendra, "where have you been that you have required that large cloak and the hat which so effectually hides your features?"

"Does it?" said Pel, mildly. "I was merely trying it out. Such hats are all the rage now in certain quarters."

"What quarters are those?" pressed Tazendra.

"Oh, why certain—"

"Come now," said Khaavren, rescuing the embarrassed Yendi. "We are reckoning what we will need for the journey."

"Money, first of all," said Pel.

"That is taken care of."

"Ah! That is good, for I confess that I am in rather poor straits just at present."

"Well then, we will get the money that is due us according to this note, and we will divide it equally."

"Ah, we have a note then?"

"I think so. From the Captain."

"Good."

"You are not surprised?"

"He said such a thing was possible. What else?"

"Tazendra will make flash-stones for us."

"Good. What else?"

"Aerich is supplying the map."

"Ah. Yes, a map. Well?"

"Bandages, an axe, warm cloaks."

"And?"

"Bread and cheese."

"Is there more?"

"No, that is all."

"Excellent. And when are we to leave?"

"To-morrow, at the first light."

"Then I will rest until then. Good night, my friends."

They all bid Pel a good night, and then, seeing the wisdom of his remarks, each retired once more to his own chamber to sleep, excepting only Tazendra, who retired to her chambers, it is true, but only to work to prepare the last flash-stone. To her credit, we must say that she spent a good many hours—six, in fact—poring over a common piece of rock, first smoothing it, then bathing it in the products of her small alembic, then using a fine stylus to carve the proper symbols upon it, and at last making arcane passes over it while chanting a few words in the language of the Serioli, of which she had at least memorized what she needed to know.

To summarize, then, she completed her work and at last put herself to bed to procure a few hours of sleep before the early morning departure.

BOOK
TWO

Chapter the Eighteenth

*In Which it is Shown That
Some Reflect, While Others Wonder,
But Many do Both at Once*

THE NEXT MORNING, after a hasty breakfast, they stopped by the Dragon treasury to draw upon the note given them by Captain G'aereth. They received, as promised, three hundred orbs, half given in gold Imperials, the rest in silver and copper. They divided it on the spot, then went and borrowed horses and a pack animal from the stables of the Guard, as well as borrowing saddles and outfits. Then Tazendra distributed the flash-stones, and they set out, passing down the streets in two ranks, with Khaavren and Aerich in the lead, Pel and Tazendra behind them.

The mist which graced the summer mornings of Dragaera City had not yet dissolved when our friends passed out by the Gate of the Flags, outside of which they stopped to splash their faces in the Foaming Pool, each leaving a few pennies in the water to bring them luck on their journey. A few drops of rain sprinkled them as they left the pool, which Tazendra claimed was a good omen. Khaavren was inclined to agree, Aerich shrugged, and Pel didn't notice, being deeply involved in thinking his own thoughts.

Since they were not in a hurry, they made traveling easy on themselves and their horses, riding, now that the road was wider than the narrow streets of the city, four abreast, so they could easily converse as they traveled, which they did after the fashion to which they had accustomed themselves in other surroundings.

They had been traveling and conversing in this manner for two or three hours when Khaavren said, "My good Tazendra, it seems to me that you are unusually silent."

"Well, I am," she said.

"Then tell me, for I am curious, what accounts for this uncharacteristic quietude?"

"I reflect," pronounced Tazendra.

"Ah! You reflect. Pel, Tazendra has been reflecting."

"That is right," said Pel. "And well she should."

"And yet," said Khaavren, addressing himself once more to the Dzurlord, "I should like to learn upon what you reflect."

"Just this," said Tazendra. "We are leaving the city."

"The Horse!" said Khaavren. "I think we are."

"I was wondering—"

"But you just said you were reflecting."

"Oh, I was, I assure you. Only—"

"Yes?"

"My reflections transformed themselves into wonderings."

"Well," said Khaavren, "mine have been known to do the same."

"It has happened to me," admitted Pel.

"I never wonder," said Aerich.

"But then," resumed Khaavren, "you say your reflections gave over to wonderings on some subject about which you had questions."

"Yes," said Tazendra, "you have hit it exactly."

"And what did you wonder?"

"Just this: we are leaving the city—"

"You had already reached the point while you were merely reflecting."

"Yes," said Tazendra determinedly. "And I began to wonder what we were leaving the city to do."

"But surely you heard that it was with the intention of finding Kathana e'Marish'Chala?"

"Well, yes, I did hear that."

"And then?"

"But I wonder *why* we are finding her."

"Oh, as to that. . . ."

"Yes?"

"Well, we are either going to arrest her or to save her from being arrested."

"But, my dear Khaavren, there is a difference, is there not?"

"What? A difference between causing her to be arrested and causing her to escape arrest? Barlen! I think so!"

"Well, but then, which is it to be?"

"I haven't the least idea in the world," said Khaavren. "We have determined, have we not, that it would be a great blow to Lanmarea if she were to be arrested?"

"That is true."

"Therefore, you perceive, we ought to arrest her."

"But then—"

"Ah, but I have been asked to save her, and that by someone who, well—" Khaavren colored slightly but continued, "—someone I think it good to listen to."

"But then, when we find her, what shall we do?"

"Do? We shall do what you have been doing since we left the city."

"We shall reflect?"

"Exactly. And, if that is not sufficient, then we shall proceed to wonder."

"To wonder," put in Pel, "is not bad, as it makes the time go quickly. But to reflect, now, reflecting is more difficult. Taro the Wise once said, 'A minute spent gathering wheat is worth a day spent sifting flour.'"

"Yes," said Tazendra. "Only, what does he mean?"

"Ah, you would know that?"

"Well, I would."

"Then I bid you reflect."

"Oh," said Aerich, in a singular tone.

Khaavren turned to him and said, "Excuse me, but do you see something?"

"I do," said Aerich. "Directly ahead of us on the road there seem to be three persons who are neither wondering nor reflecting, but rather, waiting."

"So it would seem, good Aerich. Could they be waiting for us?"

"It is possible," said Aerich laconically.

"At any rate," said Khaavren, "they are watching us closely."

"Well," said Tazendra, touching the hilt of the greatsword slung over her back. "It is all the same to me if they are waiting for us or for another, if they refuse to clear the road so we may pass. You perceive, the grass is wet, and I should dislike to have my poor horse get his feet wet, for it will make him unsteady. Therefore, if they do not get out of the road, well, I shall charge them."

"But then," said Pel, "shall we not stop and speak with them first? It would be polite."

"I think we should charge them," said Tazendra, who, we must add, had not had a fight in some time.

"Bah!" said Aerich. "Charge them? Without speaking first?" Then he addressed the two gentlemen and the lady before them, saying, "I give you good day. You seem to be blocking our path."

One of them, a slight young Dragonlord with large eyes who was dressed in sufficient ruffles and lace to have made a dance-party for the court, said, "I beg your pardon. Grant me two words, and we will step aside and allow you to pass."

"Well, that's fair enough," said Aerich. "Whom do I have the honor of addressing?"

"I am Uttrik e'Lanya, of the North Pinewood Hold."

"Well, I am called Aerich."

"I perceive that one among you is a Tiassa."

"Well?"

"Is he called Khaavren of Castlerock?"

"I am," said Khaavren, speaking in his turn. "You seem to know my name, and yet, I confess, your name has never sounded in my ears."

"That is impossible."

"Do you give me the lie, my lord?" said Khaavren. "I assure you that I have never heard your name pronounced before this moment."

"You may persist in saying that if you wish."

"I more than say it; I assert it."

"Nevertheless, I wish to exchange thoughts with you."

"Upon what subject?"

"First, allow me present my friend, Sir Wyth." Here he indicated a wide shouldered Dzurlord mounted upon a piebald gelding. "And this," he indicated the lady upon his other side, who was seated upon grey charger, "Is Cohra of Lastchance, of the House of the Hawk, who is here as an Imperial representative. You have a friend, my dear Khaavren, and I am willing to accept your other friends as witnesses."

Khaavren frowned. "You wish to play, then?"

"Exactly."

"And for what reason?"

"Reason? How, you pretend you don't know?"

"I assure you, my lord, I am entirely ignorant of how I may have offended you."

"Hunh," said Uttrik. And, apparently having done with speaking, he turned toward the gentleman called Wyth, who bowed to Khaavren and said, "Is this Lyorn gentleman your friend?"

Khaavren looked at Aerich, who shrugged. "He is," said Khaavren.

"Well then," said the Dzurlord, "we wish to propose a contest to be held here and now, with no healer present, with the game to continue until one of the players is dead."

"Dead!" murmured Khaavren. "The Horse! I seem to have offended this Dragonling."

Aerich turned to Khaavren and said, "Do you accept?"

"Well, yes," said Khaavren.

"Very well," said Aerich to Wyth, who bowed and spoke to the lady, who said to Tazendra and Pel, "Will you witness?"

"We will," they said, at which time everyone concerned dismounted. The Hawklord bowed to them all and indicated a space on the side of the road. When both seconds had agreed, she drew the circle with, Khaavren noted, the point of her dagger.

"Have a care, Khaavren," said Pel. "The grass is wet."

"Well, and is it not equally wet for him and for me?"

"Nevertheless, have a care."

"I have more than a care," said Khaavren. "I have a fine piece of skin which is wrapped around all of those charming organs that allow my breath to flow, my blood to pump, and my mind to think. I will, therefore, do my utmost to see that my epidermis finishes this conflict in the same condition in which it began it."

"That is right," said Pel.

As Khaavren watched, Aerich, who stood next to him on the other side, said, "This is absurd. Do you know him?"

"Not the least in the world."

"And you have no guess what his quarrel with you is?"

"None."

"And yet he asked for you by name."

"But he did not recognize me. You perceive, then, that he has been set upon me."

"Well, but he isn't an assassin."

"That's clear enough."

Tazendra, who had been watching the one called Uttrik as he removed his doublet, drew his sword, and began taking practice thrusts with it, said, "Good Khaavren."

"Well?"

"I do not think this gentleman will give you much sport."

"You think not?"

"Well, you perceive how, in practicing, he strikes only at the air."

"That is not unusual, when preparing for a contest."

"No, and yet he seems to miss with every third stroke."

"Yes, that is true."

"And, furthermore, you will note how stiff his back leg is, and, still, how far apart his legs are when he advances."

"Perhaps," said Aerich, "he seeks to mislead you."

"Bah! If he needs to resort to such tricks as that, you'll have little enough trouble with him."

Khaavren, for his part, agreed with the flaws Tazendra had seen, but also noticed that the Dragonlord's sword arm was very fast, and that he could change the directions of his cut with, seemingly, very little effort. He was, therefore, inclined to be prudent, as he was in all things in which his life was concerned.

"Come, then," said the Hawklord to Aerich. "Are you ready?"

Aerich looked at Khaavren, who nodded. "We are ready," said the Lyorn coolly, and escorted Khaavren to his end of the circle, and assisted him in removing his cloak and belt. Khaavren then drew his sword, saluted the judge and his opponent, and placed himself on his guard.

They were still close enough to Dragaera that the road was in heavy use, so the incident had gathered a certain crowd, who began to place bets on the probable outcome. As the two pieces of steel touched, however, the betting ceased, as did the mutterings of the crowd—that particular type of conversation peculiar to horse-races, norska fights, and duels.

The Tiassa, still fatigued from the blow to his head the night before, began the contest in his usual cautious manner, attempting to determine what sort of man he was up against. In this case, all the flaws that Tazendra had noticed seemed true, but the Dragonlord was, in fact, very fast on his feet, and moreover had a strength of arm, and a heavier sword, which forced Khaavren to work harder than he liked to parry the many ferocious attacks that Uttrik directed at his body and head. He therefore maintained a defensive posture and guarded himself closely, using the "nine-point system of aggressive protection," a product of the baroque school of the fence, which rendered his head and torso all but invulnerable while still crowding the other and forcing him to respond to a complex pattern of nine sequential feints and attacks, a pattern which Khaavren hoped to break as soon as it was established.

While doing so, he also, as was his custom, studied the countenance of his opponent. He saw, then, a gentleman with a good set of features excepting only his eyes, which were too large. His eyebrows were well separated from each other over the bridge of the nose, a sure sign of an orderly mind; his forehead was well-creased, indicating a contemplative personality, and, moreover, Khaavren detected in his eyes that the twin forces of anger and frustration vied for control of his mood. Anger, Khaavren deduced, at himself for whatever real or imaginary offense had prompted the contest, and frustration over his inability to bypass the furious defense the Tiassa offered.

It was not long, then, before Khaavren judged that Uttrik had fallen well into the complex pattern, and abruptly left it. The Dragonlord, at this time, had been making an attack for Khaavren's left flank, which his last parry had left open. Khaavren, however, twisted slightly to his right, with which same motion he struck down with the flat of his blade upon Uttrik's sword arm, and felt his own weapon shudder from the contact. Khaavren resumed his defensive posture in time to parry an attack from the other's dagger, but no such attack was forthcoming, as Uttrik groaned and stepped back, his sword falling from the numbed hand.

At this time Khaavren took a step in, deflected the dagger that the Dragonlord raised in feeble defense, and put the point of his sword against Uttrik's throat. "Well, my lord," said he, speaking in an even tone to show that the contest had not exhausted him. "Now, if you would be so good as tell me why you have attacked me, well, perhaps I will spare your life."

"Fie," said the other. "You still pretend ignorance then?"

"I assure you, my lord, I am entirely mystified."

"But then, my name means nothing to you?"

"Does that astonish you?"

"Nearly."

"Well?"

"And yet, if I were to say that I am the eldest son of the late Lord of Pepperfield, what then?"

"Ah," said Khaavren. "Then that is different."

"You know me, then?"

"That is to say, I've heard of your father, and am aware of his unfortunate death."

"Well, and does this explain my enmity for you?"

"Not the least in the world."

"What? You still claim that you have no notion of the cause of my hatred for you?"

"None at all, my lord."

"My lord, I am astounded."

"Well?"

"If you wish, I will tell you."

"Shards! I think I have been asking for nothing else for an hour."

"Well, two words will explain all."

"I await you."

"But first, if you please, remove the point of your sword from my throat, where it hampers my elocution. I am fully aware that you have won our contest, and my life now belongs to you; and I assure you that if, after I have answered your question, you still wish to kill me, well, I will not resist."

Khaavren nodded and lowered his sword. At the same time he spoke to his friends, saying, "Before we terminate our play we are going to have some speech together. Exercise patience, then, for I think it will be worth our while."

His friends bowed their assent, while the crowd, impatient for a conclusion to the duel, muttered unhappily. Khaavren turned back to Uttrik and said, "Come then, speak, for I must admit that you have excited my curiosity. I fully expect you will say things that will cause me to reflect, and perhaps even to wonder."

"Oh, as to that, it is not improbable."

"Begin then."

"Well, my argument, then, is this: the Baroness of Kaluma, that is, Kathana e'Marish'Chala, murdered my father."

"Well, of this I am aware."

"You are aware of this?"

"Indeed, yes."

"And yet you do not know my quarrel with you?"

"My lord, it is now twenty times that I have repeated it."

"But I say that it is impossible."

"My lord, I don't know the custom in the House of the Dragon, but among the Tiassa, well, we consider that when we are at a man's mercy is not the time to give him the lie."

"Your pardon, good Khaavren. You are right. I render my deepest apologies."

"But then, you perceive, you still have not answered my question."

"Well, I will tell you then. If the Baroness Kaluma murdered my father, and you wish to save her—"

"Stop."

"Eh?"

"I believe you have pronounced the words, 'wish to save her.'"

"And if I did?"

"But, why do you think we wish to save her?"

"Well, don't you?"

"Oh, as to that, I don't even know myself."

"How, don't know?"

"My lord, it is not for you to question me; do you agree?"

"Well, yes."

"Then tell me how it was that you thought I intended to assist the Baroness of Kaluma."

"Why, in the simplest possible manner."

"That being?"

"I was told."

"You were told?"

"Exactly."

"What were you told?"

"That to-day or to-morrow there would be a gentleman named Khaavren, of the House of the Tiassa, in the uniform of the Red Boot Battalion, and that this gentleman intended to assist my enemy in escaping from justice."

"Well, your information, if wrong, is not the less complete for that."

"Thank you, my lord."

"But then, who told you this?"

"Why, I hardly know."

"How, you don't know?"

"I assure you, I never met the gentleman before."

"But then, how did he explain himself?"

"Why, no explanation was necessary."

"But then, an unknown man approached you and said, 'I shan't identify myself, yet such-and-such a man will be in this place at that time and do these things?' My lord, it is not possible."

"Well then, it did not happen that way."

"Then, if you will be so good as to tell me in what way it happened, I will be very pleased."

"Well, I will."

"I assure you I shall consider myself to be in your debt if you do."

"Here it is then: I was partaking of refreshment at an inn outside of the city, in the district of Longwater."

"At what inn?"

"The sign of the small scarlet capon."

"Very well."

"And a gentleman sat down next to me."

"Of what House was this gentleman?"

"Why, I assure you I have no idea."

"Well," said Khaavren, remembering Aerich's remarks concerning Jhereg and Yendi, "what then? He sat down next to you."

"Yes, and we became engaged in conversation."

"On what subject?"

"On the death of my father. For you perceive that I had been in mourning, and consequently had touched no spirits, until that very day."

"That is clear."

"So the subject was fresh on my mind, and the wine was well placed before me."

"I understand that."

"Now this gentleman—"

"Whose House you are ignorant of."

"Yes. He had heard of my father's death, and expressed sympathy for me, which seemed well done."

"It seems so. But then?"

"Why then, he related to me that he had heard that an attempt was being made to rescue Kaluma from the authorities, in whom, until that time, I had put my trust."

"Yes, well?"

"I pressed him for details, and at last he relented."

"He relented, you say?"

"Exactly."

"And gave you my name?"

"Your name, good Khaavren, your description, and your mission."

"Well, but he was misinformed."

"So you say."

"But then, with your life in my hands, why would I conceal my intentions from you?"

"That is true."

At this time Khaavren was stuck by one of those sudden thoughts to which Tiassa are, in some measure or another, subject; those flashes of inspiration which drive some to disaster and some to wild success. Khaavren, true to his ancestry, acted upon this thought at once, saying, "Well, I will release you from the terms of this duel, and furthermore, I invite you to accompany us."

"Accompany you? But where are you going?"

"The Horse! We are going to find Kathana e'Marish'Chala!"

"But you said—"

"I did not say we were going to aid her."

"But then, are you going to arrest her?"

"Oh, I don't say that, either."

"But then, when you find her what will you do?"

"The Gods! When we find her, well, we will reflect."

Chapter the Ninteenth

*In Which Uttrik, Being Interviewed, Is Found
to be Satisfactory, and, In the course of a Meal,
Aids Tazendra in Acquiring a Lackey*

T HE DISCUSSION ENDED here, and Khaavren made
a sign to the judge that the affair was at an end,
whereupon Khaavren conducted Tazendra to
where his friends awaited him. "This gentleman will be
traveling with us," he explained.

Aerich shrugged, Pel raised his eyebrows, but Tazendra
said, "How, this gentleman?"

"None other."

"He will travel with us?"

"Yes, you have guessed it."

"He who, but a minute ago, tried to kill you?"

"Kill or wound, yes."

"Do tell me why, good Khaavren."

"Why, my dear Tazendra? Because I will have it so. Do
you protest?"

"Well, no. But I—"

"Stop, then, before your lips produce some word or
other that I have heard too often already."

Tazendra then shrugged in her turn. "Very well, be it so."

Uttrik bowed to them all, then went off to hold a conversation with Wyth. "Of what do you think they are speaking?" said Pel.

"Well, they are friends, and they are parting. No doubt that is the subject of the conversation. Or else they are communicating matters to be attended to while Uttrik is absent."

"Or," said Pel, "they are preparing something of a nature that they do not wish to disclose to us."

"Well, that is possible."

"And if it is true?"

"We shall be on our guard."

"Very well."

When Uttrik had bid farewell to Wyth and paid the judge, they mounted upon their horses and continued along the road. They had not, in fact, been traveling for more than an hour when Tazendra remarked to the world at large, or rather, to anyone who would listen, "It seems to me that Khaavren must be hungry."

"Explain to me why you think so," said Khaavren, "for I am most anxious to learn."

"Why, because you have a fought a duel."

"Well, and?"

"I have merely watched you fight, and yet I have gained sufficient hunger to go a fair way toward devouring every one of those sausages I perceive hanging in the window of the hostelry we see before us. You, then, having fought, rather than merely watching, must be even more hungry."

"If I were to disclose my true thoughts," said Khaavren, "well, I would admit that hunger would not be far from them at this moment."

"Food," said Pel reflectively, "would not hinder my enjoyment of the afternoon."

Aerich gave a shrug which indicated that he, too, would enjoy eating. Uttrik simply nodded. So saying, they entered the hostelry, which was marked by a sign containing a picture of Beed'n, the Cavalier minstrel of the early Sixteenth Cycle, easily recognized by the peacock feathers he wore trailing down from his beret.

This is the second time we have entered that peculiar institution called the rural inn since we began our history, and since we were too busy the first time to describe it, and, moreover, as we will find ourselves in such a place more than once in the course of our journeys, we will permit ourselves now to say two words about it.

If, as the Thirty-third Marquis of Goi once remarked, there is always a rebellion in progress somewhere within the Empire, then there will always be hostels to serve as the breeding grounds of sedition. If, as K'verra e'Tenith said, there are always more bandits than there are forces to contend with them, then there will always be inns to give them a place to rest between robberies. If, as Zerika II said, there are always traveling procurators, tinkers, solicitors, and peddlers on the highways to pick up anything missed by rebels and bandits, than there will always be inns to provide them with a warm place to rest before resuming their trade.

In our own happy days, when we can look back upon rebellion with a shrug, search in vain for the highwaymen who made unarmed travel impractical, and pretend that the trade of procurator, tinker, solicitor or peddler is an honest one, the character of the inn has changed markedly, and, we are forced to admit, not always for the better. In those days, it is clear from all accounts, the floors were always swept free of dirt, the tables were polished morning and evening until they fairly glistened; the glasses of wine and ale were cold and full; the plates of food were hot and plentiful, and had, moreover, always the particular characteristics of the region; and the host, who never knew if he was about to meet a rebel, a highwayman, a tinker, or one who had the duty to confound the others, took pains to be polite to all and partial to none; assuming, of course, the patron was of gentle birth.

The layout was simpler, then, as well; usually confined

to a large common room, one or more private rooms in back, and a few chambers to let on the upper story (it was a rare inn that boasted more than two stories). The benches, tables, and chairs were always simple, but built to last for a thousand years; in those ballads we hear so often which speak of brawls in which the ruffians are breaking furniture over each other, we may be sure that, in fact, a blow by a simple fireplace stool would have broken the skull of the unfortunate upon whom it was rendered without a single crack appearing on the bludgeoning instrument.

To such a place, then, our friends came and presented their horses to the stable-hands, and themselves to the hostelry, where, in a room empty save for a pair of merchants, they sat at a bench near a front window; thus being as far as possible from the cooking fire. This fire, we should say, had no purpose, the weather being still warm, but to serve the several spitted fowls, the two slabs of kethna-ribs, and the leg of mutton that were making the flames dance to the call of their dripping fat.

After the companions arranged themselves, they called first for the mutton, but, upon being told that it wanted yet two hours before it should be suitable, happily settled for two of the capons, which, along with warm poppy-seed bread, sourfruit, several kethna sausages, and a decanter of the local sweet red wine, made for a satisfactory repast.

At first the conversation was stilted; the addition of Uttrik had turned the convivial alliance into an uncomfortable association. But as they finished eating, that is, when they reached that point in the meal when it is necessary to speak in order to feed the hunger of the mind as capons will feed the hunger of the stomach, Khaavren said, "So, good Uttrik, you are from Pepperfield?"

"Well, yes."

"And have lived there all your life?"

"Oh, not at all. I spent much of my life in Dragaera City, where I have been training for a career in arms."

"But have you yet gone beyond training?"

"Only twice, Sir Khaavren."

"Tell us, then, about those two occasions."

"That is easily done," he said. "Both of these were in the south-west, and came about shortly after my father's death, which of necessity interrupted my period of mourning."

"That in understandable," said Tazendra. "But, tell us about these battles."

"Well, to be precise—"

"Precision is always good," put in Khaavren.

"—they took place in the duchy of Fautonswell."

"Ah," said Tazendra. "You then served, did you not, under the Duke of Twinoaks?"

"I had that honor."

"Against Kliburr, and the Carriage House Uprising?"

"So it has been called."

"Twinoaks is an able general, by all accounts."

"Well, I can testify to that. My first battle was a skirmish, when we were sent against a small cavalry unit to teach them to respect the supply lines that connected us with Lynch."

"Well," said Tazendra, who was becoming interested. "Did you teach them?"

"Nearly. They were coming out of the hills in an ambuscade when—"

"How many?" said Tazendra.

"Of them? Only thirty or forty."

"And you?"

"Thirty-two plus our officer, Lady Duraal."

"Well, and then?"

"Then we engaged them from the side, coming on them out of a grove of elms such as are found in abundance in that area. We left five of them dead, captured twice that number, and drove the rest away."

"And did you then give chase?"

"We were not permitted to do so."

"Well, and your casualties?"

"We were fortunate enough not to have had any."

"Well," said Tazendra nodding, "that was not bad work. And you yourself?"

"Oh, I engaged my man. He had not the skill of Sir Khaavren, I am happy to say. And, moreover, I have some knowledge of fighting on horseback. I had the honor to set my sword against the spear of an enemy, and I was able to give him a good cut on the arm and another on his leg, which convinced him to leave off the battle and retreat."

"And that was well done, I think," said Khaavren.

Uttrik bowed.

"But then," said Tazendra, "you spoke of two battles, I think?"

"The second was the Battle of Fautonswell itself."

"Ah," said the Dzurlord. "My cousin, Tynn, was wounded in that one. Not, however," she added, "before accounting for ten or twelve of the enemy."

"Well, it was a warm affair. They charged first, and our officer, Duraal, went down. That is, her horse was killed, and she was speared while she tried to recover."

"Was she killed?"

"She was mortally wounded, and died before the battle ended, but not before arranging our skirmish-line and reorganizing our force in preparation for the general's charge, and even, wounded though she was, leading our lines into the battle on the horse of an enemy swordsman she had brought down."

"Oh, that was well done."

"Those were my thoughts."

"And you," said Khaavren. "What was your role?"

"I played my part, I assure you. The General ordered our battalion to force the enemy back toward the hill, where his lancers were stationed, and, in doing so, I had the honor to bring three of the enemy to the earth; one with a flash-stone and two with my blade."

"Come, that's not bad," said Tazendra.

"Well, it was pretty hot, but we fought mercenaries, which gave us the advantage."

"That is true," put in Aerich. "They fought for pay, but you fought for the Empire."

"That is it exactly," said Uttrik. "And for the honor of our General, in whom we all took great pride. A gentleman always fights better when he is with cause, for then he is not afraid of what he will meet when he passes over Deathgate Falls."

"That is full of justice," said Aerich, who then murmured, "I think I shall end by liking this gentleman."

Pel, who overheard him, gave the sort of peculiar half-smile which was part of his nature and said softly, "I agree with you, my friend, but I say nothing on the matter of trust."

Aerich shrugged once more, and exactly as he did so, there came a cry from near the door, which sound was followed by the peculiar sound of a large sheet of thick oiled paper torn asunder. Khaavren and Tazendra were on their feet at once, looking toward the noise; Uttrik, who was facing that way, merely pushed his chair back and let his hand stray to his sword hilt; Aerich and Pel contented themselves with looking up.

The source of the cry and the cause of the sound were at once apparent, in the form of a small man in the colors of the House of the Teckla, who, contrary to the custom prevailing at all times in all public houses, had been thrown through the window *into* the inn, where he lay on his back, endeavoring to rise in spite of a certain confusion that appeared to have afflicted his brain, due, no doubt, to the effects of his means of arrival.

He was followed at once by several—Khaavren counted eleven—burly-looking men of no discernible House, save that ill-defined "House" that makes up those who are born neither to serve nor to be served, neither to make nor to sell: in other words, common riff-raff of the highways. In one of them, it is true, the sleek, pale countenance of the

Orca could be discerned, but he wore no insignia, and thus could not claim the title of gentleman.

These ruffians, then, entered the house by the door, and at once found the Teckla who had come flying through the window, with, presumably, their help. They picked him up, then, and two of them held him while a third, holding a stick of good weight, prepared to lay it upon the unfortunate. Khaavren, on seeing this, frowned; Aerich shrugged as if, since none of them were gentlemen, it was none of his affair; Pel settled himself back with a look of idle curiosity, but Tazendra, who had already risen, cleared her throat significantly, while Uttrik stood and took a position next to her.

While the sound of the Dzurlord's throat-clearing might have communicated a certain menace, in this case it failed in its object, as the sounds made by the scuffling necessary to keep the Teckla from falling over effectively blocked out any noises softer than speech. Observing this, Tazendra took the necessary action; that is, she spoke. "Excuse me, my friends."

One of the ruffians, the one, in fact, who looked like an Orca, spared her a glance. "Well?" he said.

"I hesitate to interrupt your sport, but I have certain questions to put to you. In particular, I wish to know what this Teckla has done that has caused you to treat him in this manner."

"This doesn't concern your lordship," said the Orca, in a tone that could be considered polite only by allowing the greatest possible liberty in the use of the term.

"Your pardon, but it does concern me, in that I have done you the honor to ask you the question."

"And I repeat, your ladyship, that it doesn't concern you. Our business is our own, I think, and thank the Orb the law does not require gentlemen such as ourselves to answer such questions of anyone who comes by."

"Allow me to say that you are rude," observed Tazendra. "And, moreover, you are not observant, or you would perceive these gold-colored cloaks we wear which announce that we are members of His Imperial Majesty's Guards. Now, what cause has this man given you for such treatment? I beg you to observe that I have now asked you twice; I will not ask a third time."

"That's lucky," said the Orca, and signaled his friend to begin the beating. His blow never landed, however, for before the stick could fall, there was a flash that, even in the well-lighted room, made everyone blink; the flash was accompanied, moreover, by a sharp sound, not unlike two blocks of wood clapped together, and this was followed by a bittersweet smell that filled the room, and, at the same time, a scream as the man holding the stick stared down at the black burn in the center of his chest, then collapsed to the floor like a pile of dirty linen.

"Oh," cried the Orca. "Is that it, then? Well, we are ready to answer you, meddler. Charge!" They drew knives, then, save for the leader who had a sabre, and charged Tazendra.

She, however, as cool as Aerich, said, "What is this, my man? Do you think that I only have one charge in my stone? Allow me to correct you," and fired the second in the Orca's face, leaving him stretched out dead on the spot.

She stood then, with her sword raised (the stone had been in her left hand), ready to defend her position like Lord Golgoril at Bendrock Junction. And, indeed, the brigand who held the front rank upon the fall of his leader felt something, for, though she swung her greatsword at him one handed, he had nothing but a poniard with which to deflect it, the result being that both Tazendra's sword and his own dagger cut deeply into his shoulder, leaving him moaning on his knees.

Things might have gone poorly for Tazendra nevertheless, except that Uttrik, who had likewise been offended by the injustice of the attack, had in the meantime drawn his own weapon and met the first attacker with a good thrust through the body which laid him out on the floor. Meanwhile, the Teckla, who had been released by his captors upon the order to charge, rather than running for the door, had picked up a stool that was of the sort used by those who polish the shoes of gentlemen, and proceeded, wielding it by two of its three legs, to bash in the head nearest him, which he did with good style.

"That was well struck, my good Uttrik," said Tazendra.

"Well, and yourself, I must say your sorcery is very pretty, my dear Tazendra."

"Bah, it was nothing. But look to your left, there—that's it!"

Now, while all this was going on, Pel had whispered to Aerich and Khaavren, "My friends, this has a smell about it I don't like, and spike me if I don't believe that these fine folk are here to provoke us, and for no other reason."

"Well," said Aerich. "You may be right. But, Blood of the Gods, they have succeeded!" On this, the three friends stood up, and each held his flash-stone in plain sight while Aerich called loudly, "Come now, I think we can get them all in one turn, don't you? On the count, gentlemen. Ready?"

This was too much for the remaining attackers, who, by this time, were reduced to six in number, for they at once turned and fled the room, the last to leave getting a good knock on the head by the Teckla as recompense for his tardiness. Those who remained on what had been the field, or rather, the floor of the battle, looked about them while putting away their weapons, which consisted of three flash-stones, two swords, and a barstool, which was dutifully set down by the fire. Aerich and Pel took their seats first, while Tazendra and Uttrik embraced and congratulated each other on their victory.

"Perhaps," said Pel, "we ought to question the survivors, if any are still alive, to learn who it was who set them on us."

"You persist, then," said Aerich, "in thinking this ambuscade was directed at ourselves?"

"Well, don't you?"

"It is not impossible," admitted Aerich.

"Well," said Khaavren, "we may learn something by interrogating this Teckla who wields a stool so well."

"Well thought," said Aerich. "Do you interrogate him, while I—"

"Yes? While you?"

"Blood! While I order another bottle of this fine Gegaare wine."

"Very well," said Khaavren. "You, my friend, come tell us your name."

The Teckla whom Khaavren addressed was unusually lean for a Teckla, and he was moreover of early middle years, and had a roundish face with small eyes and a protruding lower lip. His fingers were short and stubby, proclaiming his House even were it not for his straight, light brown hair and bowlegged gait. He said, "My lord, I will happily give you my name, which is Mica, and will, moreover, thank you deeply, for there is no doubt in my mind that you saved my life."

"Well," said Khaavren, "but what did those ruffians want with you?"

"As to that, I confess I have no knowledge whatsoever."

"What?" said Khaavren. "You pretend you have no notion about why they attacked you?"

"None at all, my lord."

"Well, but the thing is impossible."

"Not at all," said Pel.

"Perhaps," said Khaavren, who was as yet unconvinced, "but tell us how it came about."

"Well, my lord, three times a week I come here to this place, and am given a meal in exchange for doing whatever work Master Cleff (who is, I should mention, the host) can find for me."

"That is, then, your livelihood?"

"It is, my lord."

"And what do you do for meals on the other two days?"

"My lord, I do what Kieron the Conqueror did upon the cliffs of Adrilankha."

"That being?"

"I await the morrow."

"Decidedly, you are a clever fellow, Mica, and not lacking in courage, to judge by your treatment of your attackers. But continue your story, for I must say that you interest me."

"Well then," said Mica, bowing, "today is the day upon which I am to work, and I was arriving with that in mind, when I saw those ill-favored persons whom you have so effectively put to flight."

"And what were they doing?"

"My lord, they were standing grouped together outside the inn, speaking in low tones."

"Well, and then?"

"As I approached, one of them pointed at me, and the others turned to observe me, and nodded. I had no knowledge of their intentions, yet something made me wary, for a I took a wide path around them. You perceive, my lord, that, as I am not a gentleman, I may avoid danger without dishonoring myself."

"Yes, that is true. Go on."

"Well, they walked over in a mass, my lords, and barred my way. One of them said, 'Tell us, for we wish to know, what is your intention with regards to this public house?'

"I said, 'My lord, I intend to enter, with the plan of working here in exchange for a meal.'

" 'What?' cried the man, 'you wish to enter this place?'

" 'If it is not displeasing to you,' I said. 'If you would rather I did not,' I continued, 'I will remain without.'

" 'Oh, no,' they said, 'we are happy that you intended to go in. We will even help you to do so by providing you with the means of gaining entry.'

"And, without another word, my lords, they took me and cast me through the window, with the results of which you are acquainted.' "

"Well then," said Pel, "do you doubt that I am right? This was a snare that had been set for us, which we escaped only because our friend the Dzurlord knows how to use flash-stones, because we have with us a Dragonlord who hates injustice, and because this Teckla knows how to strike back."

"I no longer doubt what you say," said Aerich. "But who is it who so desperately wishes to stop us?"

"Why, whoever it was that attempted to convince Uttrik to kill Khaavren."

"That being?"

"The same person who attempted to warn Khaavren away."

"And that is?"

"I have no idea."

"Unfortunate," murmured Aerich.

"But," added Tazendra, "we seem to have escaped."

"And for that," said Khaavren, "we have you to thank."

"I especially, my lady," said Mica to Tazendra, "thank you. And if there is anything I can do to aid you in anything, you need only ask; henceforth, I would lay down my life for you."

Tazendra bowed, then, suddenly struck by a thought, said, "But, have you not said that you eat only three times a week?"

"Yes, my lady, but that is twice a week more than I ate before I gained this position."

"But then, would you wish for a better position; one that will allow you to eat, not three times a week, but four times a day?"

Mica's mouth seemed to water at the thought, and, to judge by the way his eyes lit up, he had no complaints to make of any plan with that as its object. He bowed to the Dzurlord and said, "My lady, that would suit my greatest wishes. Only tell me what I must do."

"Well, first you must travel with me."

"Travel with such a lady as you? Oh, that would be a fine thing."

"Good."

"But, what next?"

"Next, you must wear my livery."

"Ah, to be dressed in the arms of a Dzurlord! Such happiness is beyond me. But, what else?"

"Well, after that, you must care for my horse."

"I love horses, and have been caring for them all my life. What next?"

"You must learn to clean, polish, and sharpen my weapons."

"I sharpen the knives for Master Cleff, as well as cleaning and polishing the silver that he keeps in case a prince should honor his house, which he has never used in two hundred years, but which must, nevertheless, be polished every week against the chance that his fortune changes."

"You must help me to dress."

"My grandmother on my mother's side used to live with us when I was but a child, and she had the aryes so bad she could not dress herself, so I performed this service for her every day for three hundred years. What next?"

"You must bring food and wine for me and my friends when we require it, with the understanding that any scraps of meat or dregs of wine are yours."

"It is just this I have been doing for Master Cleff for the last year; and he is a tolerably stern taskmaster. What next?"

"That is all."

"Well, I do not conceal from you that it would bring me the greatest possible joy to hold this position."

"Then, my dear Mica, it is yours."

"But stay," said Pel, frowning, "surely you are aware that it is no longer the fashion to have lackeys."

"Blood!" said Tazendra, "That is true. I had not thought of it."

Mica trembled as all of his hopes for the future collapsed. Uttrik felt great sympathy for him, since the Dragon had, after all just saved his life, but could think of nothing to do except to lean over and whisper in Khaavren's ear, "We must do something."

"Indeed?" said Khaavren. "Why?"

"Are you not moved to tears by the look on his face?"

"Well, but what can we do?"

"The Horse! You are a Tiassa; think of something."

Khaavren had a reply ready for this: he was about to say, "You are a Dragon; kill someone," when this thought led to another, which led to still another, and he finished by addressing Tazendra.

"My dear friend, attend me."

"Well?"

"Suppose, upon wishing to enter this fine hostel, we had met with a gentleman who forbade you from entering. What would you do?"

"What would I do? Why, I should take my sword and separate his head from his body."

"Good. But then, what if, when you are in the garden taking your morning exercises, someone should say, 'Your activities offend me; I insist that you stop them.' What then?"

"Oh, then, well, then, if I had not my sword with me, I should take a flash-stone and see how large a hole I could make in his body with it."

"Good. But then, let us pretend that one day you are dining by yourself in the Longwood Arms hotel, and an individual should insist that he, rather than you, should have the table at which you are sitting, and which commands a view of the river?"

"Why, I think I should give him a better view of the river than he had asked for by sending him directly into it. But, good Khaavren, why all of these questions?"

"Because it seems to me that if you are unwilling to let individuals dictate your decisions for you, how it is you are willing to let such an abstract thing as fashion decide how you are to lead your life?"

"Well," said Tazendra, "your words are full of truth. And I have changed my mind once more; Mica, you are my man."

"Yes, my lady, and I shall only be happier than I am now on the day when you shall command me to be cut to pieces in your service."

"I must say," said Pel, "that I am also moved by these arguments; I no longer have any objections to make." But, as he said this, he frowned. After a moment he whispered to Aerich, "Do you think my idea was right in regards to those brigands with whom we have just finished arguing?"

"Yes, my dear Pel, I have told you so."

"Will you listen to my next idea?"

"You know, Cavalier, that I will listen to anything you have to say to me."

"Well then, I do not trust a Teckla who fights too well."

"So you think—?"

"That perhaps the entire purpose of this plan was to convince us to take along a spy in the person of this Mica."

Aerich furrowed his brows at the word "spy," then studied the countenance of the Teckla before him, and at last shook his head. "No, good Pel, I believe you are wrong in this. I have seen this man, and if I am any judge, and I nearly think I am, this is an honest man, though a Teckla."

"Then you think we can trust him?"

"I think so."

"Very well; I submit to your perspicacity."

"Well then, let us be off, for I begin to tire of this house, however diverting the entertainments."

It cost them three orbs to settle with Master Cleff, which amount would have been more except that they were willing to give him the despoiling of those who were left on his floor, which left him in a state of happiness only rivaled by Mica, who led the way out the door, stopping only to pick up the stool he had used in the melee, against the chance that, in this company, he should need it again, which proved that he was no fool.

They then went so far as to select the best of the horses left by the deceased brigands and gave it to Mica to use, whereupon Tazendra rendered this worthy even more happy, if it were possible, by saying, "Come along, Mica," as the Guardsmen, augmented by one Dragonlord and a lackey, set off once more.

Chapter the Twentieth

In Which the Author Believes It is Time to see What Seodra Has Been Up To

MEN HAVE INVENTED various names in which to measure distance, and have taken a certain pleasure in assigning units of one to the other, in the sense that it is so many inches to the span and so many spans to the league; or in converting one to the other, in the sense that a league in the Sorannah is almost two leagues within the ancient confines of Seawall, that is, within the barony that once held the city of Dragaera, and, at the time of which we have the honor to write, still held a portion of it; yet, for all of this measurement, it is understood by those who travel and by those who listen to travelers that the meaningful unit by which distance can be measured is *time*.

It is true, for example, that the distance from the Gate of the Darr to Ripple Point is scarcely a league, while it is a good thirty leagues from the Gate of Iron to Fosson's Well, yet, because the latter is over level ground with a good road laid on it, while the former is nearly straight up a mountainside covered in loose and crumbling rock, we may in justice assert that each of these places lies the same distance from the heart of Dragaera City, that distance being about thirty hours, or a full day and a night.

Therefore, if we say that our friends had a distance of many days ahead of them, we hope our readers will be neither offended nor confused by the apparent embarrassment of measurements.

What followed the flight at the inn, then, was a measure of time spent riding, in a leisurely way, through the beautiful Ironwood Gap of the Boiling Mountains which, while pleasant enough to those who had the leisure to travel in this way, will have, we suspect, little enough interest for those who have chosen to come along on this journey in the capacity of observers. These observers, by which, be it clearly understood, we mean the readers of these pages, might well have enjoyed the beauty of the divers mountain streams that rushed in a hundred variations through the mountains, anxious to join together to form the northern Yendi River; and might also have appreciated the way the cool, gentle winds of the pass circulated over the traveler's face; and would almost certainly have been pleased to see the explosion of red and gold from the Creeping Woods as it was spread out below Sorcerer's Rock high in the pass; and could hardly have failed to enjoy the fragrance of the tunnis and the blossoms of the late-apple; but all of these treats are reserved for those among the readers who witnessed these things before Adron's Disaster, some five hundred years after the events herein described, which took these sights, sounds, and smells away forever as it took the Palace, the city, and all those who dwelled therein. For the rest, such things are useless to describe; therefore, we shall not take up our readers' time with them, but pass on to events of more direct importance to the history we have the honor to relate.

We come, then, back to the city, some hours after the events at that hostel which was informally called Beed'n's Inn. To be more specific, we will find ourselves in the

Dragon Wing, in the lofty and spacious apartments of the Warlord, which are, as we peer at them from our invisible vantage point, occupied by Lytra, the Warlord, and an ill-favored gentleman who is distinguished both by a curious half-circle-shaped scar reaching from his right temple nearly to his lip, and by the fact that he is wearing the grey and black of House Jhereg.

"So," said Lytra, "you failed; is that what you have to tell me, Fayaavik?"

"It is, Excellency," said the Jhereg, showing no signs of embarrassment.

"Well, then, tell me of the affair."

"Excellency, my task was to prevent certain persons from continuing their journey, using any means possible."

"Save killing them, Fayaavik."

"Yes, lady, those were the orders. But that is unnecessary; I would no more countenance assassination than you would, Excellency."

"I believe you entirely, Fayaavik," said Lytra, in tones that indicated she believed him not at all. "Go on, then."

"Excellency, I found a friend with whom I was on tolerably good terms—"

"In other words, he was indebted to you?"

"If you wish."

"Very well, go on."

"My friend—"

"Had he a name?"

Fayaavik gave a sign indicating that it didn't matter. "My friend," he continued, "found ten companions, and, by means of stratagem, attempted to convince a certain one of the travelers to expose herself without the others. We would then take this opportunity to make one of them unable to continue, and so on, until we had them all, or at least, the one for whom you expressed the most desire."

"That seems to be a sound plan."

"I am glad you think so. But in brief, Excellency, the stratagem failed and they escaped."

"But how did it come to fail? That is what I wish to discover. You say there was your friend, and ten others. It seems to me that this makes eleven. The ambuscade was intended to defeat only four."

"It is true that I was told that there would be four of them."

"Well, that is the right number."

"I beg to differ with you."

"How so?"

"Because there were five of them."

"Five, Fayaavik?"

"Truly, Excellency. And moreover the Teckla, quite outside of expectation, delivered a blow or two himself, which makes six."

"But still, eleven against six, and one of them a Teckla—"

"Excellency, they had prepared themselves with flash-stones."

"Ah. I hadn't known they had such means."

"The report I received is most explicit on the point."

"But still, eleven against five. Were any of them wounded?"

"Of the enemy? No. My friend was killed, however, as were two of his companions. Three others were injured, more or less seriously."

"Incredible," muttered Lytra. Aloud she said, "But who was this fifth man?"

"That I cannot tell you."

"How, cannot?"

"Because, having no knowledge of who you expected to be there, save the Tiassa whom you described, I have no knowledge of who was unexpected."

"Well, one was a Dzurlord."

"That I know, because it was she that my friend thought to separate from the rest, as a Dzur will invariably defend someone, right or wrong, if numbers are against him."

"Still another was a Lyorn."

"Yes, it was he who was about to command his comrades to discharge their flash-stones when the survivors made a retreat."

"There was a Yendi."

"I don't deny it, but you know, my lord, that they are hard to identify. Still, there was one man who was described to me as small and handsome, very well dressed, of black hair, dark eyes, and wearing a cloak very similar to the uniform of the guards."

"That is he."

"Very good. Who else?"

"Who else, Fayaavik? Why, the Tiassa whom I had the honor to describe to you but yester-day."

"Well, and what of the Dragonlord?"

"What, you pretend there was a Dragonlord?"

"Indeed yes. He had no flash-stone, but his sword, I am informed, was tolerably long."

"I know of no Dragonlord traveling with them."

"Well, but stop, Excellency. I seem to recall, I was told by what name they called him. It was ... yes, it was Yt-something. The last sound was hard, perhaps a 'g' or a 'k'."

"Uttrik?" cried Lytra.

"That is exactly the name."

"But that is impossible."

"Very well."

"What do you mean, very well?"

"I mean, if it is impossible, then, no doubt, I was misinformed."

"But Uttrik was to have killed the Tiassa!"

"Perhaps he didn't."

"Then the Tiassa was to have killed him."

"Well, perhaps that also failed."

"Impossible."

"Very well."

"Ah, you say it again."

"Blood of the Horse, I am consistent, I think."

"Go, Fayaavik. Leave at once. By the back stairs, if you please."

"Naturally. But first, here, take this."

"What is that?"

"It is a purse, Excellency."

"I see that it is a purse, but what does it contain?"

"Barlen! It contains good Imperials, I think."

"For what purpose do you give me money, Fayaavik?"

"Well, didn't you give me money? And a good amount of it, too? Well, I have failed in my commission, hence I return the money."

"Bah! You were paid for the attempt. Keep it."

"I beg to differ with your ladyship, but only employees are paid to make attempts."

"And are you not an employee, insofar as I hired you?"

"Perhaps I was, but now I am not, for I return the money."

"Yet, I insist—"

"No, Excellency, I insist. I do not wear your livery; nor shall I. Should you wish for another attempt, you may so state, and I will then happily take your money again. Until that time, I will not have it, for unearned gold is a chain that I will not wear."

"If you will have it so, Fayaavik."

"I will. Good day, Excellency."

"Good day, Fayaavik."

The Jhereg left, as he had promised, by the back staircase. As the sound of his footsteps faded, someone else appeared in the room—the Athyra whom we have met and whom we called Seodra, which we will continue to call her because that is how Lytra referred to her, and, moreover, because that was her name.

"The Jhereg failed, then, Excellency."

"So it would seem, good Seodra."

"Amusing."

"Not so. We have been checked. We cannot allow them to arrest Kaluma; we must keep her safe so that we can destroy her at the exact moment our plan requires that we do so."

"Then we must find another way to stop them."

"That is clear, Seodra."

"We know, at least, whither they are bound."

"We know this?"

"I have been informed."

"That is good."

"You must call your Jhereg friend back to you."

"How so?"

"We have another task for him."

"That being?"

Seodra dropped her voice, as if afraid that the walls might hide spies, or, at any rate, historians; and this maneuver must have been successful, for we are unable to report what was exchanged between them for the next several moments. We can report that Lytra listened, and, after listening, nodded, and after nodding said, in a somewhat louder tone, "Yes, Seodra, you are right."

"Well, then?"

"I will have Fayaavik return to-morrow, and I will give him the instructions you have suggested."

"That would be best. I will consider what further steps must be taken."

"Very well. Good night. And please leave by the back stairs."

"Don't I always, Excellency?" she said, and, bowing ironically, she departed in the footsteps of the Jhereg before her.

Chapter the Twenty-first

In which it is Shown That Nothing,
Even Those Words That His Imperial Majesty Deigns
to Let Fall Upon the Ears Of His Discreet,
Is Safe From the Attentions Of the Historian

IT IS NOW necessary, with our readers' kind indulgence, to direct our attention toward someone who, though we have perhaps neglected him, in no wise deserves neglect, because of his role in history in general and our history in particular: that is, the Emperor Tortaalik I.

Now, at this time, that is, the beginning of the Eighteenth Cycle, Tortaalik was still a young man, with the fine fair hair of his House above eyes of which the sharpest critic could have asked that they be only a little rounder, and perhaps a shade less pale. His nose was small and straight, the nostrils having a tendency to flare when he was angry. His skin, of which he took great care, was of an agreeable bronze color and as smooth as a maiden's. His character in the early part of his reign was marked by the wild impetuosities of youth, tempered by the careful training he had received by his chief tutor, Master Yon, by whom he had been inculcated with a strict sense of responsibility. It was, in fact, the constant battle between these two tendencies—the excited young man who wanted nothing more than to be an Emperor who would be remembered by history, and the responsible gentleman who feared the excesses demanded by his own character—it was the battle between these factors, we say, that was the particular mark of his administration.

The result of this conflict was, just at this time, to find the court in turmoil. That is, the several counselors of the Emperor (those to whom he looked for guidance) were always embroiled with his several favorites (those to whom he looked for amusement). The reign, which had begun so auspiciously with the successful defeat of the Carriage House Uprising, to which we have previously had the honor to refer, began to slide into the mire of court politics, where those who had to make decisions were always afraid that the favorites would, for their own reasons, influence His Majesty against their policy, and the favorites were afraid that the intendants and ministers would, through judicious hard work, replace them in the heart of the Emperor.

One result, we have already seen: Lanmarea was given the task of arresting Kathana e'Marish'Chala for a murder that scandalized Imperial society, when in fact Lanmarea was, by virtue of being Kathana's friend, less suited to the task than another might have been. A more important decision, that is, which line of the House of the Dragon would assume command of the Pepperfield garrison, had been delayed again and again by Tortaalik, who was swayed this way and that by the words of his Consort, his favorites, and his advisors, some of whom had the interests of the Empire at heart, others of whom wished to aid friends or accomplices.

Now, any such situation is unstable; something must either break or hold that will result in a new order, a new balance, a new stability. In this case, the crises occurred while our friends were about midway on their journey to Redface.

As we look upon the Emperor, he takes his ease in the

Seven Room (so named for its peculiar form in that it had seven walls), which was snug, comfortable, and perfectly suited to intimate conversations. Here we may also observe another individual of whom history does not tell us as much as, in fact, he deserves: that being His Discretion the Duke of Wellborn, Discreet of the Imperial family. Wellborn was of the House of the Athyra, but had no desire to determine the nature of our world, or, still less, to change it. His interest had always been the secrets and desires that lie within the hearts of men, which interest had led him, as a youth, to the difficult and tedious apprenticeship of the Mysteries of Confidence. While undertaking these studies, he had discovered the works of A'jo, he who had held the Confidence of Zerik II who plotted the ruin of A'jo's family, and Confided this in A'jo, who gave him solace but never betrayed him to the Dragonlords, who wanted nothing more than a pretext to take the Orb, and who also Confided in A'jo.

To the young man, this seemed such a fine and noble act that he became thoroughly enamored of the art, and began to study it for its own sake, with the single-mindedness of which only an Athyra is capable, until by his six hundredth year he had earned the post of Imperial Discreet, which he still held a hundred and fifty years later, when Tortaalik took the throne and maintained this embodiment of trustworthiness in his old position.

Physically, we know he was sturdier than is usual for an Athyra, and that his blue-grey eyes were sharp and stood out against his dark complexion. His size, we are told, somehow inspired trust as much as his manner; as if because of his strength he would be able to bear the burden of the heaviest conscience.

And who, we must ask, will ever have a heavier conscience than the Emperor, who must make decisions every day that, while they please many, also cast many down into ruin, despair, and death? And there is, moreover, the Orb, which never lets him forget what he has done, and why. The answer is: no one, unless, perhaps, the Discreet, who willingly takes onto himself these poniards of self-loathing which would otherwise be so great that the Emperor would soon be unable to act at all, or, if he could, like Vengli the Vicious, he would make such an Emperor that he would be remembered only for the horror of his reign.

When Tortaalik entered the room, the Orb circling his head emitting a worried tan color, the Duke was already there, though he had been waiting only a moment; for Tortaalik is renowned as one of the more punctual Emperors ever produced by the House of the Phoenix. His Majesty closed the door behind him, as the Duke rose and bowed deeply. Then, while His Majesty took a seat, his Discretion took up from next to him his wand of office, and swept it with slow precision about the room, including every corner, the floor, and the ceilings. This being done, he placed it in its holder in the center of the room, with the glass tip pointing to the heavens, and the copper bottom resting gently on the floor.

When all of these complex operations were completed, he sat facing the Emperor and said, "There are none listening to us, Your Majesty."

"Very well," said the Emperor, who took a breath, closed his eyes, and intoned, "My conscience stabs me, Your Discretion."

"I will bind the wounds, Sire."

These statements duly made, Tortaalik settled back in his chair and steepled his long, perfectly manicured fingers (which, at this point in history, he had never yet painted, save for a clear gloss). He said, "My friend, I am truly troubled."

"I am glad, Sire; for that proves that you do have a conscience, and, moreover, it allows me to be of service to you."

"Yes, Wellborn, I stand in need of comforting."

"If Your Majesty will tell me why, I will do what I can."

"I have spoken harshly with my wife."

"With the Consort? Upon what occasion, Sire?"

"Upon an occasion that I do not think, in fact, she was at fault."

"Go on, Sire; I am listening intently."

"This morning, as I came in to break my fast with her, she was in deep conversation with that Lyorn, Shaltre."

"And was that wrong of her?"

"He started when I entered, as if he had not wished to be seen there."

"Well, and she?"

"She smiled and wished me a pleasant morning."

"And what did you say?"

"I smiled at them, and wished them both a pleasant morning in turn, and inquired as to the subject of the conversation, that I might join it if it should prove to be one in which I had an interest."

"And you were told?"

"Why, I was told that they were only bidding each other good morning, and that the Count, that is, Shaltre, had come to breakfast to see me, that he might beg an audience to-day on some matters of importance—probably a means of gaining the territory of Sandyhome."

"Well? And you said?"

"I said I was indisposed to-day; that he could apply again to-morrow."

"But, is there something wrong in all of this?"

"I fear there is, Your Discretion. I was not indisposed, rather, I was in a bad temper at seeing them together, and therefore did not wish to grant Shaltre anything."

"You made, then, a decision on a caprice, is that your worry?"

"That is it exactly."

"Well, Sir, I think that, if your anger could not be placated in any other way, then merely postponing an audience by a day was not so bad. Did the Count pretend this interview was in some way urgent?"

"No, he did not."

"Then I feel you have not done wrongly."

"I am glad you think so."

"You are, nevertheless, Sire, worried about the attention Shaltre pays to your consort?"

"I am not worried; I am annoyed."

"Well, but then, it would seem she had done nothing out of the ordinary."

"No, but he had."

"Yet, Sire, why should your anger be directed at her?"

"Well, listen to this."

"I am listening, Sire."

"In the afternoon, after conferring with Lytra and Windhome on the state of the uprising in the western duchies—"

"Your pardon, Sire, but I thought the uprising had been put down."

"Well, it has, but there are still garrisons there, and there has been a certain amount of damage done, and it is necessary to make the ore begin to flow once more; hence, we conferred."

"I understand now, Sire."

"Then I continue. After this conference, the thought came to me that it would be pleasant to take an hour in the Lower Baths. You are familiar with these, are you not, Duke?"

"I am, sire; they are natural alkaline baths, where hot water flows from the mouths of marble statues built in the likenesses of a Phoenix, a Dragon, a Dzur, and a Lyorn."

"Yes, that is it exactly. Then you know as well the Bath of Renewal?"

"I do, Sire, and here is the proof: it is in an alcove that is set off from the rest of the baths, and it is surrounded by ferns, where the water is even hotter, the alkali stronger, and the springs flow from directly beneath the bath."

"Well, that is where I went. I will now tell you what I discovered."

"I am anxious for Your Majesty to do so."

"I discovered Noima, that is, the Consort, in the bath, alone with—"

"With Shaltre?"

"No, Wellborn, with a certain Phoenix, whose name is Allistar, the Duke of Threewalls, and who is moreover, my cousin."

"Ah. And what was his reaction when you appeared, Your Majesty?"

"Duke, he seemed positively guilty, or I am no judge of men."

"Well, and she?"

"She was innocence itself, and pretended pleasure in seeing me."

"Well, Sire, and what did you do?"

"I sent him away, Duke, with the instructions that he ought not to return to the Palace until to-morrow."

"You banished him, then?"

"I did."

"But only for a day?"

"Exactly."

"But then, Sire, once more—"

"I am not yet done, Duke."

"Very well."

"This evening, just as I was repairing to my chambers to put on my evening dress, I thought to visit Her Majesty to ask if she wished to dine with me."

"And then, Sire?"

"There, in her very room, was the Dragon Heir, Adron e'Kieron, who seemed deep in discussion with her. The Heir, mark you, who I did not know had come to the city, and yet he involved himself with Her Majesty without so much as informing me of his presence."

"Were they alone?"

"Except for her maids of honor, entirely."

"Well, did he also appear guilty?"

"If not guilty, then startled."

"And she, Your Majesty?"

"A little surprised, that is all."

"Well, and what did you do?"

"I had become vexed, Duke, and my temper took control."

"You know, Sire, that is never good."

"It is less than ever in this case."

"Well, what did you do?"

"I asked the Prince what his business might be in the city."

"And what answer did he make, Sire?"

"He said his visit was occasioned by the length of time that had passed since he had seen the city, and that he missed it, and wished to spend some little time here, and moreover, he wished to report to me a worrisome build-up of Easterners near the Pepperfields."

"Well, that does not seem to be much of an answer, Your Majesty."

"I'm glad you think so, Wellborn, because I, well, I had the same thought."

"And what did you do then?"

"I informed His Highness that it was wrong of him to neglect his estates at this time; that he was very close to Pepperfield, which stood in danger of invasion, and that I counted on him to keep his own lands secure."

"What? You sent him away?"

"I confess it, Your Discretion. Did I do wrong?"

"Yes and no, Your Majesty."

"How, yes and no?"

"It may be that sending someone away was the right thing to do, but perhaps you have ill-chosen the culprit."

"What? Surely you do not propose that I send away Her Majesty the Consort?"

"No, I do not."

"Well then, who?"

"Will Your Majesty permit me to put to him a question?"

"Your Discretion may ask me nine."

"Very well. Tell me, Sire, if this is a new problem; that

is, one which has only to-day begun to prey upon your thoughts."

"It is not, Duke. In all truth, I have been growing more and more unhappy with respect to Noima, that is, with respect to the Consort, for some time now."

"Then why has Your Majesty only just now brought the problem to my attention?"

"Well, it has become worse."

"I beg to point out to Your Majesty that that is not an answer."

"Well then, because I thought my feelings were ignoble, unworthy, and had no foundation in fact."

"But then, all the more reason to come to me with them, Sire."

"That is true, Wellborn; you are right."

"But it is nevertheless true that this unhappiness has been growing, Sire?"

"It is true, my dear Wellborn."

"And does it seem that it is now even disrupting the functioning of the court, that is, of the Empire?"

"You have understood exactly."

"Then, do you think there could be a plan at work?"

"How, a plan? Against me? On the part of the Consort? Duke, I nearly think you go too far."

"Not at all, Sire. I beg leave to point out that it was you who suggested the plan be on the part of the Consort."

"Well, who else could it be?"

"Sire, have you ever seen a man implicated in a crime?"

"I nearly think so, Wellborn. Every day, it seems, there is another crime against someone so important that I am required to make judgment."

"Well, and has Your Majesty ever seen a man implicate himself?"

"On purpose? No, that I have never seen."

"But then, has Your Majesty ever seen one man implicate another?"

"I think I already said so."

"But then, is it not your judgement that, if one man

may implicate another, this does not constitute proof that the crime has been done?"

"It seems you are saying, Duke, that someone is attempting to implicate Noima, with the purpose of disrupting the court."

"I think the possibility should be considered, Sire."

"But with what aim, Your Discretion?"

"Oh, as to that, Sire, I have no idea."

"But come, what makes you think so?"

"Sire, to answer that, I must ask you still more questions."

"You may do so then, Duke; for you know the questions you ask always serve to answer many that I have not thought to ask myself."

"That is my purpose, Sire; I am glad that I do not fail in all cases."

"Well, begin with these questions, then."

"Very well, I will begin in this way: how many times have you broken your fast with the Consort, as you proposed to do this morning?"

"Only twice before."

"So, such a thing is unusual?"

"Well, yes. Is that wrong of me? Tell me the truth."

"In itself, no."

"But then?"

"Attend me, Sire."

"I am doing so."

"How is it that you decided to breakfast with Her Majesty this morning?"

"How? Explain what you mean."

"I mean to say, Sire, what prompted the idea?"

"Well, why should something have prompted it?"

"Because you have only done so twice before; why, then today?"

"Well, I don't know."

"Try to recall, Sire."

"I am trying, Wellborn, and I cannot."

"Well then, what prompted your decision to visit the baths?"

"Oh, that is easy; I do so often."

"Well, and the Bath of Renewal?"

"No, that rarely."

"Then, why today?"

"Do you suggest a spell had been put on me? Then what of the Orb?"

"A spell—perhaps, but not one the Orb can detect."

"Explain yourself, Wellborn."

"First, can Your Majesty tell me why you picked today to go to the Bath of Renewal?"

"Because I thought that I felt tired."

"You thought so?"

"Well, Lord Garland thought I seemed so."

"Ah!"

"Excuse me, but you say, 'ah.' "

"Well, and if I do, Sire?"

"I wish to know your thoughts."

"Your Majesty will soon know them. But first—"

"What, more questions?"

"Only this one: what gave you the notion to dine with Her Majesty this evening?"

"I can answer that, and easily."

"Well, do so, then."

"I will. It was because my attempt to breakfast with her had failed in such an awkward manner."

"So you hoped that dining together would make up for it?"

"Such was my idea."

"It was well thought, Sire."

"I cannot take credit for it."

"Who, then?"

"My advisor, Lord Garland."

"But then, it was he was also suggested that you looked tired, which caused you to visit the Bath of Renewal."

"Well, and?"

"That is all I wished to know, Sire."

"Now tell me—but wait, I have been struck with an idea."

"Tell me this idea, Sire; it is what I serve your Majesty to hear."

"It was also Lord Garland who wondered, this morning, what Her Majesty would be having for breakfast, and it was this that gave me the notion to eat in her company."

"Well, then, we see that all three cases have something in common."

"Yes, Lord Garland. But, do you think he knew—?"

"I think nothing, Sire. It is you who think, I only listen and ask questions."

"But why would he wish me to discover Her Majesty's capricious behavior?"

"Discover? You think, then, that this behavior is real, Your Majesty?"

"In truth, Duke, I no longer know. But, now that I think of it, this is not the first time Garland's ideas have led me toward suspicions of Her Majesty."

"Well, I hadn't thought it was, Sire."

"But then, is he trying to help me discover something? Or is he attempting to create a disharmony where there is no cause?"

"What do you know about him, Sire?"

"He is a Tsalmoth from the south."

"Very well."

"He is of good birth."

"Yes, and?"

"He is devoted to me."

"Ah, ah!"

"Come, you doubt it?"

"No, Sire, I merely question."

"No, no, Duke, you accuse him; say so at once."

"I accuse no one, Sire. That is not my way, as you well know. You have said that you felt unhappy about your treatment of Her Majesty the Consort. Together, we have looked for the causes of this treatment, and we have found Lord Garland."

"But, Your Discretion perceives that I do not know if Garland is using his subtle skills to show me what it is good for me to know, or attempting to harm me."

"Therefore, what should do you, Your Majesty?"

Tortaalik considered this question for a space of several moments, then he said, "It seems I must find out the truth."

"That is but just. And, what else?"

"Until I know the answer, I should send him away, so that he cannot do more harm; if he is innocent, he will be none the less welcome for having been away for a while."

"That would be well done. What else must you do?"

"What else?"

"Yes, Sire, what else?"

"Well, I do not know what else I should do."

"You do not?"

"I assure you I have no notion."

"Well, how does Your Majesty feel, now that we have spoken together?"

"In truth, Duke, little better than before. When I came to you, I was unhappy; now I am both unhappy and worried."

"But Sire, why are you unhappy?"

"Why? For just the reason I have given: first, I now fear a conspiracy to accomplish some unknown object, and second, just as before, I fear that I—ah."

"Well, Sire?"

"You think, then, that I must apologize to my lady wife?"

"Do you think so, Sire?"

"The notion is unattractive, Duke."

"What was it you told me last week day about unattractive notions?"

"That they seemed to be good indicators of the proper course."

"Well?"

"You are right as always, my dear friend. I shall apologize to Noima, and that directly. I shall also send notes to Shaltre and Threewalls, and I will re-call His Highness Lord Adron."

"Then is that all you wish of me, Sire?"

"For now it is, Wellborn. But I am certain I will see Your Discretion again, and that soon."

"Until then, Sire."

"Until then, Duke."

The interview complete, Wellborn took his wand from the stand as the Emperor left the room. Now, the Discreet's task being finished, there is little reason to follow him. We could, at this time, return to our friends as they cross the High Bridge over the Foamy River, but, excepting a few sights that are still available to any who wish to make the journey, there is little enough there. Instead, then, we shall follow His Imperial Majesty, who, for the sake of his conscience, is climbing the stairs which lead to the apartments of Noima, the Imperial Consort.

He found her in her apartments, surrounded by her maids of honor, and, as he rose to greet her, he paused to consider what her present state of mind might be, which will give us the opportunity to say two words about her who was the wife of the last Emperor before the Interregnum.

There still survive many oil portraits of her, and what is clear from them all was that she was a true child of the Phoenix; that is, her hair was that bright golden color that exists only in that House and among a few Dragonlords of the e'Kieron line; her haughty, wide-set eyes were colored a deep blue; her mouth was small with lips that usually pouted, giving her at all times the appearance of either being about to kiss or having just kissed whomever she looked at; the bones on her face were well-chiseled, almost Dzur-like in their fineness; her neck was graceful; her arms were models of smoothness and perfection, and ended in hands whose fingers were exquisitely long and graceful.

As to her character, it is well-reported that she did not

know which end of a sword to hold; that is, she had never any intention of standing to battle, hence she applied to those around her for protection. It is also undeniable that she was as surrounded by men willing to protect her as Count Brakko, in the famous ballad, was by women, and like Count Brakko, she spared no effort in her toilette or behavior to secure this attention; and there is no disagreement among historians that she received enough for any three women. It is not recorded that she took advantage of any of the offers for liaisons which she received as her due, but neither is it recorded that she was offended by these gentle suggestions. On the contrary, there are indications that she felt out of sorts on any day on which she was not forced to defend her virtue against at least two or three such requests.

Yet, we maintain that the Consort was not one of the true coquettes of her time. It is true she flirted, but it is nowhere recorded that she was ever cruel to those who fell under her sway, save with that cruelty which was necessary for a Consort who wished to maintain her virtue in the face of sieges, ambuscades, sorties, and pitched battles of all sorts. It was this virtue, in fact, that allowed her to remain calm and unblushing when, by chance or otherwise, His Majesty would discover her in close conversation with a gentleman of the court.

With this in mind, we may see at once that, upon hearing the announcement that His Majesty had deigned to enter her quarters, Noima stood respectfully but coolly and awaited his pleasure, showing no signs of embarrassment, but neither any sign of welcome.

"I bid you good evening, madam," he began.

"And a good evening to you, Sire. To what do I owe the honor of this visit?"

"Is it strange that I wish to see you, madam?"

"Strange? Perhaps not, Sire, yet I confess that I did not expect you."

"Well, am I less welcome for that?"

"Sire, you will, I hope, always be welcome here, whatever your purpose in coming."

"You pretend that I have a purpose, then?"

"Well, have you not?"

The Emperor sighed and dug his nails into the palms of his hands, for, now that he was there, he found it no easy matter to say what he had come to say. He cleared his throat, then, and said, "Well, madam, it is true; I have come here for a purpose."

"Should I, then, send my maids away?"

Tortaalik began to say yes, but then, looking at the pretty girls who stood around Noima with their faces bowed, he suddenly seemed to see Wellborn's countenance before his eyes, and he said, "No, let them stay, for it is only right that they hear what I have to tell you."

"What, Sire? You have something to tell me?" The expression on her face now resembled surprise and interest, with, indeed, some measure of anxiety.

"I have," said the Emperor.

"But tell me the, I beg of you, Sire, for you can see that I am frightened at your countenance."

"You have no need to be, madam."

"No need? Yet you seem so stern, Sire."

"Well, that is because I am wroth."

"Oh, Sire, in what way have I been so unfortunate as to incur your displeasure?"

"You have not, Noima; rather I am wroth at myself."

The Consort, on hearing him use her proper name, began to believe for the first time that she was not, in fact, about to be reprimanded before her ladies, a humiliation that would have stung a thousand times more than had it been delivered in private. Consequently, she began to breathe easier. "Well," she said, "but how can you be angry at yourself?"

"I have done something of which I am ashamed, madam, and I come here to beg your forgiveness for it."

"What? Your Majesty apologize to me? But, Sire, this is unheard of."

"Perhaps. It is nevertheless the case that I was wrong to speak harshly to you earlier to-day, and twice wrong to send Lord Adron away."

"Oh, but Sire—"

"Allow me to finish, madam. I say it was wrong, and there is no fault with you. I shall, to-morrow, send a message by post to Lord Adron and beg his forgiveness. That is all I have to say."

"Surely you go too far, Sire."

"Not the least in the world. And, that said, I will now retire. Unless—"

"Yes, Sire? Unless?"

"Unless, madam, you will permit to embrace you first."

"Ah, with pleasure, Sire. There."

"Then you forgive me, Noima."

"Oh, there is nothing to forgive your Majesty for; yet, if there were, you have surely earned forgiveness a thousand times over."

"Well then, madam, I retire the happiest of men, the happiest of husbands."

"And you take your leave of a loyal and devoted wife, Sire."

Tortaalik, who by this time really was happy and proud that he had done what he ought, bowed with pleasure and retired from the Consort's apartments, and went straightaway in search of Lord Garland.

Garland was never difficult to find, for if the Emperor always had his eye on the Empire, then Garland always had his eye on the Emperor. We know that he was a small and graceful man, with the sinewy legs and arms of the Tsalmoth, and we know he must have been better with a blade than some of his critics say, for while he was Tortaalik's favorite he fought some nine-and-twenty duels, and if he was not always victorious, he was never known to have taken a serious injury, and it is also known that, in a quarrel over certain looks the Emperor may or may not have given Jenicor e'Terics, he fought with the Marquis of Clawhills, himself a good blade, and that Garland laid the Marquis out stone dead in a single pass.

The Emperor, then, found this gentleman in one of the antechambers of Tortaalik's apartments, where he was engaged in playing dice with several other gentlemen of the court. The players rose and bowed to His Imperial Majesty, who answered only with a curt nod. He then made a sign that Garland should attend him and walked past the players into one of the lavish sitting rooms that made up his private area of the palace. Garland made haste to give his spot up to one of the gentlemen who were unengaged, and followed his liege.

He found the Emperor standing, with one hand resting on a black marble desk, the other on a shelf of folios. Garland gave His Majesty a courtesy and awaited his words.

"Lord Garland," said His Majesty, "bide a moment." Tortaalik then sat at his desk, and found parchment, a quill, ink and blotter, and, with his own hand, composed a note, which he sealed with the Imperial arms, and again with his personal signet. He then addressed the envelope and handed it to Garland, who took it, looked at the address, and could not keep an expression of surprise from crossing his countenance.

"Your Majesty, what does this mean?"

Tortaalik, still sitting at the desk, gazed up the Tsalmoth and said, "Lord Garland, it nearly seems you question me."

Garland seemed almost to choke, but he stammered out an apology, saying, "Have I somehow been so unfortunate as to displease Your Majesty?"

"I don't say that you have."

"But—"

"Hold your peace, Garland."

The Tsalmoth bowed. The Emperor continued, "The note, as you can see, is addressed to His Highness Lord Adron e'Kieron. It contains an apology I feel obligated to send him, because I so unjustly sent him away today. Do you understand, Lord Garland?"

"Sire, I—"

"You will deliver that message, personally."

"I . . . when am I to set out, Sire?"

"At once."

"Sire, it is a journey of more than a few days by carriage, and I must prepare."

"You may use the post horses. Here is a draft on the treasury for two hundred orbs, which should see you there and back."

"Still, Sire, I must beg of you still some time to prepare for the journey."

"Very well, Garland; you may postpone your departure until to-morrow morning."

"I obey, Sire. Will that be all?"

"Yes." He made a dismissing gesture, at which time Garland bowed low and backed out of the room.

We will now, with our readers' kind permission, leave the Emperor, who is, at any rate, going to do no more than finish some correspondence and then sleep; and follow Lord Garland, who is climbing up several flights of stairs and arriving in an unfurnished tower room, the very one, in fact, in which we were first introduced to the Athyra called Seodra. It should not, then, come as a complete surprise if we find, upon entering this chamber in Garland's illustrious company, that Seodra is already there.

"You have something to communicate to me, Lord Garland?"

The Tsalmoth evidently feared the Athyra, for he was able to maintain his composure only with some difficulty. He did not speak, but instead handed to her the envelope he had lately been given. Seodra took it into her withered hands and studied it, then said, "What does this mean, Lord Garland?"

"I have been sent to bring this to Lord Adron; His Majesty has done me the honor to inform me that it contains an apology."

"An apology?"

"Yes, your ladyship."

"For what?"

"His Majesty regrets that he sent Lord Adron away this morning."

"How, regrets?"

"He changed his mind about the Consort's conduct."

"That is apparent. But, why is he causing you deliver it? You are neither courier nor diplomatist."

"I fear His Majesty is angry with me, and this is a punishment."

"Then you have been discovered, haven't you?"

Garland swallowed with some difficulty, and kept his eyes on the floor. "Your ladyship—"

"Well? You *have* been discovered, haven't you?"

"I—"

"You are a fool, and, moreover, you are clumsy."

"I followed your orders, ladyship. I did the best—"

"Be silent. It is clear that you have bungled, or His Majesty would not have suspected what you were doing; and it seems certain that he does suspect, if he doesn't know it for a fact."

"What must be done now, your ladyship?"

"Well, have you not been given an order by His Majesty?"

"Yes, your ladyship."

"Then you must carry it out. When are you to leave?"

"To-morrow morning, your ladyship."

"Very well. You will do so, and, moreover, you will make such speed as no one has ever made before. Such is your zeal to carry out His Majesty's orders, that you will, in fact, arrive before Lord Adron, who has a day's start on you."

"Very well, your ladyship. What shall I do when I'm there?"

"You perceive that I am writing something?"

"I do, your ladyship."

"Well, I am writing three names, and locations where you can meet those to whom the names belong, and passwords with which to identify yourself. You are to memorize all of these things before you leave."

"I will do so."

"You will reach one or more of these people, and make certain arrangements with them."

"Yes, your ladyship."

"These arrangements regard the Tiassa and his friends, of whom we have spoken before. Do you understand?"

"Yes, your ladyship. Will they do as I say?"

"They will, if you are convincing. Here, this may help you to be convincing."

"What is it?"

"The seal of Lord Adron e'Kieron."

"The seal—! But how did your ladyship come to possess it?"

"That is not your concern, Garland. I have means, you need know no more than that."

"Very well, I will use the seal as necessary."

"When you have used it, you will return it to him, explaining that it was found in the apartments he used."

"I will do so."

She reached into the folds of her robe and emerged with a copper disk filled with peculiar engravings. "Do you know what this is, Garland?"

"No, but I hope your ladyship will tell me."

"I will. If you think about me, and begin speaking into it—"

"Well?"

"Well, I will answer you."

"Sorcery, your ladyship?"

"Exactly, Garland. Does that frighten you?"

"No, your ladyship."

"You mean to say, I frighten you more."

"Yes, your ladyship."

"That is wise, Garland. Well, then, when you have

reached Lord Adron, use it to speak with me. I may have more instructions for you then."

"I will not fail to do so, your ladyship."

"Good. Do you understand your instructions?"

"Memorize names, locations, passwords. Travel quickly. The Tiassa and his friends. The seal, to be used and returned. Deliver His Majesty's message. Communicate with you."

"Ah, apropos His Majesty's message—"

"Well?"

"As you are returning the seal, it may be that you will forget to deliver the message."

"Your ladyship!"

"We will see. If you forget, then, well, you can remember later, and no harm will come of it. I will let you know my decision on this when you are there."

"I will obey, your ladyship."

"Yes. Now get out of my sight."

Lord Garland did not need to be told twice; he bowed to Seodra and fairly fled the room, returning to his own apartments to prepare for the next day's departure. While he did this, Seodra sat for a while, considering what needed to be done, then summoned her servant and instructed him to find Lord Shaltre, who dwelt near His Majesty's apartments, and beg him to return to pay a visit.

In due time, the Lyorn was announced. Seodra stood for him. "Well?" he said. "To what do I owe the honor of this request for an interview?"

"It is to this, Count," said Seodra. "I have been thinking."

"Well, I have been known to do the same, from time to time. To what have your thoughts led you?"

"They have led me a conclusion, Count, respecting yourself."

"Well?"

"It has to do with history."

"Oh, I have never studied history."

"It might profit you to do so, Count."

"In what way?"

"You might learn of a certain Lyorn advisor, who, discredited, betrayed another Lyorn, such that the latter had become, in turn, discredited, and, moreover, his family was ruined, and he ended by blowing his head off with a flash-stone."

Shaltre took a moment to recover his composure, but he did so, then made a gesture of indifference. "An interesting story, your ladyship, but I fail to see how it concerns you or me."

"You pretend, then, that you know nothing of this?"

"I have never heard of such a thing. No doubt the survivors of the discredited Lyorn have avenged him."

"Not at all, for his family were all destroyed; the Lyorn was very thorough."

"And yet, if any in the House knew of this—"

"None of his House do. Besides, who could challenge him except a warrior? And you must know better than I, Count, that no Lyorn warrior may issue a challenge to any of his House who has not also had that special training."

"Well, that is true."

"Unless it is a case of treason."

"Which, according to your story, this was not."

"It very nearly was."

"How, giving poor advice?"

"There are times when giving poor advice can be very nearly treasonous, Count."

The Lyorn shrugged: a gesture, in fact, much like one Aerich was fond of. Then he said, "Perhaps it was close, your ladyship, but I doubt it was sufficiently close for one of my House; we are sticklers for such things. Besides, if, as you said, his family is dead, and no one else knows of it, this Lyorn, whoever he may be, is in no danger."

"And, if his family is not dead?"

"Impossible."

"I beg your pardon, Count, but it would appear that you do know of the incident after all."

Shaltre flushed, then adjusted his robes and said, "I was assuming, since you say he was thorough—"

"And it may be that the incident is known."

"By whom?"

"By His Highness Adron e'Kieron, Dragon Heir to the Throne."

"Adron? He knows, you say?"

"He knows of the incident, but, as of now, none of the names."

"How is this possible?"

"He was concerned in the battle that was won, and in the battle that was lost. He mislikes losing battles; therefore, upon losing the one, he investigated."

"Well, and—?"

"He was not able to penetrate the secret; he was, however, able to come close."

Shaltre shifted uncomfortably. "I fail to see how any of this concerns me."

"You think it does not?"

"At least, I don't see how it does."

"Very well, then let us turn to another subject."

"On the contrary, we should continue to discuss this until we have arrived at a conclusion."

"How, if it doesn't concern you?"

"I—that is, very well, then. I am at your service. What do you wish to discuss?"

"The successor to the late Marquis of Pepperfield."

"Well? What about it? The successor has not been selected."

"That is true. The e'Lanya line is interested."

"That I know."

"There is another person, also, who wants the post."

"That being?"

"Adron e'Kieron."

"Well, I hope that whoever is given the post is adequate."

"Are you aware, Count, that the Marquisate of Pepperfield is a special position?"

"Indeed yes; it is appointed specially by the Emperor."

"It is a position of great trust, Count."

"Yes, and great responsibility, due to the number of invasions by Easterners which have occurred there."

"Therefore, the Marquis is, by tradition, granted certain rights that few others nobles are ever given."

"Such as?"

"The right to directly interrogate the Orb, in matters of history."

"Ah."

"It is necessary, for strategic reasons—"

"I understand, your ladyship."

"I have reasons for wishing the e'Lanya line to be given this command."

"Well, I will support you in this."

"Support is one thing; now is the time for action."

"I am not very active by nature."

"No, but you have the ear of the Emperor, Count."

"Well, I have that honor."

"Unless you are in disgrace."

"An hour ago I was; now I am not."

"How is this?"

"It is unimportant."

"Very well. It is true, then, that if you were to ask His Majesty to have certain persons arrested, he would be likely to do so."

"Persons like His Highness Adron e'Kieron? It is not likely."

"It is not of His Highness that I am speaking."

"Well, then?"

"Certain individuals who are meddling in affairs that do not concern them, and who, if left to their own devices, might well bring about the triumph of the e'Kieron line."

"Well, I understand," said the Count.

"That is well."

"If you will give me their names, I will ask His Majesty to arrest them."

"You must do more than that, Count."

"Oh?"

"They are far from here; in fact, they are on their way now to visit Castle Redface, the home of Lord Adron."

Shaltre started. "But then, we are lost."

"Not in the least, for they are traveling slowly, and you may be able to get there before them, or even a little after, which would be all right, I think."

"And then?"

"Lord Garland will be on his way at first light; he will help you."

"Help me?"

"You must do what is necessary."

"I am not a fighter."

"You need not be; Lord Adron has many troops."

"How, Lord Adron? What would cause him to help me in this?"

"A few words from His Majesty commanding his co-operation."

"His Majesty has retired for the night; I will not be able to see him until to-morrow."

"That's as it must be. Speed, as you know, is everything. You must prevail upon His Majesty to cause Lord Adron to cooperate with you, and then—"

"I must have these persons arrested."

"That may not be sufficient; those who are arrested can be pardoned; and, even condemned, they may still speak."

"Well, I understand. I will do what is necessary."

"Very well, then, Count. I am pleased we understand each other."

"As am I, your ladyship."

While Count Shaltre prepares to visit His Majesty in the morning, with the intention of setting out immediately thereafter, we will return to those four intrepid

Guardsmen to whose actions this narrative is devoted, in the hopes that our absence from them has been sufficiently brief that our readers will not have lost patience, and will furthermore trust that this digression, as it may have seemed, was in fact necessary if we are, by and by, to bring our history to a satisfying and elegant conclusion.

Chapter the Twenty-second

In Which it is Shown That Not Only
Historians Have Prying Ears

FROM THE GATE of the Flags our friends had traveled down the mountain to the small town of Everdim where they took their rest, and proceeded early the next morning, at a good yet not frantic pace, through the Flowering Valley, crossing the Yendi River at Flatspot about noon of the following day, after which they began the trek through the *pushta*—that uncultivated, dry grassland around the edges of the desert of Suntra. We should say that this journey was made at the worst time of the year, that is, in the full heat of summer, but as the Guardsmen were not in an especial hurry, they stopped often during the worst of the heat and took their ease in the hostels of many of the villages on the *pushta*. At last they took the barge across the Adrilankha River at Guilrock Crossing and began to make their way slowly uphill again, as, even here, they were in the lap, as it were, of the Eastern Mountains where lay both their ostensible and their true destination. They continued in this manner—that is, making an easy pace and enjoying the journey—until they reached the mountain called Bli'aard and city of Bengloarafurd, which was less than a day's ride from the mountain hold of the Redface, the castle and fortress of Adron e'Kieron.

Tazendra, who had begun the journey in a reflective mood, had apparently adopted Khaavren's advice and by this time seemed to be enjoying herself thoroughly, ordering her lackey, Mica, about in fine style: which lackey, we should add, appeared to enjoy receiving the orders as much as Tazendra enjoyed giving them. He would bring wine, sharpen blades, tend the horses, serve meals, prepare bedding, and perform a thousand other tasks that the companions had been accustomed to perform by themselves and were delighted to be relieved of. Between these orders, Tazendra would banter loudly with Uttrik, disputing the aesthetics of the scenery or the nature of the roads.

Pel made the journey with his sharp eyes flashing here and there, as if he were committing everything he saw to memory; from time to time he would pause, staring, apparently, at some person or village or tree that seemed to have for him some meaning none of the others could fathom.

Uttrik, as we have said, was developing a companionable fondness for Tazendra, and seemed to be playing the game of seeing how far he could bait her without actually making her angry. He would dispute her opinions about anything she brought up, and, if she appeared about to become angry, he would immediately begin to laugh, which seemed to have the effect of removing whatever warmth had begun to build in her.

Aerich sat easily on his Cramerie gelding, taking in the sights around him, and listening to the speech of his companions, without either losing his good humor or appearing to even notice what was going on around him; that is, he was lost in his own thoughts.

Khaavren had at first enjoyed the journey a great deal, but as they drew closer to the mountains, worries seemed to hang over him until, by the time they reached the hostel, he was positively frowning, a fact which Aerich, who had become very fond of the young Tiassa, could not help noticing.

Notwithstanding that it was early in the day when they came to Bengloarafurd, they nevertheless found an inn whose sign read, in simple lettering, "The Painted Sign," and there they found rooms for the day and the night. It is worth mentioning here that Bengloarafurd lay against an unusually shallow portion of the Climbing River, one of the longest, fastest, and deepest of the streams with which the Eastern Mountains in general, and Mount Bli'aard in particular, are so abundantly supplied.

The first to discover the place were, according to legend, advance scouts of the House of the Dragon in the Fourth Cycle, who were in the vanguard of the Imperial Army which was anxious to drive the Easterners back beyond the mountains in hopes of reducing the raids to which the eastern boundaries were then being subjected. They followed the Climbing River down from the North, and found a shallow spot where there lived an independent tribe of Serioli.

What followed was ten years of almost constant war between the Dragonlords of the Empire and the Easterners, during which the Easterners occupied the area and fought from the surrounding mountains. The Serioli, who departed the area to avoid any of the unfortunate incidents that war can produce, left only the name for the place, which was "Ben," meaning "ford" in their language. The Easterners called the place "Ben Ford," or, in the Eastern tongue, "Ben gazlo."

After ten years of fierce battle, the Imperial Army won a great victory on the spot, driving the Easterners well back into the mountains. The Dragonlords who had found the place, then, began calling it "Bengazlo Ford." The Dragons, wishing to waste as little time on speech as possible, shortened this to Benglo Ford, or, in the tongue of the Dragon, which was still in use at the time, "Benglo ara." Eventually, over the course of the millennia, the tongue of the Dragon fell out of use, and the North-western language gained preeminence, which rendered the location Bengloara Ford, which was eventually shortened to Bengloarafurd. The river crossing became the Bengloar-afurd Ford, which name it held until after the Interreg-num when the river was dredged and the Bengloarafurd Bridge was built. Should anyone be interested in finding this delightful city, it still stands, and the bridge still ap-pears with the name we have cited, but the city was re-named Troe after the engineer who built the bridge, either because the citizens were proud of their new landmark, or because the engineer's name was short.

But, more remarkable than the name is the fact the city—and we do not err in calling it a city, for even at the time of which we have the honor to write, it boasted a population of eleven thousands, more than twice its ele-vation measured in meters—more remarkable than the name, we say, is the fact that the city continued to thrive in a region devoid of ore, empty of timber, and barren of land for the raising of either grain or livestock, save for the few goats that could subsist on the scanty mountain grass. At the time of the reign of Kiva VI of the House of the Jhegaala, an Imperial representative asked the Speaker how the people managed to survive there, a question to which the Speaker responded by saying, "My lord, we grow rocks."

The truth, in fact, if less witty, is no less interesting. The people of these mountains have always fiercely guarded whatever independence they could wrest from the Empire, and have done so to such an extent that it became the custom to leave Imperial troops garrisoned nearby on the pretext that if the Easterners were not, at any given time, either invading or about to invade, then no doubt the local population was either involved in an uprising or preparing one; occasionally these things hap-pened together.

The result was that there grew up a friendship between

Easterner and human that has rarely been seen elsewhere; and so the people of Bengloarafurd survived on the produce of that friendship; which is to say, by smuggling in both directions. It is no accident that, to this very day, in order to achieve combat with a resident of the area (dueling is almost unknown there; the preference is for less formal violence) all that is necessary is to refer to an individual as a "tax-man," and swords will instantly be free of their scabbards.

From the city, then, we will pass on to the inn, which was founded near the beginning of the last Jhegaala Reign by an itinerant Tsalmoth scholar named Black who was fleeing from the fall of the Teckla Republic. He fell in love with the mountains, and with the people who lived there, so he thought to serve them by keeping them drunk, and himself by becoming rich on the trade of the mountain passes. He therefore procured a supply of wine and ale, and arranged for supplies of choice victuals, and opened his inn beneath a sign on which were written letters spelling out "Black's Public House."

After nearly starving for fifty years, it occurred to this worthy gentleman to ask one of the servants who was starving with him why he never received any travelers. "Because, master, no one who passes by knows this is an inn."

"But," said Black, in some confusion, "doesn't my sign say 'Public House'?"

"I don't know," said the servant; "I can't read."

"How, can't read?"

"No, my lord."

"But then, this is intolerable. What must I do?"

"I am willing to learn, master."

"No, no, idiot. How am I to gain patrons for this house?"

"Master, it is the custom to declare an inn by putting out a sign painted with some device, by which the house will be known."

The scholar left, shaking his head and muttering, and the next day returned with a sign on which could be seen letters spelling out, "The Painted Sign." This failed to bring about the needed improvement in his business, however, and the enterprise no doubt would have failed had he not had the good fortune to be captured by mountain brigands while he was returning for supplies. Black had never had any experience with brigands, nor had the brigands any experience with scholars, hence when they took the supplies of food destined for his inn, he, in all innocence, made out a bill and humbly presented it to the leader of the bandits.

At the first the bandit-chief laughed, then he saw that the bill, which was for a good supply of wine and smoked kethna, was, in fact, rather small. He said, "Come, you don't seem to require much for your food."

"How not? It is the same I am asking at my inn."

"What, you have an inn?"

"Indeed yes. Less than two leagues along this very road, where the road splits to pass by a rock shaped like a hawk's beak, and there to the right, you will pass it upon your right side."

"Well, I've seen the place. You say it is a public house?"

"It is, sir, and I assure you you would be most welcome there."

"And these are your prices?"

"Nearly. They are a trifle more, you perceive, if I must go to the expense of putting them on plates and paying a servant to bring them to table."

"But, well, here's your money, my friend, and I will no doubt see you again."

"It will be my pleasure to serve you as it has been my pleasure to-day."

In this way, word of the inn quickly spread, and when Black died, leaving the inn to his oldest son, whose name was Brown, the family had amassed a reasonable fortune and the inn was a landmark of the region.

It was here, then, that our friends came and found food, wine, stables for their horses, and rooms in which to rest themselves while they prepared for the final stage of the journey. Along with a few other travelers, they enjoyed the noon repast, which consisted of sausages roasted on a spit, and a broth made of fresh mountain mushrooms, bacon of kethna, and certain herbs which were grown in the yard of the hostel. At the end of the meal, the host caused to be delivered a large cake made of mulberries and rednuts, topped with boiled fruit and a cream made from goat's milk.

It happened that Khaavren had eaten more of the sausages than he should have, being unused to spicy mountain cooking (which was, moreover, influenced by proximity to the Easterners), whereas Aerich never ate sweets of any kind because he pretended they would ruin his teeth, in which he took more pride than in any other aspect of his personal appearance. Therefore, while the other guests of the inn settled down to attack this cake, which, be it understood, rested upon a platter that filled an entire table, Aerich took the opportunity to make a sign to Khaavren that he wished to speak with him privately.

They adjourned, then, from the common room and strolled arm in arm about the yard of the hostel, which was laid out with a stone garden on one side, a vegetable and herb garden on another, and a high stone wall in back (enclosing a second yard), with gates in the wall whereby one could reach the outbuildings, which consisted of a pair of commodes, the stables, and the gardener's house.

As they walked, Khaavren said, "You had something to communicate to me, my friend?"

"I have observed your countenance," said Aerich.

"Well, and?"

"You seem troubled."

"I? Not the least in the world."

"Well, you say I am deceived."

"Undoubtedly, good Aerich."

"So you have not been biting your lip, so that even now I perceive it is raw?"

Khaavren licked his lips, as if to hide with his tongue the work of his teeth. "Well—"

"And you have not been digging your fingernails into the palms of your hands, so that the gouges are clearly visible?"

Khaavren flushed and quickly turned his palms inward. "That is to say—"

"And you have not been emitting sighs, increasing in number over the last four days of our journey, so that Pel and I have begun to catch each other's glances just before you are about to give another one, so predictable have they become?"

Khaavren blushed deeply this time and said, "Is it true, have I been doing all that?"

"My word, I think so."

"Well, it is true that I am troubled in my mind."

"Then, if you wish, I will listen to your troubles, and counsel you as best I can."

"I know that I can find nowhere a friend as wise, nor even in a Discreet a gentleman so perfect."

"Then, will you tell me?"

"I will. But can you not guess?"

Aerich said, "Well, I think you are worried about what to do with regards to Baroness Kaluma."

"You have hit it exactly. I made a promise—"

"Ah! A promise."

"Yes."

"To a woman?"

"Yes, to a woman."

"To a lover?"

"Oh, as to that, well—"

"Yes?"

"I don't deny it."

"You should learn, my friend, to have a care with women, lest your mouth place you in a position from which your feet cannot extricate you, nor your hands free you, but which will leave your brain confused."

"But when one's heart is engaged—"

"Then you must take even more care, for where the heart is engaged, the mind is nowhere to be found."

"The damage is done, for I have made a promise."

"Yet you have also made an oath, and that to Captain G'aereth."

"I know," said Khaavren, giving forth such a sigh as the astute Lyorn had heard him make at the shortening intervals he had mentioned. "What, then, should I do?"

Aerich shook his head. "It is as bad as I thought," he murmured. Then, aloud, he said, "Well, let us go forward, and perhaps new counsel will present itself to us."

"It would be most welcome if it did," said Khaavren, and on this philosophical reflection they began to return to the inn and to their companions. They had, by this time, walked as far as the stone wall behind the hostel, when Khaavren held up his hand for Aerich to stop, while, with his other hand, he signaled him to avoid making any sounds. Aerich, who was never curious, gave a mute shrug and obeyed.

Had Khaavren actually been a tiassa—that is, the animal—this would have been one of those occasions on which his feline ears would have, first, pricked straight up, and then pointed toward the wall, for Khaavren had heard something that seemed to him to have the greatest significance. To be precise, he had heard someone speaking in very low tones; not so low, however that he had been unable to catch the words, which, in the harsh accents of the region, were, "They're all inside fattening themselves, so we can say what we like."

Certain errors, when we catch some unknown person making them, cry out to be corrected at once. For example, should we find someone who says, in a complacent tone of voice, that the House of the Teckla has never produced a composer of note, we should at once be forced to ask if this person has ever heard of G'hair of Clyferns who composed the Nine-Hour Symphony of the Model Sevens. Should we find someone who pretends that Serioli no longer live in the world, we should desire to take this person to Jawbone Mountain, and there introduce him to Jggo!f'tha the bone-dancer, and then ask him again. Should we encounter an Eastern witch who asserts the superiority of his art over the sorcery we receive from the Orb, we are inclined, peaceable as we normally are, to suggest this claim be tested at once.

Certain other errors, however, might inspire in us the desire to leave the perpetrator in ignorance. To accidentally overhear someone say that he cannot be overheard, and thus imply to the other party that it is safe to whisper secrets, seems to fall solidly into the second category. This, at any rate, was Khaavren's opinion, which is why he signaled Aerich as he did.

We return our attention then, to the place where Khaavren's was directed; that is to say, over the stone wall which separated the yard from the gardener's hutch. The second speaker, who was either a low-voiced woman or a high-voiced man, but, in either case, spoke with a purity of accent and pronunciation that showed him to be from the environs of Dragaera city, said, "There are five of them, then?"

"Five, yes, and a lackey."

"Well, that is not too many."

"No, not if they have no sorcery."

"Well, and if they do?"

"Then, my lord, they are many more than their numbers indicate."

The second speaker, of whom we can now say with confidence that he was masculine in character, said, "Well, if they are surprised, their sorcery will be of no help to them."

"That is true with regards to sorcery."

"Then that is all, is it not?"

"My lord, you have solved only one problem."

"You pretend there is another problem?"

"A severe one, my lord."

"Well? It is?"

"It is that we are forbidden to kill them, my lord."

"How, forbidden?"

"It was in the orders I received directly from the lady."

"Well then, my orders are from the other lady, the Athyra. You know who I mean, do you not?"

"I do."

"Well, and she has no such compunctions."

"Yet, my orders—"

"These mountains are deep, and high, and wild, and accidents can easily happen to strangers. If an accident were to happen, that is, if brigands, of which these mountains are full, were to fall upon these visitors; well, as long as the Dragon suspected nothing, there would be no reason why my generosity should fail, and no reason why any ill should come to you for it."

"My lord, I am not an assassin."

"No, merely an outlaw; and an outlaw with a price upon his head."

"I nearly think you threaten me, my lord."

"And if I do?"

"Then I beg you to remember that the mountains are deep, and high, and wild, and accidents can easily happen to strangers. And, moreover, I beg you to remember that I am an outlaw, with a price upon my head."

"You reason well, Baaro."

"Thank you, my lord; I think my head is tolerably long."

"But allow me to point out something you may have overlooked."

"Well, what is that, my lord?"

"You are only able to thrive in these mountains because of the good wishes of those who live here."

"Well, that is natural."

"And those who live here are loyal to Lord Adron."

"As am I, my lord."

"But suppose he were to set the people against you?"

"He would not do so."

"But suppose he did."

"Then I would be unable to survive."

"Well?"

"Well, I repeat, he will not do that. Nor would he involve himself in anything like assassination."

"It is not necessary that he involve himself, nor that he turn against you; it is only necessary that the people of these mountains think he has turned against you."

"Do you pretend, my lord, that you can convince these people of such a thing without his knowing about it?"

"Are you not aware, good Baaro, that Lord Adron is, even now, in Dragaera City, negotiating for control of Pepperfield, and thus has no way of knowing what is declared in his name?"

"Well, that is true. All that is necessary, then, is to convince the people of this mountain that—what is it you have there?"

"How, you don't recognize it?"

"It is Lord Adron's seal!"

"Precisely."

"By the gods! How did you come upon it?"

"That doesn't concern you. What matters is that I have it."

"Well, it is clear that you do."

"Moreover, I am willing to use it."

"I believe that you are."

"And I can use it to such an effect that everyone will believe that Lord Adron has turned against you, rather than making everyone believe that he has turned against those others."

"Yes, that is possible."

"You will, then, do as I say?"

"It seems I have no choice."

"Good. Then tell me your plan."

"The strangers will set off to-morrow morning."

"That is likely."

"Just before they reach the Fordway Road, which they must take if they are to get to the castle of Lord Adron, there is a place with a stand of sycamore on one side of the road, and a line of birches on the other."

"Very well."

"Well, my men will conceal themselves there, and we will fall upon them with spear and sword."

"How many men?"

"Thirty."

"That will be enough. What else?"

"Well, we will kill them all."

"Very well. Here is the gold."

"Thank you, your lordship."

"I hope, Baaro, that, notwithstanding your resistance to my mistress's wishes, you will hold no ill-will toward me for the means I have had to use to convince you."

"My lord, I assure you that I have the highest regard for you, and this gold removes any doubts I may have had."

"That is well. I will see you again after your mission is completed, and you will receive a like amount."

"You are generous."

"The Athyra whom I serve is generous. Never forget that."

"I never shall."

"That is all, then, Baaro."

"Until to-morrow, your lordship."

Khaavren touched Aerich's shoulder at this point and made a sign that they should return to the inn, which they did, finding their companions just as they had left them, save that less of the cake was on the table. Khaavren and Aerich approached the table and bowed in a pleasant manner to all assembled (we must recall that, in addition to their companions, there were a few additional travelers there), and indicated by signs that they wished their friends to join them outside, after which signs being given and acknowledged, Khaavren and Aerich excused themselves and went back out of doors, where they awaited their companions.

Chapter the Twenty-third

In Which the Art
Of the Ambuscade is Discussed
And Examples Provided

THE FIRST TO arrive was Pel. He raised his eyebrows at Aerich, who shook his head slightly to indicate that the moment for speech had not yet arrived. Uttrik followed after a moment, then Tazendra and Mica. "Well?" said Tazendra.

"This way," said Khaavren, assuming command of the proceedings as if born to lead. He pointed up the road in the direction they were to proceed the next day, toward a place where a thick pile of stone had been built up, as if to prevent the slope of the mountain from covering the road with rocks and mud.

"Is there, then, something to see this way?" said Tazendra.

"No," said Khaavren, "but there is something to talk about."

"But then, why can't we talk in the inn, where, I must tell you, I was most comfortably stationed?"

"Because, my friend, it would be too easy for us to be overheard there."

"It is remarkable," said Aerich, "how well sound carries in these mountains."

"Well, then," persisted Tazendra, who, notwithstanding the extreme justice of Khaavren's remarks, was still annoyed at having to leave the inn, "do you pretend sound will carry less well here, along this road, than in the inn?"

"If you would be so good as to send Mica around to keep an eye and an ear open for observers, I should think we may be able to safely communicate some matters of importance."

"I will do so then," said Tazendra, and indicated to Mica that he should be about his task. The worthy Teckla nodded in a businesslike way and, still holding his barstool, began scouring the area.

After a moment, Pel said in a very quiet voice, "Come, what have you to tell us?"

"We are most anxious to hear," said Uttrik.

"I will tell you then," said Khaavren.

"What is it?" said Pel.

"Just this," said Khaavren. "Aerich and I were absent when the cake was eaten."

"Well," said Tazendra. "We knew this. In fact, I even remarked upon it, did I not, Sir Uttrik?"

"You did," said the Dragonlord.

Khaavren continued, "We took a walk behind the inn, where there is a stone path about several small clear-water pools, which it would do you good to look into, should you wish to reflect upon the infinite."

"Oh," said Tazendra, "I am done with reflecting."

"Well, but, we were not."

"And what did this reflection lead to?"

"Oh, that is unimportant. What is important, was what we heard while we were reflecting."

"Oh, you heard something?"

"That is to say, overheard."

"And what is it that you overheard?" asked Pel mildly.

Khaavren quickly described the conversation, as nearly word for word as he could, which was very nearly indeed, for he had a large head, and, as is well known, a large head gives greater capacity for memory. As he was finishing, Mica appeared and bowed to the company, "Gentlemen," he said, "I have made three circuits of the area, at widening intervals. At one time I thought I heard a listener, but a closer examination proved it to be a norska, who seemed as anxious about my intentions as I was about hers."

"Very well, Mica. You may remain here," said Tazendra.

"But then," said Uttrik, "where is this ambuscade to take place?"

"Ambuscade?" said Mica.

"Hush," said Tazendra.

"Along this very road, if I understood correctly," said Khaavren.

"That was my understanding, as well," as Aerich. "Perhaps half a league further along."

"What then ought we to do?" said Pel.

"Well, I," said Tazendra, "think we should wait above the point of the ambuscade until we find these brigands, and then carry off our own ambuscade."

"Shame," said Aerich. "A surprise attack?"

"Well," said Khaavren, "I am not far from agreeing with Tazendra. Consider that we are five against thirty, and that, furthermore, they intended to attack us in exactly that manner."

"And yet—" said Aerich.

"My dear friend," said Pel, "consider that we are dealing with brigands, not gentlemen."

"That is true," said Aerich. "Nevertheless—"

"And consider further that, if we do not, we must either admit that we have failed in our mission, which would suit my temperament but poorly, or else walk into an ambuscade, which would have results as least equally unsatisfactory, since I declare to you that I prize my skin nearly as highly as I prize success."

"Well, we could go behind them, and proceed on to the castle."

"And leave an enemy behind us?" said Uttrik.

Aerich sighed. "Very well, then. Have you a plan of battle?"

"I have one," said Uttrik.

"Tell it," said the others.

"Here it is, then. We must leave the inn as planned in the morning, only we must take care to depart in a very slow manner."

"For what reason?" said Tazendra.

"I will tell you. There is no doubt that, when we set off, there will be someone to watch us, and to inform the ambuscade that we will reach it soon. It will be good if they are told that we are not moving in a great hurry."

"And why is that, my lord?" asked Pel with the greatest courtesy.

"Because, then, you perceive, it will not be deemed suspicious if we take a great deal of time to get there."

"Well," said Tazendra, "if we are moving slowly, then it is only natural that we will not get there as soon as if we trotted our horses."

"Exactly," said Uttrik.

"That is well thought out," said Khaavren.

"But it would seem," said Tazendra, "that we must nevertheless reach the ambuscade, and if we do so slower—"

"Tazendra," said Aerich gravely, "does not comprehend."

"Well, this is true," said Tazendra.

"We intend," said Pel, "to circle behind the ambuscade. Using Uttrik's plan, with which I am in full agreement"—here he bowed to the Dragonlord, who returned the courtesy—"we will not alert them needlessly."

"Shall we divide our forces?" said Khaavren.

"Well, Tazendra, have you had the chance to charge the flash-stone you used so effectually before?"

"No, I have not had the opportunity."

"In that case—"

"Excuse me," said Pel, "but you might go on to ask if any of the rest of us have such devices."

"What? More of them?"

"Well, if one is the friend of a sorcerer"—here he bowed to Tazendra—"then it is practically the same as if one could prepare the rocks by one's self."

"So, then, how many of these famous devices are there?"

"Three, my lord," said Pel. "And mine is a very heavy load indeed, such that I might knock four of the enemy off their horses."

"Well, that one, and two others?"

"It is as I've said, my lord."

"Then do you and Tazendra take the portion of the road above them, and Khaavren, Aerich, and I will secure the road below them."

"And the signal?" said Tazendra.

"You, Pel, when you judge the time is right, will simply discharge your flash-stone at the largest group of them, whereupon we will all attack."

"Agreed," said Pel.

"And mind, we will be attacking through the woods, and using flash-stones, wherefore, if we make sufficient noise, they may believe there are more of us, and break off the engagement."

"Nevertheless," said Khaavren, frowning, "there are, to be sure, thirty of them."

"Well, yes," said Uttrik. "And?"

"I still wonder how five of us can defeat thirty of the enemy."

"Well, perhaps we will not defeat them," said Uttrik.

"But it will be a good battle," said Tazendra.

"Of that, there can be little doubt," said Pel, who smiled grimly and rested his hand upon his sword. With this they returned to the inn, for the hour had grown late as they spoke.

The Empress Undauntra I, shortly before the end of the War of the Wine Cups, that is, on the day of the battle that won for her the Orb, made the following observation as she inspected the army: "I can always tell who has never seen battle before."

A certain subaltern, in the letters from which we know the story, overheard, and asked if it was because they seemed nervous. "No," she snapped, "anyone in his right mind is nervous before a battle."

"Well then, is it that they are more eager than those of more experience?"

"In my army, everyone is eager for battle."

"Then tell me, my lady, how you can tell?"

"Because they look more tired than the rest."

No matter how many duels one has fought, or how many skirmishes of the type that arrive unexpectedly, there is still, on the even of one's first battle, a feeling unlike any other. To rest one's head upon the pillow saying to one's self, "This may be last time I sleep in this life," or to wonder, each time one's eyes begin to close, "Will I still be alive and whole at this time to-morrow?" is enough to drive any notion of sleep far into the nether reaches of possibility.

It is to Khaavren's credit that on this, the night before his first real battle, he managed at last to fall asleep some four hours before the time the host had agreed to wake them with hot, sweet klava laden with honey and goat's milk.

He awoke then, if not fully refreshed, at least, we say to his credit, eager enough to make up for the deficiency, which is to say, fully alert, and, though nervous, also cool-headed and ready for battle.

It was precisely half past the hour of eight in the morning when Khaavren reached the top of the stairs, and encountered Tazendra and Mica. The latter had a look of some worry upon his face, while the former's eyes fairly gleamed as only a Dzurlord's will when about enter a battle in which she is outnumbered. At the bottom of the stairs they met Aerich, who was sitting calmly at a table staring out the window. Uttrik was outside seeing to the horses, and Pel came down the stairs only a moment later. They settled up with the host and, on the advice of Uttrik, the most seasoned campaigner among them, took extra care to see to their saddles and gear, and made certain that their flash-stones were near at hand, and that their blades were loose and ready.

"Well then, come, gentlemen," said Uttrik.

"But slowly," said Khaavren, making no effort to speak softly. "It is a fine morning, and I wish to enjoy the ride."

"As you wish," said Pel, and they led their horses out of the yard of the inn of the painted sign.

It was, as Khaavren had remarked, a beautiful morning. Though still high summer, the mountains, as they will, cooled the air, and the constant streams and swirling breezes for which Mount Bli'aard is justly famous cooled it still more; also the orange red sky was thin, as it is in the east, and today was so far above them that it took on a faint lilac color, and the Furnace, which one can always feel but never see, was nearly visible, in that there was a direction, nearly straight ahead of them, in which one could not look without one's eyes watering and wishing to shut on their own, and giving one the strange, unaccountable desire to sneeze, which each of them did several times.

They made their slow, steady pace for a league up the road; then, just before reaching the last turn which would bring them to the place of the ambuscade, Uttrik made a sign; whereupon they rode their horses off to the sides of the road, dismounted, and tied them to trees, then slipped off, each to the place which had been prescribed.

Though there were trees on each side of the road, they were not so thickly placed that Khaavren had to worry about striking branches with his head, or tripping over extended roots. And since, for the most part, they were mountain pines, they provided excellent concealment, which Khaavren, along with Aerich and Uttrik, used to good advantage. They moved far back down the slope, circled wide, and began to come back up. They crossed what were clearly the tracks of a dragon, but, fortunately, saw no more sign of the beast than that. At last Aerich said softly, "Oh."

"What is it? Do you see them?" whispered Uttrik.

In answer, the Lyorn pointed up the slope, to where more than a dozen ill-dressed men and women waited with drawn weapons, staring at the path.

"Let us get closer," said Khaavren, in whose head the blood was beginning to pound.

"Very well," said Uttrik. "But carefully."

They maneuvered so close they could nearly make out words the brigands spoke as they whispered among themselves.

"Now," said Uttrik into Khaavren's and Aerich's ears, "we must wait for—"

But that which was to be awaited occurred, or, to be precise, there was the sudden, unmistakable *crack* that is the discharge of a flash-stone. Uttrik, who had stood to battle before, and thus could anticipate the ringing in the ears of those who were close to the sound, used the time after it to draw his sword. Khaavren and Aerich, observing this, took no longer to arm themselves, and, moreover, each took his own flash-stone into his left hand.

Uttrik said, "I believe, my lords, it is time to charge them."

"Well," said Aerich with a shrug. "I believe the honor of the command is yours."

"I agree," said Khaavren.

"Well, then I am about to give the order."

"Do so," said Khaavren, "we are with you."

"Then charge them," he cried, and, with these words, Uttrik leaped up the slope, Khaavren and Aerich at his very heels. Even before they were noticed they heard the sounds of cries and of ringing steel from the other side of the road. Those they attacked had focused their attention on the commotion on the other side of the road, and thus had their backs well exposed to the three who bore down on them.

Khaavren frowned when he realized that, whatever their position, his first blow would be to the back of a man who was not expecting such an attack. He set this consideration aside, however, and was on the point of preparing to strike, when Aerich said in loud and carrying voice, "Excuse me, gentlemen, but it would really be best if you were to surrender your weapons."

Khaavren had the distinct impression of several faces staring at him in amazement, then in disbelief, while for an instant no one moved. Then someone made a motion, small in itself, the turn of a foot, the readjustment of a hand upon a pommel, but, like the pebble that launches the rock-slide, it was enough.

Khaavren's arm, which seemed to be commanded directly by his eye without the commands having to pass through any apparatus on the way, struck out once, then again, and he felt himself suddenly in midst of a storm of steel that whirled around him and threatened to sweep him away; he entered that state where wounds, given or received, are unreal, for all that matters is the constantly evolving pattern of motion in which the broadest actions are subtleties, and finest adjustments of detail are grand strokes; here a half turn to the left, there a cut to the right, here an adjustment to ward off a blow with the dagger, there a twist to disarm, until, in what seemed to be no time at all except for the powerful though fragmented array of memory-images which assembled themselves for the consideration of his mind, all was quiet again, and Khaavren stood upon the field of battle, in the middle of the road, with his friends all whole and sound, save for a few scratches.

What actually happened was this: the ambuscade had been set up with fifteen of the enemy on either side of the road. As Uttrik had foreseen, one of them had been hidden near the inn and had raced back to tell the others that their enemies were departing, but were only walking their horses. Uttrik's plan had worked so well, in fact, that Baaro's troops, if we may so call them, had not even begun to feel impatient when Pel, having decided that enough time had passed, released the heavy charge from his flash-stone.

Barro's troops were heavily bunched together, so that the charge, while only killing one of them, stunned or wounded another five, while three more bolted down the road in terror so that there were only six of them remaining on that side of the road. It should be noted that the charge was of sufficient strength that Pel himself, in addition to being nearly deafened by the report, had to take a moment to recover, but fortunately, Tazendra did not; her greatsword was ready to hand, and before the six remaining brigands had recovered from the shock she had brought two of them to the ground, including Baaro himself, whom she killed with a single blow to the collar.

The remaining four were able to put themselves into a defensive position, and things might have gone poorly for Tazendra except that Mica, who had positioned himself on a rock ledge next to them and slightly higher than they, struck one such a blow on the head with his faithful bar-stool that the outlaw went down at once, and, at the same time, Pel, who had by now recovered and drawn his weapon, made a ferocious charge and, after dueling with one for the length of three passes, stuck his blade through the woman's thigh, so that she was stretched out full length on the road. He and Tazendra turned to the remaining two, who put up token resistance for only a moment before turning and running down the road as fast as they could.

Tazendra and Pel immediately rushed across the road. Now on that side, the battle was going in earnest, for though Khaavren had wounded one with his flash-stone (without even being aware of it), Aerich's had failed to discharge. They were at once forced into a defensive battle, with Aerich, at the point of the triangle they formed, calmly knocking away blows with his vambraces and turning to strike only when he had a clear opening; in this way he had severely wounded two attackers. Uttrik, who fought with two longswords, found himself rather cramped by the defensive nature of the engagement, yet he had managed to kill one of his opponents who had been thrown off-balance by Aerich, and injure another who had become impatient with the ferocity of the defense.

Khaavren was fighting with sword and poniard, the latter drawn without thinking as soon as his flash-stone was expended, and he made full use of the confusion brought about by the other two; that is, he darted in and out of them, ducked below thrusts to cut up, turned fully around to strike from unexpected angles, laughed in the faces of his enemies, and in this way had brought one opponent to the ground with a cut to the side while inflicting dozens of minor cuts and scratches with which to teach the enemy respect for his blades.

There were, then, nine against three, and all would have been over quickly had the brigands organized themselves rather than getting in each other's way. In fact, they were attempting to coordinate a rush at the moment when Pel and Tazendra arrived from the other side and attacked them from behind. Being attacked from behind twice in one battle was, it seems, more than they could face, for, after Tazendra had killed one with a crushing blow to the top of his head, they broke in confusion and disorder, leaving the field, as it were, to the five companions and Mica. The Teckla, we should add, seemed, after having delivered his blow, as cool as Aerich himself.

These six worthies, then, looked about them at the dead and wounded and Khaavren said, "Well, I nearly think it is time to continue our journey."

"The horses," said Aerich, "are this way."

Thus, with their first battle behind them, they retrieved their horses, mounted, and made their way safely past the scene of the carnage and continued toward Redface, home of Adron e'Kieron, and refuge, so they believed, of Kathana e'Marish'Chala.

Chapter the Twenty-fourth

In Which it is Shown that Three Copper Pennies,
Well Spent, Are More Valuable
Than Sixty Orbs,
Carelessly Applied

ONE MIGHT SUPPOSE that, having arrived at the very doorstep, as it were, of Redface Castle, the remaining few leagues would present little problem, especially as there was a road that ran in that direction. In fact, nothing could be further from the truth. The road, after a short distance, began to divide, and to divide again and then again. It was known by Uttrik, whose home in the Pepperfields had not been far from Bli'aard, that most of the roads spent themselves at farms, quarries, streams, caves, or against blank walls, and a few even ended in pits, or at the top of sudden cliffs. This was one of the means of defense devised by Maalics e'Ki-eron, who, back in the fifth cycle, had conquered the region and begun construction of the Castle. Uttrik, who was acquainted with the region in general, was no help in this problem.

Nor, we must say, were the populace in any way helpful. Several times the companions asked after directions, and even paid for them, only to have the guide disappear.

As their frustration mounted, they increased the payments, and augmented them with threats of various sorts, but to no avail.

"Do you think," said Uttrik, "that this is the way strangers are always treated in these mountains?"

"Well," said Khaavren, "you may remember that word has been out out against us. It may be that we are fortunate to avoid an attack by these peasants, rather than merely having lost some sixty orbs."

"But then," said Uttrik, "it seems we could wander these mountains for days before finding the correct path, which annoys me, inasmuch as, each time we come to place where there are no trees to block the sky, I can see the walls of the castle as plainly as I see the sky itself."

"Well," said Khaavren, "what is your plan, then?"

"We will kill a few of these peasants by hanging them up from trees, and that will make the others respect us."

"Bah," said Aerich. "We are visiting Lord Adron, whose vassals these are. He will hardly thank us. And, moreover, we might never emerge from these hills, as the peasants are many, dislike strangers, are leagued against us, and may become violent at any moment."

"Well then," said Khaavren, "what is your plan?"

"My plan is to return to the inn, send a message up to the castle, and ask to be guided. We are gentlemen; there is no reason for Lord Adron to refuse us the guide."

"I can think of one reason," said Khaavren.

"What is that?"

"That he is not here, but is, as we've been told, in Dragaera City."

"Ah, that is true," said Aerich, momentarily startled. "I had forgotten this circumstance."

"Then," said Tazendra, "listen to my plan."

"Yes," said the others, "let us listen to Tazendra's plan."

"We will send Mica to investigate, and as he is a peasant himself, the peasants will speak to him, and he will find out."

"Bah," said Pel, "he wears your livery, and will thus be recognized."

"We can remove the livery."

"That smacks of concealment," said Aerich, frowning.

"Moreover," said Pel, "to these mountain people he is still a stranger, and thus will have no better luck than we have had."

"Very well," said Khaavren, "what is your plan?"

"My plan is very simple. We will return to the inn, take the innkeeper captive, or, indeed, any of these peasants, and make our captive, on pain of his life, reveal the correct path. Moreover, we will take him with us, on the understanding that his life is forfeit if he guides us wrong. What do you think of this plan?"

"For my part," said Tazendra, "I am not far from adopting Pel's idea."

"Nor am I," said Uttrik.

Mica, who seemed relieved at any plan which did not require him to remove his livery, maintained a respectful silence, but agreement could be discerned on his features.

"And," said Aerich, coolly, "if he should believe his duty more important than his life, will you kill him, for the crime of being loyal to his master?"

"Oh," said Pel, "as to that—"

"And besides," Aerich continued, "you know how I feel about any adventure that resembles taking hostages."

"Hostages," put in Uttrik, "are a legitimate part of warfare."

"Entirely true," said Aerich. "But do you pretend that we are at war with Lord Adron?"

"Well," said Tazendra, "we are not far from it. We have thrown away sixty good silver orbs, which is enough to make me set my teeth hard in my jaw."

"Nevertheless—" began Aerich.

"But, good Aerich," began Khaavren, "we cannot wander these mountains forever."

"There is no need to," said the Lyorn with a smile.

"And why is that?"

"Because we have not yet heard your plan."

"What, my plan?"

"Yes, yes," said Tazendra. "Tell us your plan, Khaavren."

"You insist I have a plan, then?" said the Tiassa, with a small smile upon his lips.

"It is true," said Pel, "that you always have a plan."

Khaavren said, "Well, you're right, I do."

"Then," said Uttrik, "please be good enough to tell us what it is, and, if we like it, we shall adopt it."

"Well, my plan is that we take this path."

"This one?" said Tazendra. "Why this one and not any of the others."

"Because this path, and none of the others, has a dead horse lying along it at a distance of thirty yards from where we stand, and, unless I am mistaken, the saddle of that horse shows that it is from the post."

"Well?" said Uttrik. "And so?"

"And so, it looks as if the poor beast was ridden to death by a messenger, who was consequently in a hurry. Now, I would think a messenger would know the right path, and, moreover, a messenger in a hurry would be likely to be going to Redface, instead of anywhere else in the accursed mountains. There, what do you think of my plan?"

Uttrik, who had not known Khaavren as long as the others, stared at him in frank amazement. Aerich said, "Your head, my friend, is as long as your sword, and quite as sharp."

"Well," said Tazendra, "let us then take this path at once."

The castle of Redface, home of His Highness Adron e'Kieron, Dragon Heir to the Throne, Duke of Eastmanswatch, Count of Korio and Sky, etc. etc., remains one of the masterpieces of engineering, ranking with the floating castles of the e'Drien line (of which only Castle Black survives to this day) and possibly with Dzur Mountain, if the mystery behind that strange enclave is ever solved.

To begin with, it consists, quite literally, of miles of walls, with irregularly placed towers looking out in all directions. These walls, be it understood, are both thick and high, and, moreover, so perfectly match the shape of the mountain into which they are built that it is as if the mountain itself created them out of its own rock before graciously allowing the progeny of Kieron the Conqueror, oldest and proudest of the Dragon lines, to construct a home therein.

To the south, there is the Redface itself, a drop of more than two thousand feet into the Eastern River, or more exactly, onto the rocks that stick up from the river and cause its treacherous back-currents and white waters. To the west, there is the comparatively gentle slope of Mount Bli'aard leading down to the nearest city, that being Troe, or what was then called Bengloarafurd. To the north the mountain rises a little further, to a string of watch-posts that have been manned by the House of the Dragon for thousands of years, leading off to Mount Kieron, and, further, to the high plateau of Pepperfield, before dropping to the Valley of Salt, beyond which lies the region of Sandyhome. To the east there are the distant peaks of the Ironwall and Whitecrown which lead to the lands of the Easterners.

The castle consists of several large buildings, all connected by a cunning series of tunnels designed to allow supplies to move quickly and easily to any position along the wall, as well as to provide homes for both the Imperial garrison that is always stationed there and the standing army which the Duke, by custom and right, maintains to protect his position. The keep of Lord Redface, as it is sometimes called—that is, if our readers will pardon the confusion, the master of the keep is sometimes called Lord Redface, and thus his dwelling is sometimes called the keep of Lord Redface—this keep, we say, is the tallest of the structures, and located in the center of the maze of courtyards and substructures, built with nine towers, and surrounded by its own series of walls, gates, and watch-stations.

As our friends traveled the road to the castle, Khaavren, Tazendra and Pel were traveling in the front rank, with Aerich and Uttrik bringing up the rear, along with Mica, who appeared to enjoy the conversation of Aerich, consisting as it did of long silences punctuated by short silences. Shortly before arriving at the outer wall, Tazendra suddenly announced to Khaavren and Pel, "I have been wondering again."

Pel shrugged. "I had thought you had given over such activities."

"Well, I seem unable to stop myself."

"It is a sign of intelligence," said Khaavren, "to be unable to stop wondering."

"Is it indeed?" said Tazendra, who was greatly pleased by this thought.

"Entirely."

"Well, that is good; I had suspected I was intelligent, now I know that I am, and because of it—"

"Well?"

"I will continue to wonder."

"That is right," said Khaavren.

"And yet, I should like an answer to the question that has been knocking about my head so insistently."

"I understand your annoyance," said Pel, "but I beg you to reconsider."

"Reconsider?"

"Exactly."

"Why?"

"Because, if you ask your question, it might be answered."

"Well, but that is what I want."

"No," said Pel, "it is not."

"How, it is not?"

"Not the least in the world, I assure you."

"But it seems to me that is just why I want to ask the question."

"And you are wrong to do so," said Pel promptly.

"But, will you tell me why?"

"I should be delighted to do so."

"Then I am listening."

"Well, here it is: if your question is answered, you will no longer wonder."

"Well, and then?"

"Why, didn't you just say that you wished to keep wondering, because wondering is the proof of intelligence?"

"Oh, but there is no worry on that score, Pel."

"Why not, Tazendra?"

"Because, to anticipate the future as being like the past—"

"Which it often is, I think."

"Yes, exactly. Well, to anticipate the future as being like the past, I think that after you have answered my question, I will be forced to continue wondering just the same."

Pel, who could only agree with the extreme justice of this remark, fell silent, and Khaavren said, "Well then, tell us what you are wondering about."

"I will do so. It is this: what will we do when we have arrived at the castle of Redface?"

"We will ask to speak to Lord Adron," said Khaavren. "There, you see, you are answered."

"But, dear Khaavren, it is just as I expected."

"How?"

"Because it only makes me wonder more."

"What? You have more to wonder about?"

"I do, indeed. What do you say to that?"

"That I had no idea you were so intelligent."

"Well, it is true that my second cousin on my mother's side, Deraff, was a tactician."

"You say, was?"

"Yes," said Tazendra, "he was killed in an ambuscade on his first campaign."

"That is too bad."

"Yes, I have always thought so. But it shows there is intelligence in my family."

"Well, I agree with you," said Khaavren.

"And then," continued Tazendra, "it seems to me that if one is bandy-legged, or long in the arm, or tall in the body, that often one's forebears are as well; and therefore, why should not high intelligence also be something that is preserved within a family?"

"I think you are entirely correct," said Pel.

"You agree?"

"I have said so."

"Then, I am convinced of my intelligence."

"Well," said Khaavren, "of that there can be no more doubt."

"And yet," said Pel, "I am anxious to learn what Tazendra now has cause to wonder about."

"Just this," she said. "You have explained that we will ask to see Lord Adron."

"Exactly right," said Pel.

"But, I had thought that we had just learned, from the conversation which Khaavren and Aerich heard, that he was in Dragaera City, which, you observe, we left some weeks ago."

"Well," said Khaavren, "that is true."

"Then he won't be there."

"Well, that is right, too."

"But that, you perceive, is what I am wondering about: why should we ask for him, knowing, as we do, that he is not there?"

"Because," said Pel, "it is his home, and therefore, if we are visiting it, it is only proper to ask for him."

"And yet if he isn't home?"

"Then," said Khaavren, "we shall ask to wait for him."

"But then, it may be a long wait."

"In fact," said Khaavren, "we are hoping it will be."

"Oh, we are?"

"We are depending upon it."

"But then, I fail to comprehend."

"I assure you," said Khaavren, "I think none the less of your intelligence for that."

"That is good," said Tazendra. "And yet, I wonder what we will do, while we are waiting for him?"

"Well, what have we come here to do?"

"I don't know," said Tazendra. "I only know that we must find the baroness Kaluma."

"Who is where?" persisted Khaavren.

"The gods! I think she is at Redface, or we have wasted many weeks of traveling."

"Well, then, while we are awaiting Lord Adron, we shall be searching for Kathana e'Marish'Chala."

"Oh," said Tazendra, her eyes growing wide with wonder. "Now I comprehend."

"Then," said Pel, "you must find something else to wonder about."

"Oh, I will," said Tazendra. "You may rest easy on that score. Only, there is no hurry, is there?"

"No," said Pel, "I think you may take your time."

"That's good," said Tazendra.

"Here we are," said Khaavren, as they came around the last bend in the road and found the west gate was standing with both doors open, creating a break in the wall enough to admit three coaches side by side without touching in the least. They saluted the guards and rode into the central courtyard, where their horses were taken by servants, after which our friends were admitted into a comfortable antechamber of the Castle Main, where they gave their names and asked to speak with Lord Adron, if it was convenient to him to do so.

The servant bowed and asked them to wait while he inquired. After he had gone, Tazendra said, "Well, about what do you think he has gone to inquire?"

"No doubt," said Khaavren, "he has gone to inquire as to what to do about those who wish to see his master while his master is not at home. We must, then, beg to be allowed to wait for him."

"Very well," said Tazendra. "And while waiting, we will take the opportunity to search for *her*."

"Exactly," said Uttrik, with an expression of relish on his features.

"My dear Uttrik," said Aerich.

"Well?"

"However this falls out, we will be guests in Lord Adron's home, and the Baroness is another guest."

"Well, and?"

"And I trust you will observe etiquette with regard to guests."

"And yet, she is a criminal, and, moreover, she killed my father."

"She is a guest," repeated Aerich laconically.

"Well, and if I should take it into my head to confront her with her actions, and cause her to take responsibility for their consequences?"

"Then we must cross swords."

"My dear Lyorn—"

"I will regret it intensely, I assure you."

"But it seems—"

"Your pardon, gentlemen," said Khaavren, "but allow me to suggest that we refrain from launching that boat until the ground is wet."

"I agree with Khaavren entirely," said Pel.

"Very well," said Aerich.

"As you will have it," said Uttrik.

Another servant appeared at this time; only, instead of a Teckla, this was an Issola gentleman, who wore green and white robes showing that he was performing his office for Lord Adron. He said, "I am Custrin, at your service. Am I to understand that you do us the honor of requesting an interview with my master, the Prince?"

The five friends rose as one (Mica, as became a lackey, had remained standing), and bowed. Khaavren said, "You have understood us exactly. Only, as we do not wish to disturb him, and as, moreover, our errand is not urgent, we are prepared to wait until a convenient moment, whether it be to-day, to-morrow, or several weeks in the future; you perceive, my dear sir, that we are ready to be amiable."

"All the better, then, that the Prince is prepared to receive you at once."

"What?" said Khaavren, astonished. "He is here? That is, he is willing to see us now?"

"At this very moment, if that should please you. Or, if you prefer, and as the Prince is anxious that you should spend at least some little time with him, you may use our guest rooms to refresh yourselves from your journey first, however, it please you."

"No, no," said Khaavren, endeavoring to hide his confusion. "That is, we should be honored to see Lord Adron at this very moment, if he is not inconveniencing himself."

"Not at all, I assure you. He returned only yester-day from a long journey, and has rested, but not yet resumed his daily habits, so that the time is admirably suited for an interview."

"Well, then, we are at your service, my lord."

The Issola then led them from the antechamber into a well-lit hall, at the end of which was a high-ceilinged chamber furnished with paintings of various nobles of the e'Kieron line, as well as an ornate table that filled a great part of the room, and was supplied with high-backed chairs, no less ornate than the table, as well as a few stuffed chairs pushed into corners. There was a fire going in the black marble fireplace, which fire reflected against the dark wainscoting. At the far end of the room, one hand upon a chair and the other on his hip, was the Duke of Eastmanswatch, etc. etc., Lord Adron e'Kieron.

Adron was just then reaching the height of his powers, but had not yet reached the height of his fame. That is, he had already distinguished himself at the Battle of Twelve Pines, and several times during the Elde Island War, but the Rolling Rock Wars, where he constructed and led the Breath of Fire Battalion, had not yet occurred. Moreover, his studies of sorcery had reached the limits of current knowledge, and he was even then beginning to make use of the infamous blue stones which would allow him, five hundred years later, to harness the power that destroyed the Empire and replaced Dragaera City with the Lesser Sea of Flux. We should add that his eyes were blue and cold, his hair, a very light brown, was worn tied back in a knot like a Lyorn's which showed off his sharp noble's point, and he had the "Dragon chin" to such a degree that it was said, in later years, "His chin was so strong it smashed the Empire to pieces."

Notwithstanding all of this, he bowed politely to the companions and requested that they be seated at the table. He then caused a servant to appear with chilled wine, which he poured and tasted first. "Well, my lords, to what do I owe the honor of the visit with which you have graced my poor house?"

"Your Highness," said Khaavren, who had used the interval to try to clear up some of the confusion in his mind, "we are here, well, we have come to pay our respects to you."

"To pay your respects?" said Adron. "How singular. And in whose name do you do so?"

"On behalf of Captain G'aereth," said Khaavren, or, rather, said Khaavren's mouth, for it seemed to be supplying the words which his mind appeared unable to discover.

"Captain G'aereth?" said Adron, frowning. "Well, I know him."

"And he knows you, Your Highness," said Khaavren.

"And," added Pel truthfully, "he has the greatest respect for you."

"But, well, is there something he wants from me?"

"Not at all," said Khaavren, who could think of nothing the Captain might want. "He merely desired us to pay you a thousand compliments, and to then be on our way."

Uttrik shifted uncomfortably, but, like the others, was content to allow Khaavren to do the talking.

"And yet," said Adron, "that cannot be why you have

taken this journey so far from the city. Come, speak the truth, the Emperor has sent you here, has he not?"

"The Emperor!" said Khaavren.

"Well?"

"Your Highness, I assure you I have no idea what the Emperor could wish for us to do."

"But then, you are of the Guard, and I have been given to understand that His Majesty is wroth with me."

"And so you think—?"

"That you have come to arrest me, have you not? Well, I assure you that I shall accompany you happily; and will be only too glad to plead my case before the court.

"I give you my word, Your Highness—"

"Oh, you need have no fear; you may have my parole. Only allow me a few moments to gather my belongings for the journey. Shall I fetch my sword to surrender it to you?"

"Your Highness," said Aerich, coming to Khaavren's rescue. "I am a Lyorn; consequently, I cannot lie."

"I am aware of that, sir."

"Well, I tell you plainly that the mission we were entrusted with has nothing whatsoever to do with you."

"How? It does not?"

"I have said so, my lord."

"But then, what mission could you have?"

This distraction by Aerich had been sufficient to give Khaavren time to recover from his embarrassment, and it occurred to him to solve the problem by telling Adron the truth, or, at any rate, part of it. "Your Highness, the Captain, working in the interests of the Emperor, has become curious to know the actual state of affairs around Pepperfield."

"Then, you are here—"

"To investigate that area," said Pel. "That is all."

"Well, is this the truth?"

"Entirely, my lord," said Pel.

Adron studied the countenances of the five gentlemen before him and said, "Very well, then I give you welcome.

And, moreover, I should have realized it, since I made such haste on my return here that it is unlikely I could have been overtaken by anyone. In fact, my lords, I have killed three horses getting here; you may have noticed them on the road."

"We did, indeed, see such a horse, Your Highness," said Khaavren.

"Well, and as my disgrace (for such, I fear, it is) only occurred shortly before my departure, then should His Majesty wish to arrest me, well, I think that you could not be those entrusted with the mission, nor even know about it."

"Your Highness," said Khaavren, "I am relieved to see that you understand this."

"And then, in your mission to this far outpost of our Empire, you have thought to stop here merely for courtesy?" As he said this, he fixed Khaavren with a look both sharp and earnest, such that Khaavren felt himself unable to lie."

"Well," said Khaavren, "not entirely."

"How, there is, in fact, another reason?"

"Yes, exactly, another reason."

"But this does not," added Pel, "reduce in any measure the sincerity of the courtesy we offer Your Highness."

"I understand that, but, as to the second reason?"

"Oh, the second reason," said Khaavren, looking about for help.

"It is to inform Your Highness of a certain circumstance," said Pel evenly.

"Ah, there is something I ought to know, then?"

"Yes, exactly," said Pel. "And, as we were nearby, well, we wished to inform Your Highness of it."

"I assure you, I am most grateful," said Adron. "And the circumstance?"

"Oh, as to the circumstance—"

"Yes?"

"Well, this gentleman, Khaavren of Castle Rock, will communicate it to Your Highness."

"Ah," said Adron. Turning to Khaavren, he said, "Well, then, my lord?"

"Yes," said Khaavren. "I will tell Your Highness of the entire affair."

"I await you most eagerly."

Khaavren licked his lips, and, as if his ideas rested there, he imbibed the very inspiration he needed. "Your Highness, we have come to tell you that some impostor is using your device."

"How, my device? What is this?"

"It is true, Your Highness," said Aerich. "We were set upon by brigands, who believed they were acting under your orders."

"Impossible," said Adron.

"Not the least in the world."

"But, who would do such a thing?"

"Oh, as to that," said Khaavren, "we have no idea."

"But, the means?"

"Oh, as to the means, that is simple enough."

"Well, then, tell me."

"Assuredly, Your Highness," said Aerich, coolly. "But will Your Highness allow me to put a question?"

"If it will help to make matters clear."

"I believe it will."

"Then you may ask your question."

"Very well, tell me this, then: has Your Highness your seal?"

"My seal?"

"Yes. Your personal seal."

"Of course."

"May I be so bold as to ask Your Highness to allow me to see it?"

"What? You wish to see it?"

"If it would not inconvenience Your Highness."

"Not at all."

"Then, if Your Highness pleases—"

"Very well, if you will but wait a moment, I will bring it."

"What? Your Highness doesn't carry it about?"

"Ordinarily I do, but as I have just returned from a journey, well, it is still in the pack I brought with me, for, you perceive, I never allow it away from my person."

"And Your Highness does right."

"Well then, I will return with the seal."

"We will await Your Highness."

Adron left the room, a puzzled look upon his features. When his footsteps could no longer be heard, Khaavren gave an audible sigh. Tazendra said, "And yet, I had thought that he would not be here."

"Well," said Uttrik, "so did we all. I must say, Khaavren, that was skillfully played.

Khaavren did not answer, so overcome was he by the difficulty of what he had just encountered. Pel said, "But then, what are we to tell him when he returns without the seal?"

Aerich shrugged. "You may as well ask, what are we to do if he returns *with* the seal?"

"Bah," said Pel. "It is impossible."

"Well, and is it possible for him to be here?"

"And yet, we know that yesterday, someone else had the seal. So, what then?"

Khaavren sighed. "For my part, I renounced all of these intrigues. If he should have the seal, and there is more explaining to do, why, the rest of you may have your share of it."

"Yet, I say the thing is impossible," said Pel.

Aerich shrugged.

Uttrik said, "Whether he finds it or not, we still have the same problem; that is, how are we to find Kathana e'Marish'Chala."

"Indeed," said Aerich. "It is unlikely, if we should ask Lord Adron, that he will tell us."

"And yet," said Pel, "we must contrive a way to find her."

"And moreover," said Tazendra, "what are we to do when we are in her presence at last?"

"Oh, as to that," said Uttrik, "my part is clear, I assure you."

"Well, mine is not," said Khaavren. "In fact, it seems that with every moment, I find matters are more complex than I had thought."

"That delights me," said Tazendra.

"How, it delights you?"

"Yes. I had thought I was alone."

"Oh, but you aren't, I assure you. I wish to know, for example, who is it who wishes us stopped, and moreover, why?"

"Yes, why," echoed Tazendra. "For, if we do not know what we are doing, then it follows no one else does either; and, if no one knows what we are going to do, well then, why is someone so determined to prevent us from doing it?"

"You have stated the problem admirably," said Khaavren.

"It is undeniable," murmured Uttrik, "that this Dzurlord reasons like a Discreet."

"Well, then," said Pel, "perhaps I may suggest some of the answer."

"How, you?" said Khaavren. "Do you pretend that you, all this time, have known our enemy, and yet said nothing about it?"

"Not at all," said Pel coolly. "I have not known, and I still do not know. And yet, it may be that, now that I think of it, I can make a suggestion or two."

"Well, then?" said Khaavren. "I am most anxious to hear these famous suggestions."

"The cycle has turned," observed Pel. "And this was caused by the Baroness Kaluma."

"That is right," said Khaavren, to whom Pel had made this observation before.

"Well then, she is the hub about which turn the politics of the moment."

"Stay," said Tazendra. "I like that phrase: the politics of the moment. It is clever; I say so."

"Well, and I'm glad you think so."

"But go on, then. The politics of the moment—Blood, but that is a fine phrase—revolve around Kathana e'Mar-ish'Chala."

"That is right. Therefore, those with an interest in such things are striving to manipulate her, in some direction or another. That is, either to see her arrested, or to see her go free, or to see her go free until exactly the right moment for her downfall."

"But then," said Khaavren, "who are these people? For I am convinced that among them, we will find the enemy."

"No doubt you are right, Khaavren, and the reason is this: we have come along, all on our own, without any thought of any of the cabals, and have begun acting in our own interests. Anyone who sits at the table will by necessity look askance at those who pretend to walk in, unannounced, and declare that a new game is now being played. What of the plans they have been formulating for months? What of their schemes for power or favor? They do not know us, they fear we will upset everything, so they will try to stop us."

Aerich said, "Pel, I think you are entirely correct."

"But then," said Khaavren, "who are these players?"

"Cracks in the Orb," said Pel. "Who are they not? There is, first of all, our host, who wishes for his line, that is, the line of Kieron, to assume command of the Pepper-fields."

"Well, and?"

"There is the Warlord, Lytra, who wishes the Pepper-fields to be given to the line of Lanya."

"Yes, I understand that; go on."

"Then, well, do you not have a friend who is a lady of the House of the Phoenix?"

"And, if I do?"

"Well, she has a brother who has interests in these matters, and though I do not know what these interests are, no doubt they play a part."

"Well, go on, then."

"We must not forget the Athyra, Seodra."

"Who?"

"A wizard who was chief advisor to the last Emperor, who must, in order to maintain her position at court, which she likes more than a little, contrive to make herself indispensable to His Majesty."

"Very well."

"There is also Gyorg Lavode, who will do whatever he can to advance the cause of the Lavodes."

"Pel, my head is spinning. What do you think, Tazendra?"

"Oh, I stopped listening some time ago; it is all far too confusing."

"Well, I think you are right. And you, Uttrik?"

"None of this concerns me."

"On the contrary," said Pel, "it all concerns you."

"Well, that may be, but, nevertheless, I want no part in these matters. When I have found and killed the lady who killed my father—"

"Yes, then?" said Pel.

"Well, then we shall see."

"Ah," said Pel.

"Well," said Khaavren, "what is your opinion, Aerich?"

"My opinion? My opinion is that it has taken our host a great deal of time to find his seal."

"The Horse!" said Khaavren. "You are right. I wonder—"

"My lords," said Mica, who had, unnoticed by anyone, taken a position by the door. "I hear footsteps."

"A model servant," murmured Aerich.

Mica hurried back from the door, and so was standing mutely next to the fireplace when the door opened before Lord Adron, who had, in addition to a strange expression on his face, a small object in his hand; which object, we should say, greatly resembled a seal.

"Your Highness—" began Khaavren, whose mouth had already begun the task of working its way out of the embarrassment of its master.

But Adron shook his head and said, "This is a most peculiar thing."

Khaavren stopped and said, "It is, your Highness?"

"Yes. I render my apologies for having deserted you for so long, but the events of the past few moments are surprising."

"Surprising?" ventured Pel.

"Surprising indeed," said Adron. "I should even say, startling."

"Well, and of what do these events consist?" said Aerich. "If, that is, Your Highness would do us the honor of telling us."

"Well, I will, for, had it not been for you, I might have thought nothing of the incident."

"We are all listening, Your Highness," said Pel politely.

"Here it is, then. I went directly to my chambers, in order to take the seal from my pouch, for the purpose of showing it to you gentlemen. I did this, you perceive, on the assumption that you had some matter of importance to communicate to me, and that this matter involves the seal which is used to identify my official dispatches."

"And you were right, my lord," said Khaavren.

"I found my pouch at once, but, well, you may understand my amazement upon discovering that the seal was not there."

"How, not there?" said Uttrik. "Then, that is not it in your hand?"

"Yes, this is, in fact, the seal itself."

"And yet," said Tazendra, "Your Highness has done us the honor to say it was not where you had left it?"

"Not at all; and I spent some moments looking for it, I assure you."

"Well then," said Aerich, "where was it?"

"That is the strange thing. For as I was returning to this room to discover what you knew about this matter, and to learn how it might relate to the claim you have made of an outrage committed in my name, there came a visitor to the door."

"What, a visitor?" said Khaavren.

"Exactly. A visitor who announced himself as an Imperial messenger."

"Well," said Aerich, "I hope Your Highness condescended to allow him to deliver his message."

"I did exactly that, and he delivered his message."

"And would you do us the honor to relate the message?"

"I will. In fact, I will do so at once. Here it is." And, with these words, he held out his seal of office.

"What?" said Pel. "The messenger delivered the seal?"

"Exactly."

"And, excuse me for questioning Your Highness, but I am very curious. Did he explain how it came into his possession?"

"He did. He pretended that I had left it in my rooms in the Palace."

"But, is that possible?" cried Aerich, who had determined that this Dragonlord was not given to carelessness.

"Not at all."

"So, then—?"

"So, I believe it was stolen from me."

"Bah," said Aerich. "By His Majesty? Impossible."

"And yet," said Adron, "it was his confidant, Lord Garland, who delivered it."

"What?" cried Pel. "Garland? An Imperial messenger?"

"It is as I have had the honor to tell you."

"Your Highness is right; there is some intrigue in this."

"That was my opinion. I am glad to see that we are in agreement."

"Then, Your Highness believes that the seal was taken from you?" said Khaavren.

"Yes, and for no good purpose."

"Well, that is exactly what we have come to tell Your Highness."

"Then tell me, if you will, what has been done in my name, and with the use of this seal?"

"That is why we have come," said Khaavren, and hastened to describe for Lord Adron the conversation he and Aerich had overheard.

"But then," cried Adron when he had finished, "this is insupportable! It is infamous!"

"That is my opinion," said Aerich.

"You are right to tell me of it."

"We are glad of that," said Khaavren.

"But tell me, how did you avoid the trap, after you had learned of it?"

"Avoid it?" said Tazendra. "We did not avoid it. Rather, we sprang it ourselves."

"What? The five of you against thirty brigands?"

"We had," said Pel, "the advantage of surprise, and the additional advantage of several flash-stones, one of which, it is true, did not work, and yet the other two did."

"But this is amazing!" cried Adron.

"That one did not work?" asked Tazendra naively, "or that two did?"

"No, no, that the five of you survived against thirty brigands."

"Oh, we fought tolerably well," said Tazendra.

"Five of you, you say, defeated thirty of them?"

"We killed several, I think," said Khaavren. "The rest ran."

"This is a great victory!" cried Adron.

Pel bowed gracefully.

"Truly," said Adron, shaking his head, "you amaze me."

"Your Highness honors us," said Aerich.

"Come, you must stay with me for the night at least, than I can give a dinner in your honor."

"That is exceedingly kind of Your Highness," said Aerich.

"But, do you accept? I must nearly insist, for, in winning this battle, you prevented an infamy from occurring in my name. An infamy that I should have despaired of ever living down."

"Well, then," said Khaavren, "if Your Highness does us the honor to insist upon it."

"I do indeed," said Adron.

"We accept gladly," said Khaavren.

"Then do you go to your toilettes, while I give the orders for the feast. My man will show you to your rooms, and will call you when we are ready to dine."

After more courteous words, these things were done. But we do not wish to tire our readers with a description of this feast, which, at any rate, was far more entertaining to partake of then it would be to read about. Suffice it to say that there was fresh mountain poppy-bread with goat's cheese, and the meat of wild boar, and roast pheasant which had been stuffed with black mushrooms, and thin slices of kethna served in a butter-cream sauce of which even the Emperor, who prided himself on his palate, could have found no complaint.

Lord Adron had at this time no guests (excepting, presumably, the Baroness of Kaluma, who made no appearance), so it was only the six of them, but he made up for the lack by toasting them many times and praising their actions in the most complimentary way, and demanding, moreover, additional details of the battle, which he took as much delight in hearing as a child of sixty or seventy would have, and nearly as much as Tazendra, for one, took in relating. Mica was allowed to help serve the meal so that he, too, could help describe the battle in which he had played such an important role. We would not be faithful to the truth if we did not add that, while this was occurring, if there was anywhere in the Empire a happier individual than this worthy Teckla it would be hard to imagine.

When the meal was over, His Highness stood and bowed to them, saying, "You may be pleased to walk around the grounds or the castle where you will, and I will hope to see you once more in the morning, when we can break our fasts together before you depart."

"It would be a great honor, Your Highness," said Aerich, as they bowed to him.

As they left the dining hall, Khaavren said, "Well, my

friends, I think we should accept Lord Adron's offer, and avail ourselves of the lovely evening."

"That is all very well," said Tazendra, "and yet I still wonder how we are to find Kaluma?"

"Oh," said Khaavren, smiling in a manner particular to him at such times, "I have been born with foresight, and I predict we shall have no difficulty, now that we have been given the run of the grounds."

"What?" said Uttrik. "You pretend that we can search the entire grounds of Castle Redface, each room, each hall, each building, and the surrounding area, by to-morrow morning?"

"Well, I don't think that will be necessary."

"How, not?" said Tazendra.

"Observe, and you shall learn."

"Khaavren," said Pel to Aerich, "has an idea." Aerich nodded.

Khaavren said, "Come, Mica, find, if you can, a small piece of parchment, pen, ink, and blotter, and bring them to me, or, if that is not practical, bring me to them."

Mica left to do so. Pel looked at Khaavren with some curiosity, but Aerich appeared willing to merely wait contentedly. Mica returned presently and pointed the way to a small desk where Adron's secretary was accustomed to do his correspondence. Khaavren, seeing that it was not being used, sat at the desk like a veritable secretary himself, and, using the pen provided, wrote the following lines:

> *"My Dear Lady Fricorith, I have long been an ardent admirer of your work, which cause, I hope, will be sufficient to allow me to interrupt you for a few moments of conversation.*
>
> > *Your servant,*
> > *Khaavren of Castlerock."*

This done, he showed it to Pel, who said, "Well, and is Fricorith the name under which Kaluma is living here?"

"Exactly."

"But, suppose she refuses to see you?"

"There is no danger of that," said Khaavren. "Observe."

He led the way out to the courtyard, where he found a young peasant lad, whom he accosted with the words, "My friend, if you will run a brief errand for me, there are three copper pennies which will pass from my pocket to yours."

The boy seemed amenable, and said, "What errand is it, my lord? I should be most happy to oblige you, if I can."

"Well, it is just this: take this message to the artist, the lady Fricorith, and bring back her reply."

"The lady Fricorith?" said the young man, suddenly looking uneasy. "But, well—"

"Come, come, we shall not compromise her. You perceive that I know she is here; how could I know it if your master, Lord Adron, had not told me? And, moreover, how could I know under what name she is staying? Besides, I don't ask you to betray her exact whereabouts, merely to deliver a message and bring back the result."

"And yet—"

"Well, here are the pennies. Do you want them?"

At length, greed, as it so often does, won out over caution, and the lad took the message and ran off.

"And yet," said Pel, "I repeat, what if she does not wish to see you?"

"And I repeat, my good Pel, that it matters not if she does or does not. Do you pretend we are going to await her reply? That young man knows who she is, and where she is. Why are we standing here, gentlemen? To horse! Or rather, to foot! We will follow him, and, I answer for it, we will be standing before Kathana e'Marish'Chala before the sky has darkened."

Chapter the Twenty-fifth

*In Which the Reader Will, No Doubt,
Be Pleased to Meet at Last
One of the Principal Actors In Our History*

THERE IS A certain play which was written by the master playwright Villsni of Cobbletown, which is called *The Return of Duke Highwater*. The play centers around the actions of two characters, one being the Duke, the other his youngest son, the Marquis of Havenwood. As one watches this play, one begins, in about the second act, to become uncomfortably aware that the Marquis has not yet made an appearance in person, although he is industriously throwing plot twists at the other characters from off the stage—leading charges, becoming wounded, being betrayed by his mistress, and so on. And yet, the audience wonders, when will we meet him? In fact, throughout the entire work, the Marquis never does appear, and it soon becomes apparent that— but we beg the reader's pardon; it was not our intention to enter into a critique of this production, merely to draw an analogy to our present situation, in preparation for destroying that analogy for all time.

To be more precise, then, we wish to point out that the

more astute of our readers may, by this stage of our narrative, have begun to notice that someone of no small importance to our own drama has not yet appeared; that is, Kathana e'Marish'Chala. It is not our desire, then, to emulate the redoubtable Villsni, for we freely admit that his subtleties are sometimes so far beyond us as to leave us confused as to theme, plot, subplot, and, in general, what exactly the Master is trying to tell us (all the while, the reader may rest assured, we are admiring his skillfully wrought speeches and fine distinction of mood and meter).

Nevertheless, we have brought this work to our readers' attention merely to dismiss any notion that we might have thought of attempting something similar. Therefore, to utterly dispel such notions, and, moreover, because our history now absolutely requires it, we will turn our attention to the missing baroness; which we will do by following our friends to the place where, at this moment, she stands, as if awaiting our attention, with her powders, brushes, and easel, high on a bluff looking out past the Redface. Once here, we will begin by sketching the artist. We are not unaware that there is some degree of presumption in this.

Yet we are forced to ask, who can pretend to write history without, in some measure, falling victim to the sin of presumption? That is, without being arrogant enough to believe one is capable of insights others have missed? Without being bold enough to stand in the circle with those who have piled up, one after another, the great deeds upon which history itself is built? We do not attempt, in this way, to diminish either those great men and women of whom we report, nor the deeds by which they have proved themselves. It may be that we feel a certain pleasure in our actions, as if, by revealing, as faithfully as we can, the hidden ideas and motivations which lead the great ones to act as they did, we are some way above them. Yet, if we feel this, can we not be excused? The very drives which cause some to act are those which cause us to report on their actions, and if we take pride in our ability to relate these events, should that pride be any less than that felt by the do-ers themselves? And if, in our discussions, we chance to touch upon some universal fear, or some common desire, and thus enlighten our readers in some small way, should we, for this reason, take any less pride in this accomplishment than those mighty figures of history took in theirs? Or, in fact, less pride than the readers of a complex passage might take in deciphering the interrelationships and references in the passage to partake fully of what has been written, or, if we are permitted, reap all that has been sown?

Yet, we believe that none of this would be possible, for either the great ones of history, the recorders of history, or the readers of history, without a certain degree of presumption; that is, of bold, arrogant conduct. For this reason, we will not apologize if, to complete our task to our own satisfaction, we will locate that great person, the center of so many of the cogs and wheels that drove the great machine of history early in the eighteenth Phoenix reign, and, as we have had the honor of saying, sketch the artist.

This can be done in two words. She was a thin woman of medium height. Her complexion was dark for a Dragonlord, though not so dark as a Lyorn. Her features were sharp even for a Dragonlord. Her eyes were deeply set and heavily lidded indicating a sensual disposition, whereas her cheekbones were high, proving strength of character. She wore her light brown hair cut short around the sides.

But, like Kathana herself, we will not limit our picture to what can be seen, as it were, on the surface, but will go on to lay bare that which is concealed by the envelope of flesh which is worn by all mortals, and often bears only the most superficial resemblance to the shades and nuance of character which the discerning eye may discover from this surface, in much the same way that the eddies and foam on top of a stream reveal the actions of the deep currents that are the stream's true essence. These eddies and foam, be assured, never reveal the nature of the currents in a direct and obvious way, but only provide a starting point for one who is willing to penetrate the surface and uncover the true relationships, as well as the submerged boulders, that determine in exactly what way this particular waterway fulfills its unique destiny.

We feel justified in saying, then, that this ability, which men call insight, is the special attribute of the rare Dragon bloodline that is named Marish'Chala, and the Lady Kathana unquestionably had it in abundance. Yet, this quality, this insight, is not like the ether, which exists throughout the universe and provides a means for light and sound to travel from one end of the room to the other, or from one end of the world to the other. That is, it does not exist independent of other attributes, but, rather, invariably finds its expression in some certain way. In Kathana, then, it revealed itself in her ability to see, and, moreover, to show, those qualities in people, in things, even in places, which, seemingly opposites, actually determine what the thing is. That is, like the Serioli musician who makes the listener laugh while he cries and cry while he laughs, she could see, and then show, the fear that determined the bravery of the Dzurlord, the soft pliability that caused the unyielding shape of the mountain, the hidden movement in the stagnant pond, or, the opinion of the late Lord Pepperfield notwithstanding, the weakness that led to the strength of the wounded dragon protecting her young.

As for those hidden qualities within herself, it is known that she, who had, by the age of three hundred, mastered all the known techniques developed in tens of thousands of years of painting, still believed her technique was weak, and not only always strove to improve it, but believed, the results of her own hand to the contrary, that nothing except barest technique was of any importance whatever. It is known that, to her eye, the work she had created always fell so far short of the image in her mind, that she became arrogant on the subject, and would brook no criticism. It is known that she was intolerant of anyone or anything that was less than perfect, and, knowing and hating this tendency, became, when not enraged by critics, one of the most perfect ladies in the Empire, a model of courtesy and tact. It is known that, like the subject of her famous painting, *The Dzurlord Before the Charge of Knowngate*, life was so precious to her, and, consequently, her fear of death was so great, that she drove herself to acts of personal bravery that would have made her the pride of her House even if had she never touched a brush in her life.

Which of her aspects would appear at any moment? We may as well ask, as we stand in the center of the Whirling Canyon, "Which way will your winds blow tomorrow?" For it is *circumstance*, that mysterious entity, represented by a word which is so precise in its ambiguity, so vague in its precision; it is circumstance, we say, the randomly selected occurrence of events, weighted by probability, but unknown in exactitude, that determines for any painter, soldier, Emperor, peasant, or historian what his reactions will find at any specific moment on the boundless seashore of uncertainty. And if it was to these limitless but shifting sands that Kathana, at her best, returned again and again, it is also the exact lay of sand, surf, and stone on this unending beach called chance, or caprice, or *circumstance*, that determined how she would respond to events unforeseen, to company unlooked for.

This, then, was the woman whom our friends found standing before a canvas upon which a few scant lines were traced (and yet more were erased), staring out upon the pink mist fading into the orange overcast and out to the lush green of the valley below the Redface.

Such was her concentration that the young boy with Khaavren's message was nearly upon her before she was aware of him. Khaavren and his friends were at the top of a gentle slope of long grasses when she took the message, but by the time she had read it, were close enough to hear her say, "But, who is this gentleman, and what sort of reply does he wish?"

"It is I, my lady," said Khaavren, before the peasant-boy could speak. The messenger turned around in amazement, but Khaavren handed him, as promised, three pennies, and said, "I will consider the reply as having been delivered."

The boy looked from Khaavren to his friends, then to the painter, then back at Khaavren, and at last gave them a courtesy in such haste that it is barely worth noting and ran back up the hill at a good speed.

"Well," said Kathana, in a voice full of gentle inquiry. "You are called Khaavren, you say. Who are your friends, and what will you have of me?"

"My lady," said Khaavren, "it is my honor to present Lord Aerich, Lady Tazendra, the Cavalier Pel, and the lord Uttrik e'Lanya."

These worthies bowed, but Kathana said, "Uttrik e'Lanya? Stay, I know that name."

"I have the honor," said Uttrik, "to be the son of the man you murdered."

"Murdered?" said Kathana, her brows contracting. "The word is hard."

"No harder than the deed."

"I take it," said Kathana, "that your presence here concerns this pretended murder?"

"You have understood me exactly."

"And you believe, I suppose, that since you have chosen to style your father's death a murder, that there is no reason why there should not be five of you, armed, to face me when I have only a poniard with me? Well then, so be it; I have my poniard. Will you attack me one at a time, or do you fear your blades aren't long enough for that? Either way, I am ready."

With this she drew the knife she had referred to, which was straight and rather long as such knives go, and she placed herself in the guard position of a knife-fighter, bent slightly at the waist and leaning forward with her right shoulder; her left hand reaching out as if to grab or claw.

"Your pardon, my lady," said Aerich. "Forgive us for allowing you to misunderstand the situation."

"How, misunderstand?" said Kathana, without moving from her stance.

"You misunderstand," said Uttrik, "in that we will be happy to lend you a sword, and furthermore, you will be fighting only me, and, as for seconds and judges, we will—"

"Bah," said Aerich. "My friend Uttrik is speaking only for himself. We have by no means come here to fight with you, and the proof is, we will do our utmost to dissuade our friend from issuing his challenge, at least here and now."

"You will?" said Uttrik, who seemed startled by this announcement.

"Assuredly, my dear Dragon," said Khaavren.

"But then, I have told you why I wished to find her."

"Yes, and we have told you that your reasons were not ours."

"And yet—"

"But tell me," said Kathana, who passed a hand over her brow, "why the rest of you wished to find me?"

"Oh, as to that," said Khaavren. "I beg you to believe—"

"My lady," interrupted Tazendra. "We have come here only to reflect."

"How, to reflect?" said Kathana.

"And yet," said Uttrik, "in my case—"

"Be patient," said Pel, touching Uttrik's shoulder. "You will be given your chance for satisfaction."

"I will?" said Uttrik.

"He will?" said Kathana.

"I have said so," said Pel.

"Not at all," said Khaavren.

Kathana shook her head, "It seems you have arrived here without agreement as to your purpose."

Aerich said, "We have, nevertheless, arrived."

"That is true."

"Well," said Uttrik, "if we do not all agree to our purpose, I know mine, which is to kill you, if that is agreeable. So, if you will—"

"My dear Uttrik," said Aerich, "I beg you to remember that we are on Lord Adron's land, and that we have eaten his food and although we have not slept under his roof, he has offered us that honor, and we have accepted. Consider this, and remember that this lady is a guest of His Highness."

"Well," said Uttrik, frowning, "you are right; I had not thought of that."

At this point, as the proceedings seemed to Mica likely to be long ones, he seated himself in the grass, of which he pulled a stalk and began to chew it; more, we should note, from boredom than from hunger.

"But then," said Tazendra, frowning, "we cannot arrest her, either."

"Arrest?" said Kathana, on whose countenance emerged a frown much like Uttrik's. "You speak of arresting me?"

"What would you?" said Pel. "You are wanted by the Empire, and some of us are Guardsmen, who have sworn a certain oath in which the arrest of fugitives plays a role."

"So you intend to bring me back to Dragaera, like a criminal?"

"Not at all," said Aerich. "As my friend Tazendra has had the honor to explain, we cannot do so while you are on Lord Adron's land, any more than Lord Uttrik can attack you here."

"But then, to remain here would be a cowardly act."

"That's my opinion," said Uttrik.

"Whereas to leave would be a foolish act."

"A very understandable position," said Khaavren.

"How, then, shall I decide? Come," she said to Aerich. "You are a Lyorn; what is your opinion?"

Aerich shrugged, as if to say, "You are a Dragon, why should you care?"

Kathana pondered. "So, although I am safe here, you have nevertheless come to kill or arrest me, according to your inclinations, and I must decide—"

"In fact," said Khaavren, "that is not at all certain."

"What? It is not certain that Uttrik wishes to kill me?"

"Oh, as to that," said Uttrik, bowing, "you may rest assured that, not only do I wish it, but I am determined to do so at the earliest convenience to yourself."

"Well, then, is it not the case that the rest of you want to arrest me?"

"Well," said Khaavren, with some embarrassment, "that is not entirely certain."

"And yet," said Kathana, "I beg you to remember that this gentleman—what was your name?"

"Pel."

"—that Pel stated in terms clear and precise—"

"He is very well-spoken," said Khaavren.

"—that your desire was for my arrest."

"Nevertheless," said Khaavren, "you should be aware that you are not without friends."

"Oh, as to that, I know it. Lord Adron is my friend. He is more than that, he is my patron."

"Well, and he isn't your only friend."

"You know of another?"

"I do."

"But, to whom do you refer?"

"As to that, I cannot say."

"You cannot say?"

"It would be indiscreet."

"How, indiscreet to tell me the name of my friend?"

"Exactly."

"Well, go on."

"Your friend, I should say, is known to me."

"That is natural, or how could you know it is indiscreet to tell me his name?"

"Her name."

"Ah, you say her. Then I am that much closer to knowing who it is."

"Yes," said Khaavren, "you may now eliminate from consideration half of the population of the Empire."

"Which leaves the other half," pointed out Kathana, "which is still a good number."

"That is true," said Khaavren.

"Well, go on, then, my friend is a woman, and, though unknown to me, is known to you."

"More than known to me."

"More than known? She is, then, your—"

"Friend. Yes, exactly."

"Then we have the same friend."

"Precisely."

"Which nearly makes us friends."

"Nearly."

"But then, does one arrest one's friends?"

"I would think not, lady."

"But you are a Guard, and therefore must arrest fugitives."

"You have stated the problem in admirably exact terms."

"Well, I have a solution."

"I should be happy to hear it."

"I shall accompany you from Lord Adron's lands."

"Yes, and then?"

"And then? Well, Lord Uttrik will kill me, and he will he satisfied, and you need not arrest me, because I will be dead, so there will be no question of your having failed in your duty."

"An admirable plan," cried Uttrik, bowing to Kathana with a gesture full of respect.

"And yet," said Pel, "it would be sad for the world if an artist of your skill were no longer among us."

"You are full of courtesy," said Kathana. "But then, perhaps I will kill Lord Uttrik."

"But," said Tazendra, who had been following the conversation carefully, "we will be no better off than we are now; worse, in fact, for having lost a friend." At this she bowed to Uttrik.

"Well," said Kathana, "what would you have? I cannot think of a better plan. Besides," she added to Uttrik, "it is already nearly too dark to fight; by the time we will have arranged terms, we shall be unable to see each other, and have to blunder about, hitting the seconds and the judges quite as much as each other, which would be both inelegant and ineffective."

Uttrik agreed with the wisdom of this, and said, "Well, then, shall we set off in the morning?"

"It is, I think, a good plan," said Kathana. "We shall meet in the stables and set off in some direction, and, presently, we will stop and fight."

"I agree," said Uttrik.

"And I," said Tazendra.

"A satisfactory solution," said Pel.

"It will have to do," said Khaavren, frowning.

Aerich shrugged.

Chapter the Twenty-sixth

In Which the Author Resorts to a Stratagem
To Reveal the Effects Of a Stratagem

THE NEXT MORNING , as agreed, they met at the stables, where Mica, who had arisen rather before the others, busied himself in preparing the horses. Uttrik bowed to Kathana and said, "You rested well, I hope?"

"Indeed, I did," said Kathana. "And you?"

"Oh, I passed a relaxing evening, such that I now find myself entirely prepared to meet you on equal terms, and it will not be my fault if I fail to separate your head from your body, a service, you recall, that you preformed for my father without the formalities which I intend to observe toward you."

"Well," said Kathana, shrugging her shoulders. "Your loyalty does you honor. But, please to observe, he was armed."

"Armed, yes. But had he been given time to draw his blade—"

"Oh, as to that—"

"Well?"

"I confess I acted hastily. And yet—"

"And yet?"

"His blade was in his hands."

"My friends," interrupted Khaavren. "Let us be about our travels."

"Travels?" said someone who had just arrived at the service court for the stables.

Aerich bowed and said, "Indeed, Your Highness. We are just setting as out, as you see."

Adron looked around, his brow dark. "But then, the lady Fricorith has chosen to accompany you?"

"I have," she said. "And it pleases me that Your Highness has risen early, for I wished to express my thanks for Your Highness's hospitality, and yet I feared to awaken you."

"Well, you are most welcome, and yet I wonder why you have chosen to leave so precipitously."

The Guardsmen looked at each other uncomfortably, but Kathana said, "Why, I have business with these fine people, that is all."

"Business? May I inquire as to its nature?"

"Oh, as to that, well, I regret to inform your Highness that none of us are at liberty to speak of it."

Adron looked at them all for a moment, as if attempting to read their thoughts. Aerich said, "We should also like to express our gratitude for Your Highness's welcome of us."

"Yes," said Adron shortly. It was plain that he was dissatisfied with the answers he had received, yet he could find no pretext for insisting on more complete responses. At last he said, "Very well, then do me the honor to stop at the kitchens and take what you will need for your journey."

"Your offer," said Aerich, "is most generous, and we accept in the spirit in which it is made."

"So much the better," said Adron, after which he sighed, wished them all a pleasant journey, and retired.

When he had gone, Uttrik bowed low to Kathana, who

returned the gesture briefly and said, "Let us be on our way."

Without further words, they mounted and rode off, stopping only at the kitchens to procure bread, cheese, fruit, and some tough but well-seasoned dried meat. After this pause, which only required a quarter of an hour, they set out upon the road with Aerich and Khaavren in the lead, followed by Tazendra and Uttrik, then Kathana and Pel, with Mica bringing up the rear. Thus they passed below the Arch of Redface, and came to the road leading back down to Bengloarafurd.

"Kharaven, my friend," said Aerich. "Permit me to observe that you seem gloomy today."

"Well? Why should I not? Either Kathana will kill Uttrik, of whom I've grown fond, or Uttrik will kill Kathana, and I will have failed in my promise to Illista, or neither will kill the other, and I shall have to fail in my duty, for I am unlikely to arrest her."

"My young friend," said Aerich, "how you worry!"

"Well, and have I nothing worth worrying about?"

"Oh, as to that, there are many leagues between here and the city, and I have no doubt that an idea will occur to you before then."

"And yet, Aerich, I assure you that I have no ideas, and moreover feel as if my supply of ideas has been, not only used up, but promised for years in advance. No, if there is to be an idea, it must come from someone other than me."

"Well, there are always the gods. And if they should fail—"

"Well? If they fail?"

"Then there is whim, fortune, chance, or caprice, what you will."

"I should then commit my happiness to the chances of fate?"

"My friend, do we not do so at every moment?"

"And yet, Aerich, you will forgive me if this fails to comfort me."

"Comfort you? Who spoke of comfort? It is my belief—but no, you have surrendered to failure, and so you have no need of my advice. That is just as well, for advice is rarely heeded at any time, and never heeded when the advice is good."

"What, you pretend that you have advice for me?"

"What does it matter, if you have given up?"

"Well, then, if you have advice, I declare to you that I will not give up until I have heard your advice. And, if I think it good, I will follow it."

"So, you wish to hear my plan?"

"Kieron's Boots! I've been asking for nothing else for an hour!"

"Very well, here it is: instead of taking this road, turn rather to the north."

"How, the north?"

"Exactly."

"That is your advice?"

"In its entirety."

"Yet, I fail to see how that will solve the problem."

"Then I will explain."

"I am most anxious for you to do so."

"Here, then, is the explanation: Lord Adron's domain extends further to the north than it does in any other direction."

"Yes, and?"

"That is it."

"What, that is it?"

"Yes. Traveling in this way, at a slow and regular pace, we have three good days ahead of us, during which time, well, many things may happen. Perhaps Kathana will die. Perhaps Uttrik will die. Perhaps you will die. Perhaps Uttrik and Kathana will become friends. Or, perhaps the horse will—"

"Well, I admit that there is some wisdom in your plan. But, how will I explain this path to Kathana and Uttrik, both of whom are anxious to reach a place where they may honorably slaughter each other?"

"In the simplest way, good Khaavren. Have you forgotten our mission?"

"How, our mission? To arrest Kathana? I assure you, I have thought of little else for—"

"No, the mission the Captain entrusted to us."

"Oh. Egad, I had forgotten that mission."

"Well, I beg you to remember it."

"I have done so."

"Excellent."

"Now, that remembered, be good enough to explain why this mission will help justify the path we are to take, or, rather, have just taken, now that I perceive this northern trail upon which I have just set my horse."

"In this way: Pepperfield lies to the north, and the southern tip of the domain touches directly on the country of Korio, the northernmost of Lord Adron's domains."

"Well, and is it the closest path?"

"Yes and no."

"How, yes and no?"

"It is the closest path if we wish to ride."

"And, if we were to walk?"

"Oh, we could walk there by to-morrow, or even by the end of to-day if we wished to hurry."

"But we do not wish to hurry," said Khaavren.

"That is true."

"And, moreover, we would like to ride."

"I think so."

"Well, now I understand."

"Then you have ceased to worry?"

"Not entirely, I confess."

"So much the worse."

"But it is true that I am worrying less than I did a few minutes ago."

"That is well. Then let us enjoy the ride, the day, and the lovely view of the mountains that we will, I think, be granted in only a few minutes, when this path takes us around the boulder that lies just ahead."

When it came time to rest for the day, Uttrik wondered

aloud about the path they had chosen, and in this he was
seconded by Kathana. Aerich, however, coolly explained
that they were on a mission entrusted them by their Captain, and that, as they were taking the route to their destination, Uttrik and Kathana would simply have to
postpone murdering one another for a few days yet. Neither was happy at this; however, once they saw that the
four Guardsmen were determined on this route, they were
forced to accept it.

That night they rested high in the mountains, close
around a large fire built of wood that was slightly damp
and kindled with a great many pine-needles, and all of
them awoke with the feeling of vigor that only a night in
the mountains can bring. They broke their fast with bread
and goat's cheese that Lord Adron had thoughtfully supplied for their journey, and passed a peaceful day which
brought them down into the valley between Bli'aard and
Kieron, with the immensity of the Ironwall, that great
vertical slab of brown rock that might have been created
by the gods in a vain attempt to keep Easterners and
Dragaerans apart, looming ever above them to the east.

This attempt, we might say, might have been successful
were it not for the Eastern River, which, over the course
of eons, had dug for itself a passage in Mount Kieron,
until it came to a green fertile plateau which was equally
accessible from the east or the west, and was, over the
thousands of miles that the Eastern Mountains stretch,
one of only three or four places that gave any sort of easy
access between the two civilizations, if we may be permitted to use this word to describe the way the Easterners
live.

That evening, as they prepared to sleep in the compar-
ative warmth of the valley that they would, on the morrow, begin climbing up from with the same energy they
had just spent climbing down to, Kathana took the opportunity to take out her sketch pad and crayon and make
some drawings of the Ironwall, while Uttrik studied the
dark, empty sky as if to read omens there as the ancients

were said to. Aerich sat by the fire with his crochet hook, Pel sat with pen and paper composing a letter to someone whose name he did not care to divulge, Khaavren brooded, and Tazendra slept.

The last light of day was following the Eastern River out of the valley when Kathana suddenly said, "Hullo, what is this?"

Khaavren, who was taking less pleasure in his activity than any of the others were taking in theirs, and was thus more easily broken from it, said, "What have you found, Kathana?"

"I have found nothing, Khaavren. But I have seen something."

"Well," said Pel, looking up from his letter with some annoyance, "what have you seen?"

"As to that," said Kathana, "I am not entirely certain, yet it seemed to me that something moved in those rocks."

"Well?" said Khaavren. "There is no shortage of fauna in the mountains. There are, first of all, norska—"

"Well, it was larger than a norska."

"Then there are dragons."

"It was smaller than a dragon."

"There are dzur and tiassa."

"These do not walk on two feet."

"Well, there are darr."

"Not in these mountains."

"There are bear in these mountains."

"Bear do not wear hats."

"What? It was wearing a hat?"

"I am all but certain of it."

"Then perhaps it was a man."

"That is my conclusion," said Kathana. "And a man, moreover, who wishes to remain concealed, if we are to judge by the fact that I only caught a glimpse of him ducking behind the rocks, and that, since then, there has been no—ah, there he is again."

"Well, yes, I did see something," admitted Khaavren. "Brigands, do you think?"

"Brigands," said Kathana, who had unusually sharp eyes, "do do not wear the red and silver."

"The Light!" said Pel. "A Tsalmoth!"

"Well," said Uttrik, "what would a Tsalmoth be doing here?"

Tazendra opened an eye that said, "Watching us, I would think."

"That," said Aerich, "is not unlikely."

"Yet I wonder who it might be," said Kathana.

"Oh, as to that," said Pel, "I have a theory."

"Well? And that is?"

"Lord Garland."

"Garland!" said Khaavren. "The favorite?"

"The messenger," said Pel.

"That is true; we know him to be nearby. But, what might he be doing?"

"Spying on us," said Pel.

"For what purpose?"

"In order to attack us."

"How, attack us?" said Kathana.

"We have been attacked several times since we left home, 'this true," said Tazendra.

"For what reason?" said Kathana.

"Oh, as to that," said Khaavren. "I assure you we are entirely ignorant."

"And is it Lord Garland who has been directing these attacks?"

"Well, that is possible," said Pel.

"Let us ask him," said Kathana.

"We must find him first," said Uttrik.

"That is difficult," said Pel. "For, you perceive, it is already dark, and soon we will not be able to see anything beyond the range of our small fire."

"Not at all," said Tazendra. "Have you forgotten that I am a sorcerer?"

"Then," said Kathana, "you can light up the area where he is hiding?"

"It is not unlikely," said Tazendra.

"It would be a good idea to have light," said Kathana.

"Well," said Tazendra, who stood and drew her sword, "let us be about it."

"But what," said Pel, "will we do once we have light? They are doubtless preparing to massacre us, and I don't think we shall be as lucky this time as we were before."

"Oh," said Tazendra, "Khaavren will think of something."

"I assure you," said Khaavren, "that I have entirely exhausted my store of ideas."

"Well then," said Aerich carelessly, "someone else will. Come, make the light."

"And yet," said Khaavren, "they may have an entire army ready to attack us, and I, for one, am loathe to begin a fight against any army until we have managed to equip ourselves with one as well."

"Do you know," said Tazendra, "that gives me an idea."

"I am not startled," said Aerich. "I have always believed that you do yourself too little credit in the matter of ideas, merely because you are slower than some in the matter of comprehension."

"So you think," said Tazendra, "that ideas and comprehension are not co-related?"

"Where did you learn that word, Tazendra?" said Pel.

"I have no idea," said Tazendra.

"And yet," said Uttrik, "I had thought you just said you had an idea."

"Come," said Kathana. "Let us hear this famous idea before we are attacked and it becomes, like our souls, immaterial."

"But," persisted Uttrik, "she said she had no idea."

"Well, this is it, then," said Tazendra, ignoring Uttrik. "But first, who has a loud voice?"

"I have," said Kathana.

"Very well, then here it is." And she quickly sketched out a plan which, after a few additions by Uttrik and Kathana, was agreed upon.

"Make the light then," said Kathana.

"Very well," said Tazendra.

And while it would be possible for us to simply relate all that followed the casting of this simplest of spells, we must admit that we would find it more amusing to delay this revelation; or rather, to find an indirect method of describing it. While the amusement of the historian may be insufficient reason to take such a circuitous route to relation of facts, rest assured we have another reason as well, that being the necessity of describing another conversation in which these very events were announced.

It would seem, therefore, that if we were to allow our readers, by virtue of being in the company of the historian, to eavesdrop on this interchange, we will have, in one scene, discharged two obligations; a sacrifice, if we may say so, to the god Brevity, whom all historians, indeed, all who work with the written word, ought to worship. We cannot say too little on this subject.

This having been stated, then, we will carry our worship of the afore-mentioned god so far as to dwell no longer on explanations, but instead will at once bear our readers to a place some two leagues back toward Redface and an hour in the future, where Lord Garland (Pel was correct concerning the identity of the Tsalmoth) is staring hard at the gold disk that we watched him receive from Seodra.

After a few minutes, it seemed to him that he heard her voice, as if in his very ear, saying, "Is that you, Garland?"

"It is, your ladyship."

"Well? Have you something to report?"

"I do, your ladyship."

"Have you, then, completed your task?"

"Not yet, your ladyship."

"How, not? Were my instructions not explicit enough?"

"Oh, no, your ladyship. There was no flaw in the instructions, except—"

"Well?"

"Except, we were betrayed, your ladyship."

"Betrayed? Impossible!"

"It is true."

"By whom?"

"I can only think by the dweller in the house with stones like crooked teeth, your ladyship."

"The notion is absurd. Confess, Garland, that you bungled the mission."

"Your ladyship that may be. Yet, had we not been betrayed—"

"You use that word again, Garland."

"Well, and is it not a perfectly good word, your ladyship?"

"Oh, I have no quarrel with the word."

"And then?"

"But its application in this case."

"I must hold to it, your ladyship."

"And yet I declare that the thing is impossible."

"Well, I will relate that happened to you, and you may then judge for yourself."

"And at once, I hope."

"Without delay."

"Begin then."

"Well, your ladyship, your instructions after the failure of the attack outside The Painted Sign—"

"Which failure I still do not understand, Garland."

"No more do I, your ladyship."

"Very well, continue. After the attack—"

"Yes, your ladyship. After the attack, I was to return the seal to Lord Adron."

"And did you do so?"

"I did."

"And did he invite you to remain?"

"Yes, your ladyship, just as you said he would."

"And did you do so?"

"No, your ladyship, since your orders were to plead that I was in a hurry to return to His Majesty, I did so, and excused myself."

"Very well. And did you give him His Majesty's letter?"

"No, I still hold it, as your ladyship instructed."

"Very well. And then?"

"And then, I was to travel to a small hamlet below Redface, which is called FourCrossings, and there I was to locate a certain unmarked house, identified by three large stones set in front of it, pointing up and outward like crooked teeth."

"You have an excellent memory, Garland."

"I have come to rely upon it, your ladyship."

"Well, and did you find the house?"

"Exactly as you said."

"And did you speak to him who was within?"

"I did more than speak to him. As instructed, I showed him this very disk which is now allowing me to communicate with your ladyship."

"Very well. And he?"

"He put himself entirely at my, that is to say, your service."

"Well, and what did you do then?"

"I instructed him to deliver to me a flash-stone of sufficient strength to destroy nine men."

"How, nine? They were only five and a lackey."

"And yet, your ladyship, it seemed wise to prepare for surprises."

"Well, I accept that. Go on. Did he deliver the stone?"

"Within minutes, your ladyship. He seemed to have had one ready."

"So, and you?"

"I then asked him to gather sixty warriors he could trust, and, with himself, to accompany me, and to use both the flash-stone and the warriors against those I indicated."

"Well, and he?"

"He only asked leave to call his comrades and to gather supplies for the journey."

"Did he ask any questions?"

"He asked how long he would be away, so he might know what to bring."

"And you told him?"

"That I didn't know."

"And he?"

"He did not seem disturbed, but instantly gathered his troop together, after which we set off."

"Well, and how much time was involved in this gathering?"

"Scarcely three hours, your ladyship."

"Well, and then?"

"Then we set off, your ladyship."

"And what were the results of the journey?"

"The very next morning, your ladyship, as we were positioned in a spot overlooking Castle Redfare, we saw the six of them leave."

"Six. You mean, five plus the lackey."

"I beg your pardon, your ladyship. There were six plus the lackey."

"How, six?"

"I counted them several times to see if I was mistaken."

"Well, and?"

"And there were six of them, as well as the lackey."

"But, who was the sixth?"

"The sixth was the Baroness Kaluma, that is, Kathana e'Marish'Chala."

"What? She traveled with them?"

"It is as I have had the honor to inform your ladyship."

"But then, you knew not to kill her, I hope."

"I had no sooner observed her presence, then I informed my battalion, if I may use such a word, that she was under no circumstances to be killed."

"That is not so bad, then."

"Well, I have the honor to inform your ladyship that it didn't matter."

"How, it didn't matter?"

"No, because we were unable to touch them."

"What, they were protected?"

"In a most formidable way, your ladyship."

"In what way was that, Garland."

"They had an army."

"How, an army?"

"A brigade at least, preparing an ambuscade for us."

"And were you caught in it?"

"No, we were able to escape with little injury."

"But, how did it come about?"

"Well, we were taking a position around their camp, which was near the Floating Bridge."

"Yes, I know the area. What were your positions?"

"Your ladyship, we had surrounded them."

"Well, and what time was it?"

"Dusk was falling."

"A good time for an attack, I think."

"So I thought, your ladyship."

"Well, and then?"

"It was at that moment, your ladyship, just as we were about to discharge the flash-stone and commence the attack—"

"A heavy flash-stone and a troop of sixty, you say."

"Yes, exactly. At that moment, the sky was lit up, and we were, instead of being hidden, terribly illuminated."

"Bah. The simplest of sorceries. Was that all?"

"Not in the least."

"What else, then?"

"At that moment, we were attacked by their brigade."

"You were attacked you say?"

"Yes. At least, the order was given."

"By whom?"

"I believe that I recognized the voice of the Baroness of Kaluma giving the orders."

"Well, what were these famous orders?"

"She was deploying her forces for a counter-attack."

"In what manner?"

"Well, first she cried to her lancers to be at the ready."

"Lancers?"

"Yes, your ladyship."

"Well, what else?"

"She required her archers to remain in position."

"Archers? Are you certain?"

"She spoke in a loud voice, your ladyship, so that her brigade could hear her, as a consequence of which, we could, also."

"What then?"

"Then she commanded her cavalry to prepare to charge."

"Is that all?"

"No, for she also ordered her sorcerers to prepare counterspells, in case any were needed, and to lead the attack as well, from which I deduced there were a good number of them."

"Sorcerers?"

"Well, there were loud noises and bright flashes of light, such that I can see no other way than sorcery to achieve the explosions that must have caused them."

"But you did not see the arrows, or the lancers, or the cavalry?"

"Your ladyship, it seemed that we were caught in an ambuscade, and, to avoid a massacre, I ordered that we retreat at once."

"Well, and did your troop obey?"

"They more than obeyed, most of them were gone before I gave the command."

"I see."

"But, as we were attempting to leave, some of our brigade must have stumbled across the enemy forces, for three did not return."

"Three, you say."

"So, your ladyship, we must have been betrayed."

"You are right, Garland, you were betrayed."

"I am glad your ladyship understands."

"I more than understand, I can tell you who betrayed you."

"Well, I am most anxious to learn."

"Your own foolishness betrayed you, Garland."

"How—?"

"There were no lancers, there were no pikeman, there

were no archers, there were no sorcerers, and there was no cavalry; there was only a quick-thinking Dragonlord who spotted someone moving in to attack, a sorcerer who knew how to perform a light-spell, and a fool who believes everything he hears."

"But the lights, and the explosions—"

"What explosions? Any fool of a sorcerer can make a flash and a loud noise. Was anyone injured in these explosions?"

"Well, no. And yet—"

"Be still, idiot. I must consider what is to be done."

"Very well, your ladyship. And I?"

"You? Well, after I have considered, I will have instructions for you."

"I will carry them out, your ladyship."

"I hope so, Garland."

"When shall I endeavor to speak with you again?"

"Give me two hours."

"Until then, your ladyship."

And with this, we will, with our readers' permission, leave Seodra to consider her next action, while we follow our friends across the Floating Bridge and on to Mount Kieron, and so on toward the Pepperfields.

Chapter the Twenty-seventh

In Which it is Shown
That Some are made Unhappy by Reflection,
While others are made Unhappy By Projection

I N ORDER TO cross the Eastern River, which is, at its best, far too cold to swim and far too fast to ford, it was necessary to cross the Floating Bridge. Duraj e'Kieron, Duchess of Eastmanswatch during the Pioneer Wars, had caused this cunning feat of engineering to be built to provide access to the forts and strongholds the rebels had built and inhabited along the southern slopes of Mount Kieron. It did not, we should say at once, actually float; it was merely so low that, viewed from the passes on either Mount Kieron or Mount Bli'aard it seemed as if it were, in fact, floating freely on the river, an effect that was enhanced by its curious shape—the mystery of which we propose to solve.

There have been many stories to account for the peculiar pattern in which the bridge was laid out—the twistings and turnings, esses and half-loops of its length. We have heard it proposed that the form was due to some particular spell of preservation which was laid beneath it; we have heard that it was intended to frighten the enemy so he wouldn't use it himself; we have heard that the engineer who designed the bridge had a weakness for imbibing know-not weed which affected his judgement; and there are other stories besides these.

Yet, had anyone taken the trouble to study the letters and papers of Lady Duraj at the time and compared these to the accounts of the battles then being fought, he would have noticed that, even as the bridge was constructed, the engineers who built it were constantly under attack from the rebels, attacks that consisted of infantry charges, bow shots, catapulted boulders, and other things. The notion of a permanent bridge was, at first, far from the mind of the Duchess; she, in fact, merely wanted access to the other side as quickly as possible. Her solution was, then, to cause boulders to be rolled down from Mount Bli'aard and to cause them further to be pushed or dragged into the river, after which planks were set on them wherever they happened to fall. This is how Duraj was able to secure a foothold on Mount Kieron.

After this time, there was never a chance to design the bridge in a proper manner, it simply had to be maintained as it was to allow for a possible retreat, then strengthened to allow for the passing of reinforcements, and finally widened to allow supply wagons to cross. It was toward the end of the war (in fact, shortly before the abdication of the Issola Emperor Juzai XI) that Duraj spoke of her men tying ropes during a heavy engagement to allow the passing of an ambulance. That is, with the war nearly over, the bridge was still of rope and wood; the first iron beams were probably not added until twenty or thirty years later, by which time no one thought of going to all the work necessary to take down the bridge and re-design it; it was easier (although more expensive in material) to simply strengthen what was there. As the rocks which supported the structure began to sink deeper into the river they were replaced, first with wood, then with iron struts, finally with bricks, which were connected to the structure by means of thick iron chains.

The result, then, was a bridge built of odd, unexpected curves and angles, fully three times as long across as the distance an arrow would make; that, at the height of the rainy season, lay almost fully on the water itself, so even now one cannot traverse it and expect to arrive on the other side with one's feet entirely dry, and during unusually rainy years the bridge is impassable for weeks at a time.

This bridge is famous for many things. We may number among them, first, its vital role in the Pioneer Wars we have already had the honor to mention. Next, there are the suicides which have been committed nearby, especially those of lovers who jump from Deppa's Fang into the icy water the bridge traverses; in such a way did the Issola noble Chalora and his Tiassa lover Auiri die, in spite of the more gruesome and poetic means of mutual destruction ascribed to them in the ballad that bears their names. There have been, as well, so many duels fought along the bridge that it would be tiring to list them, but it should be pointed out that it was on the Floating Bridge that the poet Barracsk and his chief critic, V'rono, killed each other to end an artistic siege that had lasted nearly two millennia. We may add, as an historical footnote, that the critic Norra, who served as Imperial Witness, wryly remarked of this duel, "Barracsk's end was as dramatic as he could manage at his age, but he suffered from allowing his desire for emphatic statement to dominate his movement; whereas V'rono seemed unable to put aside his own ideas of the fence long enough to understand what his opponent was engaged in bringing off; the result was therefore curiously inevitable, yet artistically satisfying."

It was to this bridge, then, that our friends came after having, through Kathana's subterfuge, escaped from the surrounding forces; or, rather, after having allowed the surrounding forces to escape them. As they walked their horses along its peculiar length (another thing the bridge is justly famous for is the dislike it arouses in horses, which is how the Cavalier Joroli of Bridden Cove came to be drowned), Khaavren said, "Well, we all agree, do we not, that this Tazendra is clever enough?"

"Indeed yes," said the others.

Tazendra bowed. "We must add, however, that this Kathana is surely brave enough."

"And quick-eyed as well," said Khaavren.

"Norska's Teeth!" said Pel. "I think so! I would surely have been spitted like a game hen had she not seen those three brigands who stumbled upon us so unexpectedly when we thought all was over."

"And I," said Khaavren, bowing to Kathana, "would have found my head cloven in two, which would have made thinking impractical, if she had not so elegantly struck down the one who had caught me at such a disadvantage."

"And," added Uttrik, "though it pains me to admit it, I saw that, in doing so, she exposed herself to the attacks of the third, who would surely have wounded her severely had Tazendra not interrupted his attack by treating him in exactly the manner his friend proposed to treat Khaavren." And he, too, bowed to Kathana, though he did so somewhat stiffly.

"And yet it seems to me," said Kathana, bowing in return, "that we ought to determine why we were to be attacked, and then discover a way to prevent such attacks in the future."

"Well," said Tazendra, "that is only right. Who knows, but that next time they will have an army."

"And," said Pel, "they will be less likely to be fooled a second time."

"We could," said Khaavren, "request help from Lord Adron, who is your friend, Kathana, and does indeed have an army."

"I am loathe to do so," said Kathana. "Because such a thing might compromise his position in the discussion he is engaged in with the Emperor to earn command of the Pepperfield. He would certainly send help if I asked, but, you perceive, it would be an unkindness."

"Then we must not do so," said Aerich, as if to be discourteous to the Dragon Heir ended the discussion for all time.

"And yet," said Uttrik, "I am not convinced that we require any help at all."

"How?" said Pel. "Explain your reasoning."

"I will be glad to do so. To-morrow we will have arrived in the Pepperfields."

"Well, and?"

"And then, Kathana and I will have the honor of touching steel with steel, and it seems to me that, however the encounter ends, there will be no need for the survivors to remain here. And, furthermore, it may well be that the cause of the attacks will have vanished."

"Well," said Kathana, "there is some justice in this remark."

"Well then," said Khaavren, "as I perceive we are now at the end of the bridge, let us mount once more and continue," which excellent and practical suggestion they followed at once, taking the mountain paths, which, like those leading up to Castle Redface, were steep, but well within the capabilities of the horses.

Khaavren took the lead himself, and for a while Aerich rode with him, but then, with the great sensitivity this Lyorn possessed, he determined that the young Tiassa wished to be alone with his thoughts and so Aerich allowed his horse to fall back to where Tazendra and Uttrik were involved in a discussion comparing the merits of various sorts of stirrups when used in melee versus in mounted duels (which had not yet fallen entirely out of fashion, though they were becoming rare). Aerich astounded them both with his knowledge of the intricacies of this subtle art, and with his wisdom on the necessity of relating the style of stirrup to the precise task the cavalry officer intends to perform; but, as we suspect our readers will have rather less interest in this subject than the participants, we will return our attention to Khaavren, in his blue and white, gold half-cloak down his back, as he rides his mare and soliloquizes.

"Now," Khaavren was saying to himself, "I must decide between betraying my Emperor and betraying my love. Well, when put this way, the choice becomes simple after all: the love of one obscure Guardsman must always give way before the needs of the Empire, that is the principal upon which men live together under his banner. But no, I must think again. The choice is not between love and the Empire, it is between two oaths that I have made and which contradict each other, so the problem is really one of choosing to whom I am to be forsworn. Forsworn! Ah, now there is an ugly word. And why am I to be forsworn? Because my mouth has made a promise that my heart directed it to make, without first consulting my brain, which it ought not to have done, because it is certainly my brain's proper function to keep a check on my mouth's activities, whereas my heart should limit itself to pumping blood through my body. But never mind that, the case is still clear: it is far more important to keep an oath to one's Emperor than to one's love.

"But, if this is true, why does my heart say so differently? Well, that is easy, it is because my heart, quite properly ashamed of what it has done, is denying blood to my brain, so that the brain, instead of thinking clearly, allows everything to become muddled and confused. Perhaps I will be so fortunate in our next encounter that this treacherous heart will deny blood to my arms, and then it will find itself properly pierced with holes and my dilemma will then end, albeit in a rather droll way. Oaths must come from somewhere, after all, and my heart knows it has no business making them when they contradict those that have been prompted by my brain, or, at any rate, by my viscera.

"This being the case, my choices are to fall sick at heart, or, in the other case, either sick to my stomach or develop the headache. I have been sick to my stomach, and I have had the headache, perhaps it is now time to become sick at heart, after which I will have had the experience of feeling illness in all major regions of the body, and I will be that much more complete for it. Bah, as Aerich would say. There must be a better way to make choices than by determining where the illness caused by the decision will fall. Well, that is an interesting question; let us examine it.

"To live," Khaavren continued to himself, "is to be faced with choices. This must be, because to be dead is to be faced with no choices whatsoever, save those that exist beyond Deathgate, and which the philosophers believe are nothing but a recapitulation of all the choices one has taken in life.

"But then, if life is to be filled with choices, many of them difficult, one ought to have a method with which to approach the art of decision-making. But no, I have left something out. One *always* has such a method; it is merely the case that one is not always aware of it. So, then, what is my method? Simply this: to fail to make any decision at all, to worry it the way a dog worries a scrap of leather, and then, by Undauntra's Garters, to be forced into some hateful actions or inaction that I'd never have contemplated a month before. Cha! That's no way to live!

"But, to return to the question, there ought to be a way to decide, clearly and explicitly, where one's duty lies, and yet so often there is not. In this case, for example, to fail in my duty toward my lover will give me, and in faith, I think her, too, great pain, whereas to fail in my duty to his Majesty will not cause any damage to the Empire itself, it will merely cause some slight annoyance in a man who, if truth be told, is just like me, except that over his head circles the Orb, whereas over mine circle only these infernal clouds which will not stop producing these thin droplets of mountain rain until, I suppose, we have reached such heights that they will begin producing snow. Cha! If nature cannot make up her mind about such a simple, practical question, that is, to rain, or mist, or snow, then how am I to make a moral choice knowing I shall be miserable whichever way I decide?

"So, when there is no right thing to do, how does one decide which course to take? It seems my mother and father, whose duty it was to instruct me, ought to have told me the answer to this; unless it is one of those lessons which, if they can be learned, cannot, at any rate, be taught. If so, then I am a fool for thinking I can simply decide, and I must go on my way and prepare myself for the instruction of events, which, I am certain, make the best teachers, at least when one is prepared to learn from them."

At this point, Khaavren broke off his monologue, for he noticed that Mica had come up next to him, and was looking around with a melancholy expression on his normally cheerful face.

"Well," said Khaavren, happy to be distracted by someone else's misery, "you are looking mournful."

"It is true, my lord."

"But then, have you a reason for this look? Or is it due to the rain that is soaking us to the skin and making us fear our horses will slip on this treacherous mountain path and lead us to break our necks? Do you know, we had planned to bring oiled cloaks with us, we even counted on it, but somehow we forgot to bring them. It is a sad comment on the human condition when even correct planning is of no benefit. Is it this that saddens you, good Mica? For, if so, I am in full agreement."

"No, it is not that at all, my lord."

"Well, what is it then?"

"You wish me to tell you?"

"I do."

"Then I will."

"Go on, then, I await you."

"Well, this is it: I have been doing sums in head."

"But then," said Khaavren, "I have done sums in my head, and it never makes me sad; on the contrary, it sharpens my wits, which, in turn, increases my amusement with the world, and that makes the hours go by in a very pleasurable way."

"I will try to follow your example, my lord."

"You will be pleased with the results, Mica, I assure you."

"But I have been doing more than sums, my lord; I have been making *projections*."

"Ah, *projections*. Well, that is another matter entirely."

"I am pleased that you think so, my lord."

"Oh, I do indeed. Projections are fare more serious matters than sums."

"And moreover—"

"What, there is more?"

"There is, my lord, and, if you want to hear it, I shall tell you."

"I should enjoy hearing it if for other reason than because the clipped tones of your accent tickle me; you speak so differently from the northern twang of the city or the lilt of my own country."

"Well, my lord, it may be that the subject upon which you calculate sums is different from the subject upon which I make projections."

"Well, that may be, Mica, because I had not known you were making projections on a particular subject."

"I have been, my lord."

"And what, then, is this famous subject?"

"It is soldiers, my lord."

"How, soldiers?"

"Exactly. Attend: were you not, before I had the honor to meet you, attacked by one man?"

"Well, yes, I was, and the proof is, it was Uttrik, who now rides with us."

"And then, at Beed'n's Inn, were there not twelve brigands who attacked us?"

"Why, that is exactly the number, Mica."

"And then, when we were leaving The Painted Sign, were we not set on by some thirty of the enemy?"

"That is to say, we set on them, but your numbers are correct."

"Well, and, were there not at least a hundred of the enemy who were driven off by my lady's stratagem?"

"This time, I think, you may be in error."

"But at least, my lord, there were a good deal more than thirty."

"With this I agree."

"Well then, it is upon this subject that I have been making projections, toward the goal of determining how many enemies will face us next time."

"I see. Well, and what have you determined, Mica?"

"That there will be many more of them than there are of us."

"Well, I don't doubt that you are correct."

"An army, my lord. I fear they will bring an army."

"It could happen, good Mica."

"My lord, I know you are brave and strong, and my mistress fights like a dzur, and I perceive that Lord Aerich is very cool under fire, while the Cavalier Pel is both clever and fierce, and both Lord Uttrik and Lady Kathana are Dragons, and I, though a Teckla, can keep my head well enough when matters become hot and I have a bar-stool in my hand—"

"I know it well, good Mica, for I have seen it."

"Thanks, my lord. And yet, well, an army, my lord?"

"What, then, you are afraid of dying?"

"Afraid? Oh, no, my lord, I beg you to believe that I wouldn't dare to be afraid. But I am sad, because serving my lady has seemed to be such a fine thing for me, that I hate to see my life end at the very moment it has become sweet."

Khaavren reached out his hand and patted Mica on the shoulder. "Take heart, good Mica," he said. "All is not lost, and, who knows, but something may, as Aerich has suggested, occur that will save both of us—you from death, and me from something worse. Besides, you have only made a projection; perhaps they have given up and will make no more attempts."

"Oh, do you believe it, my lord?"

"Cha! It is possible. And, in any case, I have no idea where they could find an army even if they desired to raise one."

"I hope you're right, my lord," said Mica, but he shook his head as if to say, "I put no faith in it, however."

Chapter the Twenty-eighth

In Which Both Stage And Players
are Put Into Position for The Conclusion
of Something Like a Tragedy

AND, IN FACT, Mica was not far wrong, for at that moment, some few leagues behind them a certain nobleman was causing his name to be announced to Lord Adron, and in his hand was piece of paper, a mere scrap, which, by the time it had finished its business, would have irrevocably altered the destinies of everyone with whom our history concerns itself.

The nobleman was admitted at once upon giving his name, and was led into the same room that we have already visited, where Lord Adron rose, bowed and studied him. "Good day to you, Count Shaltre," he said.

"And to you, Your Highness," said the Lyorn, bowing low out of deference to the Dragonlord's rank, but not so low as he might have, since he came as a messenger from his Majesty.

Adron, who was able to interpret this bow, said, "You have something to convey to me?"

"I have that honor, Your Highness," said Shaltre.

"Well, I await you."

"Here it is, then: I require a thousand troops, with you to lead them, in order to capture certain fugitives."

"Fugitives? That is to say, criminals?"

"I don't say they are criminals, Your Highness, yet they must be taken or killed."

"Well, and how many of these fugitives are there?"

"There are, at present, six."

"How, six? You require a thousand men to capture six fugitives?"

"There are many miles of mountain to search, Your Highness."

"Ah, you require a search, then. But I assure you, my lord, that a search can be far more effectively carried out by a few trackers than by a thousand soldiers."

"It may require many soldiers to bring them home once the trackers have found them, Your Highness."

"Then they are dangerous, my lord?"

"Exceedingly."

"And their names?"

"I do not know all of their names, Your Highness. There is one called Khaavren, and another called Uttrik."

"Those gentlemen?"

"None other."

"They are fugitives?"

"Indeed they are, and even very much so."

"Well, I know them. They have been my guests, and departed my home two days ago. I am afraid that by now they are far from here—too far for soldiers to catch them."

"Not at all, Your Highness. We have reason to believe that they have taken the road to the Floating Bridge."

"Well, but then?"

"They have, for reasons best known to themselves, taken a lengthy route; perhaps so they could keep their horses. If we leave within the hour, and you direct us through the high passes, we could in nine hours be where they are now."

"You know the terrain very well, Count."

"Your Highness is kind."

"I'm sorry, then, but I must refuse."

"How, refuse?"

"They have been my guests, and, moreover, they have with them one—"

"Whose name need not be mentioned, Your Highness. Not all of them need be taken or killed; that is why you must lead the troops yourself, to be certain no mistakes are made on this score."

Adron frowned, trying to puzzle out the complex interrelations of policy and intrigue which had led to this particular Imperial request. At last, unable to guess, he said, "Nevertheless, as I have had the honor of telling you, I must refuse His Majesty in this case. If for no other reason, than because I was informed, while in the city, of a build-up of Easterners near the Pepperfields, and I must bring my troops there lest we be faced with an invasion."

"Allow me to remind your Highness that you are not Marquis of Pepperfield."

"Well, nor is anyone else. Yet I assure you that the Easterners will not delay any invasion they may have planned because His Majesty has delayed designating a Marquis for that estate."

"It is, nevertheless, an Imperial matter at this time, and some may wonder at your determination to place your own forces there."

"The Easterners, I assure you, will not wonder."

"So you are determined to bring your forces to the Pepperfields, rather than to submit to His Majesty's request?"

"Blood! I think so; I have killed two horses in order to return here for that purpose."

"Yet, I declare the thing is impossible, Your Highness," said Shaltre.

"How, impossible?"

"When His Majesty makes a request—"

"It is still a request; therefore, I may act upon it or not. While I am not anxious to offend His Majesty, nevertheless—"

"But if it were not a request, rather, if it were an order?"

"Well, that is another matter. Then, in my capacity as Duke of Eastmanswatch, a position which bears Imperial signets, I must obey."

"Exactly."

"Well?"

"Well, it is an order."

"And yet, you explained that it was a request."

"It was a request, Your Highness, until the moment you refused; it then became an order."

Adron studied the Lyorn carefully. Then he said, "You have, I suppose, some proof of His Majesty's will?"

"If your Highness would deign to read this paper?"

Adron's frown deepened, but he took the paper that Shaltre presented him, and he read, "Lord Adron: By our will, you are to follow Shaltre's instructions exactly in all matters regarding the capture of Khaavren of Castlerock and his companions.—Tortaalik." Adron checked the seal and the signature, and fought to keep his face expressionless. Finally he bowed, because he did not trust himself to speak.

"Is it sufficiently clear, Your Highness?" said Shaltre.

After a moment to regain his composure, he said, "We will be ready to leave within the hour, my lord."

"I will await Your Highness without."

We will now return to our friends, who knew nothing of this interchange of ideas. By the time the daylight began to fail, they had reached a place within two leagues of the Pepperfields. Uttrik was for pressing on and finishing his affair with Kaluma that very night, but at last Khaavren convinced him to wait for full light, so that they settled in for one last rest before the morning, at which time they expected to resolve the issues before them.

It was, we should note, quite cold, as they had reached an elevated position, but there was still no lack of firewood, so after seeing to the horses, they built the fire up very high and had a meal of bread and cheese, during which even Tazendra seemed silent and brooding. They sat thus, well wrapped in cloaks and blankets, huddled about the fire, yet saying nothing to each other, all of them aware that the next day would see an end, among some of them, of certain friendships they had grown accustomed to and comfortable with. From time to time, Kathana would look at Uttrik speculatively, as if wondering what sort of friends they might have been had circumstances been different. Uttrik, for his part, avoided looking at Kathana, as if, though bound by his word and his duty, he no longer relished the thought of mortal combat with her.

Khaavren sighed, and said, "My friends, I will tell you that I am not happy about what we are doing. In Dragaera, it seemed a fine idea to go off on a campaign, win favor, and become heroes, but now that we are here, nothing seems as simple as it did."

"Well," said Tazendra, "you are right, and I, for one, freely admit that I do not understand why."

"It is," said Aerich, "because we have embroiled ourselves in the affairs of the Empire, and we have done so for our own reasons, rather than to serve the Empire. This was an error, and I confess myself to be guilty of it."

"Oh, bah," said Pel. "Yes, it is because we are involved in Imperial matters, but there is no fault in that if the Emperor is strong; it is exactly thus that a gentleman discovers his own strength. But when the Emperor is weak, gentlemen who serve him discover only their weaknesses."

Khaavren frowned. "The Emperor is weak, you say? I fail to see how."

"Do you?" said Pel. "But look at our own affair. We four—I must excuse you, Uttrik, and you, Kathana—we four left our homes in Dragaera City on the Imperial service. That is, we serve the Empire, which is personified by his Majesty and the court."

"All you say is clear," said Khaavren. "Go on, then."

"Well, this court, like a chreotha web whose ropes have come undone in the wind, waves tendrils of intrigue about in a fashion which is so haphazard one might not err in using the term anarchistic. It has been our misfortune to find ourselves caught in these tendrils as if by accident. These tendrils have no central mind controlling them, else we would have been well snared before we left the city. The central mind that ought to be controlling them is that of the Emperor. If he does not, then we know that he is weak."

"But then," said Khaavren, "what makes the Emperor weak?"

"Well, in the first place, he is young."

"But well intentioned," said Aerich.

"Oh, I don't deny that. But he is young, and, moreover, has the worst failing an Emperor may have."

"That being?" said Khaavren.

"Poor advisors, to whom he listens."

"Well, he must listen to someone."

"Yes, but he must gain experience in order to determine to whom he ought to listen."

"And how is he to know who these people are?" said Khaavren, who was fascinated by this novel look at Imperial politics.

"In exactly the way Aerich has said: he must find advisors who have, at their heart, the interest of the Empire."

"Well, and what has he now?"

"Now he has advisors who look after their own positions, and seek to advise him only in such a way as to gain his favor, thus they contradict one another needlessly, and leave policy, which ought to be the force which unites all of the Imperial decisions into a single direction, scattered and uncertain. Hence we see the Pepperfields undefended, the Baroness"—here he bowed his head to Kathana—"unarrested, and campaigns that exist only to capture baubles with which to please his love of bright stones."

"Well," said Aerich, with a smile, "if only he had you as an advisor—"

"Oh," said Pel, perhaps too quickly, "I have no such ambition as that, I assure you."

Aerich and Khaavren caught each other's eye, and exchanged a fleeting smile.

"Nevertheless," said Tazendra, who had missed this interchange, "If you were an advisor, what would you tell His Majesty?"

But Pel merely shook his head, as if aware that, lulled by the cold night and warm fire, he had said more than he had intended to. Aerich said, "I must confess, that were I an advisor, a post for which I hold no more ambition than does Pel, I should advise him, first of all, to arrest the lady Kathana."

The lady referred to started at this, but Aerich's attitude was so polite that she could not take offense. Uttrik stared at him, but said nothing. Khaavren, who felt suddenly uncomfortable, said, "Well, my lady, what will you? Ashes! We cannot go around killing those who don't like our paintings."

"You do not paint," said Kathana coldly.

"Well, that is true, so I will say no more."

After an interval, she spoke again, very softly, as if her words were intended for none but herself. "He was too arrogant," she said. "I had worked on that painting for thirty-nine years, of which eleven were spent in the jungles watching dragons, sometimes sneaking into their lairs. For five years I worked on the background, so that every plant, every stone, every shadow was more real than the models from which I drew them, and yet supported the theme of my work. And for fifteen years I sketched dragons, until I could read the expression on a dragon's face, and, moreover, show it to one who didn't know dragons had such expressions. And then I painted and painted, and then I glossed and finished, and then I very humbly brought it to my Lord e'Drien, and, as I stood there, prepared to present it, this person walks by and, in one glance, dismissed it as unworthy of comment."

She fell silent again. Tazendra coughed and said, "You are saying, then, that you were angry?"

Kathana smiled and said, "Well, if truth be known, I regret what I did."

"How," said Uttrik, "you regret it?"

"Yes. I wish I had not killed him; or, at least, that I had taken more time to insure that he was prepared to defend himself. Yet, I was so angry."

"Well," said Uttrik, "I understand anger."

"That's well," said Kathana. "I, in my turn, understand vengeance."

"We understand each other then," said Uttrik.

"Entirely," said Kathana.

"But, the matter of the paint-brushes—"

"Paint-brushes?"

"In his eyes."

"Bah. That never happened."

"What, are you certain?"

"My dear Uttrik, I think I would know if I had stuck paint-brushes into someone's eyes. Besides, I was presenting the painting, I had no paint-brushes with me."

"But the story—"

"You know how stories grow with everyone who repeats it."

"Well, that is true."

"I am pleased you understand."

"I understand entirely. And, should I kill you tomorrow, I assure you I will hold no more animosity toward you."

"And if I kill you, the same."

"Your hand?"

"Here it is."

"Well, until to-morrow, then."

"Until to-morrow."

With this resolve, they closed their eyes and, one after the other, drifted off to sleep.

Chapter the Twenty-ninth

In Which Our Friends Realize
with Great Pleasure That the Situation
has Become Hopeless

THE DOMAIN OF Pepperfield, a large, fertile plateau nestled between Mount Kieron and the Ironwall, was named for scores of varieties of natural peppers which grow there unattended, and for the dozens more, which, owing to the suitability of the land, due to soil and climate, are so readily cultivated. On the northern side there is a sheer wall some five hundred feet high, upon which is built the Looming Fortress, where the Marquis of Pepperfield dwelt, and behind it the North Pinewood Hold which had, until recently, been Uttrik's home. There is a steep, winding path from the Fortress down to the plateau, which is one of the four ways of reaching Pepperfield from the outside world; that is, if one is able to reach the Looming Fortress, which is unlikely, as it is inaccessible except through the Pepperfields themselves.

Another entrance is from the east, where a long, gentle slope rises from a gap in the Ironwall some four leagues to the north. Still another approach is from the southeast, a steep climb, and one unsuitable for horses, yet only a bow-shot away, as it were, from Redface. The final approach, that of the south-west, is the one our friends took, which was to follow a narrow but well-trodden path up from the valley of the Eastern River, only a few leagues below its source at the Thundering Falls in the Ironwall.

This last approach more closely resembles a road than the others, in that there are high stone ridges on either side, which end abruptly in a small grove of trees, after which one is standing on the seemingly endless plain upon which so much blood, human and Eastern, has been spilled since its discovery by the Dzurlord Brionn, who named the mountain after her hero, Kieron the Conqueror.

Early in the morning, then, the companions found themselves looking out at these gentle fields. Uttrik said, "My friends, we are now in the domain of Pepperfield; that is, we have left the holdings of Lord Adron."

"Well," said Kathana laconically.

Uttrik now took the lead, bringing them through the place where a few poplars had sprung up as if to celebrate the few score of years that had passed since the Easterners had been there—for it has always been the Easterners who cultivated those fields, humans being content with those peppers nature chose to provide on her own.

"Here," said Uttrik, "in this small depression, is where my ancestor, Ziver the Tall, made his last stand in the Tsalmoth reign in the eleventh Cycle. Over that hill we observe on our right is where Cli'dha's cavalry lay concealed, their horses made to lie upon the ground, before the charge of the Sundered Trees, that won the Pepperfields back in the Dzur reign in the sixteenth Cycle.

"To the left, up ahead, upon that small hill," Uttrik continued, "is where the Defense of the Running Circle was first developed, which came about accidentally in the fourteenth Issola reign as a desperate measure to save Taalini the Three-Fisted, who had been wounded up ahead there, behind the rock shaped like a mushroom, and was pulled back to the hillock by his esquire, whose name escapes me just at the moment. And here," he added, stopping his horse by the least movement of his knees, "is where my father made me swear the Oath of Protection, and, moreover, where he first belted my sword upon me. You perceive," he added, "that the ground is flat and smooth, with only a few pepper plants just beginning to emerge to greet the summer, bearing only the potentialities of their fruit, which I believe to be of the curving white variety, pungent, sweet, with few seeds and an agreeable tang upon the tongue."

He dismounted and gave his horse to the care of Mica, indicating a lone cherry tree some eighty meters distant where the horses might be tied. He said, "Tazendra, will you stand for me?"

"I will," said Tazendra, "though I must add that this means I hold no animosity toward Kathana, which I beg she will do me the honor to believe."

"I understand," said Kathana, whose throat seemed to have become dry during Uttrik's recital. She then dismounted, handed her horse in turn to Mica, and, turning to Pel, said, "Will you stand for me?"

"I should be honored," said the cavalier, "with the same understanding with respect to Uttrik."

"Well, I agree," said Uttrik.

"And the judge?" said Tazendra.

"Aerich, of course," said Pel.

The Lyorn bowed over his horse's neck, and he, too, dismounted. "For the witness," said Tazendra, "we have Khaavren."

"I will do it," said Khaavren, who felt himself nearly choking with emotion. "I will witness the more willingly because I have no preference for a victor, but the less willingly because I would see neither of you die. The gods know that I love you both."

Uttrik and Kathana hung their heads at this speech, so frank and full of such heartfelt tenderness. Tazendra, Pel, Aerich, and Khaavren then dismounted and gave their horses into the care of Mica, who brought them to the cherry tree and tethered them there. Khaavren murmured, "It is likely that we will need one fewer on the return; my only prayer is that our requirements are not diminished by two."

"Draw the circle, Khaavren," said Aerich.

Khaavren, with a look at the Lyorn that is impossible to describe, drew his poniard, and, his heart nearly breaking, bent over and walked the rectangle, his knife inscribing it with cut grasses, making a circle which was, if difficult to see, at least sufficient for a duel in which it was unlikely either combatant would retreat very often or very far.

Aerich said softly, "The terms?"

Tazendra looked at Uttrik, who returned her a brief nod, as if to say, "You know very well what the terms must be." Tazendra bowed to Pel and said, "Plain steel only, to the death."

Pel looked at Kathana who nodded to him as if to say, "It must be so." He then returned Tazendra's bow and said, "We accept these terms."

"Then," said Aerich, "let us be about it."

Khaavren came to stand near to the Lyorn, his head hanging down. Mica, in his turn, standing next to Khaavren, shook his head sadly and murmured, "If this is what it means to be a gentleman, well, I'm glad that I, at least, am fortunate enough not to be one."

The combatants took their positions, and Aerich said, "Will you not be reconciled?"

Uttrik, looking at the ground, signed that he would not. Kathana shrugged.

"I ask again," said Aerich, his voice trembling with emotion. "Will you not be reconciled?"

The assembled party looked at him in amazement; such a breach of propriety being ten times as amazing, coming as it did from the Lyorn. Once again, they each signed that the duel was necessary.

Aerich sighed audibly. "Inspect the weapons," he said in a voice so low it could only be heard because of the awful stillness of the fields, where even the wind seemed to have stopped out of respect for the tragedy that was brewing on its lap.

Tazendra gave a cursory glance at Uttrik's longswords, while Pel made a brief examination of Kathana's longsword and poniard. They returned the weapons and signed to Aerich that all was in order.

"Take your weapons," said Aerich.

Tazendra gave Kathana her steel, while Uttrik took his from Pel.

"Place yourselves within the circle," said Aerich, whose voice was now barely above a whisper. The combatants did so, the Lyorn taking his place between them. He indicated by signs, apparently unable to speak, where each should stand. Then, with an effort, he said, "Have either of you anything to say before we commence?"

"For my part," said Uttrik, "I declare to you that it is only duty which forces me to attempt to take your life, and, at this moment, I say if you kill me, you will be rendering me the greatest service."

"And I say," said Kathana, "that you are one of the finest gentleman I have ever met, and I now so bitterly regret killing your father, which was a low act and one unworthy of a Dragon, that I say that if I am so unfortunate as to kill you, I will place myself at once in the hands of the Empire."

Khaavren, who was shaking with emotion, said, "You may do so if you wish, but it will not be me who brings you to the Issola Wing, and for my part, you will be free if you win, and mourned if you die. And you, Uttrik, I say again that I love you like a brother, and I hope you bear me no malice if I say I will betray my oath to my Captain and to the Emperor if it should happen that it is Kathana who walks away from this hated combat."

"I bear you no malice for that," said Uttrik. "In fact, I assure you that I will die happier, if I should die, in thinking that Kathana, whom I esteem as a sister, will, hereafter, be free from all effects of her actions, even remorse."

"The only way I should be free of remorse," said Kathana, "is if you will do me the honor to take my life."

"Well," said Uttrik, "I will try to do so, but, I beg you to believe, not happily."

"Then," said Kathana, "let us begin."

"I am ready," said Uttrik.

"Be on your guards," whispered Aerich.

Kathana stood with her sword-arm, that is, her right, to the front, but her right leg behind. The point of her sword was directed at Uttrik's eye, while her poniard was placed to strike at his midsection. Uttrik, meanwhile, had positioned himself with his left leg forward, one longsword held back and over his head, in order to strike down and across at the first opportunity presented, the other pointing at Kathana's eye.

Khaavren, though the Imperial Witness, could not, at first, watch the dreadful scene, and, telling himself that he would look again at the first sound of steel, cast his eyes eastward over the fecundity of the Pepperfields, where one more death, insignificant compared to the thousands that had preceded it in this place, would soon be added to the tally of that beautiful, horrible, fate-filled plateau.

"Hullo," said Khaavren, suddenly.

Aerich, who had gone so far as to take in the very breath which would have exhaled the word, "Begin," stopped, and looked at Khaavren, whose eyes were now fixed upon some point out in the distance. He, Aerich, very slowly let his breath out and followed the imaginary line penciled by the intensity of Khaavren's gaze.

Seeing this, Pel, Tazendra and Mica looked, then Uttrik, who stood facing the east, and, last of all, Kathana turned around and stared herself.

After a few moments, Pel murmured, "Easterners, if I am not mistaken. See how they sit bent over their horses?"

"Thousands of them," said Khaavren.

"The invasion has begun," said Uttrik, as if he could not believe it himself.

"Then," said Tazendra, "instead of having to watch one of our friends die, we shall all die together. How splendid!"

"Splendid, mistress?" said Mica, amazed that she should be positively glowing with pleasure at the thought of her imminent demise.

"Compared to the alternative," said Khaavren, drawing his sword, "a pleasure indeed."

Pel said, "I admit that it pleases me also."

"It is just the sort of thing I had been hoping for," said Aerich.

"For my part," said Kathana, "I quite agree."

"As do I," said Uttrik.

Mica looked at the lot of them and shook his head, then looking back at the growing line of Easterners, he said, "There is time to reach the horses and escape, if we hurry."

The others stared at him. "How," said Tazendra. "And miss a battle of six against thousands? When will such a chance come again?"

"Not to mention," said Uttrik, "that, if we escape, Kathana and I will simply have to fight, and I assure you that I haven't the heart to experience once more what I felt just now as I prepared to try my best to slay her."

"Far better to die in battle with honest foes," said Kathana, "than to be forced to kill a friend. Ah! It is not Easterners out there, it is expiation!"

"Well," said Uttrik. "Let us spread out in a good line, and see what they can do."

Mica, trembling, took into his hand the poniard Tazendra had given him, but kept his trusty bar-stool in the other. Aerich looked at him and said, "Tazendra, I fully share your desire to fight this battle, but, is it not true that we must give some thought to warning Lord Adron?"

"Ah," said Tazendra, "I had not thought of that. You are right. What must we do?"

"Why," said Uttrik, "we shall order Mica back to Castle Redface, by the fastest route, which, if I am not mistaken, is the footpath that begins between a pair of watch-stations which are called Nilk'arf's Tower and which are built upon a tall pair of rocks. To reach it, you must only follow this brook, which is called the Slipknot, and which flows over the ridge very near to the towers."

"Well, Mica?" said Tazendra.

Mica drew himself up and shook his head. "Oh, mistress, leave your side, now, in such a circumstance? I cannot."

"Your courage does you honor," said Tazendra, "but you must, for there is no one else."

"And yet, I should prefer—"

"No more speech," said Tazendra, sternly. "In twenty minutes they will be here; and every second counts. Go."

"Mistress—"

"Go!"

Mica, almost in tears, bowed his head, and, without another word, ran toward the indicated rocks.

"Well, and now?" said Khaavren, coolly surveying the Easterners who approached at a walk."

"Now," said Uttrik, "there is no better place for waiting, the nature of these fields being such that nowhere can we force them to attack with fewer numbers, so I propose that we await them here."

"Well," said Tazendra, "I have one flash-stone, with a single charge, which I prepared while in Castle Redface. Here, Khaavren, you take it, and attempt to kill their leader; that should give them a few moments of concern."

"Excellent," said Kathana. "And the rest of us will endeavor to give Khaavren time to do so."

Aerich, Pel, and Tazendra drew their swords, and, there being nothing else to do, they waited.

Chapter the Thirtieth

*In Which Khaavren is Amazed To Discover
an Easterner Who Speaks the Dragaeran Language,
Albeit With an Accent, And, Out of Necessity,
The Tiassa Becomes a Diplomatist*

A S IT WILL be some few moments before the Eastern army arrives at the place where Khaavren and his friends await them, let us make use of the interval to follow Mica along his route toward Castle Redface. We should say that there had been no hint of subterfuge in Mica's reluctance to desert his lady and the others; though he had no taste for war, he already developed such a strong attachment to her that the thought of leaving her to die unattended was repugnant to him, even to the point where he would have preferred to die at her side. And then, it was also true that she represented to him his first chance of a life above the level of the most abject poverty, a life for which he had already acquired such a taste that he would have preferred to die rather than to be forced to return to his previous condition. Conversely, his attachment to his lady and to his present circumstances gave him a greater reason than he had ever had for wishing to remain alive.

All of this confusion in his mind, however, did nothing

to diminish the speed with which his feet, driven by his legs, traversed the path which, as Uttrik had said, began between two rocks upon which watch-stations had been built, and which were called Nilk'arf's Tower (the one on the right being named for Nilk e'Terics, the one on the left for her brother, Narf), which he could just barely see in the distance. He ran for them, then, with the intention of passing between them and following the path thus revealed until, in some fifteen or sixteen hours, he reached Castle Redface, exhausted, dying perhaps, but able at least to warn anyone who would listen that the demons from the east had crossed the mountains again.

This, we say, was his intention. What actually happened was that, some time before he reached the rocks that marked the beginning of the descent into the hidden valley between the mountains of Kieron and Bli'aard, he stopped, his mouth hanging so far open that it was just as well for him that bees did not live in these mountains.

What was it he saw that caused this abrupt alteration in his gait and confusion in his thinking? It was, emerging from between these very rocks which were his destination, what could only be an army, and that of foot-soldiers, marching, as nearly as he could tell from the distance, directly toward him. He was unable to determine their numbers, because of the distance, and moreover, because they were still appearing, as if the ground was spitting them forth the way Dzur Mountain, according to the mood of The Enchantress, will sometimes spit forth fire.

He stood then, watching this army come forth, and, after his first moment of shock, he realized that before him was the answer to his prayers. And this was the more remarkable, he realized, in that it had not occurred to him to utter any prayers. He began to reflect upon the nature of the gods, wondering how useful prayer was, since, in spite of all the things he had prayed for at one time or another in his life, the blessings he had received all seemed to come at times when prayer had been the farthest thing from his mind. These reflections ended abruptly, however, when he realized that the army was still appearing, and that, moreover, now was the time for action, or at least the consideration of action, rather than for the sort of thoughts that were best appreciated during days of travel or hours of leisure.

After a moment, then, during which Mica stood rooted to the ground, he came to himself enough to consider what he ought to do. "I could return at once to my lady, and tell her that there is help on the way along the Slip-knot from Nilk'arf's Tower, upon which intelligence she would, perhaps, fall back and allow her rescuers time to arrive. But then, she seems determined to die, and might well ignore such a solution. I could, instead, continue on toward the advancing army, and try to convince them to hurry, and thus save my lady, which plan has the advantage that, if, as I suspect, these troops are arrived from Redface, I will have fulfilled my commission, and done so with such dispatch that no one could have anything to say against me. Well, that is the plan, I think; now, to action."

This decision having been reached, the clever and devoted servant at once rushed forward, with all the speed of which he was capable, toward the troops, a thousand in number, who seemed to have formed ranks and were marching precisely in his direction. In no time at all, it seemed, he had reached the front ranks, who at first put their hands to their weapons, then, upon seeing it was only a single Teckla who approached them, waited. Their officer evidently perceived that this Teckla had something important to say, for he gave the command to halt, at which time Mica suddenly found himself face to face with Lord Adron.

"Well, my man?" said Adron.

"Your Highness," said Mica, bowing to the very ground.

"You have something to tell me?"

"I do, my lord."

"Well then—but stay," he said suddenly as Mica dared

to raise his head at last, "I know you; you were the lackey of one of those who did me the honor to stay beneath my roof some few days ago."

"Yes, my lord. I am called Mica, if it please Your Highness."

"Very well, Mica, then—"

The conversation was joined at this time by two gentlemen who did not wear the uniform and insignia of Lord Adron. By their bearing, Mica took them to be high nobles. By their dress, one seemed to be a Tsalmoth, the other a Lyorn.

"Your Highness," said the Lyorn, "I perceive that the column has stopped."

"You are correct, Count," said Adron.

"Well, I am most anxious to learn the reason."

"I am speaking with this Teckla."

"I see that."

"Then you understand."

"Your pardon, my lord," said the other with a curtly bow, "but we wish especially to learn why the column should stop so that Your Highness may converse with this Teckla."

"For the simplest possible reason, Lord Garland," said Adron. "It is because he is the lackey of one of those we pursue."

"Lackey?" said Garland, laughing slightly. "How quaint."

The other frowned and said, "You are interrogating him, then? Good."

Mica said, "My lord? May I presume to ask Your Highness a question?"

"Very well, ask."

"Excuse me, but I nearly think I heard Your Highness use the word pursue with respect to my lady."

"Well, and if I did?"

"Your Highness is pursuing my lady?"

"The Horse," said Adron, "what did you think I might be doing out here with a thousand men at my back?"

"I had thought, Your Highness—"

"Well, you had thought?"

"That, with the invasion, you had come to—"

"Invasion!" said Adron.

"The Easterners, Your Highness."

"Easterners have invaded the Empire?"

"They are doing so even now, my lord."

"How many of them?"

"Two or three thousands, my lord."

"Where are they?"

"There. Your Highness can nearly see them."

"Blood of the Horse, I do indeed. And your lady and her friends, where are they?"

"They are in front of the Easterners."

"In front! Leading them?"

"Oh, no, your Highness. They are about to engage them."

"What? The six of them? Against an army? Odds of three against a thousand?"

"I am certain, my lord, that they would have preferred to fight a more even battle, only—"

"Yes?"

"Well, there were no more of them, and no fewer of the Easterners, so the matter was taken out of their hands."

"Did they not think to fall back?" said the Lyorn.

Mica frowned. "Fall back, my lord? Before Easterners? My lady and her friends never considered it."

"Well," said Adron, "it seems we are called upon to rescue them."

"Not at all," said the one called Garland.

Adron looked coldly at him, and turned to the Lyorn. "Well?" he said.

Shaltre moved a little distance away from the troops so that they might not hear him, and motioned for Garland and Adron to follow. Mica followed as well, although, because he was a Teckla, none of them paid any attention to him. When they had approached Shaltre, that worthy said, "Your Highness."

"Well?" said Adron once more, in an even more menacing tone of voice, which did not appear to upset Shaltre in the least.

"I do myself the honor to remind Your Highness that we are on a mission from His Majesty."

"Well, that is true," said Adron. "Detestable as I find this mission, I was forced to set out upon it. But now, you perceive, the situation has changed."

"Not the least in the world."

"How, not?"

"Well, we will simply bring the Baroness back with us, and allow these Easterners to slaughter the rest, and all is said."

"And the invasion?" said Adron, ironically.

"That is hardly your affair," said Shaltre, "considering that Pepperfield is not numbered among your estates."

"You would allow these Easterners to invade, merely to—"

"Obey His Majesty's will? Of a certainty, your Highness. I will more than allow it, I will insist upon it."

"And do you think His Majesty would approve of such a course?"

"His Majesty is not here; therefore, I must do as I think best."

"And when I inform His Majesty of your decision?"

Shaltre looked quickly at Garland, and it seemed they exchanged a sort of communication with their eyes, for Shaltre said, "Your Highness is, perhaps, correct; I must confer with my friend to see if we can, together, reach a decision regarding what His Majesty would have us do."

"You must live with the results."

"Well, I know; I trust, therefore, you will permit us a moment to make such an important decision."

"Very well; a moment."

Shaltre took Garland aside, and, after being certain they were out of Adron's earshot, they spoke together for some few minutes, after which they returned together.

Shaltre said, "I am afraid, Your Highness, that we have determined that His Majesty would much prefer these criminals dead—all of them, including Kaluma, who is, as you know, wanted for murder; if this requires us to permit a small force of Easterners to temporarily inhabit a few hectares of useless fields, then, well, so be it. I therefore call upon you to hold your forces here, where we will remain and witness the execution of these enemies of the state by the hands of the Eastern rabble; it will be amusing. After they are dead, we will then return to make our report to His Majesty, and if you wish to send your warriors against the Easterners at that time, well, we will not be here to object."

"You are aware, I think, that by then they will hold the field?"

"Bah," said Shaltre. "It is a field. An army can hold it only by occupying it; it can then be displaced by another army."

"I beg to differ," said Adron. "By placing a few men along the Ritmoro Levee, where the Slipknot turns and becomes wide, and then again by building and manning fortifications on Splittop Hill, that would only leave the Wood of Twelve Pines to be defended, and I suspect you will have heard of the latest battle to be fought there."

"That is not our concern," said Shaltre.

"What you suggest is impossible," said Adron.

"Not at all," said Shaltre.

"And, if I tell the Emperor?"

"That's as it must be."

Adron bit his lips until the blood ran, and cast his eyes again and again at the Eastern army. There is no question that five hundred years later he would, without hesitation, have disobeyed the Emperor's orders, as he thought them, in order to do what he considered his duty. But at this time, he was still loyal; that is, he still considered that he must obey his Emperor under any conditions. He therefore called over to him an officer, and gave the command for his troops to relax, but to hold themselves ready.

He turned back, then, and looked once more at the Easterners, who, though they were moving slowly, nevertheless had closed the distance between themselves and the six individuals whom Adron could just barely distinguish in the distance. He said, "Well, what could that be?"

Shaltre said, "I do not understand what Your Highness does me the honor to ask me."

"Do you not see someone running from us?"

"You are right."

"It is their lackey," said Garland, "no doubt returning to tell them that we will not save them. It's all the same."

In fact, Garland was right; as soon as Mica had heard the decision, he had set off as fast as he could run back toward his lady and her friends, there to give them what news he could. It is to his credit that he arrived well before the Easterners.

"What?" said Tazendra, when she saw him. "You are back?"

"I am, my lady," he said, gasping for breath.

"Well, how have you returned without completing your mission?"

"Oh, there is no question of completing my mission," he said.

"How, no question?"

"Well, I have done so, my lady."

"What, you have informed Lord Adron of the invasion?"

"Yes, my lady."

"But, then, he is several leagues away."

"Oh, not at all; scarcely a league."

"What?" cried all of the friends, and they looked around, and, indeed, they were able to make out in the distance the banner of Lord Adron flapping in the vigorous mountain winds.

"We are saved," cried Tazendra.

"You are lost, my lady," said Mica.

"How, lost? What does this mean?"

"They will not come to your aid."

"Impossible," said Aerich.

"Not in the least," said Mica.

"Well," demanded Khaavren, "tell us what has happened; and speak quickly, for you perceive that the Easterners are nearly upon us."

"This is it, then," said Mica, and he told all that he had heard. When he mentioned the name, "Count Shaltre," Aerich's brows came together, which for him was what a string of curses would be for another.

At length, when Mica had finished, Khaavren said, "So, they mean to let us die."

"So it seems," said Pel.

"It must grieve Lord Adron," said Kathana.

"The Horse," said Uttrik. "It nearly grieves me."

"Bah," said Tazendra, using Aerich's favorite expression. "It is just as it was a few minutes ago."

"True enough," said Khaavren. "Only now, we have a thousand witnesses."

"For which reason," said Tazendra, "we should fight all the better."

"Those are exactly my thoughts," said Khaavren.

"Eyes front, my friends," said Kathana. "They are almost upon us. Khaavren, is the flash-stone ready?"

"It is."

"And you know what to do with it?"

"Nearly."

"Well?"

"I am to kill their leader."

"And will you recognize him?"

"I think I already do."

"How?"

"Do you see a white horse, and upon it a rider who sits straight in the saddle like a human, and seems, moreover, to be in advance of the regiment?"

"Well, you're right, there is such a man."

"I take him for the leader."

"Well, can you hit him from this distance."

"Cha! Without speaking first? Is this battle, Kathana, or assassination?"

"Sometimes the difference is not entirely clear," she said ironically.

"Nevertheless, I do not like to strike from a distance, without warning."

"Yet, with the disparity of numbers—"

"Khaavren is right," said Aerich in a tone that indicated no further argument was possible.

"Besides," added Pel, "they seem to be slowing down."

"Perhaps they fear us," said Tazendra.

Uttrik laughed. "Well, they wouldn't be far wrong in doing so."

"Shall we speak to them, do you think?" said Pel, addressing Aerich.

"Certainly, if they wish it," said the Lyorn.

"Well, and who shall speak for us? For, as they have one leader, we ought to have one speaker."

"Oh," said Khaavren. "Allow me. For, now that I no longer face that dismal duel, my tongue is quite loose in my head, and I feel my wits to be well about me."

"Very well," said Kathana. "For my part, you may speak for us."

"And I agree," said Uttrik. "I know, in all events, that it would not be proper for me to do so, since we once held these lands, but do no longer."

"Come," said Tazendra, "it is decided then."

"And none too soon," said Pel. "For I perceive they are, indeed, stopping before us."

In fact, the Easterner whom Khaavren had noticed had stopped the advance of his army some twenty paces from where the six humans awaited them. He studied them with a bemused expression, or at least what would have been a bemused expression had he been human. Khaavren, in turn, studied him, and likewise the brigade which rode in some twenty-five files, each file being a hundred or more deep. There seemed to be a great variety in the makeup of this army; some were very tall compared to the others (though quite short compared to humans), while others were extremely short, almost the size of Serioli. A few had light-colored hair, and some had no hair at all, while most had hair that was dark brown or black, and, in fact, many had this hair of whatever color spread over their faces, sometimes covering the lower half of the face, other times only here and there, as if cut into certain ritual patterns.

Their horses looked like many that Khaavran knew (which was no surprise, for he knew that these horses were common in the East, and, in fact, had heard that the Marquis of Pepperfield often organized expeditions into the East to procure breeding stock), except for the one their leader rode, which, in addition to being all white, and a stallion (which, if truth be told, impressed Khaavren very much), was larger and prouder than any horse he had seen before.

The Easterner himself was wide in the shoulders, and had dark hair and dark eyes, so that he looked not unlike Pel, allowing for the difference in species. His height was impossible to determine as he sat on his horse, yet Khaavren suspected he was rather short even for an Easterner. For weapons, he bore two swords, oddly slung on the same side of his belt, as if he fought with only one at a time, but desired to choose which to use on any occasion.

The unknown Easterner spoke then, to Khaavren's amazement, in passable Dragaeran, although with unnaturally trilled r's, g's that sounded like k's, w's that sounded like v's, and an oddly musical cadence to his sentences. He said, in the manner we have described, which we will not attempt to render here, "I am called Crionofenarr; whom do I have the honor of addressing?"

"I am called Khaavren of Castle Rock, and these are my friends, Aerich, Pel, Tazendra, Uttrik e'Lanya, and Kathana e'Marish'Chala. And allow me to say, sir, that you speak our language very well."

"Thanks, my lord. I lived among you for some time, in these very mountains, as vassal to a certain Viscount of the House of the Iorich."

"That must be where you acquired a name which does

not offend my ears as, if you will pardon me, most names of Easterners seem to do."

"You are right, my lord; my own name should be very difficult for you to pronounce, but I have chosen Crion-ofenarr because, whenever I hear it, I recall my life of servitude, and this inspires me in my task."

"Ah. You say it inspires you."

"Exactly."

"And in your task?"

"Precisely."

"But, if I may inquire, what task is this?"

"The re-taking of these lands which have been taken from us, and so nearly join my own, and for which, I assure you, we have more use than you."

"Not at all," said Khaavren.

"Well, and what use have you for these lands?"

"Why, to prevent you from invading us," said Khaavren with a bow.

"And yet," said Crionofenarr, "we have never invaded you; we have merely taken back, from time to time, a few of those fields you have stolen, for which you have no use, and yet we have great use."

"Ah, but there it is; to one it is an invasion, to another it is merely an effort to reclaim what has been stolen. It's all the same."

"It is, indeed, my lord. But, now that I have told you of my affairs, tell me of yours."

"That is only just," said Khaavren. "What do you wish to know?"

"I wish to know, my lord, what the six of you are doing here."

"Doing here, my good Crionofenarr? Why, we have given ourselves the honor of being here to welcome you."

"Welcome us?" said the Easterner.

"Welcome them?" murmured Tazendra.

"Hush," said Aerich.

"Naturally, welcome you; you are on Dragaeran soil, hence you must have come to pay homage to the Empire and to become vassals of whichever lord is in need of such service. It is a wise decision, and, not only do I welcome you, but, moreover, I salute you." And, true to his word, Khaavren saluted the Easterner, though not without a certain amount of irony in the gesture.

"Nevertheless—" said Tazendra.

"You are insupportable," said Pel.

"Hush," repeated Aerich.

"I must assume," said Crionofenarr, "that you are jesting."

"You may observe by my countenance whether I am jesting," said Khaavren.

"Then I must affirm that you are under a misapprehension."

"How? You cannot be here to invade, therefore—"

"But, my lord, why can we not?"

"Well, because, as you have done us the honor to observe, there are six of us."

"Well, and?"

"Therefore, you perceive, you are outnumbered."

"Oh, well spoken," murmured Aerich.

A grimace, which was probably anger, passed across Crionofenarr's face, and he said, "We shall see who is outnumbered, and that in a few minutes."

"Then you intend to attack us?"

"I nearly think so," said the Easterner.

"Well, you will understand, I hope, if I do my utmost to kill you."

"Oh, I would expect nothing less."

"In that case, when you please."

"Now will do very well, my arrogant friend," cried Crionofenarr, and with this he charged at Khaavren, as if to run him down with his horse.

Khaavren, however, had been waiting for exactly this, and coolly raised his flash-stone and discharged it at Crionofenarr's head. It may be that the Easterner's horse had more experience than its master had, or it may have been the merest chance, but the horse reared up, and so the discharge, intended for the rider, struck the horse instead, which rolled its eyes wildly and collapsed to the ground. Crionofenarr was, for an instant, pinned beneath it, but after a moment its throes caused it to roll over, and the Easterner stood. At that moment, the horse ceased its moving, and Crionofenarr knelt down next to it in an attitude of great sorrow.

There was silence, then, for a moment, and at last the Easterner stood, and, looking at Khaavren with an expression impossible to describe, said, "You killed my horse."

"I assure you," said Khaavren, "that I had no intention of doing so, and, moreover, that I am in despair at having killed such a fine beast. I beg you to believe that I was aiming for you." He shrugged and dropped the now-useless stone at his feet.

The Easterner stared at the flash-stone the way a city-dweller would look at a stuffed yendi; as if, though dead, it might still have the means of biting once more. "I do believe you," he said at last. "Nevertheless, you have killed my horse, whom I loved more than anything or anyone else, therefore, I will kill you."

"That is only right," said Khaavren, with a bow.

"Place yourself on your guard, my lord."

"I will do so, directly, sir, but first, if you please, allow me to say two words to my friends."

"You will be laconic, I trust."

"You will be satisfied with my brevity, believe me."

"Very well."

Khaavren turned then, and said, "My friends, I must say that this Easterner pleases me."

"Well," said Uttrik. "And then?"

"You will be doing me a great favor if you will allow us to fight without coming to my aid."

"Providing," said Pel, "that he receives no help from his army, well, I agree."

Khaavren glanced quickly at the proud Easterner and said, "I think he will not."

"Very well," said Tazendra. "Only—"

"Yes?"

"If he defeats you—"

"Well?"

"I shall kill him."

"That," said Khaavren, "is as it may be. But remember that I do not intend to allow him to kill me."

"And you are right not to," said Pel. "The gods, there are enough of them already, we have no reason to make it easy for them."

"Well, if we are agreed, then that is all."

The others signified that this plan was acceptable to them, and Khaavren turned back to Crionofenarr with a bow.

"Be on your guard, then," said the Easterner.

Khaavren, whose sword was out, and who, moreover, hated to be paid this sort of compliment twice, drew his poniard with his left hand and took his favorite guard position. The Easterner drew what was, for his size, a very large sword and stood squarely facing Khaavren, holding the blade in both hands.

The moment Crionofenarr drew, however, Khaavren felt a sensation very much like that which some experience when standing on cliffs, or else on the top of very tall buildings; a certain lassitude, combined with disorientation, as well as a fear that seemed to pass directly to his knees, making them tremble as if from fatigue. He was barely able to hold his hands steady, and, looking into his enemy's eyes, as was his custom, he saw there a look of hatred and triumph.

Evidently, Khaavren's friends felt it too, for he heard Aerich mutter "Morganti," in a tone of great scorn, and in that instant he understood everything. He was facing one of those hateful weapons which are the shame of a world filled with shameful things—a weapon whose merest scratch will kill, not only the body, but the soul of its victim.

Khaavren drew back in spite of himself, but not quickly

enough, for Crionofenarr leapt close and, with a single blow, knocked both weapons from Khaavren's weak, trembling hands, after which the Easterner held the point of the sword directly at Khaavren's breast.

Khaavren stared down into the Easterner's eyes, and felt himself the scorn and disgust that Aerich had expressed in the single hated word, "Morganti." He said, "Sir, no gentleman would use such a weapon."

"Ah," said the other, "but, you perceive, I am no gentleman, I am an Easterner, hence, beneath contempt; is that not what you think?"

"Well, do what you will, then, but I promise you my friends will kill you without pity the instant you strike."

And, indeed, Khaavren's five friends had gathered around and were preparing to do so, even as those in the front rank of Crionofenarr's army drew their weapons in preparation for falling upon the Dragaerans the instant their chieftain fell.

"That's all right," said the Easterner. "They may do so, for I will have killed you already, and, moreover, your soul."

"Do it, then," said Khaavren, drawing himself up in order to die as bravely as he could, to thus give the barbarians something to remember, as well as the troops of Lord Adron whom he knew to be watching.

"And yet," said Aerich, who had taken a position behind Crionofenarr, thus exposing his back to his foe's army. "You may wish to consider, who will command your brigade when you are dead?"

"What does it matter?" said the Easterner. "We have won the field, and—"

"I beg to differ," said Aerich.

"You think the six of you—"

"There are, if I am not mistaken, a thousand of us."

"A thousand? Where?"

"Cast your eyes where mine are; that is, behind Khaavren's shoulder."

"By the Demon-Goddess!" cried Crionofenarr. "Whence

came those troops I see upon that field, which was empty an hour ago?"

"As to that," said Khaavren, "I promise I have not the least idea in the world."

"Well," said Crionofenarr, "they do not seem to be advancing."

"No, they are waiting," said Khaavren.

"Well, and what are they waiting for?"

"Kieron's Boots!" said Khaavren. "They are waiting to see if they are needed."

Crionofenarr smiled. "By the River, but you are stubborn. I could come to like you, friend Khaavren, if I were not forced to kill you, and if, moreover, you had not killed my horse."

"Well," said Khaavren. "If we are all to die, we may as well be about it, although if you will satisfy my curiosity, I will die all the happier for it."

"I see nothing against answering a question or two before I kill you."

"You are generous."

"Not at all."

"Then I will ask."

"I await you."

"Well, I recall in my conversation with you a moment ago, you said that your reasons for wanting this land were greater than our reasons."

"Well, and if I did?" said Crionofenarr.

"Then," said Khaavren, "I should be most anxious to learn what the reasons are."

"Well, they are easily told," said Crionofenarr. "In the first place, because we no longer wish this passage through the mountains to be in the hands of those who use it to steal our horses."

"Well, that is a good reason," said Khaavren.

"I am pleased that you think so."

"Next?"

"The other reason is because this is the only place where we may grow the particular variety of peppers with which we flavor many of our foods, and which give our dishes their special character, and which, besides, many of us believe impart wisdom, long life, fertility, virility, and strength, and moreover, cure fever, falltooth, and pox."

"For peppers?" cried Uttrik, in voice of amazement, echoing the thoughts of the others. "That is why, for thousands of years, you have been invading the Empire?"

"I am forced to admit, my dear Uttrik," said Khaavren, "that it is a better reason for war than many I have heard of."

"And I," said Kathana, "am entirely of Khaavren's opinion."

"Well, then," said Khaavren, "I am satisfied."

"That is well. Have you anything else to say before I destroy you?"

"Only this, my dear Easterner—it is all unnecessary."

"How, unnecessary?"

"Well, there is about to be a great slaughter here. First me, then you, then my friends, and finally, well, there are two armies, after all."

"But," said Crionofenarr, "you perceive that they are too far away to interfere with our intentions of establishing ourselves along the Dike of Orveny and on Torthalom and throughout the woods. And you must say that they are too few to drive us off once we have occupied these positions."

"Oh, as to that, you may be right, but do you think they will fail to attack for all of that?"

"Well, if they do?"

"I would beg to point out that your leader, that is, you, will be dead."

"That is certain," said Aerich, who coolly stood behind him, while the others watched Aerich's back to see that none of Crionofenarr's warriors took any precipitous action.

"Well, I will be dead."

"And many of your men besides."

"Well, and?"

"And, instead, you could have what you want without battle."

"How is that?"

"In faith, my dear Easterner. I can assure you that, if you withdrew once more beyond the mountains, you will be subject to no more raids."

"You have the authority to tell me this, upon your word of honor?"

"Not in the least," said Khaavren. "But there is a gentleman over there who does, and, if we were to send for him, I will undertake to arrange matters."

"Impossible," said the Easterner.

"Not at all," said the Tiassa.

"What are you thinking?" said Tazendra.

"Hold your tongue," said Pel.

"Do as you think best," said Kathana and Uttrik.

Aerich shrugged.

"What will we be required to give up?"

"Oh, as to that, we can see. But, by the cracks in the Orb, there is no harm in discussing it, is there?"

Crionofenarr smiled. "Is it your fear speaking?" he said. At this Tazendra made a motion, but Pel held her back with a gesture.

Khaavren said, "Oh, it is well for you, who hold a Morganti sword at my breast, to speak of courage. Cha! Look at me, then, in the face, you who have lived among us, and tell me if I speak from fear for my life, or from the desire to avoid spilling more blood on this unhappy soil that has seen so much already."

Crionofenarr looked, and, Easterner though he was, he read so much loyalty and frankness in Khaavren's face, that he was instantly convinced. "Very well," he said, "I believe that you mean what you say, but I still doubt that it can be done."

"Well, are you willing to try?"

"What will you do?"

"I will send someone to bring back Lord Adron, and the three of us will speak together."

"And there will be no deceit or trickery?"

"None, on the word of a gentleman."

The Easterner lowered his sword. "Very well, bring this Lord Adron, and we will see what we see."

Khaavren breathed once more, now that the Morganti blade was no longer poised at his breast. "Who shall we send?" he asked.

"Heh," said Kathana. "I will go; for I am the only one we know they will not cut down at once."

"Very well," said Khaavren. "Go and try to bring back Lord Adron."

"No," said Pel, "we must send Mica once more."

"How," said Kathana. "And why is that?"

"Because, not being a gentleman, he may be permitted to lie."

"Well, and what lie must he tell?"

"I will explain," said Pel.

Since Khaavren was no longer threatened, Aerich removed himself from behind Crionofenarr and the friends spoke together at some length, by the end of which they had agreed to Pel's plan, and made certain that Mica understood.

"My lords," said the Teckla, "I assure you that I would rather die than fail in this commission."

"Very well," said Tazendra. "Here are ten orbs for you, and, if you return with Lord Adron, there are another ten like it."

"Well, I depart at once," said Mica, and true to his words, he was running back along the Slipknot before the echo of his words had faded from their ears.

While they waited, Khaavren observed, "I am truly sorry to have killed your horse, and, in faith, if there is anything I can do—"

"His name was Wisdom," said the Easterner, "and he was my only companion for many years of wandering.

But, if we truly can achieve an end to the fighting over these fields, well, it will not be too great a price to pay."

"Then I hope we do," said Khaavren.

Mica reached Lord Adron, and bowed to him, while he recovered his breath. Garland and Shaltre looked at him, but before they could speak, Adron said, "Why is it they have not killed them?"

"That is what I have been sent to inform your Highness, if Your Highness will do me the honor to listen to the message with which I have been entrusted."

"Message?" said Adron. "Well, what is this message?"

"This is it: the Easterners have negotiated a peace, wherewith they will not harm Lord Khaavren or his friends."

"What, that is the message?"

"That is it, your Highness."

"Then, they are safe?"

"As if they were beneath the Orb, my lord."

"But, what peace have they negotiated?"

"Oh, as to that, I was not allowed to listen, my lord."

Shaltre frowned. "Then we must take them ourselves, as we'd planned."

"But this truce," said Adron. "I must know what they have agreed to, and in whose name."

"Your Highness may find out by returning with me."

"Very well. With my army?"

"That is as you wish; only your safety has been pledged."

"Then, it would be dishonorable to bring them. Sudi," he said, addressing his officer, "have them wait here."

"Very well, Your Highness," said the officer.

"Garland and I will accompany you," said Shaltre.

"Very well," said Adron with a shrug, and they set off once more across the fields.

When they arrived, they found Khaavren and Criono-fenarr complaisantly engaging in conversation, which, to be sure, they broke off long enough for Khaavren to perform introductions. Aerich, upon seeing Shaltre, stared directly through him as though he weren't there.

"Well, then," said Adron. "You have, you say, concluded a peace?"

Before Crionofenarr could speak, Khaavren said, "How, concluded? Without your Highness? Impossible." He turned to Mica with pretended harshness and said, "Is that what you said, idiot?"

"My lord, I had thought—"

"Quiet, fool." While Khaavren turned back to Lord Adron, Tazendra quietly slipped ten orbs into the Teckla's pocket, and patted him on the back.

"Well, then?" said Adron.

"Your Highness, we were only awaiting you to begin negotiations."

Shaltre seemed ready to speak, but at that moment, Uttrik, Kathana, Tazendra, and Pel slipped behind him and Garland and whispered in their ears words to this effect: "You have claimed we are fugitives, well then, if you do or say anything that interferes with these negotiations, we will cut your throats without a second thought." Needless to say, Shaltre and Garland, though neither appeared to be coward, had no wish to put these words to the test, and they held their silence as meekly as norska.

Adron, who had no notion of what was happening behind him, said, "Well, you pretend we can settle matters without fighting, then?"

"I nearly think we can," said Khaavren.

"I hope so," said Crionofenarr.

"And how will we do this?"

"Because," said Khaavren, "the Empire will agree not to make any more raids into the land of the Easterners."

"Heh," said Adron. "For whom do you pretend to speak?"

"Heh," said Crionofenarr. "Will you no longer need horses?"

"If we need horses," said Khaavren, "we will buy them. Better, we will trade for them. And I speak for your Highness, who will, unless my powers of prophecy have failed me, be made Marquis of Pepperfield within a few weeks."

"Well," said Adron, "I don't say you're wrong, but nevertheless—"

"What do you pretend you could trade?" interrupted the Easterner.

"You understand, sir, that we need very few, only to improve our breeding stock."

"Well?"

"We could trade horses of our own, some of which are certain to please you. And, moreover, we could trade—"

"Well?"

"The right to grow peppers," said Khaavren coolly.

Silence stretched over the field, and so great was the Easterner's amazement at this answer, that for a moment he found nothing to say.

"But that is the same as if you were giving up these lands."

"Nearly," said Khaavren.

"Impossible," said Adron.

"Not at all," said Khaavren.

"But we must have these lands."

"Oh, that, of a certainty we will."

"And yet," said Crionofenarr, "you have just said—"

"Cha," said Khaavren. "A detail only. His Highness will not mind if you remove a portion of your people hither to work these fields."

"How," said Adron. "I will not?"

"Assuredly not, lord, because your own troops, stationed in places overlooking these fields, will see that there are no weapons among them, and because they will swear an oath that they will never make war nor raids upon us, nor allow anyone to use this place to do so."

"We will do this?" said Crionofenarr. "It is a great deal, it seems to me."

"Well, but you will then receive this land," said Khaavren, "that is, the right to work it as you would, and to carry off from it what you will, and you will receive a promise that the Empire will make no more sorties into your lands."

"That is too much," said Adron. "Why should we give up these lands, which we now hold?"

"I do not think you hold them," said Crionofenarr, glancing back at his army.

"Well," said Adron, "I think, at any rate, that you do not."

"That can be mended," said the Easterner.

"Bah," said Khaavren. "Why fight, Your Highness, when this worthy Easterner is giving us so much?"

"How, so much?"

"Indeed. He will surrender to the Empire certain lands some forty or fifty leagues to the north, which are held by Easterners, but are of no possible value to him, save for their location."

"I will do all of this?" said Crionofenarr doubtfully.

"Well, it is that or war, I think."

"To what lands do you refer?" asked the Easterner.

"I wish also to know that," said Adron.

"Oh, a mere nothing," said Khaavren. "A place of shifting sand, where nothing grows except plants too stringy to eat, and nothing lives save the poisonous yendi. In our tongue, we call it Sandyhome."

Adron's eyes widened as he realized what the Tiassa had just proposed, and he said, "Well, if these terms are agreeable to Crionofenarr, and if I am to become the Marquis of Pepperfield, then I accept the terms, with one additional condition."

"And what is that?" said the Easterner.

"Your sword."

"How, you expect me to surrender my sword? And yet I beg to remind your lordship that you have not beaten me."

"That is true. But, nevertheless, it is not right for an Easterner to bear a Morganti weapon."

"How," said Crionofenarr with a smile. "It frightens you?"

"It disgusts me," said Adron.

The Easterner's eyes narrowed, and Khaavren feared that all would be lost just as everything was nearly agreed to. He stepped forward then, and handed Crionofenarr his sword. "This is a very good weapon, my dear sir," he said. "And, as you have, in fact, beaten me, why, I surrender it to you."

"Well, and then?"

"As to that, I leave to you, but I beg to point out to you that you now have three swords, which are two more than you are likely to need."

"Well," said the Easterner, frowning, "I prefer this arrangement to seeing our warriors kill one another. Yet if I am not mistaken, you used, in your speech, the word, 'if.' "

"Well," said Adron, "and why not? It is a perfectly good word."

"Oh, as to the word, there is no question. But as to its meaning—"

"Well?"

"It seems to indicate some doubt."

"It does, because how can I know that I will become the Marquis of these lands? And, if I am not, how can I know the truce will be held?"

"I answer for it," said Khaavren.

The Easterner looked at Khaavren with an expression of speculation. "You answer for it?" he said doubtfully.

"I more than answer for it, I swear that, if does not come about, well, I will place myself in your hands for you to do with as you would."

"You swear to this, you say?"

"I swear to it by ... by ..." Khaavren cast his eyes around for something to swear by, and at last he found it. "I swear to it," he said, "by the blood of your horse."

Evidently, he had, by chance, found the right answer, for Crionofenarr, after expressing surprise, nodded and said, "I believe you. Give me your hand."

"Here it is."

"And here is mine."

"That is well."

"And yours, Lord Adron?"

"Here it is."

"That is good. And to you, Sir Khaavren, I give over this sword. And, moreover, here is your own back. By the Goddess, what would I do with it? It is too long and heavy for me in any event."

Khaavren took his own weapon back gratefully, and the Morganti blade with some hesitation, even though, in its sheath, it seemed no different from any other sword. He quickly handed it to Lord Adron, who said, "Then it is settled."

"Yes," said Crionofenarr. "Let us retire from this field for an hour, and then, after we have rested, we will finish by agreeing upon the exact details."

"To this I agree."

Crionofenarr had a horse brought to him, and, mounted once more, led his army back away from the place where the battle had nearly been fought. When Adron turned around, he perceived that Shaltre and Garland were being held in a very threatening manner. "What is this?" he demanded.

Khaavren bowed. "We were merely insuring that the negotiations could be carried off evenly."

"Well," said Garland in an ironic tone of voice. "You have proved an able negotiator, and the Empire ought to be grateful to you."

"I hope so, my lord," said Khaavren, bowing and ignoring the way in which this compliment was delivered.

"Nevertheless," said Shaltre, "we have our orders, and moreover, an army at our backs, and you are our prisoners."

"I think not," said a new voice, that being Aerich, who picked that moment to step forward, his eyes flashing.

"Who are you and what do you want?" said Shaltre, frowning.

Aerich had long since sheathed his sword and now

held out his hands, palms open. He spoke slowly and clearly, saying, "My friends call me Aerich, but I should be called Temma, Duke of Arylle, Count of Bra-moor, which titles I hold by birth and blood, and I challenge you, Count Shaltre."

Shaltre fell back half a step, amazed. "Impossible," he said. "The last Duke of Arylle took his own life."

"Not the last," said Aerich. "I am his son."

"He had no son."

"I was carried away from the destruction of our chateau, and my existence was concealed from you, for my father knew you for the coward and traitor that you are, and wished to spare my life. He hoped I might avenge him; that hope is now to be realized."

Shaltre said, "You cannot challenge me, for, by the ancient laws, you, trained as a warrior, cannot—"

"Do you know," interrupted Aerich coldly, "that no one ever seems to notice Teckla. There may be one practically hiding in your fine silk stockings without your ever being aware of him."

"What do you say?" said Shaltre, frowning still more.

"Back there, you spoke privately with His Highness and with Lord Garland; you did not notice our friend Mica, lackey to the lady Tazendra, for no one ever seems to notice a Teckla."

"Well," said Shaltre, "and if he heard our conversation, what then? You know, then, what we wish for you."

"And, moreover, you then had a conversation without His Highness."

"And, if I did?" Count Shaltre, we should say, appeared a little less sure of himself than he had a few moments before; Garland had become pale.

"As I have had the honor to inform you, Count, no one ever notices a Teckla, and yet, some Teckla, such as Mica here, are perfectly capable of overhearing a conversation."

Shaltre looked shaken for a moment, but recovered himself. "You are lying," he said coolly.

"I? I have no history of lying. There is no one in the world who can ever say that I have told a lie. But in your case, that is not true. Would you like to question Mica here? Do you wish him to say, in plain, simple words, all that you and Garland told each other?"

Shaltre became quite pale, which showed sharply with his bronzed complexion, but only repeated, "You are lying."

"Teckla can not only hear," continued Aerich impassively, "but they can also report what they have heard. They can discuss matters of court intrigue, matters of secret arrangements with certain Athyra, the hiring of Jhereg, conspiracies against Lord Adron—"

"All lies," insisted Shaltre, although he was clearly quite shaken by the charges.

"What is this?" said Adron. "What did they say when I couldn't hear them?"

"He is lying," said Shaltre.

"They said," continued Aerich coolly, "that if all the witnesses of this deed were killed in battle with the Easterners, including Your Highness, there would be no need to keep Kathana alive, as Pepperfield would naturally fall into the hands of the e'Lanya line, which is what Garland's master, Seodra, wants, and what Shaltre wants as well, since he has evidently made some sort of pact with Seodra, perhaps in order to keep the shameful secret of his past."

"You are lying!" cried Shaltre, while Garland gave Mica such a look of hatred that it was a wonder he didn't fall dead on the spot.

"Assassination is an ugly word," said Adron, looking at Shaltre coldly, "but proofs are required."

"Treason is an uglier word," said Aerich coolly. "It is so ugly, that, by the custom of my House, I am released, under such circumstances, from the oath that forbids warriors of our House to challenge those who are not so trained."

"I declare that this Teckla was lying!" said Shaltre. "He is a Teckla, and—"

"I declare," said Aerich, "that you are lying; and, I declare further that I am about to kill you; this very moment, in fact."

"You cannot touch me!" cried Shaltre, panic in his voice, drawing his sword and springing back.

"On the contrary," said Tazendra, "I think that, if he is willing to dirty his hands, he can touch you quite easily."

"In your pride and ambition," said Aerich, "you dishonored my family, have given poor counsel to his Majesty, and you are now prepared to commit treason outright, and to cause to be assassinated friends whom I love. You will die, and, if my voice is heard, you will be denied Deathgate. What have you to say?"

"No," whispered Shaltre. "I will exile myself. I will leave the Empire for the Islands."

"Where you will use the knowledge you have gained at court as a poniard in the back of His Majesty."

"I will not."

"No, you will not," said Aerich, letting each word fall like a single drop of water falling into a rain-pail after a storm. "You will not, because I am going to kill you now."

"No, I swear—" and, at these words, thinking, perhaps, to catch Aerich off guard, he sprung, his sword swinging to cut at Aerich's neck. The first thing his sword did was come near to decapitating Garland, who stood behind him. In point of fact, the blade sliced through the leather cord that held Garland's pouch, before coming around to strike at Aerich.

There was a brief clang as Aerich deflected the cut with one of his vambraces, then, with the same hand, he took Shaltre by the throat. The older Lyorn swung again, and once more Aerich deflected the blade, this time with his other vambrace, after which he gripped Shaltre's throat with his other hand. Then he squeezed and twisted. There came a stifled cry, and the sound of breaking bones, and

Count Shaltre fell unmoving to the ground, his neck at an odd angle.

Adron and Aerich looked at each other, then, as if with a single thought, looked at Garland, who, brave though he was, stood trembling like a Teckla. Suddenly he turned and bolted away from them back toward the southwestern path down from the plateau.

"And him?" said Adron.

Aerich shrugged. "Let him go, Your Highness. His mission has failed, let him survive Seodra's wrath as best he may."

"Very well," said Adron. "So be it."

These worthies studied the body of Shaltre as if it would tell them something. Then Aerich's head rose, and he looked as someone will who, without being aware of it, has for years been walking with his back slightly bent; when he suddenly straightens up. He reached into his pocket, took out his crochet work, and held it up. "The Arylle coat of arms," he said. "And it is almost completed."

When Garland was out of sight, Khaavren turned back to Lord Adron and said, "We must write out the terms of the treaty, and your Highness may endorse them on the understanding that His Majesty must ratify them, or that they will become official if you are granted the estate of the Pepperfields. You must have a scribe."

"It will be seen to," said Adron. "To that end, let us rejoin my troops, who are, no doubt, awaiting anxiously to hear what has befallen us."

"Yes," said Aerich. "Let us go."

Aerich seemed to have changed after his encounter with Count Shaltre; his eyes were alive, his head was high, and all traces of his melancholy disposition seemed to have vanished. He and Khaavren embraced. Khaavren said, "I am delighted for you, Duke," and sighed.

"Well, I accept your compliments, and do you, in your turn, accept mine, for you have well served the Empire today."

Khaavren sighed again.

"Khaavren," said Pel, "accept my compliments as well; what you have done here is nothing short of miraculous."

Khaavren sighed for the third time.

Tazendra said, "Excuse me, Khaavren, but you seem unhappy, and I am at a loss to know why. Are you, like me, annoyed that we were not able to die gloriously?"

"Not that; I am unhappy because we have survived."

"Well, and what is wrong with that?"

"Ah," said Aerich, "he is right."

"I had forgotten," said Pel.

"Oh," said Kathana.

"Ah, now I recall," said Tazendra, and, one at a time, they turned their glances toward Uttrik.

The Dragonlord shook his head. "No, you have nothing to fear. Perhaps it dishonors me, but, if so, I will live with it, for, after what we have been through together, I declare that I would sooner jump from some of these cliffs than to cross swords with someone whom I love and revere as I do Kathana, and the rest of you as well."

"So," said the baroness, "we need not fight?"

"I have said so, and now I repeat it. For my part, we are no longer enemies."

And, for the first time in many days, Khaavren felt a smile growing on his face, while such pleasure ran through him that he felt like shouting for joy. "And I assure you I shall not arrest you, either," he said. "So my love will still love me, and, as for the Empire, well, I think I have done enough to-day that the Emperor cannot complain about such a small thing."

"He will have no need," said Kathana, "for I will surrender myself, and I will ask for pardon. If you, Uttrik, will speak for me, well, he cannot fail to grant it."

"We will all speak for you," said Aerich. "And I believe I can say as much for Lord Adron as well."

"But, are we not forgetting the true hero of the day?" said Khaavren.

"Ah," said Uttrik. "You are right; our clever Mica, who overhears conversations so well."

"Oh," said Mica, blushing, "It was very little. In fact," he added with a sly glance at Aerich, "it was less than perhaps you think it was."

"Well," said Tazendra, "you heard what Garland and Shaltre said to His Highness, and were thus able to warn us."

"That is true," said Mica. "I heard all of that, and I told you all that I heard. But I must confess that I heard nothing beyond that."

"What?" said Kathana, smiling. "You pretend you didn't hear what Count Shaltre said to Lord Garland, so that you then went and told Aerich?"

"Not at all. I tried to, but I couldn't get close enough; that is what I told him."

Khaavren turned to Aerich, "Do you mean you lied, my friend?"

"I?" said Aerich. "Not at all. I never said that Mica had overheard the conversation, I merely pointed out that no one ever thinks about whether a Teckla might overhear what he says, which is an entirely different thing, I assure you."

"And yet," Khaavren persisted, "you claimed to know what they said to each other."

"Oh, as to that, well, I did."

"But if Mica didn't overhear them—"

"It was not necessary that he overhear them," said Aerich. "Because, some time ago, Pel happened to overhear a conversation between Count Shaltre and Captain G'aereth, and he recently related to me the substance of that conversation."

"Well," said Khaavren, "I remember the occasion; it was the day upon which we joined the guards, was it not?"

"Your memory is excellent, my dear Khaavren."

"Well, then, what was said?"

"It was simple enough," said Pel. "Shaltre explained to our Captain that it was the desire of the Emperor that Kathana not be arrested."

"Well," said Khaavren, "then it is just as well he didn't know the real purpose of our journey."

"That may be," said Pel. "But that is not the end of the matter."

"Well, and?"

"I discovered, before we left, that Shaltre must have been lying, because it became clear that it was the Consort who wanted Kathana to remain free."

"Well, not only the Consort," said Khaavren.

"No, but it was only the Consort who was acting out of friendship. Everyone else was acting to advance his own interests by being the one who eventually killed or arrested Kathana, in the hopes that this would put him into the graces of His Majesty, especially if the arrest could be contrived to be both public and spectacular."

"That may be," said Khaavren, thinking uncomfortably of Illista.

"In any case," continued Pel, "it was clear that His Majesty had no such opinion; on the contrary, he desired that the Baroness be arrested as quickly as possible, and was even vexed with Lanmarea that she was still at large."

"Go on, Pel," said Khaavren, "for I must say this conversation interests me exceedingly."

"You have now heard the whole of it, for my part."

"Well, and you, Duke, will you tell me the rest?"

"Only," said the Lyorn, "on the condition that you continue to call me Aerich."

"Very well, I submit."

"Then I will tell you."

"I am waiting most anxiously."

"Here it is, then: knowing that Shaltre was lying, I was able to form certain conclusions about why he was lying, and I presented these to him, and, as you saw, he confirmed my guesses by his reaction."

"And this is the entire affair?"

"That is all."

"But then, if he had not attacked you?"

"In that case," said Aerich, "I should have been embarrassed."

"Blood of the Horse," said Khaavren.

Chapter the Thirty-first

*In Which the Reader Will, No Doubt,
Be As Surprised As Our Heroes
to Learn That All is Not Over*

"**M**Y FRIENDS," SAID Lord Adron "it is my great hope that you will return with me to my home to allow me to bestow upon you the honors you have earned." They were, at this time, alone on the field once more, for Lord Adron's troops had been directed back home by Sudi, Adron's lieutenant, and the Easterners had withdrawn, taking with them, Khaavren noticed, the corpse of the poor horse, which Crionofenarr had caused, with much difficulty, to be loaded onto one of the wains that had been in the rear of the army.

"On the contrary," said Aerich in response to Adron's proposals. "Allow me to suggest that Your Highness return with us to the city, where we will intercede with you before the court."

"He is right," declared Pel. "For, if we have been fortunate enough to have gained some notoriety here, well, it is entirely at Your Highness's disposal."

"And, moreover," said Kathana, "I am going back to

surrender myself to the court, and the company of Your Highness would please me immensely."

"I should also say," added Khaavren, "that we ought to hurry, for I think it would be well if we could arrive before Lord Garland, who might endeavor to poison the ears of His Majesty against us."

"All of this is well thought," said Adron. "Only I have been exiled by His Majesty, and it would be wrong of me to return."

"Ah, I had not understood that," said Aerich, who was well-acquainted with propriety in all situations. "That is another matter, and I entirely agree with Your Highness."

"In that case," said Khaavren, "we will return and do what we can for Your Highness."

"Well," said Tazendra, who was beginning to recover from her annoyance at not dying gloriously, and was now looking proudly about the field, "I think we should have built up some small degree of credit."

"And yet," said Uttrik, "I am worried that—but stay a moment. Tazendra, what is it that your lackey is holding?"

"Eh? Why, yes. What are holding, Mica?"

"A letter, my lady."

"A letter?"

"So it seems to be."

"And to whom is it addressed?"

"To Lord Adron," said the clever Teckla, who had learned his ciphers sometime during his early career, a fact which even Aerich did not hold against him.

"How?" said Adron. " A letter for me?"

"So it seems to be, Your Highness."

"From whom?"

"As to that, I have no idea, Your Highness."

"But," said Khaavren, "where did you find it?"

"In Lord Garland's pouch, which he left behind him after it was cut from his waist by Count Shaltre."

"What is this," said Tazendra sternly. "You have looked through the gentleman's pouch?"

"Yes, exactly, my lady," said Mica complacently. "There is no crime in that, for I am not a gentleman."

"That is true," said Aerich, after which he murmured, "This notion of Tazendra's lackey, will, in time, get entirely out of hand; I must mention it to her."

"And there was a letter for me in it?" said Adron.

"Yes, and the proof is, here is the letter."

Mica handed the letter to Tazendra to give to His Highness, which she promptly did, but only after glancing at the seal. "Why, faith," she said, "it is from His Majesty."

"His Majesty?" said Adron. "Garland had a letter for me from His Majesty which he failed to give to me?"

"I think," said Aerich to Pel, "that it will go hard with Garland when this is communicated to His Majesty."

"And when it is communicated to Seodra," said Pel.

Adron broke the seal and read the letter, then read it a second time, and even a third time. When he began to read it a fourth time, Khaavren said to Tazendra, "I nearly think His Highness is startled."

Adron, who happened to overhear his remark, said, "Well, I am. Look, His Majesty not only forgives me, but apologizes to me; it is remarkable."

Pel said, "If this letter was to be given to Your Highness by Garland, and if Garland is Seodra's creature, well, I am not surprised that he was slow in giving it."

"Well," said Adron with a shrug, "I have it now."

"And will Your Highness," asked Aerich politely, "condescend to accompany us back to the city?"

"I will," said Adron, "for I think that there are events stirring of which I ought to be a part, and I accompany you the more gladly because of the esteem in which I hold you."

"Well, then," said Khaavren, "it remains for us to find another horse. The one Mica has been riding will do for me, and I will happily surrender mine to His Highness, but, unless we wish to leave our servant in the dust, we had best procure another."

Uttrik said, "There is a post-station a short distance

down the mountain which, as it is maintained by the Empire rather than by the Marquis, ought to still be manned."

"It will be enough," said Tazendra, "if it is horsed."

There was nothing to say after this profound observation, so they set off across the field, walking their horses, and in this way arrived at the post, where Aerich showed the Captain's letter to the officer. In this way they procured the additional horse, which was, in fact, such a fine animal that Adron took it, after which they continued back the way they had come, returning to Mount Bli'aard and Bengloarafurd. We should note that certain of the residents seemed surprised to see His Highness happily riding knee-to-knee with individuals whom he had proscribed and condemned a week before, but no one said anything, presumably attributing this change in attitude to the right of princes to be as capricious as they wished.

When they neared The Painted Sign, they stopped their horses, as if by a common thought, and looked over the site of the battle. Lord Adron took his hat off out of respect, and studied the grounds. "I perceive the marks of a flash-stone," he said, pointing to a place above the hill.

"That was mine, I believe," said Pel. "It seems to have scored the rock upon which Mica was stationed, and where he delivered the famous blow to the head of one of our attackers. The Horse, but I think he nearly cracked the scoundrel's skull for him, which was no more than he deserved."

Mica shivered with pleasure at the honor he had been paid by this reference to his deed, while Khaavren looked the other way along the path and said, "There, that is the tree we used for a rear-guard, Uttrik and Aerich and I. In faith, I had thought it rather larger than that."

"It was large enough," said Aerich.

"I wish I had been with you," sighed Kathana.

"As do I," said Adron.

"Bah," said Tazendra. "It would no longer have been fair. Besides, Aerich would have then required us make a frontal assault, and, in faith, well, some of us might have been injured."

"You are not far wrong," said Aerich, and they continued on their way.

They stopped at The Painted Sign to enjoy a repast and for Lord Adron to consider if he ought to return to Redface for any reason, or whether it was enough to write to his steward about his plans. They were treated quite royally by the host, who very rarely had to do with an Heir at his inn, so the wines were all back-of-the-cellar and the meats were prepared with especial care. Lord Adron, in between eating and thinking, which activities he was, in any case, accustomed to perform together, told the host and anyone else who would listen of the recent exploits of his traveling companions, which caused Aerich to shrug, Pel to smile, Khaavren to blush, Kathana to consider more closely her food, Uttrik to look nervous, Tazendra to look haughty, and Mica to positively glow.

Adron had come to the decision to write, and was on the point of calling for pen, ink, parchment, and blotter, when he was interrupted by the arrival of a small girl, who did him a courtesy, placed a scrap of paper in his hand, and dashed off without waiting for a reply.

Adron frowned and said, "Well, that is peculiar."

"How peculiar?" said Tazendra, who had been so intent on her meal that she had not noticed the arrival of the messenger. "It is merely a duck which has been covered with wild plums before being baked like a loaf of bread. For my part, I find it excellent."

"How?" said Pel, ignoring Tazendra. "Your Highness doesn't know this messenger?"

"Not the least in the world."

"Then she was merely a messenger," suggested Khaavren.

"But from whom, and for what? For, you perceive, we had not been here so long that my presence could have become generally known; not, at any rate, at the fort." Such was the way, we should point out, that Adron always referred to his home. "Nor, certainly," he added, "to the Empire."

"Well," said Kathana, "perhaps if Your Highness would read the message, it would explain."

"Perhaps not, too," said Pel.

"I will read it," said Adron.

"We shall await Your Highness," said Pel.

"I shall do more than wait," said Khaavren, "I shall eat this famous duck, and at the same time, I declare that I shall tear off pieces of this heavy, dark bread and allow these pieces to absorb the sauce, and then eat them along with it."

"And," added Uttrik, "if you will drink from some of these five bottles of Furnia wine which we have ordered to accompany our repast, I think the time will go all the more quickly."

"You are wisdom incarnate," said Khaavren. "I tell you so."

As Adron read the letter, his frown deepened, and he said, "What nonsense is this?"

He held out the note to Aerich, who took it and said, "Does Your Highness desire me to read this?"

"Yes, yes," said Adron, impatiently. "Read it aloud, and tell me what you think."

"Very well, Your Highness," said Aerich, and he first studied the almost impossibly elegant handwriting, then read: "Your Highness ought to return home directly if he wishes to have his daughter presented to him."

"Well," said Khaavren, "that is clear enough, I think."

"Not at all," said Adron. "For I have no daughter."

"Perhaps none you know about," said Tazendra carelessly, then realized what she had said and blushed deeply, while Aerich gave her a look full of reproach.

Adron, however, did not appear to notice the blunder, so engrossed was he in contemplation. "It is impossible," he said, "for I have not—ah."

At this word, the others, who did not dare to say anything, looked at each other significantly. "Well," he amended, "it is not altogether impossible, yet, for such a thing to be—" His voice trailed off, and Khaavren would have sworn that he was trembling as if from some great emotion.

We should say here that certain discoveries in the High Art which provide safeguards that are common today were less common then, although they were available, thus the existence of bastards and even half-breeds was not unknown. However, the stigma which such unfortunates must suffer today was in existence even then, though perhaps with less vigor. Still, it should be said that any gentleman who was informed, especially publicly, of the existence of a child whose birth he didn't expect was almost certain to feel embarrassment to a greater or lesser degree; yet, to judge by Adron's countenance, the emotion he was feeling had less of embarrassment or shame about it and more of excitement or wonder, which reaction did not escape Khaavren's notice.

"Well, then," said Pel. "What are Your Highness's wishes?"

"My wishes?" said Adron, frowning. "It seems that, in all cases, I must return to the fort."

"I assure Your Highness," said Aerich, "that we are entirely at your service, should you wish us to accompany you."

"Oh, as to that," said Adron. "I think you had best return to the city with all speed, and, when you appear before His Majesty, as I have no doubt you will, you must inform him that I have been delayed by unusual circumstances and will return as soon as it is possible to do so, and will then present myself before him."

"We will fulfill your commission with the greatest pleasure," said Aerich.

"And at once, too," said Tazendra, "for, in faith, I am taken with the desire to see the city again."

"And I, also," said Kathana. "For if I am to stand to trial before His Majesty, well, I should like it to be finished sooner rather than later."

"In that case," said Adron, "we will part at once. Yet I think we will see each other again, and I assure you that I hold you all in the highest esteem."

"Your Highness does us too much honor," said Aerich.

"Not at all," said Adron.

"Then let us be off," said Pel and Uttrik together.

They settled up with the host, which honor Adron insisted upon for himself, even over the protestations of the host, who wished to have for himself the honor of providing the Heir's repast, and afterward they caused their horses to be saddled and brought to the yard. Then, with only a few more words, they took their separate ways: Adron back to Redface, the others toward the city.

This time they made better speed; for they all felt that they had been gone a long time and needed to report the results of their mission, as well as to find out what had been happening while they were away, and Khaavren, moreover, was anxious to see the fair Illista once more, and to explain how it had happened that he had fulfilled his promise without breaking his oath; therefore, though they were careful not to exhaust their horses in the blistering summer heat, they made stages of twenty or twenty-five leagues across the *pushta*, sometimes not stopping until full dark had fallen.

The return, notwithstanding that it took place during what was still the height of summer, and that, therefore, it was unpleasantly hot, was passed in a happier mode than the journey out had been.

Tazendra, though still annoyed that the chance for a glorious death had passed her by, was in some measure reconciled to it, and ran over and over in her mind the battles in which she had fought and been triumphant.

Uttrik's mood was that of one who has happily put aside a vengeance, so he rode with a light heart, and, moreover, he, too, took pleasure in recalling the victories which, in retrospect, had seemed to come so easily and naturally.

Kathana had, if truth be known, been growing increasingly dissatisfied with hiding, and was now happy and content to be "face toward the fire," as the saying is, and was composing speeches which she might have the honor to deliver before His Majesty.

Pel was ruminating all the events that had taken place, and considering how they might be turned into lasting advantages, these being more important to him than glory, which is so fleeting in any event.

Aerich, normally the most moody of companions, was, since he had killed Shaltre, always amiable and pleasant; smiling calmly to all and even sometimes engaging in small conversations with Khaavren on the people and sights they rode by.

Khaavren was constructing daydreams of Illista, and, moreover, of the honors and promotions he might achieve as a result the events of the last few days, and was even trying on the name, "Lieutenant Khaavren," to see how it sounded in his ears.

Mica, we may be sure, was awash in pleasure at the dzur which they had had embroidered upon the breast of his tunic by a tailor they had happened to meet at a hostel at the foot of Bli'aard.

In this way, then, the return journey took its course, and before many days had passed they found themselves once more in sight of Beed'n's Inn, which caused Mica, first, to tremble, as he remembered the beating he had received, and then smile, as he recalled what the results of the affair were. Khaavren, who, as we should comprehend by now, noticed everything, observed this reaction and said, "Well, we have made good time, and are nearly home; let us, then, celebrate in advance by stopping here for jug of Khaav'n, or a bottle of Ailor."

To this they all agreed, and, finding the place nearly empty, they claimed the largest table, placed, as Khaavren preferred, by a window, so he could amuse himself by watching the passersby. They did, in fact, consume a certain quantity of Khaav'n, which Khaavren preferred to most other wines, because it came from his own region, and shared a name with him, and was, besides, neither too sweet nor too dry; and although in fact it was rather fuller in body than Pel preferred, he made no complaint and drank in such a way as to keep up with his companions.

They had been at it for some time, when Khaavren said, "Well, it is clear we are nearly home, for I have observed more than one Imperial messenger travel along the road of which I have such a fine view through this window, as well as such a multitude of bourgeois and clerks that the issue cannot be in doubt."

"Well then," said Aerich, "if you are enjoying the view, it is just as well the landlord has not repaired the window which good Mica broke with his head. Otherwise, I think I would have preferred that it had been repaired, since the paper would do well to keep the heat out."

"Bah," said Uttrik. "After passing through the *pushta*, where we had to find water for our horses every three leagues, I declare that this heat doesn't bother me all, but rather, it feels as cool as the mountains by comparison."

"And yet," said Khaavren, "It must still be hot, for here is a troop of Guardsmen, wearing our uniforms but Lanmarea's badges, which must have determined to take a rest here, for, though it is not a mealtime, they are nevertheless stopping."

"Well," said Tazendra, "that is good; we shall get news of the city from them."

"Perhaps not," said Khaavren, "for, now that I look, they are merely tethering their horses, as if they don't expect to remain long."

"Indeed, you are right," observed Pel, leaning over and looking out the window. "It is as if they have only stopped to ask questions, for, see, the officer alone is coming in."

"But why," asked Kathana, "are the rest of them moving around to the sides of the hostelry, as if to surround it?"

"I confess," said Pel, "that I've no idea, unless they are searching for someone and suspect he may be here, and don't wish to let him escape."

"Well," said Tazendra, "I've seen no one who looks suspicious."

"There could be someone hiding upstairs," said Khaavren, "and for my part, I declare that I will put aside all rivalry that might exist between their service and our own, and give them all the help I can."

"They don't seem likely to need help," said Aerich.

"Oh, you are doubtless correct," said Khaavren, "but it is only right to offer, and, if they need no help, why, I've no doubt we will be told of it. Hullo, Sergeant," he called to the lady who entered at that moment. "We are both servants of His Majesty, and you seem to be intent upon some business, therefore we will offer you our services, and, if these services are not needed, then, by the Shards, you may come and have a glass with us, and we will drink to the health of His Majesty and Captains G'aereth and Lanmarea, and the Warlord herself."

"Well," said the Sergeant, bowing to those at the table, "you may, indeed, be able to do me a service, and, if not, I will accept your kind offer."

"That is all we ask, Sergeant," said Khaavren. "How may we help you?"

"I am called Lebouru," she said, "Sergeant, as you have perceived, of the Imperial Guard, and if you would do me honor of telling me your names, I will happily tell you how you could be of help to me."

"Very well," said the Tiassa. "I am called Khaavren, and these are my friends, Aerich, Tazendra, and Pel, as well as our companion Uttrik, and the Lady Fricorith." He gave Kathana her assumed name because, as she intended to surrender herself, he had no wish to compromise her ahead of time.

"Your name, you say, is Khaavren?" said Lebouru.

"Exactly," said the Tiassa.

"That falls out remarkably well, and you can indeed, do me a great favor."

"Then I am anxious to do so."

"That is most kind of you."

"I wait to hear what this service is."

"Well, I will tell you."

"You will please me by doing so."

"Well, this is it: if you will do me the honor to surrender your sword to me, and to cause your companions to do likewise, and then to accompany me to the city, well, I will ask for nothing further, and, moreover, will consider myself in your debt."

"How," cried Khaavren. "Surrender my sword?"

"Yes, exactly."

"And accompany you?"

"I am pleased to see that I have to do with a gentleman of understanding."

"You pretend, then, that we are arrested?"

"Nearly so."

"On what charge?"

"As to that, I assure you I have no idea in the world. But I was told to take a troop of twenty, and to follow this road, and to question every passerby, and to stop at every inn, and to find a Guardsman, who was called Khaavren of Castlerock, and who was, moreover, a Tiassa, and I was directed to arrest him and whatever companions happened to be with him. You see that I am about performing my duty."

Uttrik, who had just begun to recover from the shock that Lebouru's words had given him, said, "This is insupportable."

Tazendra said, "Indeed. Bah! A troop of twenty? It is an insult."

The Sergeant shrugged and said, "My troop is deployed around this house, so that, you perceive, escape is impossible. Furthermore, in addition to our swords, we have each a flash-stone of two charges, so that, if you resist, you will doubtless be killed. Now, I was told to return you alive if possible, but dead if necessary, so, in order to complete my task in the best way, I would prefer if you made no resistance."

"Will you," said Khaavren, "allow us a few moments to

confer, so we can reach agreement on whether we wish to do ourselves the honor of resisting you?"

"Certainly," said Lebouru. "There is nothing against that. Only I am under strict orders not to allow you to communicate with anyone outside of this inn. So, if you will give me your word not to do so, and will, moreover, allow me to call to my men and inform them of the state of things, well, you may take whatever time you need."

"We give you our word," said Khaavren, "which ought to convince you the more readily as there is no one here to communicate to."

"Very well," said the Sergeant, and she stepped to the doorway and called, "Hullo, we have found them. Stand ready to battle, if it should prove necessary, but take no action until you receive my order, or hear the discharge of my flash-stone."

While she was doing this, Khaavren said, "Well, this is a turn of events that I did not, I confess, anticipate."

"For my part," said Tazendra, "I think we should fight. The Horse! There are only twenty of them."

"And," said Pel, "to be arrested, well, it is humiliating."

"This," said Kathana, "will console me for the fights I have missed."

Uttrik said, "To die here, to die another place, well, it's all the same to me. Besides, we might win, and think of how it would be to defeat twenty of his Majesty's Phoenix Guards, armed with flash-stones?"

Aerich said, "And you, Khaavren, what is your idea?"

Khaavren sighed. "It is, my dear friend, the same as yours, I think. If we fight, win or lose, we shall be rebels."

"That is my thought exactly," said Aerich.

"Rebels!" said Pel. "The word is hard."

"But none the less accurate for that," said Aerich. "Do you agree?"

"But to allow ourselves to be arrested," said Tazendra.

"Yes," said Uttrik. "To be arrested, well, it is not a thing I like the sound of."

"Well, what would you?" said Aerich, addressing Uttrik. "Are you not of the line of Lanya?"

"Well, yes."

"And was not Lanya herself, then called Lanya e'Kieron, arrested in the third Cycle by the Athyra Emperor, Soori-Laino-Kri, for refusing to assault the fortress of the Issola, Muranda?"

"Well, that is true."

"So, you perceive, there is no shame in being arrested."

Uttrik sighed, "If Lanya could do it, well, I can submit as well."

Kathana said, "For my part, I should have preferred to give myself willingly into the hands of the Guard, but since they have come, well, it will have to do."

Aerich stood and bowed to Lebouru, "My lady, here is my sword."

"Well, I accept it with pleasure."

"And here is mine," said Khaavren. "Cha! What you will do with so many swords is your affair, but for all of that, here they are."

And, one by one, the others surrendered their swords to the Sergeant, who handed them to her men and said, "If you will do me the honor to accompany me, we may return to the city, whither, I think, you were bound in any case, only now you shall have more company than you had thought to."

"That is right," said Pel, "only allow us first to settle matters with our host."

"I cannot permit that," said Lebouru, "when I have been given six hundred orbs to see that my men are fed and their horses watered, and I have had no need to use the tenth part of it." She called the host over to her, determined the score to be settled, and paid it to the last penny. "Now, I think, we are ready."

"We are at your service, Sergeant," said Khaavren.

The troop had formed by this time, except for seven who stood by, six of them to hold the horses for the prisoners and assist them to mount, the seventh to perform this service for the sergeant. In this way they left the inn, with ten Guardsmen riding ahead of the prisoners and ten behind. It should be added that, as Khaavren and his friends still wore their uniform cloaks and Uttrik and Kathana were deep in the middle of the troop, no one who saw them would perceive that these Guardsmen were escorting prisoners.

In this way, then, they traveled until they had arrived at a place in the road where Uttrik observed to Khaavren, "It is remarkable to consider that, in this spot, I attempted to take your life."

"Well," said Khaavren. "I am glad that you didn't, and equally glad that I didn't take yours."

"Oh, indeed yes," said Uttrik. "Either would have been too droll compared to what actually happened."

"Cha! And what is continuing to happen even now, for I, at least, am unable to foresee where this will end."

"Nowhere good, I'm afraid," said Mica, who had been as crushed by recent events as the others were rigorously cheerful; as if he was assuming to himself all the melancholy that was the rightful property of the entire band. This can be more readily understood when we consider that, a few hours before, he had been about to take his place as a lackey for a valiant Dzurlord, and he was now only the servant of a prisoner; a position which, so far as we know, has never been actively sought by anyone.

As for the others, they were, as we mentioned above, doing their best to maintain their spirits. Tazendra was involved in a discussion with a Guardsman on her right, explaining to him how, if they had chosen to fight, it would have been a simple matter after all to have scattered and defeated a mere twenty of the enemy.

"And our flash-stones?" inquired the gentleman politely. "What of them?"

"Oh, bah," said Tazendra, using an expression she enjoyed from Pel and admired from Aerich. "What are flash-stones? They would have failed to discharge. And if by chance they went off, well, Blood of the Horse, it isn't for nothing that I am a sorcerer. I should have rendered them useless in an instant."

"Well, that may be true of the flash-stones, but we had still our swords."

"Mere nothings," said Tazendra. "Sticks. I'd have brushed away three of them at the first, inflicting, I should add, good wounds on their holders."

"Well, that is three," said the other. "But it leaves seventeen of us, not to mention the sergeant, who is a skilled player, as I happen to know."

"But you forget our servant, Mica, who is handy with a bar-stool, but delights especially in striking officers, for, as a child, he was ill used by soldiers, and consequently he bears a grudge."

"And, as for the other seventeen of us?"

"Well, had I not companions?"

"You had indeed; five of them. That means three for each of you, if I am not mistaken."

"And yet, there were but three windows, each only big enough for one, and the door, where we could have stationed two, leaving one of us free to dance around as chance offered."

And so the discussion continued, accomplishing nothing, it is true, but providing Tazendra with great amusement.

As for Pel, he took the opportunity to question one of his captors and thus learn what he could of what had transpired at court during his absence.

Uttrik and Kathana happily and loudly discussed the history of Lanya e'Kiernon, which Aerich had brought to their minds. She had been considered a rebel for her opposition to the Athyra emperor, and then again for engineering the Coup of the Bureaucrats against the Phoenix Jessier the Fearful, when, first backed by and then opposing a conspiracy led by a Tsalmoth noble called Seawall, she, that is, Lanya, took the Palace, the Throne, and the Orb with an army composed of fifty soldiers and two thousand privately trained functionaries, an action which gave her a permanent place in history and started the War of the Streets. The War lasted some two hundred years, off and on, during which time Lanya caused the Inner Palace to be designed and built: the only part of the Palace which could be held against attackers.

Aerich seemed content with his own thoughts, whatever they might be, and Khaavren constructed dreams in which Illista figured prominently, only this time, in his dreams, she rescued him from prison and contrived to bring him before His Majesty, where together they pleaded their case and, not only won the release of all the companions, but were awarded promotions and medals enough to satisfy a Dzurlord.

Of the companions, only Mica, as we have said, was downcast. And so it was a complacent group which, surrounded by Guards, passed through the Gate of the Flags in the early afternoon, and turned up the Old Miller's Road toward the Palace district.

About this time, Khaavren became curious about their destination, accordingly he asked the sergeant.

"The Dragon Wing, first," she said. "After that, I am entirely ignorant."

"Well, it must either be a prison or the Emperor."

"That seems likely, Sir Khaavren."

"For my part, I must confess that I don't much care. If it is His Majesty, well, we will have the chance to find out why we have been arrested, and I think we can convince him to change his mind with respect to ourselves. And if it is prison, well, in faith, I can use the rest."

"Well, I am happy that you are so complaisant, for I should hate to resort to extreme measures with a gentleman like yourself."

"Oh, there will be no call for that, I promise."

"Good."

"But you ought to tell me if there are any special instructions, so that we may be certain not to unintentionally cause you any difficulty."

"Oh, be easy on that score. The only special orders were in the case of resistance."

"And, had we done so?"

"Well, then I was ordered to have all of you killed."

"What, killed? All of us?"

"Exactly."

"Impossible."

"No, my word of honor on it. And, as such a slaughter would have been distasteful to me, well, I am only glad that you did not resist."

"Well, in faith, so am I. And that was the only special order you were given?"

"Yes, only that, except that I am also to prevent you from escaping, and to be certain you communicate with no one."

"How, we are forbidden to speak with anyone along the way?"

"Exactly."

"Well," said Khaavren, to whom this request presented all sorts of meat upon which the teeth of his thoughts could masticate, "then, if you will excuse me, I must inform my companions of this, lest, upon seeing a familiar face, someone unintentionally causes you some difficulty."

"Well, I will be most grateful if you do."

"I will do so at once."

"I assure you, I am entirely your servant."

"Excuse me, then." Khaavren allowed his horse to drop back until he rode next to Pel, whom he judged to have the best sort of mind for problems of this nature. He interrupted the Yendi's discourse, saying, "I beg your pardon, Cavalier, but I wish to have a moment's conversation with you."

"As you wish," said Pel, excusing himself from the Guardsman he had been questioning. Then speaking in a low voice so as not to be overheard, he said, "Well, what is it?"

"Do you know that our captors have orders to prevent

us from making any sort of communication with anyone along our route?"

"Blood! Do they?"

"I have it from the Sergeant herself."

"But, what can this mean?"

"It can only mean that our arrest is to be kept secret, and moreover—"

"Yes?"

"That we are not to be given a chance to defend ourselves."

"But then, you think—?"

"That we will put in some dungeon somewhere, and no one will know what has become of us, and, presently, well, we will disappear."

"Bah. Impossible. And what of our escort?"

"They will be put under orders not to mention our names nor the circumstances of our capture."

"But, who would have given such an order, and moreover, why?"

"Who? Who else but Seodra. Why? Because they have despaired of assassinating us, and, since we failed to resist them, the Sergeant could not have us killed as she had been ordered to in such a case—"

"What? Killed?"

"Those were her orders, if we had resisted."

"Cracks in the Orb!"

"Well?"

"I think you are right, Khaavren; they wish us to vanish with no chance to defend ourselves."

"That is my opinion. It is why I have spoken to you, for you are sufficiently clever, I thought you might have a plan."

"Well, I nearly think you are right."

"What, you have one already?"

"Almost."

"What is it?"

Pel shook his head. "Leave me for a few minutes; I must gather my thoughts."

"Very well, but I beg you to observe that we are passing the ruins of the Towers of Sorcery, and are very nearly at Watchers Hill, which means we will soon be arriving at the Dragon Wing."

"I understand. Leave everything to me."

"I will do so."

"Very well."

Pel returned then to the side of the Guardsman with whom he had been speaking. "Your pardon, my dear sir," he said. "I had to speak a few words of comfort to my friend who is in some despair over our predicament."

"Well, that is only natural," said the Guardsman, whose name, it turned out, was Thack. "But, come, we ought not to talk about that."

"Oh, I am in complete agreement. Besides, it is hardly so amusing when compared to the escapades of the Consort. But come, do you think that she is very close with Threewalls?"

"How," said Thack with a smile. "What do you mean by close?"

"Oh, you know very well what I mean."

"I assure you, I have no idea in the world, Cavalier."

"But to be close, well, that is clear enough. We are close now, you and I."

"Not so very close, Cavalier; we are not touching."

"Yes we could, if one or the other of us was to reach out a hand, my good Thack."

"And yet, you perceive, neither of us has done so."

"But if either of us could, then—"

"Yes, then?"

"Well, that is being close."

"Not in the least. My opinion is that, to be close, one must touch."

"Very well, then," said Pel. "By your terms then, is the Consort close to Threewalls?"

"Well," said the Guardsman with a wink. "Close, at least, by your terms."

"Bah," said Pel. "That isn't so much."

"Yet," laughed the other, "for my part, I think it a great deal."

"To be close by your terms, Thack, well, that would be better."

"Oh, with that I should make no argument, good Pel."

"I imagine you know well enough, Thack."

"I? Not the least in the world, and I am ashamed to admit it."

"Bah! Your mistress, at least, would have a different story."

"Oh, if I had a mistress, that might be true."

"How, if? You mean you don't have a mistress? And yet, you are handsome enough; and you have an excellent air about you; I should have thought the ladies would faint for you by the score."

"Oh, all you say is true, yet I am too shy to take advantage of it."

"Oh, then you require a woman who knows in what way to treat a shy gentleman."

"Well, that would certainly please me, only—"

"Only?"

"Well, she would have to be well-born, in addition."

"That need not be said; I know with whom I am speaking after all."

"And, in addition, it is necessary that she be beautiful."

"That is only just."

"You perceive, then, that I am extraordinarily particular, and that is why I am alone."

"Well, let us recapitulate."

"Very well."

"First of all, she must be beautiful."

"Yes, that is right."

"Then, she must be of birth suitable to an excellent gentleman such as yourself."

"Continue, Cavalier, for you are correct on all counts."

"Third, she must be willing to become close, as we mean the word."

"Yes, by my meaning in particular."

"That is understood."

"Very well."

"And, finally, she must be able to overcome your shyness."

"That is, she must not object to my natural reticence and timidity, for, as you perceive, I am extremely modest."

"Yes," said Pel, biting his cheeks to keep from laughing. "I had noticed this about you."

"Well, so you see the problem, Cavalier."

"Your pardon, Thack, but I do not."

"How, you do not?"

"Not at all."

"Shall I explain it to you?"

"If you wish me to understand it, yes."

"Very well, then, in two words: where am I to find such a woman?"

"That is your problem?"

"That is it exactly."

"Well, but I know the answer."

"How, you know it?"

"Certainly."

"And you will tell me?"

"If you would like me to."

"Like you to? I have been asking for an hour."

"Well, then, the answer is called Jenicor e'Terics."

"How, Jenicor?"

"Yes, exactly."

"You know her yourself, Cavalier?"

"I?" said Pel. "Not at all. Do you?"

"Well, that is, I know of her, and I have seen her."

"Well, then," said Pel, "she is of high enough birth, I hope."

"I nearly think so; she is almost the Heir."

"And she is beautiful."

"Of that, there is no question."

"Well, what else?"

"What else? Why she must be willing to become close, and, moreover, close with a gentleman of my retiring disposition."

"Well, that is the special mark of her character."

"Bah! It is unlikely."

"Not at all, for I heard exactly this, and in no uncertain terms. In fact, it is known that, upon meeting a gentleman who is both handsome and shy, well, she loses control of herself entirely, and cannot refrain from taking the sorts of long couch-rides where intimacies are whispered into the ear, and the sort of walks where pauses are frequent and of long duration."

"You know this?"

"As much as if I had been following her about the city."

"Well, and from whom?"

"Why, from Captain G'aereth, none other."

"How, he told you this was her character?"

"Exactly, and in terms that left no room for doubt. He is also a shy gentleman, you perceive."

"Well, I had not remarked that, but no doubt you are correct."

"Oh, I am, of that there can be no question."

"Well, I shall consider this."

"Not too long, I hope; for you know about such women, one turns around, and they have been taken away. The Captain himself would have married her, only he is, as you know, a Dzurlord, which prevents him from marrying a Dragon, and, moreover, he is already married."

"Well, those are two good reasons."

"But they do not apply to you, good Thack."

"Oh, as to that, I have no thought of marriage."

"Well, no, but you know about women, I hope. Once they are married, well, it is sometimes a hundred years before they are willing to become close friends with anyone else."

"Do you know, I had remarked that very thing."

"Well, then, you perceive, you ought not to lose a day."

"I think you are right, Cavalier, and I assure you I am deeply in your debt."

"Bah. When I am released, well, you may buy me dinner and a few bottles of Ailor and tell me of the entire affair, and I promise I will be satisfied."

"You think you will be released then?"

"As I have committed no crime, I am certain of it."

"How, you have committed no crime?"

"None at all."

"But then, why are you arrested?"

"I assure you, I have not the least idea in the world."

"But then, you are right, they will doubtless release you soon."

"That is my opinion."

"And when they do, well, perhaps I will have something to tell you."

"I would be most pleased to hear it."

"Ah, Cavalier, I wish we could continue our conversation, but it seems we have arrived at the Dragon Wing, and the sergeant has already gone within, and is just now returning, so we are doubtless to escort you somewhere, which means our conversation must end."

"Until later then, my dear captor."

"Until later, Cavalier."

Pel went up, then, and rejoined Khaavren, saying, "It is all arranged."

"What is arranged, my dear Pel?"

"You shall see."

"Well, I hope so, for we seem bound for the Iorich Wing, where the justicers live."

"Are we, then, afraid of the justicers?"

"Not at all, but also in the Iorich Wing is the Imperial Prison, where prisoners of state are kept, as are those who are to be executed. And, while I hope we do not fall into the latter category, at least we fall into the former."

In this Khaavren was not mistaken, and all he expected, in fact, occurred. But as it would be too painful to witness the process of locking the prisoners, for such all of our friends were, into the dungeons below the Iorich Wing, we will, instead, skip this matter entirely and proceed on to other things, wherefore we will, without further ado, end this chapter of our history.

Chapter the Thirty-second

*In Which Having Already Seen
a Bloodless Battle, The Reader
is Shown a Bloodless Duel*

W E WILL NOW turn our attention to a gentleman who has been neglected since the early portions of our history; that is, Captain G'aereth, he who sent our friends on the mission that had ended by bearing such unusual fruit. We should say that the Captain was by no means Pel's dupe; he understood that the Cavalier's reason for wanting to take this journey had not been stated in exactly truthful terms, but he understood as well that he would be likely to get useful information from the affair, and he was, moreover, always willing to go out of his way to help his Guardsmen, whom he thought of as the patriarch of a large family might think of his grandchildren.

His thoughts, therefore, turned more than once toward those he had sent, or rather, had permitted to go, east, and he wondered what events might be transpiring there. But he also waited with confidence that he would, by and by, learn many interesting things; for just as one cannot throw a bag of gold into the Almshouse of Chatier without expecting a certain amount of commotion, one cannot throw a Yendi, a Dzur, a Lyorn, and a Tiassa into the place where all of the political maneuvering of the court is centered without being certain that something or other will come of it.

To the left, however, we must consider that the Captain was still the Captain, and therefore, always busy, and that the court had not stood by patiently awaiting the results of events happening hundreds of leagues away. The Captain had continued with his duties, of which the primary one, although he was not aware of it, was to slowly transform the Imperial Guard from an elite fighting unit to a police force. As for the court, from what G'aereth had seen (and, while not an intriguer, he was nevertheless well informed) it had been concerning itself more and more with the scandals of the Consort, to which the Emperor appeared to have turned a blind eye. Lord Adron e'Kieron had been summoned, Lord Garland had vanished, and the Athyra, Seodra, seemed to be functioning as His Majesty's chief advisor, while the courtiers watched anxiously to see in what direction she might impel the Emperor with regard to an invasion of Sandyhome, the disposition of the Pepperfields, and a score of matters of less importance except to those with interest direct.

In addition to all of this, he had found that his time was taken by a series of incidents and complaints against his Guardsmen, all coming from unlikely quarters, and, upon being investigated, all of which proved false, in that the individuals who had purportedly made the claims vigorously denied them, so that the Captain came to the conclusion, at first, that Lanmarea was attempting to slander his command, and, after, that someone unknown was merely working to keep him busy. While this puzzled him, there was little he could do about it.

Word had reached the Captain's ears that certain arrests had been made of some unknown gentlemen on certain charges involving a conspiracy of some sort, but as no names were attached to these rumors, nor the fact they were Guardsmen at all (in fact, the Guards who had arrested our friends were not even given their names, and none of our friends, except the clever Yendi, had thought to insure that his or her name was known), G'aereth spent no time considering the matter, which seemed to be none of his affair, and for which he had no time to spare in any event.

Therefore, we find him, some two days after the close of the previous chapter, in the apartments where he was accustomed to conduct his business; that is, the same closet in which he had the famous interviews with our friends. At about an hour after the ringing of the noon-bells from the Spiked Tower of the Issola Wing, which could, despite the intervention of walls and distance, still be discerned in the interior of the Dragon Wing, a certain Dragonlord who was on duty begged the Captain to receive the Marquis of Bothways, called Diesep e'Lanya, who asked to speak to the Captain on a personal matter.

"Very well," said the Captain. "I know the gentleman; you may show him in."

The Marquis was admitted, and bowed courteously to G'aereth, who invited him to sit. The Marquis politely refused the courtesy, at which refusal the Captain grunted, as if to say, "Well, then, so this call has some element to it that is not entirely friendly."

The Marquis said, "My lord Captain G'aereth, I am here as a friend of the lady Jenicor e'Terics."

"Why, yes, I know the lady."

"Of that, there is no doubt."

"Well, and what does she wish of me?"

"What, you do not know?"

The Captain grunted, as if to say, "How should I know?"

"Well then," persisted Diesep, "can you not guess?"

This time the Captain was so moved that he spoke, saying, "I assure you that I cannot."

"Well, but that is strange, my lord Captain."

The Captain grunted, and spoke in addition, saying, "You speak in enigmas."

"Well, would you have me speak plainer?"

"I desire nothing better."

"And you wish me to state my mission?"

"I assure you I have been waiting for nothing else for an hour."

"And it signifies nothing that I am here on behalf of Jenicor e'Terics? I repeat, Jenicor e'Terics?"

"Well, that tells me on whose behalf you have come, but nothing else. And yet, from the manner in which you speak, it seems that you are here for a particular purpose."

"You are perspicacious, my lord."

"And should I find a friend with whom you can arrange matters?"

"You have understood everything."

"Well, although I have no knowledge of any quarrel she might have with me, still, she does me great honor to make this request, and I assure you she will no have cause to complain of my response."

"I am surprised that you pretend to no knowledge of the complaint, my lord, yet I am delighted that you understand so well our desire in this matter."

"Shall we arrange things quickly, sir?"

"I am convinced that would be best."

"Very well, then—but excuse me, I am called for." Indeed, at that moment, the Guardsman who had the honor that day to be the Captain's doorman, requested an audience on behalf of the Duke of Threewalls. The Captain solicited and received permission of Diesep to attend to the Duke first, whereupon Lord Allistar was admitted, and introductions were made, although unnecessarily since the Duke and the Marquis had had occasion to encounter one another before.

"You have requested to see me?" said the Captain.

"Indeed yes; I come on behalf of my sister, the lady Illista."

The Captain frowned. "How is this? Another affair of honor? Can I have been offending every lady in the Empire without being aware of it?"

Lord Diesep at first smiled at this, then frowned and said, "I must insist, Duke, that, as I was first, my affair must be concluded first."

"You misunderstand," said Threewalls, bowing. "I am here on behalf of my sister, but only to ask you a simple question."

"Ah, that is all? Well, that is much more easily managed."

"Then you will entertain my question?"

"I will more than entertain it, my dear Duke, I will, if it is in my power, answer it."

"So much the better."

"Ask, then."

"My sister is interested, for reasons we need not discuss, in a certain Guardsman who is in your brigade."

"Well, and?"

"She has not heard from him in some time, and is desirous of knowing his state and his whereabouts."

"Perhaps," said G'aereth, "he has been busy."

"It is possible, but, under the circumstances, not likely."

"Well then, who is he?"

"He is a Tiassa named Khaavren."

"Ah, yes. Well, the gentleman is on a mission, I am not at liberty to say where, and he has not yet returned."

"And you have heard nothing from him?"

"He is, as you have observed, a Tiassa. I am unlikely to hear from him until he is able to make a complete report."

"Well," said Allistar, bowing, "that is all then. And if I can in any way be of service to you, you need only ask."

"In that case," said G'aereth, with a glint of humor in his eyes, "I will ask now."

"Now? Then am I to be granted the happiness of serving you in some manner?"

"If it will not trouble you."

"Well, tell me what you wish, and, even if it does trouble me, you may keep on asking."

"This gentleman," G'aereth nodded toward Diesep,

"conveys a challenge from Jenicor e'Terics, and, to arrange matters, I stand in need of a second."

"And you are asking me to stand for you?"

"Yes, that is it exactly."

"Well, if you will allow me to dispatch a messenger to my sister, in order to inform her of the results of the interrogatories to which you have done me the honor of replying, I will stand for you with pleasure, my lord Captain."

"Very well, then, let us arrange things."

"For my part," said Diesep with a bow to Threewalls, "I ask nothing better."

The matter was quickly settled; they agreed to fight with longswords, until one or the other was unable to continue. The seconds, it was agreed, would merely observe. They dispatched a messenger to Lytra e'Tenith to inquire if she would honor them by judging, and Diesep agreed to accept a pair of Guardsmen as witnesses. While they awaited Lytra's response, they sat amiably as two old friends speaking only on inconsequential matters.

Presently the messenger returned bringing not only Lytra's reply, but Lytra herself, who embraced G'aereth as an old friend and greeted Diesep cordially enough, after which the same messenger was dispatched, this time to bring Jenicor to the Sycamore Pavilion, which place had been agreed upon as the sight of the engagement.

In order for our readers to have an understanding of the scene, it is necessary to say that the Pavilion of the Sycamores was not, as one might think, a covered terrace surrounded by those trees for which it was named; rather, it was an uncovered area with a flooring of grass and surrounded by a low stone wall, with a small fountain in the middle and a few marble tables at odd distances about it. It had been named for the twentieth Baron of Sycamore, Warlord to the sixteenth Issola Emperor. This Baron had caused it to be built in order to please a certain lady of whom he was enamored, and who complained that the Dragon Wing was lacking in elegance. It was rather long in form, looking not unlike a shotball court save for the lack of goals and nets, and the existence of doors on either end. The fountain, we should say, had not seen use for five hundred years and was in poor condition.

G'aereth, Lytra, Allistar, and Diesep arrived with the witnesses, and had to wait only a short time before Jenicor arrived. She was dressed in the manner of the high Dragonlord she was, that is, in black with silver trim, wearing clothes cut for fighting. After a brief discussion, in which it was agreed that the entire length and width of the Pavilion would serve as the circle, saving only one side, which was set aside for the witnesses, the combatants took their positions.

Lytra said, "Jenicor e'Terics, will you be reconciled to Captain my lord G'aereth?"

She cast a haughty look upon her opponent and said, "Only if he will consent to apologize before the entire court, and to retract his words and admit that he lied."

Lytra then turned to G'aereth and said, "Well, and will you consent to make this apology and these statements?"

G'aereth shrugged. "That is unlikely, as I am entirely ignorant of the statements the lady pretends I have made."

"Impossible," said Jenicor, glaring at the Dzurlord.

"How," said G'aereth, drawing himself up to his full height. "You give me the lie?"

"Well, I nearly think I do," she said coolly.

"Then, if we had not had cause enough before, well, on my honor, we do now."

"Oh, I assure you, my lord, we had cause before."

"That may be, my lady, yet I am entirely ignorant of it."

"Then you deny—"

"No matter," said G'aereth. "You say there is cause on your part, and I declare there is cause on mine. On your guard, then, and we will settle the matter pleasantly enough."

Jenicor, rather than advancing, as one would expect her to do after having been paid such a compliment, lowered her sword and frowned. "Could it be," she said, "that you are telling the truth?"

"Eh? I declare it, I affirm it, and I will even fight on that basis."

"You have no knowledge of how you have offended me?"

"I know how you have offended me, and that is quite sufficient, I assure you."

"Not at all."

"How, not?"

"Because, as it is my intention to kill you, I wish you to be entirely clear on why you are about to die."

"Well," said G'aereth, lowering his own sword, "that is only right, and if you wish to tell me, well, I will listen."

"Very well. I refer to certain words you have spoken about me of an extremely personal, I should even say, intimate nature."

G'aereth grunted, as if to say, "I remain entirely ignorant."

"Then," said Jenicor, "you deny having made any such remarks?"

"I do."

"It is odd," said she, "for of all that I have ever heard of you, no one, even your enemies (for you must be aware, my lord, that you have some), has spoken of you as anything but a loyal and honest gentleman."

"That is my hope, my lady."

"But consider," she said, "is there nothing you might have said, even to an intimate?"

"Your name has never come up in my presence except in the highest terms."

"But, perhaps you were drunk."

"I do not drink."

Jenicor lowered her sword the rest of the way and her frown deepened. "My lord, I mislike mystery when it is a matter of someone's life."

"Well, as do I. How should we make things right?"

Jenicor said, "Allow me to approach you."

"Very well. For what reason?"

"To whisper in your ear the slanders I have been informed of, and which I do not wish to spread."

"I await you then."

"Well, I am approaching."

"I will listen."

"Here it is, then."

Jenicor whispered to G'aereth, whose eyes grew wide, while a flush spread over his countenance. "My lady," he cried at last, "such words never came from me, I swear it by the Orb."

"Well, but then—"

"From whose mouth did you get such things?"

"Why, from a Guardsman named Thack, who thought to take advantage of these supposed characteristics."

"Well, and where is he now?"

"Oh, he is recovering. I stopped short of slaying him that I might question him and learn where his ideas of me came from."

"And he said?"

"They came from you."

"But I have never even met him."

"How, not met him? A Dragonlord with light hair and thin brows, who carries a rose in his collar and has a baldrick with gold trim, and walks as if there were stones in the toes of his boots?"

"I have never even seen this man."

"Well, but then, even wounded and near death, he lied to me?"

"He must have, or else he was deceived."

"Well, I will speak with him again, I think."

"If you will do me the honor to allow me to accompany you, well, I think it appropriate that I be there, as it concerns me closely."

"I am in complete agreement," said Jenicor. "And while I don't think our seconds will be needed any longer, still if the lady Lytra will do us the honor to accompany us, it may be that some good will come of it, for, as Warlord, she can hardly be uninterested in any matters concerning her command."

"I am in full agreement," said Lytra, "and, to help resolve this issue, would follow you beneath the sea."

"So much the better, then," said Jenicor, "that you need only follow us for a few leagues."

Allistar indicated an interest the proceedings, and no one made any objections. As for Diesep, he indicated that he had no need to see the matter played out, and so, with courteous words on both sides, he walked out of the pavilion and out of our history.

Without wasting time, then, these worthies left the Dragon Wing and followed the Street of the Dragon to the Street of the Six Towers, and so came to a small house in the Coronet district where, after gaining admittance, they were brought to the sickbed of the Guardsman called Thack.

Now, he was in a bad way, for if the offended Jenicor had stopped short of killing him, she had done so by only the narrowest of margins. He had, then, been given a cut in the forehead, one on either leg, and had received a good thrust through the body, as a result of which almost all of his blood had been lost. He had been attended by doctors both medical and sorcerous, which is why he was still alive, and was even, scarcely a day after being wounded, pronounced out of danger by the sorcerer; but he still slept most of the time.

The coalescence of aristocracy clustered around the sickbed and, by tapping earnestly on Thack's forehead, in order to bring about the circulation of blood to his brain, succeeded in waking him, upon which he evidently thought he was dreaming, for he smiled at most of the faces around him, grimaced upon seeing Jenicor, and settled himself once more among his pillows.

Lytra said, "Cavalier Thack, I bid you wake and have speech with us."

Upon hearing this voice, Thack opened his eyes once more, startled, then seemed to shake his head and blink his eyes several times, as if he expected the visions before him to dissolve into the dream fabric from which he evidently thought they had emerged. When the phantasmata failed to behave as expected, he opened his mouth, gagged, swallowed, and said, "Is Your Excellency really here?"

"We are all here," said Lytra.

"Well, that is, forgive me if I do not rise, but, you perceive, I am confined to this cursed bed."

"Yes, we know you have been wounded," said Lytra.

"But then, may I ask the reason for this visit?"

"No," said G'aereth sternly, "it is for us to put the questions to you, young man."

From this answer, Thack perceived that the matter was serious, and there was no question of joking; and in his weakened state it was almost more than he could endure, but he rallied and said, "Well, I will do my best to answer; the more honestly since the doctor says my life is still at stake, and I have no wish to pass over Deathgate Falls, if such is my fate, with a lie fresh upon my lips."

"That is wise," said Lytra, "and we ask nothing better. Indeed, it may be that, should you live, only the truth will now save you from disgrace."

Thack swallowed heavily and said, "Then ask your questions, for I am ready, and I will attempt to satisfy you before I faint again. Ah, curse this weakness! My lady," he added to Jenicor, "when you give wounds, well, you don't stop at half measures. I declare that I have never been more effectually pierced."

Jenicor, though somewhat moved to pity by the condition of the wounded man, was still angry from the insult she had received, and so she bowed to acknowledge the compliment, but said nothing.

"To begin, then," said G'aereth, "you had certain information concerning the character of this lady, Jenicor e'Terics."

"Well, but it seems the information was wrong."

"So that?"

"So that I no longer hold the opinion I used to hold concerning her disposition."

"That is well," said G'aereth. "But, we are anxious to learn how you came to be misinformed?"

Thack, insofar as he could, frowned. "Will your lordship permit me to speak freely?"

"We will more than permit it," said G'aereth. "I even think we require it."

"Then I will tell you."

"Well?"

"It was from your lordship, Captain."

Jenicor turned her gaze fiercely on the astounded Captain, who said, "How, from me?"

"Yes, exactly."

"From my own lips?"

"Well, I did not hear it myself, but it was told to me as coming from your lordship."

"Well, that is an entirely different matter."

"Not at all," said Thack. "I was given to understand it in the most definite terms."

"And yet," said the Captain, looking at Jenicor. "We have never met, have we?"

"No, I have never had that honor until now."

"So, someone told you that I had said these things?"

"Yes, indeed."

"Well, and who was that person?"

"Oh, as to that, I cannot say."

"How, cannot say?"

"I truly regret it, your lordship, because I see plainly that you want to know."

"I more than want to, I demand to," cried G'aereth.

"And yet, orders—"

"Orders? And by whom were these famous orders issued?"

"By my Captain, Lanmarea."

"She told you not to tell me the name of the individual who had slandered the Lady Jenicor?"

"Yes. Well, we were ordered not to reveal the names of the prisoners."

"Prisoners!" said G'aereth and Lytra together.

"Well, yes, those we had arrested."

"What is this?" said Lytra. "You have made an arrest?"

"Well, I am a Guardsman," said Thack. "It is my duty, when ordered, to make arrests."

"And you were further ordered not to reveal the names of those you arrested?"

"You have understood exactly. I—ah," he stopped for a moment, overcome with pain or fatigue, then said, "I beg forgiveness of your lordships. Yes, yes, that was it; we were to perform these arrests, and make sure none of the arrested had any communication with anyone, and we were not to reveal the names or identities, or even the Houses of those we arrested."

"Well, the numbers, then?" said Lytra.

"Oh, as to that, nothing was said, so I may tell your Excellency that there were four gentleman, two ladies, and a lackey."

"How, a lackey?" said Lytra, frowning.

"So he seemed to be, Excellency," said Thack.

Somehow, as is sometimes the case when someone presents a surprising detail, this served to increase rather than to diminish the credibility of his tale.

"But," said G'aereth, "you may not reveal their names?"

"I regret it to your lordship. And, moreover, with the exception of the one who gave me this advice, which now appears to me not so good as it did two days ago, I do not even know who they were."

"Two days ago?" said G'aereth. "That is when you made these arrests?"

"Exactly."

"But then," said Lytra, "who gave this infamous order?"

"Why, Lanmarea, none other."

"So, then, if she were to order you to tell me this name, you would do so?"

"Gladly, Excellency."

"Well, you perceive, do you not, that I am her commander?"

"Oh, that is clear enough."

"So, then, if I were to give her an order, she would obey, would she not?"

"Well, I nearly think so, Excellency."

"Then, if I were to give you an order, that would have as much force as if she had given it, would it not?"

"Even more, I think, Excellency."

"Very well. Tell me the name, and do so at once."

Thack stared. "How, Your Excellency commands me to do so?"

"Exactly, and at once."

"This is, then, an order?"

"It is, and one that I do not care to do myself the honor of repeating."

Thack considered this, then said, "Well, it seems I must capitulate."

"That's best," said G'aereth. "Believe me."

"I will tell you then."

"Do so," said Lytra in tone that allowed for no discussion.

"This is it, then: I do not know his House, but his name is Pel."

There came a gasp from Jenicor, while G'aereth started. "Pel?" he said.

"So he called himself."

"And was he a Guardsman?"

"Well, he seemed to be, although his cloak, while it had the color and insignia, was not of regulation cut."

"And," said G'aereth, "was he of rather small build, although well proportioned?"

"And," said Jenicor, "with fine, delicate hands?"

"A firm gait upon his horse?"

"Deep black eyes?"

"Wearing a light sword of the Neobi style, with a dueler's grip and a ruby set into the hilt?"

"And a nervous smile?"

"A complexion as dark as a Jhegaala's?"

"Manners that are at once gentle and sensuous?"

"Well," said Thack to both of them, "you have described him exactly, although—"

"Yes?" said Jenicor.

"I had not remarked his smile."

"What?" cried G'aereth. "Pel has been arrested?"

"You know him, then?" said Lytra.

"I think so; he is one of my regiment, and not the least able."

"And," said Lytra to Thack, "you do not know on what charge he was arrested?"

"I assure you, my lady, I have no idea at all."

"Well," said G'aereth, "my way is clear, and that is to see His Majesty."

"For my part," said Lytra, "I will accompany you."

Allistar, who had been listening to the conversation carefully, shifted uncomfortably and seemed about to speak, but then evidently thought better of it.

Suddenly Jenicor, who had been deep in thought, burst out laughing.

"Well?" said Lytra.

"Ah, Excellency, it is too droll. I understand everything now."

"You do?"

"Yes, indeed. Come, my friends, we have no more business here. And as for you, my lord," she said, addressing Thack, "I assure you that you have my complete pardon."

"How, you pardon me?"

"I do, and more, I wish you a quick and complete recovery."

"You are too kind, my lady."

"Not at all, my friend, not at all."

While she spoke, Allistar, who had said nothing the entire time, took Lytra aside and spoke to her for some few minutes in a quiet tone, during which time the Warlord's countenance turned dark. At the conclusion of the conversation, she shrugged, as if to say, "It is now out of my hands," after which they rejoined G'aereth and proceeded from the house.

As for Jenicor, she remarked, looking into the distance as if speaking to someone who wasn't present, "Ah, Cavalier, you are truly a Yendi."

Chapter the Thirty-third

In Which our Friends
Spend some time in Prison

AT THIS TIME, as Lytra, Jenicor, and G'aereth leave the ailing Guardsman, we will turn our attention once more to those personages whom we have so patiently followed across the continent and back.

Aerich and Khaavren had been given the same cell, and Khaavren, who was convinced that Pel's idea, whatever it was, would bear fruit, was attempting to remain as calm as Aerich, who was placidly crocheting. We would be less than honest if we allowed our readers to infer that Khaavren was to any degree successful at this. First, he walked the length of his cell in that activity which has been the prerogative of prisoners as long as the class has existed. Then he studied the cell, which had two small windows high on the wall.

"Aerich," he said.

"Well?"

"Could either of us fit through those windows?"

The Lyorn glanced at them. "No, and, moreover, they are barred."

"Well, I'm just as glad we have been given a room with windows anyway."

"It is because we are gentleman."

"Suppose we were princes?"

"Then we'd be a floor higher."

"Well, and?"

"And we would not only have windows, but they would be placed so we could see out of them."

"Well, I understand. But what of poor Mica?"

"He doubtless has no window at all."

"Cha! This is intolerable."

"Well, didn't you tell me yourself that our friend Pel had a plan?"

"Yes, or so he pretended to me."

"Then we need only wait."

"Wait, by the Orb! Wait! How I loathe waiting!"

Aerich shrugged.

Khaavren continued to pace and wonder, but, as Aerich is truly as calm as he seems, and Khaavren is imbibing hope of release with every breath, let us pass on.

Tazendra was in the same cell as Kathana, because it was the custom of the time to separate prisoners, first by class, and afterwards according to sex, and finally by the type of crime. Since the governor of the prison had not been informed of what crime these gentlesouls were accused, he at least knew enough to put them together.

Tazendra had at once sat down on one of the straw pallets, crossed her legs, and frowned mightily. Kathana's first action was to request a visit from the jailer, a small Iorich named Guinn. "Did your ladyship do me the honor to summon me?" he asked with a bow.

"Oh, summon," said Kathana. "That is too strong a word. I merely asked that you might attend me for a moment."

"Well, it's all the same," said Guinn, who seemed, nevertheless, pleased with the courtesy. "If there is something that I, in my capacity as host, can do to make your stay here more pleasant, why, insofar as it lies within my ability and does not conflict with my duties, I will do it."

"Well," said Kathana, "since you make such a frank and generous offer, I will be equally frank in accepting it."

"I ask nothing better," said the jailer, who was, moreover, becoming curious. We should say that Tazendra was as well, for she stared in amazement at this powerful Dragonlord who was speaking in such friendly terms to the Iorich.

"Well then, I have called you over that I might find out the terms of imprisonment."

"That is only right," said the jailer. "They are: no communication with anyone outside, or even anyone inside, with the exception of your host"; here he bowed to indicate himself.

"Very well, pass on."

"With that understanding, no paper or writing utensils are to be permitted."

"I understand. And next?"

"You are to be given four meals every day, which meals are to be served at the eighth hour past midnight, again at the thirteenth, then at the third hour past noon, and at the eighth hour past noon, and which meals will consist of roasted meats, fresh bread, any fruits which are in season, along with suitable wine; and you are in addition to be allowed two hours each day in which to exercise in the yard, with said exercise to begin at exactly noon."

"That is sufficient for me, I think, the more so as the cell is large enough for calisthenics, if these are not forbidden."

"Not in the least."

"Well, and next?"

"You must not speak, even to me, of whatever crime brought you here; these are particular orders for you and your friends, and do not apply to other prisoners."

"Very well, then, I understand. What else?"

"Those are the only restrictions, madam."

"Very well, but may I say something?"

"Of course, as your host, you may tell me anything at all, so long as it relates to your accommodations."

"Well, I must tell you that this cell displeases me."

"How, it displeases you? In what way?"

"Oh, several ways."

"Well, perhaps we can see about another, my lady."

"Oh, that isn't necessary, this one can be put in good order, I think."

"Well, let us see, then, what needs to be done."

"First, we need a little wood for the fire."

"In the summer?"

"Yes. My companion suffers from the chill."

"How?" said Tazendra. "The chill? I suffer from no chill."

Kathana shot Tazendra a looking imploring her to keep silent, and said, "Yes, yes, the chill. She doesn't realize it herself, my good Guinn, but she has been shivering in a most alarming manner."

"In fact," said Tazendra, "I do feel slightly cold."

"There, you see how it is? For her health, a fire is indispensable."

"Well, as you are a lady, you are allowed nine fagots of wood each day, and bark and twigs as needed. This is generally only granted when the weather is cold, but there is no rule that says you may not have it now."

"Then you will see to it?"

"I will do so at once."

"We shall be in your debt."

"So, that is the fire seen to. What else?"

"Well, next, the walls are not clean to my standards."

"Ah, ah, you are fastidious?"

"It is a failing, but after all, we cannot change what we are."

"Well, that is true. But the servants, you perceive, are all busy."

"Well, then, don't trouble yourself about the servants; if you supply me with a bucket of water and a scrub-brush, I will clean them myself."

"Well," said Guinn, "there is no difficulty in that. What next?"

"That is all, my dear jailer. If you could supply these things, well, I will be in your debt, I promise you."

"I will attend to them at once."

When the jailer had gone, Tazendra said, "I assure you, Kathana, I have no notion at all of what you are about."

"Oh, it is not such a great thing, but, as we may be here for some time, I must find amusement where I can."

"How, it amuses you to send our jailer for a pail of water and a few fagots?"

"No, but it will amuse me to get them."

"Why is that?"

"You will see by and by."

The jailer returned with the water, brush, and the wood. Kathana, after thanking him, lost no time in starting a small fire, which, because of its size, did not make the cell intolerably hot. When the fire was well going, she at once applied the brush and the water to the walls, with a thoroughness that indicated she may indeed have been a charwoman in some previous lifetime. Tazendra soon became bored with watching her, and so, for no other reason, called for a second brush, with which, upon being given it, she began to work with the Dragonlord in making the walls fairly shine.

When this had been done, the jailer returned to collect the bucket and brushes. Kathana begged to be allowed to keep the bucket, which she pretended made a more comfortable chair than the pallet. Guinn allowed her to do so, and, when he had gone, she gave a satisfied smile.

"Well?" said Tazendra. "And now?"

"Now, observe. Do you see these?"

"They seem to be a few bristles from the brushes."

"Exactly. And this?"

"A piece of straw from your pallet."

"Well, observe what I am doing."

"You are pouring a small quantity of our drinking water into the bucket."

"And now?"

"You are adding ash from the fire, thus rendering the water unfit to drink."

"Exactly. And now?"

"Now you are dipping the straw into the water, and—the Orb! You are drawing on the walls!"

"Exactly. It will make the time pass quickly, don't you think?"

"You are as clever as, as Khaavren! And that is no small thing, for I know of no one more clever than he is."

Kathana bowed, and offered straw and bristles to Tazendra, who said, "But I do not paint."

"Well, but this is, as you yourself have remarked, more akin to drawing, and, by the gods, everyone draws a little."

"Well, you are right, and I shall be honored to draw with you. Only—"

"Yes?"

"What shall we draw?"

"Why, scenes depicting our experience in the last few weeks."

"Well, yes, we could do that."

"We more than could, we ought to."

"And the reason, good Kathana?"

"The reason is that someone may ask about these drawings, and we will then tell him, and in this way, word might get out of our predicament."

"It does not seem likely."

"With this I agree. But then, have you a better plan?"

"I admit that I do not."

"Well, and then?"

"Then, my dear Baroness, let us draw."

Accordingly, the two women at once set to work to make the cell, if not more beautiful, at least more interesting, and to amuse themselves in the meantime.

Neither Uttrik nor Pel had the least interest in the cell they occupied. Pel took the opportunity to question his jailer, first, about the conditions under which they were incarcerated, next, upon the goings-on in the city, such as the jailer might know. As Pel was both clever and charming, he accordingly found out much more than the jailer realized. As for Uttrik, he was a campaigner, and, as such, knew how to make the time pass under circumstances when he could do nothing else; accordingly, he slept.

And let us not forget Mica, who, not being a gentleman, was imprisoned in a room with a score of Teckla, many of them ruffians of one sort or another, as well as a good number of drunkards, tax-evaders, and debtors. One might suppose that, of the entire group, he would have been the most miserable, but nothing could be further from the truth. The fact that he wore livery made him of interest to all, and that he wore the livery of a Dzurlord was even more interesting. When we also consider that this clever Teckla was a gifted speaker, and was both willing and able to relate to his fellow-prisoners the details of the adventures he had been a part of, we may see that his status soon rose directly to the top of prison hierarchy. He enjoyed this status with the honest pleasure a Teckla always takes in simple enjoyments, and thus, though he would have preferred to be free, he was, in fact, the happiest of the seven souls who had been incarcerated at the same time.

Yet, what a difference sixty hours can make, when those hours are spent in prison or in jail. To better understand this, we must make clear that there is a difference. Prison is where those who have been sentence await execution of that sentence, or take up residency if the judges have condemned them to confinement for a greater or lesser period. Jail, on the other hand, is where those who are arrested but not yet convicted wait for the judges to determine their fate. There is no difference in treatment, nor is there a difference even in location, but the difference in the psychology of the prisoner is everything. While in jail, it is difficult to become resigned; while in prison, it is difficult to hope. For those, like our friends, who did

not know in which situation they were, the hours become
burdens in increments that would require a mathemati-
cian to explain.

By the time they had been in for two days and two
nights, Khaavren had given up even trying to remain calm,
and Aerich, the coolest of the Guardsmen, was still engaged in crocheting, but his fingers trembled slightly as
he worked.

Kathana and Tazendra had quite filled the walls of their
cell with studies of each other and reminiscences of their
recent adventures, and had fallen into the unhappy stage
of criticizing their own work, after which it would only
be a matter of a short time before they took to criticizing
each other's, with unpleasant results sure to follow.

Pel had become gloomy and silent, and sat brooding
upon all the ways his plan might miscarry; he had even
taking to chewing his lip. Uttrik, still trying to sleep but
no longer able to, turned and moaned and twenty times
adjusted the straw in his pallet.

Mica, though still not entirely unhappy, and still enjoying the glory of his status among the other prisoners,
had begun to reflect that he didn't know how long he
would be imprisoned, if indeed, he was ever to be released at all, and these thoughts had taken much of the
pleasure out of the enthusiasms with which his stories
were greeted; stories, moreover, that had nearly run out,
for, as our readers ought to be aware by now, such deeds
are much briefer in the telling than in the doing.

It was at just this point that Khaavren was disturbed—
if such a word may be used in the case of a gentleman to
whom any break in the dreary itinerary was a relief—by
the arrival of Guinn, who informed Khaavren that he
ought to accompany him to a chamber of questions,
where a certain lady wished to speak with him.

It came to his mind that perhaps the lady was Illista;
he therefore accompanied Guinn with such alacrity that
the Iorich was forced to hurry to keep up with him, and
there is no doubt that Khaavren would have left him be-

hind if the Tiassa had known where to go. Guinn, therefore, pointed out the room to him, indicated that he
should enter at once, and explained that he would wait
outside until the interview was at an end.

In this instance, Khaavren was not mistaken; upon being admitted to the questioning room, he saw Illista herself, who was looking at him with an expression of
indescribable tenderness. Her toilette, it must be said, ill
became her surroundings, for she had put on a blue ball-
gown, with a lace collar and high shoulders that set off
her graceful neck and wide eyes, while on her feet were
the sort of dainty slippers that would belong rather to a
parlor than a prison, yet all of this, as far as Khaavren
was concerned, only increased her charm, and in an instant all of the emotions which she had first inspired in
him, and which had, perhaps, faded slightly from absence, came roaring back like the waves of the Sundering
Beach.

He rushed forward, and threw himself at her feet and
covered her hands with a hundred kisses, while murmuring a thousand endearments. After allowing these
protestations of his devotion to continue for some few
moments, Illista bid Khaavren rise, and said, "Well, I had
hoped you might be here."

"How, you had I hoped I might be here? In prison?"

"That is, I meant that I had hoped to be able to find
you, and, since you were nowhere else, I had hoped that
I might have the chance to speak with you."

"Well, and you have that chance, and I, I have the
chance to see you."

"Well, and so you do. But we haven't much time, and
there are matters I wish to communicate to you."

Khaavren frowned. "Then you didn't come here to see
me?"

"Well, yes, that first, and other things after."

"Other things? Such as, I hope, my release?"

"Yes, yes, that is what I intend, and, if you do what I
say, I hope it will have that happy result."

"How, do what you say?"

"Well, haven't you said you would help me?"

"I did, and, moreover, I have done so, or nearly. Kathana, had we not been arrested for reasons of which I am entirely ignorant, was about to surrender herself to His Majesty. You understand, then, that the commission with which you entrusted me was, if not entirely successful—"

"Oh, that is of no consequence now."

"What? Of no consequence?"

"Exactly."

"You no longer care about whether your friend has been arrested?"

"Oh, I care, it is merely that things have changed."

"How, changed?"

"We now have other matters to consider."

"What other matters, then?"

Illista frowned, as if she feared to say too much, or didn't wish to say more than she had to in order to accomplish her objective. "Tell me first about your mission. You say Kaluma returned with you?"

"Indeed, yes, and she is in this very prison; no doubt, if you have managed to gain entry to see me, you could arrange to see her as well."

"Yes, yes, I will certainly do so. But, you were saying?"

"I? What was I saying?"

"That is what I am asking you."

"Well, it must have been about the mission with which you entrusted me."

"Yes, that was it."

"Well, we have returned with Kathana, who is a charming lady—"

"Is she?"

"What, you don't know? I thought she was your friend."

"Well, yes, I know that she is charming. But what else?"

"What else? Well, she is also brave, and tolerably quick-thinking, and—"

"No, that is not what I meant to ask."

"Well?"

"What else about your mission?"

"Oh, well, we have secured peace with the Easterners, and—"

"What, peace?"

"Exactly; we have concluded a treaty with them."

"Upon what terms?"

"Well, in part they must surrender Sandyhome to the Empire—"

"What?" cried Illista, in great distress. "They agreed to that?"

"They insisted upon it as a condition."

"But then—" she interrupted herself in order to bite her lip, either to keep herself from speaking or in response to some great emotion.

"Well?" said Khaavren, becoming more and more curious. "But then—"

"Oh, it is nothing."

"My dear Illista, you have now said that several times, and, if you will permit me to speak—"

"Oh, yes, speak freely."

"Well, it seems from the expression on your countenance that all of these nothings, when taken together, amount to a great deal."

"Perhaps you are right."

"It also seems as if you are in some distress."

"What, I?"

"Well, perhaps I am in error. But, if you are—"

"Well, if I am?"

"Then I hope you will tell me what I can do, for, if I am to be released from here soon, I will once more have the freedom to throw myself into the fire in order to serve you."

Illista smiled at this and said, "Then, do you love me a little?"

"Oh, you know that I do!"

"You will do what I ask of you, then?"

"Anything!"

"Then perhaps you can help me."

"I can imagine no greater happiness than that. Only—"

"Yes?"

"You must tell me what I am to do."

"Oh, you may rest assured, I will tell you."

"Then I am ready to obey."

"Without question?"

"Without question."

"No matter what you must do?"

"Anything!"

"So much the better."

"Well, but tell me, for I am dying to know."

"This is it, then: you must kill a man."

"What, that is all? Cha! Once I am free, the thing is easily done."

"You will do so, then?"

"For you, with the greatest pleasure."

"Ah, that's all right then."

"Has he insulted you?"

"Yes," she said quickly. "That is it. He has insulted me, in a most cowardly manner."

"Well, you have then only to name him, and I will find him and I will say, 'You have offended the Lady Illista, you will die now,' and then, by the Light, I will strike him through the heart," and, as he spoke, he made a pantomime of executing exactly the thrust of which he spoke.

"Well," said Illista, "but suppose he is far from here?"

"Cha! That is of no consequence; I have just returned from the Eastern Mountains, I could go back, if necessary."

"So much the better," said Illista.

"And his name?"

"What if it is someone who is known to you?"

"Well, then he will be that much easier to find."

"And you will find him, and kill him?"

"I have said so, I say it again. What is his name?"

"Adron e'Kieron."

"How, him?" said Khaavren, staring in amazement. "The protector of your friend, Kathana."

"Oh, he is a base coward, I assure you."

Khaavren frowned, endeavoring to clear up the confusion of his mind. "Well, but, are you sure?"

"Sure? I think I should know when I have been insulted."

"But, how did he insult you?"

"You said you would ask no questions."

"Well, that is true."

"And so?"

Khaavren frowned, and, for the first time, certain questions came into his mind. That Adron could have insulted Illista did not startle him, for anyone can feel insulted by anything; but he had seen Adron, and the thought that he was a coward was difficult for Khaavren to entertain. And yet, to think ill of Illista was beyond him. For a moment he was completely befuddled, but this is a condition which can never exist for long within a mind like Khaavren's, a mind which acts like a fallow field, in which it is only necessary for a seed to touch it before this seed will sprout, although with what fruit is not always apparent.

Khaavren's idea, in this instance, was to play his hand closer to his body, that is, to pretend to cooperate, and, as he did so, to ask a few more questions, for he was certain that if he but gave Illista the chance, she would at once put his suspicions to rest. Therefore, he answered her last question by saying, "I do not ask. Arrange for my freedom, and the freedom of my friends, and His Highness will die."

"Oh, your friends?"

"Well, that is only a small thing, and I am better with them, and in addition, I am certain that you wish to free your friend, Kathana e'Marish'Chala."

"Oh, yes, of a certainty, but that can be attended to later."

Khaavren frowned once more. "Very well, at all events,

once I am free I will solicit an audience with His Majesty and inform him of the treaty, and he cannot fail, then, to release—"

"Oh, no," said Illista. "You must not mention the treaty."

"How, not mention it?"

"No, you must forget it entirely."

"But it will surely be known."

"How?"

"Why, Lord Adron—"

"You will kill him."

"Oh, that is true, I had forgotten. And yet, he will have the treaty upon his person."

"Well, after killing him, you will search him, and you will find this famous treaty, and you will bring it to me, or else destroy it."

"But, for what reason?"

"Have you forgotten again that you had promised to ask no questions?"

"Well, but what you ask is extraordinary."

"Extraordinary?"

"Think, Illista—peace with the Easterners for the first time, and diamonds for His Majesty without useless bloodshed—"

"That is unimportant."

"How, unimportant?"

"Yes, we are what matters, you and I. If we are to be together—"

"Yes?"

"You must do what I ask."

"And yet, in order to insure my friends' release from this prison—"

"Well, what does that matter, if you are free, and we are together?"

Now, ordinarily the thought that Illista had as much as promised herself to him if he completed his mission would have filled Khaavren's heart to bursting, but his ideas had been thrown into such confusion by her last statements that he scarcely noticed this remark. It seemed to him that, if he did not possess this woman, he would die, and yet, if he did, he must consent to leaving his friends in prison. The seed had sprouted into that most wonderful and horrible of fruits: doubt, which, like the strawberry, has a succulent taste, but has also a tendency to spread and spread, until it dominates whatever garden it has taken root in.

Illista's words served rather to fertilize these doubts than to inhibit them, and Khaavren bit his lips, while wondering how he ought to proceed.

The changes that flitted across his countenance were not entirely lost on Illista, who said, "Listen, my friend, if we are to be lovers, for that is what you want, is it not? Well, I assure you that you are the sole keeper of my passion, and if we are to fulfill this mutual longing, well, certain sacrifices must be made. You understand, do you not?"

She put forth all of her charms of voice and face, and they were considerable, and we would not be truthful if we did not admit that Khaavren was moved; yet he could not forget how Uttrik had given up his vengeance out of love for Kathana, and the most unselfish sort of love at that; and how Kathana, for the same reason, had determined to surrender herself to the Emperor, at the risk, perhaps of her life. He thought of deserting his friends, and, with these examples before him, it seemed repugnant to do so.

In fact, the Tiassa was thinking furiously, recalling this latest conversation from an entirely different view. It was as if Pel were softly urging him to question everything, while Tazendra touched his shoulder, reminding him of the duties of friendship, and Aerich looked at him somberly, as if asking if he ought, at the bidding of this woman, to murder a man who had shown him kindness. And yet—

And yet, there is no question that she was lovely beyond his dreams, and she had the sort of coquettish smile in her eyes that drives men mad. The thought that she was within his reach burned, so that he still hesitated for a moment, filled with that strange emotion that lies midway between true love and the desire to possess, yet balancing this with the memories of all that he had shared with his friends.

At last he sighed. "I cannot," he said.

"How, you cannot?"

"I cannot leave my friends. We must all leave here together. Surely you can arrange that—"

"But, they will speak, and no word of this agreement with the Easterners must be allowed to escape, or—"

"Well, or?"

"Or all my plans will be undone."

"What plans are these?"

"Ah, you persist with the questions."

"Well, and if I do?"

"Yet, you said—"

"Bah. You had said nothing about asking me to leave my friends to rot in prison."

"Well, you will not do that for me?"

"Not in a thousand years."

"Then you will allow my enemies to triumph over me? You, who claim you love me, who claim you will do anything for me, who—"

"Friends who have saved my life a hundred times over? With whom I have fought, have killed, have bled, have eaten and drank? And you, who wish for my love, desire to consign them to prison? Impossible!"

She drew herself up and stared at him coldly. "Prison? No, the Executioner's Star."

Khaavren felt himself trembling as this awful name was pronounced. "What do you say?"

"They will not languish long before they are brought to Justicer's Square, and you with them. I might have saved you from that, but now it is too late."

"All of this for an insult?"

She looked at him with such an expression of mingled hate and contempt that any lesser man might have crumbled merely from the blow to self-love, coming, as the look did, from one to whom he had poured out all the sincere devotion of his heart. And, moreover, to accompany this look, she said, "You are a fool. There was no insult; it is policy. This treaty must never be consummated; therefore, all who know of it must die. Do you think you have saved that fool, Adron? No, only now I must call in Seodra, who knows Jhereg who will perform for money the task you would not perform for love. And with him will die the last, for your heads will already be sealed beneath the marble slabs of the Square."

By now, Khaavren was filled with so many emotions, and those all locked in battle with each other, that the fear of the ignominious death with which he was threatened meant nothing to him. His love for Illista was as strong as ever, yet now was combined with hatred and contempt in that oddest of appositions to which we are sometimes subjected. He adored her, yet he despised her, as if, looking upon her visage, she was at once a goddess whom he ought to worship, and a reptile he ought to strike down.

He said, "Cha, you venomous yendi, I will denounce you."

"You? Denounce me? Ha. You will remain here, unable to communicate with anyone, until you are brought to the Square, and that will not be long, I assure you; two words to Seodra, a message to the Warlord, his Majesty's seal on a scrap of paper, and all is done."

"Perhaps," said Khaavren. "But I will denounce you from the Star as I am strapped down."

"No," she said, smiling the way the chreotha might smile at the norska which had blundered into its net. "For you will be gagged; it can be managed, and it will be. You could have had several days of pleasure with me before I cast you aside; instead you will have nothing except the axe. I hope you are happy with your choice." As she finished, she pulled a cord that was hanging near her head, at the same time crying out, "Guinn! Come, escort me out of here, for I have nothing more to say to this wretch." She rose, turned her back on Khaavren, and walked to the door. When it was opened, she turned back and gave one last glance of withering contempt, and left the room in flurry of skirts and hair.

Khaavren, unable to speak, was escorted back to his cell. Aerich, who could see that something was amiss with his friend, was unable to find out what it was, for Khaavren was too stunned to speak, and, moreover, could find no reason for sharing the hopelessness of the situation with his friend. In fact, more than a few tears fell from Khaavren's eyes as he lay on the straw pallet in his cell, nursing a grief rendered ten times worse by his unwillingness to share it. And we should add that Aerich, puzzled by Khaavren's misery, nevertheless partook of it to such a degree that his recent joy at having avenged himself on Shaltre was all but wiped away.

It would not be unfair, then, to say that our friends were unanimous in being miserable, if to different degrees and in different ways. Happily, it was not long after Khaavren's interview with Illista that they were called by Guinn to make themselves as presentable as circumstances permitted, for they were to appear before an august personage.

When Khaavren and Aerich were so informed, Khaavren's eyes flashed, and he said, "The executioner is an august personage?"

"How," said Guinn. "The executioner?"

"Well, is that not the individual to whom you have just done us the honor to refer?"

"I assure you I know nothing about it."

"Then you have no reason to think I'm wrong."

"Well, but I hope you are."

"That's kind of you."

"It is more likely," said Aerich, "to be the Emperor himself."

Khaavren shook his head, but would not explain the reasons for his conviction that Aerich was deceived. He made up his mind, however, to face the Star bravely, beginning with that very moment, so no one would be able to say he had shown fear. Accordingly, after they had made the best toilette possible in a cell without soaps or perfumes, Khaavren drew himself up and made a sign to Guinn and the other guards that they could proceed.

They were first brought into the light of day on what were called the Dark Stairs, which was an extremely wide, straight stairway that was one of three entrances into the Wing; the others being the Justicer's Door and the Winged Stairs. The Dark Stairs lead down into the dungeons of the Wing, or, more precisely in this case, up from the dungeons to the Pavilion of the Iorich. It was always watched by six pair of guards, each consisting of one Phoenix Guard in the gold cloak, and the other an Iorich Guard wearing a black hood and carrying a halberd. We should say that Khaavren, Aerich, Pel, and Tazendra had each, at one time or another, had this duty, and it was one of the least favored, as the Iorich Guards were silent and grim, off duty as well as on. But, tedious as it was, it had never occurred to them that would soon be passing by on their way to captivity, nor returning past them in the hope of freedom or expectation of immediate death, according to the thoughts of the individual.

Fortunately, this week was the turn of Lanmarea's battalion to stand this duty, so neither in arriving nor departing had they seen anyone they recognized, which would have embarrassed all concerned.

From the Dark Stairs they were invited into two carriages with the Iorich arms. Pel, Uttrik, Aerich, and Khaavren were bidden to enter the first, while the second was for Tazendra and Kathana. Mica was required to walk the distance, with two silent Iorich Guardsmen flanking him, though it is only fair to say that seeing the daylight again more than made up for the walk, which was not of a greater distance than he had been accustomed to in any case.

Once in the coaches, they were informed that all speech

was forbidden them, which Khaavren took as the final slab of marble over his head, though he said nothing of the matter to his friends. There were six Iorich Guards, four in the coach and two on top, to see that this rule was obeyed, and that, furthermore, no attempt was made by the prisoners at communication with the outside or at escape. They contented themselves, therefore, with such greetings and communications as could be given by smiles and grimaces. It should also be said that the windows of the carriages were not only barred, but also enclosed in slatted iron coverings, so that they were not only stuffy, but almost completely dark, and, moreover, our friends could not see where they were going, from which Khaavren assumed the worst.

At the end of the ride they were commanded to quit the carriage and, still flanked by Guards, they discovered that they were outside the Imperial Wing.

"What is this?" cried Khaavren, almost afraid to hope.

"Why," said Uttrik, "it is the Imperial Wing. Where had you thought—"

"Silence," commanded the guard.

Aerich shrugged. They were brought into the Wing, where, after a wait of some few minutes, during which time Mica was reunited with them, and also during which time Khaavren began to feel hope returning to him in all its effusion, they were brought into the presence of His Majesty, the Emperor.

Chapter the Thirty-fourth

*In Which His Majesty Attempts to Pick a Strand
Of Justice from a Nest Of Accusation,
And is Fortunate to Receive Help*

O UR FRIENDS, WITH the exception of Mica, were
admitted to His imperial Majesty's presence in
the Balcony Room, which was a narrow sitting
room which overlooked the Embassy Hall. The Embassy
Hall was one of the principal residences of the courtiers,
being a place where His Majesty was accustomed to greet
official visitors on matters of State. Any time His Majesty
deigned to appear there, the affair was a serious, or at
least, a formal one; therefore to be seen near His Majesty
in that room bequeathed a certain status. Hence, a good
number of those anxious to achieve this status, that is, to
be considered someone upon whom it was worthwhile to
bestow favors, would often spend their time wearying
themselves against the hope that the Emperor would appear.

The Balcony Room was a long, narrow place painted
in light colors, dimly lit, and sparsely furnished. It looked
down upon the scene we have described, and, though
little used by many Emperors, had become a favorite place

for Tortaalik to have face-to-face meetings, because the fire was small, the furniture comfortable, and the general atmosphere more confined than spacious, which allowed him to feel a certain intimacy from which he pretended he could better judge the true thoughts and feelings of those whom he questioned.

Khaavren, along with his friends, was brought into this room, and directed to stand before His Majesty. Also present, we should add, were Lytra e'Tenith and Captain G'a-ereth, at the left and right hand of the Emperor. The Captain's face was without expression, whereas the Warlord stared at Kathana with a look of cool calculation.

Now, although Khaavren didn't know the thoughts of the Warlord, it is worth while to say two words about her state of mind. We have witnessed the quiet conversation between Lytra and Allistar, during which he had informed her, that, whatever happened, it was vital that nothing of the truth come out; that is, although neither of them knew what had happened in the east, Allistar had become convinced that Khaavren and his friends knew enough to compromise their plans, and had informed the Warlord of this circumstance. Lytra had, by this time, gone too far with G'aereth to permit her to back out of her agreement to press for an audience with His Majesty, and, to her credit, had sufficient interest in justice to wish to see this interview take place, but now that it came to the point, as it were, her agile mine was filled with thoughts on how to prevent these troublesome individuals from ruining everything.

The prisoners filed in, and, as one person, bowed to His Majesty. Khaavren, with great difficulty, managed to conceal perhaps half of the agitation he felt at being for the first time in the presence of the Emperor. Uttrik, if he felt any dis-ease at all, was able to conceal the whole of it. Tazendra was too concerned with the sort of impression she was making to allow room for anything as pedestrian as intimidation. Pel was deep in thought, and all of the wheels, if we may be permitted such an expression, were turning rapidly as he made the various calculations his quick mind suggested to him. Kathana had been in the presence of the Emperor several times before his ascension to the throne, on the occasion of His Majesty doing her the honor to view certain of her works, as he fancied himself a connoisseur of painting. Aerich, knowing exactly the position his rank entitled him to with respect to his Majesty, had that confidence which comes from secure knowledge of one's place and the duties attendant upon it. Mica, as we have said, was not present.

The reader ought to understand that, at the time of which we have the honor to write, matters were often handled in a manner that today we would consider "high-handed," that is, the question of what degree of formality was appropriate to certain cases was left to the Emperor's own sense of propriety. He could, if he chose, convene a full court of justicers and peers to hear the confession or testimony of a prisoner, or he could, protected as he was by the Orb, simply listen and decide himself. The magnanimous and equal justice such as flows from our own Empress, whom the gods preserve, was then, if not entirely unknown, at least not expected as a matter of course.

In this case, the Warlord and the Captain had come before His Majesty and made claims of injustice, and begged him humbly to hear the matter himself. Now, as Tortaalik as well acquainted with history, and as "injustice" has been the most common pretext which the House of the Dragon has used to make war upon the throne, His Majesty felt inclined to give the Warlord complete satisfaction. Yet not so much, as we may have implied, from fear of the consequences—it was as yet far too early in the Phoenix reign for any such considerations to be appropriate—as from the certain knowledge that he would find himself explaining his conduct to His Discretion the Duke of Wellborn, and he knew very well how unpleasant such discussions could be if he had not acted in a manner that he, himself, would consider correct and honorable.

His Majesty, therefore, after bringing together those who had brought the complaint with those to whom the complaint referred, was disposed to listen with as much impartiality as he could bring to bear. The Orb, slowly circling his head, reflected this impartiality by emitting a pale yellow color.

"Well, then, my lords and ladies," he said. "I know some of you. You are the Baroness Kaluma, who stand accused of the murder of the Marquis of Pepperfield. And you are the Marquis's son, are you not? I believe you are called Uttrik, and, until recently, dwelt in the North Pinewood Hold, on the estates of the Pepperfields, and are Baronet of Kurakai."

These two bowed to acknowledge His Majesty's perspicacity, but said nothing.

"As to the rest of you, I perceive that you are Guardsmen, and, from certain insignia, that you are of the Red Boot Battalion, commanded by our own Captain G'aereth. But I do not know your names, and I wish to, for I am greatly interested in what you have to tell me."

Aerich spoke first, giving his name and protesting his devotion to His Majesty.

"How, Aerich? That is not the name of a Lyorn."

"I beg Your Majesty's pardon. It is the name under which I have taken service in the Guards. Otherwise, if it please Your Majesty, I am Temma, Duke Arylle, Count of Bra-moor, and before Your Majesty I also lay claim, at this moment, to the county of Shaltre, which is mine according to the customs of my House."

At this his Majesty started, and narrowed his eyes. The Orb darkened for a moment, becoming faintly red, then returned to its neutral yellow. Tortaalik said, "We will see about that by and by. And you?"

"I am Tazendra," said the Dzurlord. This time, it was Lytra e'Tenith who started, and then an expression of anger crossed her features, as this name was not only known to her, but had unpleasant associations.

Tortaalik frowned. "What, another assumed name?"

"I have renounced my titles, Sire."

"Renounced them? Well, but tell me the titles you have renounced."

Tazendra looked unhappy and said, "Does Your Majesty truly command this?"

"And if I do?"

"Then, I will tell you, although I am not proud of my name, Sire, wherefore I have renounced it for all time."

His Majesty shrugged and said, "We will call you Tazendra, then. And next?"

"I am Pel," said the Yendi, bowing gracefully.

"Ah," said the Emperor, with a small smile. "Well, I will not question your name further, for that is the name that has come to my ears, and it has sounded in connection with actions that were, if perhaps not entirely noble, at least not lacking finesse."

Pel bowed.

Tortaalik said, "And you, my good Tiassa?"

"I am Khaavren of Castlerock."

"What is this?" said His Majesty, laughing. "A Guardsman who gives his true name?"

"It is the only one I have, Sire," said Khaavren.

"Well, well, and no titles to go with it?"

"Our lands were sold ten hundreds of years ago, Sire," said Khaavren.

"Ah, well, there is no shame in that," said His Majesty. "But now, it seems to me you have stories to tell?"

"If it please Your Majesty," said Pel, "we hope to make them good ones."

"I ask nothing better. Who is to begin?"

Kathana stepped forward and said, "I am willing, for I came to the city with the intention of surrendering myself to Your Majesty, and, for me, to be arrested is no more than I expected."

"Very well, what have you to say? For you are, you know, charged with nothing short of murder."

"I can only say, Sire, that I am guilty, that I repent of my action, and am entirely willing to submit to whatever justice Your Majesty may require."

"That is clear enough. What does the son of the murdered man say to this?"

"Sire," said Uttrik. "For my part, since she repents, I absolve her."

"You absolve her?" said Tortaalik.

"If it please Your Majesty, I even forgive her, for she is honestly repentant, and, moreover, we have fought side by side, so that I know something of her character, and I believe, though I do not say it without pain, that she was provoked."

"Well, well," said His Majesty. "We will consider this later. Let us pass on to the rest of you. Who will speak next in answer to the charges?"

Khaavren bowed and said, "Sire, we cannot speak, for we are entirely ignorant of what these charges consist."

"How, you don't know of what crimes you stand accused?"

"Not the least in the world," said Khaavren.

"But," said Pel, bowing, "we are anxious to find out."

"Well, it is easily stated. You are accused of the murders of Count Shaltre and Lord Garland."

"How, murder?" said Tazendra. "Impossible."

"I think, my lady," said the Emperor, the Orb turning a cold blue, "that you are disputing with me."

"We humbly beg Your Majesty's pardon," said Pel coolly. "It was amazement at these charges that caused my companion's outburst. We assure you that no disrespect was intended."

While he spoke, Lytra was whispering in the Emperor's ears, and the Orb's color turned into a blue that was like ice. His Majesty said, "Well, and what, also, of the murder of the Cavalier Kurich, the younger brother of the Warlord, which took place in the seclusion of the archery range attached to the sub-wing of the Imperial Guard shortly before these gentlemen left the city?"

"How, murder?" said Tazendra.

Aerich said, "Sire, the word is hard."

"Well, what then of the deed?"

"Oh," said Tazendra carelessly. "The deed was easy enough."

Lytra turned pale, and shot a glance full of anger, first, at Tazendra, then at G'aereth, who withstood the shot with the cool silence he had maintained since the interview began.

Khaavren said, "If Your Majesty will permit me?"

Tortaalik scowled, but nodded.

"It seems to me that there are, at issue, four murders, which are: Pepperfield, Kurich, Shaltre, and Garland."

"Yes, yes," said the Emperor impatiently. "What then?"

"May I have permission to speak of them individually?"

"Very well."

"As to the first, then, the Baroness has, as you have heard, confessed her guilt, but I hope to show Your Majesty that she has more than made up for her error."

"We will see. Go on."

"As to Kurich, well, Sire, I saw the entire affair, and if it had not all the trimmings of a duel, well, Kurich asked for the meeting, and agreed to the terms, and he fought tolerably well, and died bravely. I do not think he would have wished to see a prosecution against the Lady Tazendra. Moreover, if Your Majesty will condescend to question his seconds, the Cavaliers Uilliv and Rekov, we believe so firmly that they are honorable gentlemen, that we will stand by whatever they might say on the matter."

Lytra bit her lip and looked at his Majesty, who said, "We will come back to this, too. What of Shaltre?"

"I beg you to believe that this was in no sense a murder, Sire. Aerich challenged him before witnesses, those being ourselves, as well as Lord Garland and Lord Adron e'Kieron, all of whom can testify that, in response to this challenge, Shaltre initiated a cowardly attack on Aerich, who merely defended himself."

"As for Adron," said his Majesty grimly, "we will have our own dealings with him. Garland cannot so testify, for he has also been murdered. What have you to say to that?"

"That we are entirely unaware of it. He was alive when we saw him last, and running on foot through the mountains. It may be that some mischance happened to him, but I assure you we are unaware of it, and had no part in it."

Tortaalik frowned and said, "In fact, it may be that he still lives, we have no certain knowledge beyond the fact that he has neither returned, nor has there been any message from him. But it could be that he will appear."

"We ask nothing better, Sire," said Khaavren.

"Well, and, concerning the accusations with respect to Kurich, Garland, and Shaltre, will all of you be willing to testify under the Orb?"

Aerich looked at the Orb coldly, then bowed to His Majesty. "If the word of a gentleman is not deemed sufficient, Sire, well, I will submit."

"As will we all," said the others.

Lytra leaned over and whispered to the Emperor, who nodded. "Only one will be necessary, I think," said His Majesty. Lytra whispered once more, after which His Majesty said, "It is our pleasure that this gentleman, Khaavren, answer our questions."

"Well," said Khaavren, "I will be happy to stand below the Orb and answer any questions Your Majesty may wish to put to me."

"I will not ask the questions, I will allow Her Excellency the Warlord that honor."

Khaavren bowed to Lytra, and as Khaavren studied the expression on her face, her realized that she would be directing all of her resources to attempting to trap him, or to prevent him from telling what he knew. He glanced at G'aereth, who stood mutely, but, by his expression, warned Khaavren to be careful.

"Well, and is this acceptable to the rest of you?"

"It is, Sire," they said.

"That's well, then. Apropos, you may await without, and you will be informed when I have made a decision." There was nothing to say to this, so Khaavren's friends left. On the way out, Pel whispered, "Have a care; this Dragon is tricky."

"Well, I will be careful."

"That is right," said Pel.

Khaavren bowed to signify that he was ready, noting with pleasure that G'aereth had been retained as witness. The Orb moved away from the Emperor and began circling Khaavren's head. He did not even glance at it, but rather looked at Lytra with a patient and frank expression.

"I await Your Excellency," he said.

"Well, then, I will begin."

"I am anxious for you to do so."

"This, then, is my first question, when you last saw Lord Garland, what was his condition?"

"His condition, Excellency?" said Khaavren. "Well, he was healthy. I do not think health would excuse his failure to deliver—"

"You will confine yourself to answering the questions, young Sir," said Lytra.

"And yet—" began Khaavren.

"Stop," said Tortaalik sternly. "The Warlord is conducting this investigation. You must only answer the questions Her Excellency does you the honor to ask."

"Yes, Sire," said Khaavren, who began to tremble with frustration.

Lytra, who either did not notice or did not care about Khaavren's condition, said, "You say he was healthy?"

Khaavren took a deep breath in an effort to recover his composure. "It seemed likely," he said.

"How could you tell?"

"Well, he was not wounded, and he was running."

"How, running? Where was he running to?"

"The mountains, Excellency."

"Well, and what was he running from?"

Khaavren winced; the bolt had struck its mark. "From us, Excellency."

"Running from you?"

"It is as I have the honor to tell Your Excellency."

"But then, he was frightened?"

"It seemed likely, Excellency."

"As if his life was in danger?"

"That was exactly it, Excellency; he ran as if he feared for his life."

"From you?"

"And my friends, yes, Excellency."

"Well, then, let us pass on."

"How, pass on? But it seems to me—"

"You must merely answer the questions you are asked," said the Warlord.

Khaavren looked at His Majesty, who was frowning as he considered the matter, and at G'aereth, who was biting his lips so hard the blood ran, and he saw the sort of game this Dragonlord was playing. "Ah, you fool," he said to himself. "You should never have let them trap you into answering this way. This is Pel's sort of match, he would have talked this asker-of-pointed-questions into circles. Aerich would have astounded them with his dignity, and made her ask the necessary questions, and Tazendra would have burst out with the truth before they could stop her."

"As to Count Shaltre," said the Warlord, smiling as if she had her prey trapped. "You say he attacked the Duke of Arylle."

"Oh, yes, Excellency; he drew his blade and swung at Aerich's head as if he would send it over the cliff, some two leagues distant."

"But then," said Lytra, "did he seem frightened?"

"Well, in fact, Excellency, he did appear to me to be terrified."

"And what reason could you give for his terror?"

"Well, Aerich had challenged him, and—"

"In what terms was the challenge issued?"

"Well, Aerich said he would kill him."

"But then, Arylle is a Lyorn warrior, and did Shaltre not insist that, by the customs of his House, his Lordship could not attack Shaltre."

"Yes, but Aerich explained—"

The Emperor said, "Only answer the question, young man."

"Yes, Sire," said Khaavren, trembling.

"Well," said Lytra, "and was Arylle, that is, your accomplice Aerich, prepared to attack him anyway?"

"That is, he—"

"Yes or no, Sir Khaavren."

"Well, yes." G'aereth had turned completely white, and was trembling from head to foot.

"So that," continued Lytra, "in fact, Shaltre only made his attack from desperation, as he thought he was about to die, struck down by one who he knew was handily able to kill him, is that not the case?"

"It is," said Khaavren, grimacing.

Lytra turned to the Emperor. "Your Majesty can plainly see that Shaltre, though he struck the first blow, was murdered in effect, and Garland driven off in fear for his life, no doubt to die in the mountains."

Khaavren started to speak, but the Emperor cut him off with a gesture and addressed the Captain. "Lord G'aereth, have you anything to say before I pronounce the sentence?"

The Captain's face had become very pale. It was clear that he knew what Lytra was doing, but as he did not know what had actually occurred, he was unable to formulate a question that would allow Khaavren to make the necessary explanations. The others in the room, at that moment, also looked at the Captain, with curiosity or triumph, according to their interest and nature.

The Emperor opened his mouth, and the Tiassa, for a moment, could almost read the future: His Majesty would call for the Guards to take him away, and he and his friends would be imprisoned for a short time, and then they would be executed, their story untold, the treaty unfulfilled, and their enemies laughing as the headman's axe fell.

It is undeniable that, in this imperfect world, examples of injustice abound, and, in this regard, perhaps Khaavren ought not to have been astonished at what was taking place, yet he had never, himself, been in the presence of such monstrous undertakings; much less had he been the victim. And, in the agony of his mind, not knowing what he was doing, he fastened his last, imploring look on the Captain, his last remaining hope, and silently mouthed the name, "Kurich."

The Captain had, in fact, been looking at him, but, to Khaavren's dismay, G'aereth did not seem to have noticed; even if he had, it is no simple matter to read a name from silent lips, and the sending of thought from mind to mind requires both training and a closer connection between people than they had had time to build up, in spite of Khaavren's hope that desperation would serve to make up for the lack of these requirements.

The captain grunted, as if he were surrendering to fate, and Khaavren's last hope died as G'aereth said, "Well, Sire, I must confess I think them guilty one and all."

"I agree," said Tortaalik, "and I am happy to see that you don't defend murderers merely because they wear your uniform."

"Well, so far am I from wishing to defend them, that I will go further than your Majesty has, and say they must be guilty as well of killing poor Kurich."

Khaavren's heart began beating once more, as the feint breath of hope came once more to his veins.

"Oh," said Lytra, hastily, looking at G'aereth suspiciously. "For my part, I believe them on that score."

"How?" said G'aereth, with an incredulous expression on his face. "You would let them escape justice for that crime?"

"If they are to be hanged at the Corner of Tears or beheaded in Justicers Square," said Lytra, shrugging, "then it matters little how many crimes we hang or behead them for."

Khaavren held his breath, trembling, hardly daring to listen as his fate hung in the balance, not knowing if this final card he had played was high enough to win the stake.

"Well, I don't agree," said G'aereth. "And, when they are brought to the gallows, or the Star, I wish to hear the charges read in their entirety."

"Oh, I have no quarrel with that," said Lytra. "Let us include, then, the matter of Kurich."

"You can not mean that," said G'aereth.

"How, not?"

"We cannot charge them thus without proving the crime as we have so effectually proved the others."

"But then—"

"No, my lady, I insist, with His Majesty's permission, that you interrogate him on the subject of Kurich's death."

"Yes, yes," said Tortaalik, who had not at all understood the significance of this interplay. "Let us be complete by all means."

Lytra said, "Well, then, I will do so."

"It will be for the best," said G'aereth.

"Sir Khaavren," said Lytra.

"I am ready, Excellency," said Khaavren, who had understood the Captain's gambit, and was racking his brains to find a way to make use of it.

"Was Kurich killed in a fair and just fight?"

"Yes, my lady," said Khaavren.

"Well," said Lytra, breathing a sigh of relief, "there it is done, and it seems we were wrong."

"Bah," said the Captain. "Impossible."

"But you have heard what he said, and the Orb showed no falsehood."

"Well, but perhaps your Excellency didn't question him as thoroughly as she could have. Perhaps they sought a quarrel with Kurich for just the purpose fo finding an excuse to kill him."

"Nevertheless, it is true that, if it was a fair fight, my poor brother would have not wished the lady to be held accountable as if it were murder."

"Bah," said G'aereth once more. "Come, Excellency, ask about the cause of the quarrel, then we will know everything, and there will be no more doubts on any subject."

Lytra bit her lip, but at last she said, "Well, then, Cavalier Khaavren, what did Tazendra and Kurich quarrel about?"

"Excellency, Tazendra happened to disturb Kurich while he was on duty guarding a private conversation between yourself and—"

"That will do."

"How," said G'aereth, "you do not wish him to complete his thought?"

"We have our answer."

"And yet, I am curious."

"Oh, but it has no bearing—"

"Well," said Tortaalik, "if it comes to it, I am curious, too. Finish what you were saying, young man."

Khaavren bowed, took a deep breath, and said, "a private conversation between the lady Lytra and Garland's master."

The Emperor frowned. "Garland's master? That is to say, me?"

"No, Sire."

"How, Garland had another master than me?"

"Yes, Sire."

"Who?"

"The lady Seodra."

"How, Seodra? My chief advisor?"

"Yes, Sire."

"What do you tell me?"

"That Garland obeyed the orders of Seodra."

"What orders?"

Lytra said, "SIre—"

"Hold your tongue, Lytra," said the Emperor. "Sir Khaa-vren, I say again, what orders?"

"Why, the same orders she gave Count Shaltre."

"She gave orders to Count Shaltre?"

"Orders, or requests for help in her intrigues, Sire; I am not always aware of the differences."

Tortaalik stared at the Orb, but it was emitting a pure red glow of truth.

"What sort of order, then?"

"Such as the order to allow my friends and myself to be killed by the Easterners, Sire."

"What Easterners?"

"The ones who invaded Pepperfield."

"How, Easterners invaded Pepperfield?"

"Yes, Sire, it is as I have had the honor to tell your Majesty."

"Impossible," said Lytra, who was, this time, truly astounded.

G'aereth shrugged. "The Orb cannot be fooled," he said complacently.

"But then," said Tortaalik, "was there no one to stop the invasion?"

"There was Lord Adron, Sire, who had brought with him an army with which to capture us, and then wished to fight the Easterners."

"Well, and it was well thought. Did he then, engage them?"

"He was prevented, Sire."

"How, prevented? By whom?"

"Lord Garland and Count Shaltre, who had been given power over him, and used it to keep him from engaging the Easterners."

"What power?"

"I believe it was a piece of paper with Your Majesty's seal."

"Ah, the Horse, that is true. They ordered him not to fight the Easterners?"

"As I have had the honor to inform Your Majesty."

"But then, why?"

"Because they wished to allow the Easterners to kill us."

"To kill you? For what reason?"

"Because we were bringing Kathana e'Marish'Chala back with us, and this disrupted their plans."

"What plans?"

"To see to it that the e'Kieron line was not given the estate of Pepperfields."

"Why should they care which line of Dragons is given the estate?"

"Because they, that is, Seodra, had made bargains with certain Dragonlords."

"What sort of bargains?"

"Ones that would allow her to remain in power as Your Majesty's advisor, and would, moreover, embroil the Empire in a war over the diamond mines."

Tortaalik shook his head as if to clear it, and studied the Orb once more, but it continued to argue the truth of Khaavren's words. At last he said, "So, then, Lord Adron did not attack the Easterners?"

"He wished to, but, once he saw the orders from Your Majesty's hands, he could not disobey."

Tortaalik wiped sweat off his forehead with the cuff of his golden robe. "So, then, Lord Adron withdrew?"

"No, Sire."

"He did not? But, why?"

"Because then, Sire, Aerich accused Shaltre of treason, which gave him grounds to challenge him, and he further accused Garland of the same."

"And that is when Shaltre attacked him?"

"And when Garland ran off, yes, Sire."

"Well, and then Adron attacked the Easterners?"

"Oh, by then it was unnecessary."

"How, unnecessary?"

"We had concluded a peace agreement, saving only Your Majesty's willingness to partake in it."

Tortaalik stared at this complacent young Tiassa who was announcing these amazing things as if he spoke of matters of no importance. "A peace agreement?"

"Yes, Sire. With the Empire."

"Of what sort?"

"That we would no longer raid their country for horses, that they would no longer invade, that we would allow them to grow peppers, and—"

"Yes, and—?"

"That they would deliver to us the country of Sandy-home."

"What? And they agreed to this?"

"As I have the honor to inform your Majesty."

"But, who concluded this agreement?"

"I had that honor, Sire."

"What? You negotiated this peace?"

Khaavren bowed.

"And for this, you were arrested?"

"No, Sire, we were arrested to make sure we didn't tell Your Majesty of what we had done, because that would have compromised Seodra to Your Majesty. She therefore caused Lanmarea to have us arrested and, moreover, to keep us silent."

"Which was why," put in G'aereth, "the orders were that the prisoners could speak to no one, and why, had it not been for our good fortune, Pel's cleverness and Your Majesty's willingness to hear the case, these brave souls would have died without ever being able to tell you of the peace they had concluded."

Tortaalik was, by this time, shaking. He said, "Well, is that all?"

"Nearly," said Khaavren.

"What, there is more?"

"Only this: Lord Garland never delivered the letter to

Lord Adron from your Majesty, which is why he did not return with us. We found the letter in Garland's pouch, which he left behind when he ran."

"Then, Lord Adron is coming?"

"He asked us to beg his excuses for a short time, Sire, for he was just setting out for the city, as Your Majesty commanded, when he was informed of the birth of his first child."

"Ah, ah," said the Emperor. "Well, that is worth a little delay."

Khaavren bowed. "I am glad Your Majesty thinks so."

The Emperor then turned to Lytra. "And you," he said. "What have you to say to all of this?"

Lytra had, during Khaavren's speech, been growing more and more pale, until, by the end, she looked the way G'aereth had a few minutes before. But she said, "Sire, it is true that I have been involved with Seodra in attempting to win the Pepperfield estates for my line, but I assure your Majesty that I had no notion that she had gone so far. I will happily testify under the Orb, if you wish."

"That is exactly my desire," said Tortaalik coldly. Lytra bowed.

G'aereth said, "I beg leave to point out to Your Majesty that Her Excellency was instrumental in bringing these prisoners before Your Majesty, rather than allowing them to be killed unheard."

"Hmmm. That is true. Very well, Lytra, we will, for now, accept that you are innocent of treason."

"Thank you, Sire," she said, giving G'aereth a look full of gratitude.

"Well, then," said the Emperor, "call in your friends."

Aerich, Tazendra, Pel, Uttrik, and Kathana were brought in, and Tortaalik said, "Well, my friends, you have been busy, haven't you?"

They bowed, not knowing what to say.

"I caution you, however, concerning the matter of history."

"History, Sire?" said Pel.

"Yes, indeed. I wish to be remembered as a great Emperor. Well, if you continue doing the sorts of things you've been doing, The Horse, no one will remember me at all." He laughed. "Come now, here are your swords back; I had taken the precaution of having them brought in case they would be needed, and, in faith, I'm glad I did. Put them on, you look naked without them."

"Thank you, Sire," they said, and hastened to do as he had asked. "In faith," said Tazendra, strapping her greatsword over her back, "I *felt* naked without it."

"Sire," said Kathana, "even me?"

"Ah, yes. Well, in your case, Baroness, I have had to consider."

"I will be honored to hear the results of your Majesty's considerations."

"This is it, then: you are pardoned, on the condition that you serve fifty-seven years in the Phoenix Guards; which should not be much of a hardship, as you seem to have some friends there."

"Your Majesty is wise as well as merciful," said Kathana, bowing her face both from respect and because his Majesty's decision had filled her with emotion.

"Well, and the rest of you, as you have gathered, you are held innocent of all charges, and are free from this moment."

"Thank you, Sire," they said with one voice.

"And, as it is my wish that you should drink to my health, here," dug around his pockets and found a purse, which he handed to Khaavren. "I give you these ten Imperials in the hopes that you will drink my health many times in they days to come, for I shall be drinking yours before the entire court."

He silenced their protestations of thanks with a gesture, and said, "That is all. But, apropos, keep your ears to the sky, and your eyes to the ground, as the Hawks say, for you will be hearing from me."

Once outside the chamber, Khaavren was at once asked to detail all that had transpired with his Majesty.

"There is time for that later," he said.

"You mean," said Tazendra, "when we have returned home?"

"Yes, but I don't mean to return home directly."

"Well, and why not?" said Uttrik.

"Because, my friends, we are not yet finished."

"How, there is more to be done?" said Tazendra.

"Indeed there is."

Uttrik laughed. "Let us be about it then; in faith, at this moment I should be willing to battle the Enchantress of Dzur Mountain."

"Well," said Khaavren, "you may not be far from doing so. Come with me; I will explain as we walk."

'But," said Tazendra, "to where are we walking?"

"Why, through these doors, and up this stairway."

"Which leads?"

"To another stairway."

"Well, and then?"

"And then, down a pretty little hallway."

Tazendra shrugged, as if realizing that she was not to get an answer to her question, and should resign herself to waiting for it. When they arrived, Khaavren said, "Remember, all of you, that the countersign will be, 'Crionofenarr.' "

"Countersign?" said Tazendra.

"Hush," said Khaavren. "You will understand all soon enough."

Khaavren came to a door, and, desiring his friends to remain hidden for the moment, he clapped. The door was opened by a rather young chambermaid, who inquired what he could want.

"To see your mistress."

"Well, and whom should I announce?"

"A messenger."

"From?"

"From a certain Jhereg, whose name I am unwilling to give, but with whom I am certain she is acquainted."

"Very well, I will deliver this message."

In less time than it takes to tell of it, the Athyra came to the door, and, judging by her countenance, her ire had been roused. Upon seeing Khaavren, who had placed his cloak out of sight beside the door, she said, "What sort of game is Fayaavik playing, to send a messenger to me, here?"

At which Khaavren bowed, saying, "Fayaavik? Thanks, madam, that is all I wished to know."

He bowed again and made as if to leave, but Seodra called him back, saying, "Who are you?"

"How, you don't know me?"

"Not the least in the world."

"You have had me threatened, beaten, nearly assassinated, and brought me within an inch of the Executioner's Star, and yet you do not know my countenance?"

Her eyes grew wide. "You are—"

"Khaavren, madam."

Her eyes narrowed, and she looked like some sort of loathsome beast as she raised her hands as if she would cast a spell on the Tiassa, but at that moment, Aerich appeared next to him, while Tazendra, Pel, Uttrik, and Kathana took positions behind him.

"Gently, madam," said Khaavren, drawing his blade. "I should hate to have to taint my sword with your blood."

Seodra looked at the numbers ranged against her, and the grim expressions on their faces, and realized that her position was hopeless. Khaavren forced her back, and the companions entered her apartments. "Well," he said. "We had thought to leave after having learned what we wished to learn, but it is clear that you cannot be trusted. No matter. This gentleman, the Cavalier Pel, is going to visit your friend Fayaavik with me, while these others will wait for you. When I have repeated to you the countersign, which these gentlemen already know, you will tell them, and they will courteously depart. Do you understand?"

Seodra glared at him, but only said, "How will you give me the countersign if you are not here?"

Khaavren pulled a small disk from his pocket. "Why, madam, I will use this charming device, which I took from Lord Garland's pouch, and which, no doubt he used to ask you how to go about killing me. I am entirely certain that, if I try my utmost, it will direct my thoughts in your direction such that you will hear them. Cha! If it worked across half the continent, it will work across half the city, don't you think?"

Seodra gritted her teeth but said nothing. Accordingly, Khaavren took Pel and two of them left the Palace together. Pel said, "Khaavren, you are a great man, I tell you so. But tell me, how are you going to find Fayaavik? Do you know him?"

Khaavren smiled ingeniously. "I will find him in the easiest possible manner; I will ask you."

"How, you pretend I know him?"

"Perhaps. In any case, you know Jhereg who know him."

"You think so?"

"Well, it is not for nothing that you have spent your turns of duty making friends with every Jhereg in town; you must know something."

Pel smiled, "Well, I think you are nearly correct."

In fact, it took Pel only a couple of tries before he found someone who was willing to direct them to Fayaavik, who lived, or, at any rate, worked out of a small room above a cabaret on Blind Street. Gold cloaks flashing, they had no trouble gaining admission to him.

Fayaavik, on seeing the two Guardsmen, was courtesy personified, asking if there were any service he could perform for them.

"Nothing, I hope," said Khaavren pleasantly. "But we can perform one for you."

"For me? What have I done to deserve this honor?"

"I hope nothing," said Khaavren. "And, moreover, I hope you will continue to do nothing."

The Jhereg, who was no one's dupe, said, "With respect to what?"

"With respect to Seodra's request that you cause to be assassinated his Highness Adron e'Kieron."

"What?" cried Fayaavik. "Do you pretend—"

"Do not trouble yourself to deny it, Sir Jhereg," said Khaavren. "For we have no interest in hearing your protestations. We have only this to say: If anything happens to his Highness, we will come for you; and if you escape the Justicers, I promise that you will not escape us."

This being said, they turned and left, stopping only long enough for Khaavren to make use of the disk in order to reach Seodra and to say to her the word, "Crionofenarr." After she had repeated it to be certain she had it right, Khaavren and Pel turned toward home.

Meanwhile, Aerich, Tazendra, Kathana, and Uttrik took their leave of Seodra, and found Mica patiently and confidently awaiting them. They took him back to their house on the Street of the Glass Cutters, where they met up with Khaavren and Pel, who were just arriving.

Srahi had, to their surprise, kept the house in some semblance of order. They introduced the two Teckla, who looked at other with suspicion, whereupon they left them to work out whatever differences or similarities they might find in each other's character, after arranging for a pallet for Mica and couches for Uttrik and Kathana, who they insisted be their guests.

Early the next morning, our friends, that is, those four with whom we began our study, were awakened by a messenger who required their presence at the Dragon Wing, in the closet of Captain G'aereth. They arrived with a promptness that gave credit to their youthful powers of recuperation, and made their reports. The Captain, after admitting them, made no mention whatsoever of their journey, except to say that, now that they were back, they ought to resume their duties at once.

"Well," said Aerich mildly. "You have, then, a duty for us?"

"I do, and I expect it to be carried out at once, with dispatch and precision."

"We only await your orders, Captain," said Pel.

"Then I shall you give you the first of the orders I have received from his Majesty. Here it is." And he put into Tazendra's hand, for she happened to be closest, a written order. The Dzur read it, then read it a second time, and yet a third.

Pel said, "Read it aloud, if you please."

"Well then," said Tazendra. "Here it is: 'Order to arrest the Lady Seodra wherever she may be found, and to convey her to the prisons in the Iorich Wing. (Signed) Tortaalik.'"

"Well," said Khaavren. "And the second?"

"Here it is."

This time Tazendra read, "'Order to hold the Lady Seodra in my prisons in the Issola Wing. (Signed) Tortaalik.'"

"Well?" said the Captain.

"It will be a pleasure," said Khaavren, and—it is to their credit we say it—in less than an hour Seodra had been arrested in her apartments and conveyed to the prison which, thirty hours before, had contained our friends.

The arrest being complete, the companions, as they had promised, repaired to their favorite hostel, where, being joined by Kathana and Uttrik, with Mica serving at the table, Khaavren related the entire conversation with Tortaalik, after which they drank the health of his Majesty until well into night.

Conclusion

S OME MONTHS AFTER the events we have had the honor to relate, we can find our friends, Khaavren, Aerich, Tazendra, Pel, and Mica, once more riding on the long road across the *pushta*, back toward Dragaera City from the Eastern Mountains. In their pockets are leaves of absence which are due to expire soon.

Pel, who happened to be riding next to Aerich, said, "I think the journey has been a good one; our young friend seems to have recovered from the blow."

Aerich shrugged, as if to say, "One never fully recovers from the first betrayal of love."

Tazendra, who rode next to Khaavren, said, "Well, my lord Ensign, I hope you were delighted with the ceremony."

"Indeed yes," said Khaavren with a bit of a start, for he had not quite gotten used to his new rank. "Lord Adron carried it off in fine style; it was kind of him, after all that has happened, to allow Uttrik to be his child's name-giver."

"And to allow Kathana to stand for the mother."

Pel, who had heard this remark said, "That is true, but it gives one to wonder who the child's mother really is. I cannot help remembering the look on Lord Adron's face when he thought he knew. Do you recall, Aerich?"

"As if I were still seeing it," said the Lyorn.

"Well, what then?" said Tazendra. "We'll never know, I think."

Mica said, "The gossip in the kitchens is that the child's mother was a goddess."

"No doubt Lord Adron thought so at the time," said Khaavren with a trace of bitterness. "And yet, where was she?"

"If she was a goddess," said Pel, "then no doubt she had her own reasons for her absence. And if she was not, well, then no doubt she had reasons as well."

Tazendra shook her head. "For my part, it gives me great cause to think, however: the offspring of Adron e'Ki-eron and a goddess, with the Reign of the Dragon perhaps only a few hundred years away. I think we shall hear more of—stay, what is the child's name?"

"Aliera," said Pel.

"That is it. Well, I think we shall hear more from her."

"Cha!" said Khaavren. "More than we would have heard, I think, if we had allowed her father to be assassinated as that Seodra had planned."

"Oh, there is no question of that," said Pel.

"It is a shame," said Khaavren, "that Uttrik did not choose to join our battalion.'

"For us, yes," said Pel. "But it is better for him. He has the stewardship of the Pepperfields, which he loves, and serves under Lord Adron, whom he nearly worships."

"Apropos the Pepperfields," said Tazendra. "Did you not hear Uttrik remark that the negotiations were nearly complete?"

"It seems likely," said Pel.

"Imagine," said Tazendra. "Peace with the Easterners.

That such a thing should happen in our lifetimes, and to consider that we, ourselves, were responsible."

"It is," said Khaavren, "certainly something with which one may console one's self on lonely nights."

Something in the way he said this caused Pel and Aerich to look at each other, as if both had the thought that Khaavren had been experiencing many of these lonely nights of late. Aerich sighed.

In an effort to turn the conversation, Aerich said, "His Majesty seems determined to have done with intriguers at court."

Pel said, "For my part, I think it a doomed cause; intrigues are as much a part of the court as blood is a part of battle."

Tazendra laughed. "And you love the one as much as the other, do you not, my good Yendi?"

"In faith," said Pel, smiling. "I don't deny it."

"And you," said Tazendra, looking at Aerich. "What now? You have your name back; there is no reason to remain in the service any longer."

Aerich said, "Well, to be truthful, I have been thinking of leaving the service and returning to my estates. A career as a soldier is worthy for a gentleman, but, and I'm sorry to say it, I think that in a few years the Phoenix Guards will be nothing more than police, and I confess that I am too proud to be a police-officer."

Khaavren, to whom these words brought a pang that was not the less painful because it was expected, said, "I will be sorry to see you go."

"And I will be sorry to leave; in faith, it is only love for you, my friends, that has held me here so long."

"Nevertheless," said Tazendra, "it must be a pleasure to have the burden of shame lifted. And, I must say, you lifted it in a most elegant manner. Ah, I can still see your hands upon that wretch Shaltre! If only—"

She stopped, and turned her face away. Khaavren reached over and pressed her hand.

"Well, come," said Khaavren, who was nearly able to

read her thoughts as one reads the pages of a book. "In a few years we will have accumulated some leave, and we will go looking for these famous estates of yours, and at least settle matters with them. No doubt Aerich, wherever he is, will join us in this quest."

"Gladly," said Aerich. "We will search together for, what was the name of your duchy?"

"It was a barony," said Tazendra. "I know not where, only that it is called Daavya, and—"

"Daavya!" said Aerich. "Well, but that lies within the duchy of Arylle."

"How, Arylle?" said Tazendra. She laughed. "But then, if I were to take my title, I should be your vassal."

"Bah," said Aerich. "It means nothing."

"On the contrary," said Tazendra. "I should be honored to have you as overlord."

"And yet," said Aerich. "There is a circumstance that I wish to remember."

"Well," said Tazendra, "I hope you do."

"I was told of it by my nurse at a time when I was very young."

"So then?"

"I remember everything that was important to me then, but, what would you? Not everything that is important when one is young is the same as what is important when one is older."

"I know that well, dear Aerich, yet tell us what you can."

"It seems that, upon learning of his disgrace, my father anticipated what would follow, and made certain preparations."

"That was well thought," said Tazendra. "But what were the preparations against?"

"Against an attack on my life."

"It is good that you were protected."

"Do you think so?"

"I do indeed."

"Well, I am glad of that."

"Only, what were the preparations?"

"That is what I am trying to recall. Ah, yes; I remember now."

"Well, and I hope you will tell me."

"I will, the more readily because it concerns you."

"How, concerns me?"

"Yes, and very much so."

"Then I will listen closely."

"I am glad that you will."

"Speak, then, for I am hanging upon your words."

"Here it is, then: upon determining that my life was at risk—"

"Yes, yes, I understand that."

"And learning that the Count of Shaltre—"

"He whom you killed."

"Yes."

"Well, go on."

"Upon learning that he had received permission from her Majesty Cherova, the last Empress, to hire a mercenary army of Dragonlords—"

"Well, yes?"

"He made arrangements with certain vassals for my protection."

"That was well done."

"You think so?"

"I have said it already, and I repeat it, dear Aerich."

"He knew these vassals were the best for this task, because they were discreet, and understood duty, and were without fear."

"A good choice, it seems."

"They were, in fact, Dzurlords."

"Well, but go on."

"How, you don't see?"

"No, not at all."

"But they were the Baron and Baroness of Daavya."

"How, my mother and father?"

"Exactly."

"But then, they were killed."

"Yes, only not running from battle; rather, they had already placed me beyond Shaltre's reach, after which they allowed themselves to be killed to that the secret would be safe."

"So, you mean—?"

"Yes, that is why they ran when their holdings were attacked; they knew the attack meant that my father was about to be set upon, and they had made a vow to see to my safety."

"Then, they were not cowards!"

"Far from it, good Tazendra, they were heroes, and I will so testify before your House. They did not run from battle, but toward duty and honor."

Tazendra's eyes were glowing like the fire from Dzur Mountain. "There is no shame in that."

"Not in the least, Tazendra."

"Bah. Call me Daavya."

"As you wish, my lady Barnoess."

"At your service, my lord Duke."

Khaavren said, "I am delighted for you, Baroness."

"Thank you, Ensign."

Khaavren sighed.

Pel said, "What is it, Khaavren? You seem unhappy."

"Well, I am pleased for Tazendra, pardon me, for the Baroness, and I am pleased for Aerich, and yet—"

"Well, and yet?" said Tazendra (for so we, at least, will continue to call her, lest our readers become confused).

"There is no doubt that both of our friends will be leaving the service, and I, for one, will miss them. Will you not miss them also, Pel? Speak truly."

"In faith I will, Khaavren. And yet—"

"Well, and yet?"

"I am afraid that I, too, will not be staying in the service much longer."

"How," said Khaavren, both surprised and hurt. "You, too?"

"I have petitioned his Majesty, who has expressed some

interest in me, to request of His Discretion the Duke of Wellborn that I be granted an apprenticeship in his art."

Khaavren sighed, "Well, you will be a great Discreet, my friend, and yet—"

"Well?"

"I cannot see what else there is for me. You, Aerich, can say that the Guards will become mere police, and no doubt you are right, but what choice have I? And, without you, my friends, it will be a melancholy sort of life."

"Bah," said Pel. "You are young; friendship turns up everywhere. Besides, though I will be busy, I will still be at court, and we will no doubt meet each other from time to time."

Khaavren made no answer to this, and for some leagues no one spoke. Then, at last, Khaavren said, "Well, so be it. You will all leave me to pursue your fortunes, and I wish you well. But now I have the income of an ensign, and that is good for one thing at least."

"What is that," said Tazendra.

"I can afford to maintain our house, and I declare that I will continue to live there, and to hold your rooms ready in case you should ever wish for them."

"That is well done," said the others.

"And, who knows," said Khaavren, looking at the road before them as if he were peering into the future. "Fate might well bring us together for reasons we have no inkling of."

Aerich said, "Khaavren, I have heard you say that you have sometimes the gift of prophecy, and in this case, well, I think I am convinced of it. And, moreover—"

"Yes, moreover?"

"As Pel told the Captain so long ago—"

"Well?"

"We ask nothing better."

Epilogue

AS IT TURNED out, Seodra retained too much influence at court for her execution to be practical, but she remained in prison until she died some four hundred years later. Lytra was able to hold her position as Warlord until, some ninety years after the events we have had the honor to relate, she was caught up in the matter of the White Goblets, which cost her both her position and her head.

Illista and her brother were exiled, and they were believed to have lived out the remainder of their lives on an island kingdom to the west.

Lanmarea was dismissed from the service, and G'aereth was promoted to Brigadier of the Phoenix Guards, and took command of both troops. He turned the White Sash Battalion into what was effectively a police force, which allowed him to keep the Red Boots, with Khaavren as ensign, as the elite palace guard and fighting corps which Khaavren had thought he had joined. While this did not diminish the rivalry between the two brigades, it did take them out of contact with each other, and a potentially problematical situation was thus resolved before it could become serious. Whether this was good or bad is left to the judgement of the reader; the historian makes no choice, seeing his task, as Master Hunter has so aptly put it, as merely the shedding of light into the dark spaces of the past.

Aerich, true to his word, left the Phoenix Guards before the end of the year, taking Tazendra with him, who, in turn, took Mica. Pel remained a little longer, but, eventually his petition was granted and he began his apprenticeship in the art of Discretion, whereupon he took quarters within the Athyra Wing of the Palace. Despite his words to Khaavren, they rarely saw each other after that, and, when they did, it was only to exchange greetings and a few words as Pel would pass by where Khaavren was on duty in the Palace.

In the fourth year of Tortaalik's reign, in the month of the Orca, the entire court traveled to the Pepperfields to conclude the treaty with Crionofenarr; the matter having been arranged with extreme haste out of consideration to the short-lived Easterners. Khaavren was present in his role as ensign of the Red Boot Battalion.

Kathana e'Marish'Chala, to Khaavren's delight, remained in his brigade for thirty-eight years of the fifty-seven she had agreed to, after which, upon presenting her painting, "The Consort by the Fireside" to his Majesty, he granted her permission to return to her vocation.

Khaavren, true to his word, continued in the house he had rented upon the Street of the Glass Cutters and retained the worthy Srahi to keep the house in order, and, as he had promised, he maintained all of the rooms his friends had once occupied, hoping that, someday, they would be of use once more.

In this, we should add as a last note, he was not deceived, but as the details would be beyond the scope of this history, with which we hope our readers are not too dissatisfied, we shall, with regret mingled with some sense of satisfaction in the completion of a task, leave it to another time.

About the Author

Paarfi of Roundwood is the creation of a writer who, at first, wished the style of the French Romantics (Dumas, Sabatini, etc.) was still popular, then decided he didn't care, and he'd bloody well write like that anyway. Paarfi is not really intended to look like one of those individuals; merely to sound something like them. For those with an interest in Dragaeran "history," or rather, continuity, he can be placed at roughly the same period as the books of the Vlad Taltos series, or about a thousand years after the events he is supposed to be writing about.

If I've set him up as a bit pompous, that shouldn't be construed as a slam at the writers I'm imitating. It's just that, as I spent a whole novel with his voice running through my fingers, he developed his own personality, for which I can take no more or less responsibility than I can for any of my other characters. Take that how you will.

He keeps trying to refer to himself as an historian, which is okay, but it seems to me that he is making up more than he is willing to let on, his protests in the Preface notwithstanding. His true love is, I think, history, and he isn't really bad at it, but the era in which he is writing, only a few hundred years after the Interregnum, is not one where there is much call for historians; everyone is too preoccupied with rebuilding the Empire to have the leisure to look backward. In other words, everyone is too busy repeating past mistakes to take the time to look at those mistakes, much to Paarfi's frustration. Therefore, to support himself, he had to find a patron, the Lady Parachai, who enjoyed reading the sort of books that passed on Dragaera for historical romances.

Think of Paarfi, then, as a bit like Arthur Conan Doyle; he isn't making his living doing what he really wants to do, but rather doing what he is good at: telling stories. In Paarfi's case, his manner of telling stories may be a bit overblown and pretentious—and it is certainly wordy—but it's his own. If Dumas developed his style, at least in part, because he was paid by the word (rather like Dickens, only Dumas had more fun), then Paarfi's style is just as understandable: on Dragaera, all the scholars write like that.

As for my own reasons, well, the fact is, I was having too much fun to stop. I enjoyed working with him a great deal, both for his own sake, and as homage to some great writers of the past. I hope you like him, as well.

Steven Brust, P.J.F.
April, 1990
Minneapolis, Minnesota

About the Author

Mr. Steven Brust (while we are not familiar with the title, "Mister," it is thus we find him called, and we will not take it upon ourselves to change it) lives in a place called Minneapolis, which name, we are given to understand, means either, "Place of Blowing and Drifting Snow," or, "Land of Almost Constant Road Repair." He was born one thousand, nine hundred, and fifty-five years after the founding of the temple of one of the more popular local deities, on the twenty-third day of a month called "November," which name, we are given to understand, means either, "Time of the Start of Blowing and Drifting Snow," or, "Time of Short-Lived Hiatus in Road Repair."

He has supplied us with a rather lengthy list of activities in which he has engaged in order to support himself, but as we are unable to make any sort of sense out of any of them, we will omit the list entirely, confident that the reader is missing nothing of any importance by the omission.

While his personal life is, in some measure, beyond

the scope of our studies, we may say that he is the author of four children and ten novels; the book which you have the honor of holding in your hands being the tenth. We consider our task to be one of recording what has been, rather than predicting what will be, yet we feel confident in asserting that the number of children is not likely to increase, whereas the number of novels might well have grown even before this present volume goes forth into the public, where it is destined, according to Mr. Brust, to perform some arcane service called, "Leveling Washing Machines."

When Mr. Brust is not writing, he is likely to be found striking, either with his hands or with sticks, imitation hides stretched across shells of various sizes, which act he engages in in hopes of bringing forth musically pleasing sounds. While we are at a loss to understand how one might imitate hide or why one would wish to—we are unwilling to judge without having witnessed the attempt, which, considering the circumstances, seems unlikely.

It should be noted, however, that he does this in conjunction with several other persons, most notably including a certain Lady Emma of the House of the Bull, and that this coincidence of musical personalities refers to itself as "Cats Laughing," for reasons upon which we will not speculate. Should the reader wish to continue his researches into this federation of performers, he ought to write his address on an envelope, along with whatever seals are required for delivery by the post, place this envelope into a second, or rather, a first envelope, also with appropriate postal seals, and send this package to:

Cats Laughing
P.O. Box 7253
Minneapolis, Minnesota, 55407

Let us add, on our own behalf, that we have been accused of having had more of a creative than an historical role with regard to the persons of whom we have had the honor to write; there are even those have suggested that these individuals have never existed except in our imaginings. While we do not, in general, consider such charges worth responding to, we may assure the reader that, if he were to follow the above instructions, he will receive proof that Mr. Brust, at least, has nothing fictitious about him; and, if we may be permitted a last opinion, it seems that, of all the characters who have done us the honor of appearing before us in this work, Mr. Brust is by far the most improbable.

Paarfi of Roundwood
2/1/2/3
Adrilankha, Whitecrest

FANTASY BESTSELLERS
FROM TOR